S0-ASI-985

Books By The Author

The Captive Series

Captured (Book 1)

Renegade (Book 2)

Refugee (Book 3)

Salvation (Book 4)

Redemption (Book 5)

Broken (The Captive Series prequel)

Vengeance (Book 6)

Unbound (Book 7)

The Fire & Ice Series

Frost Burn (Book 1)

Arctic Fire (Book 2)

Scorched Ice (Book 3) Coming November 15th 2016

The Kindred Series

Kindred (Book 1)

Ashes (Book 2)

Kindled (Book 3)

Inferno (Book 4)

Phoenix Rising (Book 5)

The Ravening Series

Ravenous (Book 1)

Taken Over (Book 2)

Reclamation (Book 3)

The Survivor Chronicles

Book 1: The Upheaval

Book 2: The Divide

Book 3: The Forsaken

Book 4: The Risen

Books written under the penname Brenda K. Davies

The Road to Hell Series

Good Intentions (Book 1)

Carved (Book 2) Coming 10/11/16

The Road (Book 3) Coming January 2017

Into Hell (Book 4) Coming 2017

The Vampire Awakenings Series

Awakened (Book 1)

Destined (Book 2)

Untamed (Book 3)

Enraptured (Book 4)

Undone (Book 5)

Fractured (Book 6) Coming Winter 2016/2017.

Historical Romance

A Stolen Heart

Dedication

To all the fans
who loved and followed this series for so long.

Your support has meant the world to me and I
couldn't have done any of this without all of you!

Thank you so much for loving these characters as
much as I do and making this such a wonderful ride
with them and with you!

Here is to many more adventures together!

CHAPTER 1

Aria

"Wait." Aria said to Braith and pulled back on her horse's reins as she surveyed the skeletal trees surrounding her. The breeze drifting through the woods caused the swaying tree branches to clack together, setting her already frazzled nerves that much more on edge. Above her, thin clouds slipped through the sky, momentarily blocking out the late afternoon sun shining down on the snow covering the forest floor.

They were almost thirty miles from the palace, in the area of the forest where she'd spent most of her life as a rebel, before she'd married Braith and become queen. That tree over there was the one she and Max had climbed in order to avoid a group of vampires on the hunt for rebels. The two of them had stood in those branches, afraid to even breathe, as they watched Caleb and Braith pass beneath them. She recalled Braith stopping below them and tipping his head back to look at her. He'd still worn his dark glasses at the time, but she'd known the instant he'd spotted her standing above him and Caleb.

The remembrance of Braith's younger and extremely twisted brother, Caleb, gave her chills. However, those chills were nothing compared to the ones currently consuming her as she looked around the sparse woods.

She focused on the many evergreens within the forest. Their pine scent tickled her nostrils as it drifted through the air. Normally it was a comforting, constant aroma, but now it was too sharp. Someone or something had trampled some of the smaller pines, or torn away their branches, which made their smell more potent.

Aria's gaze flicked toward the sky when a pair of mourning doves took flight, their wings whistling in the wind. Her hands tightened on the reins, and panic struck her so forcefully she nearly cried out. Ever since William had told her about the vampire woman he'd encountered who claimed to be the rightful queen, she couldn't rid herself of the feeling something awful was about to happen.

That feeling of impending doom now kicked around in her stomach and caused a clammy sweat to break out on her icy skin.

She wanted to grab hold of Braith, yank their mounts back, and flee from here as fast as they could. Despite the driving impulse, she remained unmoving. She didn't know where those who had made the pine scent more potent were; if they fled now, they could alert possible enemies to their presence or stumble across them. There was still the smallest chance they hadn't been spotted yet. Any sudden movement could destroy that.

Her small group had been moving with exceptional care through the trees. They were scouting the forest ahead of the assembly of vampires and humans who made up the survivors of Tempest's town of Badwin and the inhabitants of Hannah's town of Chippman.

"What is it?" Braith asked from beside her as he moved his mount closer to hers.

Aria turned her head to him, her heart swelling with love as she gazed at his magnificent face. He was so handsome he could make her deadened heart feel as if it raced every time she looked at him. Her fingers itched to brush back the black hair falling to the corner of his gray eyes. A band of pure blue encircled his now dilated pupils.

Faint white scars surrounded his eyes, but they had faded further over the nearly two years she'd known him, and Braith said they'd probably disappear completely over the next fifty or hundred years. Those scars remained a testament to a time when he'd been completely blind. Then, she had walked into his life and the strength of their bloodlink, a deep bond that developed between vampires, had given him his vision back.

He sat proudly in his saddle, his broad shoulders back and the noble air of a king surrounding him. Since he'd become king, he'd grown to be a mighty and fair ruler. One who was respected and admired, one who was loved by those who followed him.

He'd put to right many of the atrocities his father had committed over his years as king. Humans and vampires now worked side by side, fear and brutality no longer reigned, and the practice of vampires owning blood slaves had been put to an end.

Now a new threat had risen, and she sought to destroy everything they had so tirelessly worked and sacrificed for.

Leaning across the small space between them, Aria rested her hand on his stubble-roughened jaw. For a second, the world around her stilled as the brief contact soothed the tumult of emotions spiraling through her. Love, deep and intense, welled within her. She would *not* lose him.

"There is someone or something in these woods," she whispered.

His head turned toward the trees. Xavier, her friend and bodyguard, moved his horse so he was positioned before her.

"Are you sure?" Ashby asked from behind her.

Aria pulled her bow from her back and an arrow from her quiver. She swung them around so they were in front of her. "Yes."

Aria's attention shifted from Braith to her brother-in-law. Ashby's bloodlink and Braith's sister, Melinda, sat on the horse beside him. Melinda's normally fair skin became paler as she surveyed the woods.

Braith's brother, Jack, nudged his horse forward to position himself ahead of his wife's mount. Hannah shot him a disgruntled look, but refrained from protesting his protective gesture.

William cursed and rode forward so that his mount flanked her other side. Aria glanced at her twin's hard profile, as his crystalline blue eyes narrowed to take in the woods. His dark auburn hair, so similar in hue to hers, shone in the fading winter sun. He'd shaved his beard off when he'd been in Badwin, but already the thick, dark auburn hair had grown in across his square jaw and over his upper lip. His nostrils flared as he scented the air.

"The pine," he commented.

"Yes," Aria said.

"Can we turn back?" Tempest asked.

Turning in the saddle, William looked back at his blood-link, Tempest. He'd just found her; she was the one who had helped him to get past his anger over having been stabbed through the back by Kane. Aria had been able to give William her blood and save him before he died, but his mortal life had ended that day and his life as a vampire had begun. There had been a time when Aria worried she would lose William to his desire to destroy Kane. Now she worried she would lose him to whatever was in the woods with them.

"There is no turning back right now," Daniel replied.

Aria glanced over to where her older brother sat on his horse with Max and Timber at his sides. Behind him, sat the five king's men who had been picked to make this scouting trip with them. The king's men rode forward, spreading out to flank her and Braith within a protective circle.

"If we can get to the caves, we can take shelter," William said and Aria suppressed a shudder.

She'd gotten better with it over the past couple of years, but she hated being anywhere enclosed. However, they had no choice, not right now.

"Aria, go," Braith said.

"I know these woods better than you," she told him. "I'm not going anywhere without you."

"I'll be right behind you. Go."

She opened her mouth to protest, but it was silenced by the motion she caught out of the corner of her right eye. Spinning in the saddle, Aria pulled her bow and an arrow from her back. With rapid speed, she nocked the arrow and released it. William jerked back when the arrow whistled past his ear and directly into the heart of the vampire who had been trying to slink from one tree to another.

The force of the arrow knocked the vamp off his feet and into the snow. Wearing a solid white cloak, the vampire would have been nearly invisible to anyone who didn't know every subtle shift and flow within these woods. His now still form almost completely blended in with the mound of snow he'd been moving through only seconds ago.

Ashby spun in his saddle to face her. "You don't know that he was an enemy!"

"Our allies aren't going to be slinking through the woods trying to go unnoticed," Jack replied.

"White cloak," William murmured. "It's them or it's *her*."

Another chill ran down Aria's spine as she tugged a second arrow from her quiver. William had told them the vampires following the woman claiming to be the rightful queen wore white cloaks. It had been one of the reasons she'd shot without hesitation. Their allies wouldn't be slinking through the woods.

Braith grabbed the reins of her mount and pulled her back. "Fall back," he commanded the others as he pulled her closer to him.

Before she could react, he wrapped his arm around her waist and plucked her from her horse. The thick muscles of his biceps rippled against her as he swung her onto his saddle and tucked her firmly against his chest. He slapped his hand against the rump of her horse, sending it bolting into the woods as a distraction.

Gathering his reins, Braith spun his horse in one fluid motion. Snow kicked up from the horse's hooves to splatter against the bottom of her boots. Out of habit, she tried to take a calming breath, but then recalled she didn't breathe air anymore.

We're not going to make it.

She hated the bleak thought the minute it crossed her mind, but she knew it was true.

Her fingers curled into the chiseled muscle of Braith's forearm as a *twang* echoed in the air around them. The bow and arrow had been her favored weapon since she'd been old enough to lift one; it was a sound she normally loved. Now, it caused terror to spike through her as the whistle of arrows erupted in the air around them.

The first wave of arrows soared into the clearing, burying into the ground in front of Braith's horse and causing the animal to reel back as the whites of its eyes became clearly visible. Aria bit back a scream when one of the arrows struck Timber in his shoulder. The mountain of a man nearly tumbled from his saddle, but managed to catch himself before he did.

Despite the wave of arrows that had flooded the small area they were in, Timber was the only one who had been hit. Those arrows had been meant to keep them where they were.

They want us alive, but why?

***

Braith

Braith enfolded Aria against his body, attempting to keep her as protected as he could from the figures moving through the trees toward them. The deep auburn strands of hair escaping her braid tickled his nose; her intricate, woodsy aroma filled his nostrils. Her scent was something he would never get enough of, much like the woman herself, and now someone was threatening her.

A snarl rumbled through his chest as his fangs slid free. He'd tear every one of them to shreds before he ever allowed one of them to touch her. She was *his* bloodlink, his wife, his queen, and someone was conspiring to try to take her away from him, again. It would never happen.

"Don't move," he growled in her ear when she tried to pull away.

"I need to be able to shoot," she protested.

"Too many, stay still." He couldn't get full sentences out through the fury boiling within his veins.

She became immobile against him as more figures slid through the trees around them. They weren't attacking, not yet. For some reason, they were waiting; Braith had a feeling they would discover that reason soon enough. Jack moved closer to Hannah; he extended his hand to her and pulled her from her saddle and onto his. William dragged Tempest's mount closer to his and positioned himself so he was in front of her with his bow and arrow aimed at the figures closing in around them.

"Don't shoot," Jack said to William.

William scowled at him before focusing on the forest once more. "I haven't yet, have I?"

Ashby pulled Melinda from her horse, tucking her against his chest as he surveyed the encroaching vampires with haughty disdain. Xavier tugged on the reins of his horse, positioning himself directly in front of Aria. The fading sunlight gleamed across Xavier's dark skin and bald head, illuminating the tribal tattoos on his arms, hands, and neck. His deep brown eyes were troubled when they met Braith's before falling to Aria.

Xavier had been the vampire history keeper for most of his life, yet he had stepped aside from taking his rightful seat at The Council table in favor of being Aria's bodyguard when the war with Braith's father ended. Braith didn't have any concerns Xavier might have romantic feelings for his wife. Xavier would be far more likely to be attracted to him. However, Xavier did care for Aria, deeply. They had become extremely close and Braith knew Xavier would lay down his life in order to save hers.

Braith hugged her against him; he would do whatever it took to get her out of here. She had literally brought light and color back into his life. She was his everything, and he would not allow her bright soul to be taken from this world.

Max and Daniel moved closer to Timber as he broke off the shaft of the arrow embedded in his shoulder and tossed it aside. The king's men moved closer to him and Aria. The other king's men had remained with the residents of Chippman and the survivors from Badwin. They were over a mile back, awaiting word it was safe to progress.

They were going to be waiting longer than he'd anticipated.

"Braith," William hissed under his breath. "It is *her*."

Braith followed William's gaze to a small grouping of pines where a woman leisurely emerged from between the snow-encrusted limbs. It was impossible to miss her, as instead of the white cloaks of her followers, she wore a blood red cloak that emphasized her pale complexion and vivid green eyes. Black hair tumbled behind her to brush against the snowy ground with every step she took. Her face was perfect in its beauty, but malevolence oozed from her pores, making her one of the ugliest women he'd ever encountered.

Braith's gaze ran over her slender figure and refined features. He'd never seen her before, but as William had said, there *was* something familiar about her broad cheekbones and full lips. He felt as if he should know her, yet he couldn't figure out how or why.

Aria's hand flew to her mouth as some of the color faded from her sun-kissed skin. When she tried to sit up in order to see the woman better, he pulled her back, refusing to let her be more exposed in any way.

The vampire men and women in the white cloaks fell back and bowed their heads in deference when the woman passed by them. Timber, Max, and Daniel pulled their mounts back, edging away from the woman who stopped at the edge of the small clearing.

Braith's skin tingled, and the hair on his arms rose as waves of power crackled against him. He'd assumed William had exaggerated, or been mistaken, about the amount of power this woman possessed. Staring at her now, he realized William had been right.

She may be the most powerful vampire he'd ever encountered.

CHAPTER 2

Braith

The sharp, ozone scent of her power permeated the crisp air as the woman's gaze landed on Braith.

"She's powerful," William had said to him. *"And old. She felt as powerful as you, perhaps more so."*

Definitely old and powerful. More so than him? Maybe. Where had she come from?

It didn't matter; he'd destroyed other vampires that were more powerful than him before, he would do so again. This woman may be older and stronger than him—for the life of him he couldn't figure out how that was possible when he was supposed to be the oldest vampire in existence. One thing was for certain, she didn't have a bloodlink to strengthen her like Aria strengthened him. This woman had no idea who she was messing with, but she soon would.

Aria's head tilted back to look up at him. Her rounded cheeks somehow appeared more hollow as she bit on her full bottom lip. The freckles on the bridge of her nose stood out starkly as she gazed at him.

"Braith—"

"It will be okay, love," he whispered.

She stared at him for a minute more before giving a brisk nod. A small tremor went through her and into him. He lifted his gaze to take in the woman across from him once more. His

UNBOUND

ERICA STEVENS

Copyright © 2016 Erica Stevens
All rights reserved.

horse released an uneasy snort, a plume of air coiling up from its nostrils as the sun dipped behind the trees. The woman continued to stare at him as another vampire emerged from between the pines behind her.

If not for his red cloak, the man would have blended in with the snow around him with his white blond hair, pale skin, and eyes so light a blue they were almost white. His bushy white eyebrows nearly touched. He had a prominent roman nose, thin lips, and a rail-thin frame that made him look deceptively frail despite his six-three height and the aura of strength he emitted, though one not nearly as intense as that of the woman he stopped beside. The ruby rings on all the fingers of his right hand cast sparkling red flashes of color across the snow.

"Goran," William whispered.

William had mentioned this man before, said he might be the false queen's second-in-command, but Braith had never heard of him, and neither had Xavier despite his extensive knowledge of vampire history and lineage. Braith exchanged a look with Xavier who gave a subtle shake of his head. He still had no idea who either of them were either.

Braith turned his attention back to the woman. "I'm only going to tell you once to leave here, now."

The woman lifted an elegant black brow and tossed back a strand of her midnight hair with her pointed, blood-red nails. Her air of superiority was one he'd encountered before, from the many royal vampires he'd known throughout his life. Aristocrat, without a doubt, but how did they not know of her?

"Awfully arrogant for someone who is completely surrounded," the woman replied. The laughter in her surprisingly girlish voice rankled his nerves.

Aria shifted before him. His hand dug deeper into Aria's flesh when the woman's eyes were drawn to her. The woman's lips skimmed back to reveal her fangs as loathing washed off her in waves. Braith nearly leapt from the saddle to attack the woman, but he couldn't leave Aria exposed in such a way. They would kill her immediately if he did.

"We've faced far worse odds, yet we're still standing," Braith grated through his teeth at the woman. "Do you wish to add your name to the list of those who have fallen?"

Her head canted to the side in such a way that Braith saw a flash of something or some*one* in her features. Who *was* this woman? A tremor went through Aria; he felt her trying to take a hitching breath, something she used to do when she was first turned, but had stopped doing as of late.

Did she somehow know who this woman was? He didn't see how that was possible when he didn't even know her, but something about Aria's demeanor led him to believe it was more than terror over their current situation rattling her right now.

When the woman smiled smugly at them, Braith managed to restrain his temper enough to keep from going after her. Something he suspected she was trying to provoke him into doing. Why was this woman not attacking? She couldn't possibly plan to keep him alive and kill Aria? Did she think he would make *her* his queen if Aria died?

The woman had no concept of bloodlinks, or his deep bond to Arianna, if she believed that could ever happen. If she ever hurt Aria, he'd leisurely pull every hair from her head before working on removing every other piece of her body.

Did she intend to try to capture them and then... do what? Use Aria to bend him to her will? That would be a much more likely scenario than this woman becoming his queen, but he would never allow Aria to go through the hell of imprisonment again, and he would never fall into line with anyone who sought to use her in such a way.

Or did this woman simply believe she was too powerful to fall to him and merely played with them now? He felt that was exactly what she was trying to do as her eyes surveyed him with amusement.

Her gaze fell to Aria again, who met the woman's malicious gaze head-on. "You taint the line with a turned human as your queen," the woman replied. "An imposter queen."

"Such words are punishable by death," Braith replied.

The woman chuckled. "Death is not so frightening for some." Her gaze slid back and forth between Aria and William, before settling on Braith once more. "This perversion of vampire blood cannot be allowed to continue. It most certainly cannot be allowed to reproduce."

"Enough!" Braith roared as Aria's fingers dug into his arm.

"Braith," Aria whispered warningly.

The woman's gaze slid to Jack, who pulled Hannah more firmly against his chest. His gray eyes were focused on the woman as a muscle twitched in his cheek. "The younger brother," the woman murmured before her gaze slid over the group once more. It finally settled on Melinda. "And the youngest child, I'm assuming. You look very much like your mother."

Xavier shot Braith another questioning look at the revelation this woman had somehow known their mother. Ashby backed his mount further away from the woman with Melinda pressed close against his chest. The others all looked to him, but Braith had no answers for any of them about this woman's identity.

"Kill them all," the woman commanded flippantly before pointing a finger at Braith. "But bring me his head."

"William, fire now!" Braith commanded.

At the last second, William spun his arrow away from the woman and fired at Goran. Goran twisted to the side, but not fast enough to avoid taking the arrow to the center of his chest, centimeters off his heart. William never would have been able to hit the woman with an arrow, but he'd distracted them all by hitting Goran.

Aria sat up before him and pulled another arrow from her quiver as the white-cloaked vampires surged forward. Max fought against the hands grasping at him, but he was torn from his mount. Timber kept his reins in the hand of his injured arm as he swung at the vampires swarming him. Ashby launched a fist at one trying to grab at Melinda and caught him in the jaw, knocking him away. Two other vampires ripped him from his horse. Melinda lurched toward Ashby, but he had vanished from view within the sea of white.

"No!" Aria screamed when Daniel was pulled from his horse.

She plucked three arrows from her quiver and released them in rapid fire, taking out the two who had captured Daniel and the one who had grabbed Max. Ashby remerged from the crush of vamps, swinging and punching his way back toward Melinda. Throwing herself from the saddle, Melinda attacked the vampires who were still trying to drag Ashby beneath them. Ashby remained on his feet as he moved to position Melinda behind him.

More bowstrings twanged from the vampires attacking them, the feathers of the arrows whistled as they soared through the air. Unlike the first wave of arrows, which were meant to corral them into one spot, these arrows had targets. An arrow pierced straight through Xavier's throat, knocking him back. Braith jerked Aria against his chest when she lurched toward Xavier as he tumbled from his saddle.

"No!" he hissed in her ear. "Stay against *me*."

Jack pulled Hannah from their horse when another wave of arrows erupted into the clearing. He hadn't been fast enough to get clear of the saddle though as an arrow pierced his right thigh. His momentum out of the saddle was the only thing that kept him from being pinned against the horse by the arrow.

Diving backward, William wrapped his arm around Tempest's waist and pulled her out of the back of the saddle. His body twisted to take the impact on the ground before he rolled over to pin Tempest beneath him. His horse, Achilles, spooked and charged toward a grouping of vampires, knocking them all back.

Kicking his feet free of the stirrups, Braith lifted Aria from the saddle and leapt out at the same time his hand swung down to hit his horse on the rump. The horse charged into the fray, creating more chaos and disorganization amongst the group of attackers. Around them, he saw the rest of the horses taking off into the woods, looking to escape the blood and noise of the unfolding battle.

Reluctantly, he released Aria from his grasp. He couldn't keep her against him and defend her at the same time. Aria kept her back to his as she spun away and released a new volley of arrows into the hearts of the vampires closing in on them.

"William!" she shouted. "I need your arrows!"

Rolling over with Tempest, William lifted Tempest to her feet with an arm around her waist. He pushed her down to a crouched position and remained bent over her as he ran toward Aria through the stream of arrows flying across the small clearing. Braith grabbed two vampires closing in on him and bashed their skulls together before tearing the head off one and using the body of the other to beat back a vamp who lunged at Aria.

Knowing that his sister was better with a bow and arrow than he was, William tossed Aria his quiver and pushed Tempest down so she knelt in the center of the three of them. "Make sure they all count," he said to Aria.

"I always do," she murmured and took out two more vampires.

"Stay close to me," Braith commanded them. "We have to move toward the others."

Tempest rose in the center of them as Braith backed them steadily toward where Jack was trying to defend Hannah. No matter how hard he fought the influx of vamps closing in on him, the vampires were steadily overrunning his brother. Jack released a furious shout when an arrow pierced straight through his right calf and out the other side.

Around them, the men and women of the king's guard were falling. There were only two left and they'd been separated and surrounded. There would be no getting them out of here, but Braith would get the others to safety if it was the last thing he did. Steadily pushing them back, he kept his body in between theirs and the main influx of white-cloaked vampires encroaching on them.

Reaching where Xavier lay, Braith took hold of his arm and helped him to his feet. The arrow was still embedded straight through his throat, and fire burned in Xavier's eyes when they met Braith's.

Through the turmoil surrounding them, Braith spotted the woman once more, smiling as she watched the bloodshed. *I'll enjoy killing her.* As soon as they were out of this mess and Aria was somewhere safe, he would hunt this woman down and destroy her.

Aria cried out from behind him, the scent of her blood filled the air. Red shaded his vision as he spun to find her tearing an arrow from her chest. William grabbed for her, but Braith seized her arms first, dragging her toward him.

So close. It had been so close to her heart. Saliva dripped from his fangs as he roared in fury.

"Braith, I'm fine!" Aria blurted.

His head tilted up, his gaze locked on the woman across from him. He hadn't felt this encompassing, insatiable need to kill since his father and Caleb had dared to hurt her, but it was there now.

He would make that woman pay for this if it was the last thing he did. He dragged Aria against his chest, cradling her there. The flow of her blood wet his shirt before he released her. Spinning at the sound of footsteps, he drove his fist into the chest of the vampire running toward him. He enclosed his hand around the vamp's heart, tore it from his chest, and discarded it on the ground.

Tempest stomped on the heart as William swung out with his bow and caught the next vampire under the chin with it. The scent of Aria's blood burning into his nostrils fueled Braith's wrath. A fresh wave of arrows unleashed, and cries of pain filled the air as more of them found their targets and the last of the king's guard fell.

Braith dodged to the side and snagged an arrow out of the air that would have pierced through his chest. He handed it to William who set it against his bow and fired to take out a vamp leaping at Xavier. The vamp fell and Xavier tore the arrow in his throat free. Blood pooled from the hole in his throat as another arrow pierced through his shoulder.

"Xavier!" Aria's hands slid under his armpits to catch him before he crumpled to the ground.

"Arianna!" Braith shouted and lurched toward her when two other vamps ran at her.

Red filled her blue eyes, and she fell back as the vampires grabbed at her arms. Braith grasped the arm of one, placed his foot into the vampire's chest, and tore back with enough force to rend muscle and bone from the vampire who howled his agony. Braith used the arm to bash in the cheek of the next one, before thrusting his hand into the vamp's chest and tearing his heart free.

Xavier stumbled to his feet, wrapped his arms around Aria's waist, and launched them both backward into the snow seconds before the tip of a sword would have sliced her head from her shoulders. Braith thrust his hand out to grip the blade of the sword; he ignored the biting sting of the metal cutting deep into his palm as he jerked it from the vampire's hands.

Blood reddened the snow around his feet as he whirled the sword around and sliced the vamp's head from his shoulders. "Braith, look out!" Aria screamed.

Turning, he swung out with the sword, separating two more vampires from their heads as more arrows were loosed into the air. Something slammed into his back; the impact knocked him forward a step. Braith gritted his teeth against the pain blooming over his back and spun to face the next vamp charging at him. An arrow struck the vamp through the cheek. Braith turned to see William only feet away, his reddened eyes glaring at the squirming vamp as he lowered his bow.

A break in the line of white-cloaked vamps had appeared behind William. The last thing Braith wanted to do was retreat, but they were vastly outnumbered, badly injured, and he had to get Aria out of here.

Braith took a step toward Aria as she rose to her feet just as a fresh wave of arrows released. He realized this time, they had all marked *him* as their target. Darting to the side, he dodged the first wave. Three of the arrows pierced through the forearm he flung up to batter the rest away, and one caught him in his chest, just off his heart.

When the arrows stopped flying, he launched toward Aria, determined to get her and the others to safety. Wrapping his arm around her waist, he lifted her off the ground. Ten feet away from them, Jack and Ashby battled back the vampires enclosing them. Jack limped as he moved. Ashby had blood streaking his cheek and a hole in his shirt as he tore the heart from the chest of another vamp. They were vastly outnumbered and steadily losing ground as they sought to protect Melinda and Hannah.

Charging forward, Braith lowered his shoulder and curled his arm protectively around Aria's head. He barreled into the wave of vamps pushing against Jack and Ashby, flinging them all backward. Jack's reddened eyes met his before he grabbed Hannah and lifted her off the ground. Melinda flung herself into Ashby's arms.

Setting Aria down, Braith positioned his body in front of hers before clutching the cloaks of two vamps and plucking them off Daniel and Max. Both their faces were already bruising. They had bite marks on their necks and blood staining their clothes, but the vampires deciding to feed from them before killing them had saved their lives. They would survive, if he could get them out of here.

He tossed aside the two vamps as Timber stumbled toward them and fell into the snow. His shoulders heaved; his shirt was covered in blood, but he wasn't as badly beaten as the other two. Not yet anyway. Braith spun back to Aria and lifted her into his arms once more. Her mouth pressed against his neck as he held her flush against him.

"This way!" Braith shouted to the others. Lowering his shoulder, he plowed through the vampires enclosing on them, clearing the way toward the break in the line he'd seen before.

They were only five feet from the break when he heard the sound of a fresh wave of arrows unleashing into the air. Bending over, he covered Aria's body with his. Thuds sounded in his ears, and his body jerked as he took the brunt of the arrows in his back. He clamped his teeth together to keep from making any sound that would alert Aria to what had happened. Aria gasped when one arrow pierced through his side and the tip of it cut across her.

Her voice wavered when she spoke, "Braith—"

"Fine, I'm fine," he grated in her ear, trying to control his rage over more of her blood spilling.

Rising back up, he ignored the discomfort of the arrows digging into his back and scraping against his ribs with every step he took. One had caught the corner of his heart. It wasn't a mortal wound, not if he could heal, but warm blood seeped from his chest and dripped down his back.

Keeping his head down, he again charged toward where he'd seen the opening. He drove his shoulder into any vampires who stepped into his way, throwing them aside. He could hear the others following behind him, but he didn't look back.

"Stop him!" the woman shouted.

He was almost to the opening when another volley of arrows released. They drove into his back, piercing repeatedly through his skin and deep into his body.

This time, he knew, one had not missed.

Cradling Aria closer, he continued forward as the wood of an arrow shifted and bit into the center of his heart. Every step made it feel as if his bones would splinter to pieces. Weakness seeped through his muscles, but he couldn't stop, not until Aria was safe.

Fresh anguish twisted in his heart, but this had nothing to do with the arrow shredding the organ and everything to do with Aria. He couldn't die; he *refused* to die. She'd be alone if he died, and without him, she would also die or go mad. She was his light; he'd been born to love her. He would *not* be the cause of her destruction.

No matter what it took, he would stay alive, for her.

CHAPTER 3

Aria

Aria felt the hesitation in Braith's step, yet he kept charging toward the woods with her secured within his arms. She knew he'd been hit, but he didn't ease his grip on her so she could see how badly he'd been hurt.

Terror battered at her as the scent of his blood filled her nostrils, but she didn't struggle to try to see his wounds. Fighting against his hold would only slow him down. Once they were somewhere safe, she would be able to ascertain the extent of the damage and give him blood to help him heal. She didn't care if it took every last drop in her body.

A vampire stepped forward to stop them. Ashby crashed into the vamp's side, flinging him out of the way and sending him hurtling into a tree with the crunch of bone.

"Braith!" she cried when his step faltered again. "Are you okay?"

He didn't say a word but kept going through the opening in the vamps. He plunged into the woods and down an embankment. Aria bit back a cry when his foot caught on something and they plummeted forward. Braith grunted again, but remained enveloped around her to take the brunt of the trees and rocks they bounced off of and against. Fury and fear suffused her as the sharp tip of arrowheads pressed against her belly when they were pushed through his body. He was hurt, badly, and there was nothing she could do to help him right now.

His back crashed against a tree, spinning them around and sending them rolling down the hill head over heels. Her hands dug into his arms, clinging to him as the world flashed by in a blur that made her head spin. She prayed for their rapid descent to come to an end soon. If one of those arrows should drive through him the wrong way…

Finally, their plunge came to an abrupt halt with him on top of her. From beneath his arm, she could see the corner of the boulder they'd come to a stop against.

"Braith?" she whispered.

She knew every inch of his body, every detail of his chiseled abs and broad chest. Every hollow, every dip, every sound he made when she touched him, and never before had he been so still.

"Braith?"

Tears choked her throat as her hands pushed against his chest as his body remained unmoving over hers.

Don't panic. Don't panic. Don't panic.

The words became a mantra in her head; her eyes burned with tears and a scream lodged firmly in her throat.

Careful not to throw him onto his back and drive the arrows embedded within his flesh even deeper, Aria managed to squirm her way out from underneath his heavy weight. Settling her back against the boulder, her body shook as her gaze fell on Braith's still form.

A choked sound escaped her. She was going to throw up. She was going to pass out. No, she was going to *die*. She nearly doubled into a ball, but despite the fact he remained so unmoving, and there was no way *that* arrow wasn't embedded in his heart, she still felt the faint wave of a connection to him through their bloodlink.

My blood flows within him, his within me. I am him and he is me. I'll know if the bloodlink breaks. It wasn't broken yet, but if she didn't do something to get him away from here, it would be soon.

Her gaze lifted to the hillside they had tumbled down. They'd plunged nearly two hundred feet down the rocky, steep terrain into a gulley. Near the top of the hill, she spotted the others from their group skidding down the snow-slickened hill as they tried to flee the group of white-cloaked vampires chasing them.

Arrows fired into the trees around her friends and family. Timber cried out when leaves and dirt gave way beneath him and he tumbled down the hill much like she and Braith had. He smashed into a tree halfway down, getting caught up on it instead of plunging all the way to the bottom of the gulch.

Aria glanced back and forth down the snowy gulch. Sheltered by the trees surrounding it, there was only a coating of snow to be found in this part of the forest. *Her* woods. She knew where they were, knew where to find shelter in order to keep Braith protected, and she had to get him there, now.

Braith outweighed her by more than a hundred pounds, but it didn't matter. Even if she'd still been human, she would have found a way to pick him up and carry him away before their enemies could get to them.

Her gaze went back to the others making their way toward her. No matter how badly she wanted to make sure they were safe too, she couldn't wait for them. It would mean certain death for Braith if she did. They would understand, and Daniel and William would know where she went. *If* they made it to the bottom of the canyon.

She couldn't think of that. Her main focus now had to be Braith. He was vulnerable, and if he died, then everything they'd fought so hard to achieve would be ruined. He was her everything, but not only that, so many others counted on him as well. His many loyal followers would die without him, as she knew that woman wouldn't permit any of them to live, and Aria refused to let that happen.

Grabbing hold of Braith's wrist, she brought his arm around her shoulder. She ignored the wrenching pain in her chest from where the arrow had pierced her. She pulled him over her back and around her shoulders. A bloodlink made a vampire stronger. It had made it possible for Braith to see when he was around her, and for Hannah to walk in the sun after drinking from Jack. Now, she easily lifted Braith as she rose to her feet.

She ignored every protesting ache in her battered body as she turned to the right and ran down the gulch toward the cave a couple miles away. She hadn't known she could run so fast, but fear drove her to speeds she'd never attained before.

Despite the fact her wounds were healing and she no longer felt blood seeping down her chest or side, her legs quaked from exhaustion and blood loss by the time she stopped a mile away from the cave.

Carefully, she laid Braith on his side to avoid the arrows and brushed her fingers over his pale face. The sight of all those arrows in his back caused her to wince, but she couldn't pull them out yet. They would only bleed more if she did, and right now they had too much blood trailing them here.

He'd lost the brown cloak he'd been wearing during the battle, so she didn't have to try to remove it from him now. Taking hold of one of the numerous holes in his shirt, she tore it further. Her hands trembled as she worked to carefully pull the material away from his battered body and set the shirt on the ground.

His flesh was mottled and red from where the arrows had punctured him over and over again. He'd always had flawless skin, smooth to the touch, so strong and warm beneath her hands. Now it was chilled beneath her fingers and there was a weakness in him she'd never seen before. The cold of his body wasn't from the snow beneath him and the winter air flowing over him, but from the life steadily seeping away from him.

She would *crave* death without him. She knew what the loss of a bloodlink had done to his father, Atticus. She would never allow herself to become that kind of a monster.

She'd informed William she might have to be destroyed. Now, the possibility loomed over her like a guillotine preparing to fall. She could almost feel the sharp steel edge kissing the back of her neck.

However, like Atticus, she wouldn't die or allow herself to be destroyed before exacting her revenge against Braith's killer. She would not rest until she knew the woman who destroyed her husband was dead. That woman was far stronger than she was, but Aria would find a way to watch her screaming in agony before she allowed death to claim her.

Braith had taken those arrows to keep her alive. It should have been her lying there now, not him. She brushed a strand of black hair off his forehead. His face was lax, making him appear more vulnerable than she'd ever seen him, and right now, he was vulnerable. Like him, she would risk everything to keep him protected.

Aria hastily removed her bow, quiver, and cloak before taking her bloody shirt off. The cold air cut through the thin undershirt she wore as she lifted Braith's shirt from the ground.

"Keep working," she muttered to herself. "Keep going."

Bunching up the ruined clothes, she rose to her feet and ran up the side of the embankment on the other side of the gulch. She dipped the clothes onto the ground every couple of feet, leaving blood stains on the snow as she went. Halfway up the hillside, she fell to her hands and knees. She dug through a patch of snow to uncover the leaves and earth beyond. Tearing away the dirt, she created a small hole and stuffed the shirts inside before burying them.

She ran back and forth over the area, kicking snow up to cover her digging. When she was done, she turned and walked backwards down the hill, giving the appearance of someone going up the hill, but no one coming back down. It might not distract their pursuers for long, but it would buy her some time to navigate the traps within the cave safely. If she knew her brothers, they would realize what she'd done and not go to the caves the same way she planned to go.

A sense of urgency drove her as she raced back to Braith's side. *The bloodlink between us is still there...*

However, she could feel a wavering within the bond connecting them. "Don't leave me," she whispered to him.

She threw her cloak back around her shoulders and pinned it in place with the silver horsehead brooch her father had left for her before he died. She would have put the cloak around Braith to try to warm him, but it would never fit his large frame. Kneeling at Braith's side, she ran her fingers over his cherished face before lifting him onto her shoulders once more. She didn't look back as she raced through the snow to the entrance of the cave.

The musty scent of the cave filled her nostrils when she plunged into its gloomy depths. She carefully placed Braith on the rocky ground twenty feet within before returning to the entrance. She searched the gulch and the trees lining the sides of it for any hint of danger. Everything remained calm for as far as she could see, and she scented nothing out of the ordinary on the breeze shaking the trees.

Satisfied they were still alone, she stripped her cloak off once more and raced out into the open. She ran half a mile back; it was as far as she dared to go without chancing being spotted. Lowering her cloak into the snow, she walked backwards and wiped away her footprints leading to the cave.

There was nothing she could do to completely mask their scent, but with the buried clothes, she hoped to leave their enemies confused enough about their location that she would have a better chance of leading them away from the cave system later.

If their enemies did find the cave and decided to investigate, there was a good chance they would be driven back, killed, or at least maimed by Daniel's booby traps. It had been nearly a year and a half since they'd had to use the caves to hide from vampires, but she didn't doubt her brother's designs had held up during that time.

Returning to the entrance of the cave, she fled back to where she'd left Braith and knelt by his side before lifting him onto her shoulders once more. Her legs, back, and chest protested the movement, but she'd carry him a thousand more miles if she had to.

CHAPTER 4

William

"This way," William said and fled down the center of the gulch after his sister's footprints. On her own, Aria barely would have left a mark behind in the snow, but Braith's weight on her shoulders had made her normally agile step far more pronounced.

He kept hold of Tempest's hand as he ran through the snow in pursuit of Aria. Her hand warmed his as he slid his fingers across the delicate bones in the back of it. Tempest was strong, nimble, and smart, but he'd felt the power of the vampire woman claiming to be the rightful queen and experienced her cruelty when he'd allowed himself to be captured in Badwin.

He shuddered at the possibility of anything happening to Tempest. She was *his*; she'd made him forget the wrath that had festered inside him after he'd lost his mortality and become a vampire, one of the creatures he'd spent most of his life hating.

But with Tempest, his life as a vampire had finally made sense. He would have endured the agony and uncertainty of his death as a human and transition into a vampire a thousand times over again to have her in his life. Now he may lose it all if they didn't get away from their trackers soon.

He glanced over his shoulder as the vampires in white chased them down the hill. At least the hill was too steep for their followers to get a good shot off with their bows, but it didn't mean some of them weren't still trying. The others in their scouting party were close behind him, laboring to keep up. He had no idea how Xavier was still on his feet, as blood covered him from head to toe.

William couldn't fully process what had happened, and how quickly it had all unfolded. They had to regroup, plan, and get away from their attackers.

Braith looked dead. William winced as the image of the arrows protruding from Braith's back went through his mind once more. Many of those arrows were clustered around his heart. If Braith had been lost, then that meant Aria would be too...

Don't think it. Just keep moving.

The whistle of a fresh wave of arrows being released filled the air before someone else grunted in pain. Glancing over his shoulder, he saw Xavier tear an arrow from his thigh and toss it aside.

The trail of Aria and Braith's blood in the snow suddenly disappeared, but Aria's footprints continued. On the hillside opposite of the one they'd fled down, he spotted beads of blood amid the snow and his sister's footprints going halfway up the hill.

"Which way?" Jack asked hoarsely from beside him.

"Aria didn't continue to the top of the hill here, but she's trying to throw them off her trail. I'd be willing to bet the footprints continuing through the gulch ahead of us stop at some point too. She wouldn't have led them straight to the cave. We have to find where her tracks end, then go up the hill there."

He glanced at Daniel to find his older brother's blue eyes on him. Sweat plastered Daniel's wheat blond hair to his flushed face. Bruises shadowed his eyes and jaw; blood seeped from his nose and bite marks marred his neck. He was beaten and battered, but his gaze was filled with steely resolve.

"You're right. We can't continue on this way to the cave once her tracks stop. We'll go up the hill then," Daniel said.

William's heart sank at Daniel's words. Daniel was faster than most humans. Their entire family had always been faster than normal, thanks to what was most likely partial vampire DNA from a distant ancestor. However, as humans, they weren't fast enough to evade a pack of vampires for much longer. Daniel knew it too, knew going up the hill could spell his death, but he was much like their father with his unfailing devotion to doing what must be done and protecting those he loved. Their father was gone though, and William would *not* lose his brother too.

"Standing here isn't helping," Ashby said impatiently. "The king and queen must be protected above all else, no matter what."

William inhaled deeply, a habit he still hadn't managed to break from the days when he'd been a human. Gripping Tempest's hand tighter, he fled further down the gulch. When he found where Aria's tracks ended in the snow, he turned to face the steep hillside. Thick trees covered the embankment, allowing only a little snow to have slipped through during the last storm.

The ground would be loose beneath their feet, but at least it wouldn't be slippery, and the trees would help shelter them from any arrows unleashed on them. Hopefully the top of the hill would be as thick with trees so they could hide their tracks and lose themselves in the forest.

Tempest's almond-shaped, doe brown eyes were apprehensive when she tilted her head back to look at him. Her silvery blonde hair tumbled about her shoulders. The press of her full lips had caused them to thin out, and her pretty face radiated strain, but she remained stoic as she watched him.

"We've been in worse than this before," he said and drew her forward to kiss her forehead.

"Yes," she agreed.

Releasing her, he stepped back and gestured toward the hill. He kept Tempest in front of him to shelter her as he nudged her up the hillside. "Don't look back."

Her feet slipped in the leaves and loose dirt, but she kept her gaze focused ahead as she climbed before him.

"We'll carry you once we get to the top," William said over his shoulder to Daniel.

"I'm not riding anyone's back," Timber grumbled as he struggled up the hillside.

"I don't think anything short of a horse could carry you," Ashby replied. Placing his hand on the small of Timber's back, he propelled the man faster up the side of the hill.

William had to agree. Timber was by far the largest man he'd ever seen at nearly seven feet, if not seven. His broad back and thighs the size of tree trunks made him the biggest target. Despite his massive size, he moved with relative ease up the hill, though his permanently crooked nose whistled with every ragged inhalation he made. His shaggy brown hair fell forward over his shoulders to nearly trail in the snow as he remained low to the ground.

They made it to the top of the hill as the twang of more arrows being released filled the air. Diving forward, William enclosed his arm around Tempest's waist and shoved her to the ground. He rolled toward a white pine. The needles pricked his back when he came up against it, but no arrows pierced his flesh.

Rolling over, he discovered Ashby and Melinda rising to their feet beside him. Usually immaculate, Ashby had leaves and pine needles sticking to his face and dark blond hair. His green eyes were flashing with red when they met William's. Melinda's knee-length, golden blonde hair was a tangled mess as she pushed it back from her forehead. Her normally dove-gray eyes were the color of rubies.

"They're coming," Melinda said as she stared down the hill. "When the time comes, I'm going to enjoy killing every one of these bastards."

"All in due time, dear," Ashby replied in his unruffled manner as he slid his arm through Melinda's and hurried her forward. "But first let's work on getting you away from them."

William glanced back down the hill at the vampires already making their way up. Their white cloaks were far more noticeable in the growing night. They were as loud as if they were riding a dozen horses through the trees.

"You won't have to carry anyone. We'll lose them easily in the dark," Daniel said from beside him.

"Yes," William agreed. "Let's go."

He reclaimed Tempest's hand and fled through the forest. All of those with him were accustomed to having to move through the trees with stealth. He barely detected their movement. Behind him, trees and branches snapped as the vampire's trailing topped the hill and came for them.

**

Aria

It took Aria almost two hours to safely navigate all of Daniel's traps inside the cave with Braith across her shoulders. Despite the cool air surrounding her, sweat covered her body and adhered her clothes to her skin. Every inch of her hurt in ways she hadn't believed possible, but her physical discomfort was nothing compared to the growing pain in her chest.

Finally, she reached the end of the narrow cave. The iron gate built into the wall there was closed and locked, but like all the cave systems in the area, she knew there was a key hidden nearby. *Unless someone took it with them...*

She broke the thought off. There was no need for humans to hide within these caves anymore. Or at least there hadn't been a reason before that vampire woman had arrived. If that woman won, the humans would be forced into a life of slavery or back to a life hidden in these caves once more.

Her father had given his life in the last war to help attain peace. Many more would die and the peace would be shattered if that woman had her way. Aria wouldn't allow her father's death, and all of the other lives lost during the war with Atticus, to be for nothing.

Walking back ten feet, Aria bent and pushed aside a small rock tucked within the cave wall. She reached her fingers in and pulled out the key hidden behind the rock. Drawing it out, she kept her ears attuned for any hint of someone approaching, but the cave remained hushed. Not even the drip of water could be heard amongst the rocks enclosing her.

Enclosing... Stop it!

She'd gotten much better with her fear of confined spaces. However, every once in a while, it would creep back in. She couldn't allow this to be one of those times. The mineral scent of the rocks surrounding her filled her nostrils, but she kept her attention focused on her task and Braith's limp body around her shoulders. Her hand enveloped Braith's wrist, seeking comfort from touching him.

Turning away, she walked back to the gate, slid the key into the lock, and pushed it open. The hinges squeaked from disuse and she had to shove at the gate to get it to open enough so she could slip past. She put the key back in its hiding spot before returning to the gate, slipping inside, and closing it behind her.

On the other side, about twenty feet in, she shifted Braith's weight as she knelt to retrieve some matches hidden within a small hole years ago. She pulled the matches free of the hole and pulled back the protective, waterproof canvas they'd been wrapped in. Rising, the jagged, cool rocks brushed roughly over her fingertips as she made her way forward until she came across a torch propped against the wall. With her enhanced vampire vision, she could see far more than she ever had as a human, but *no* light penetrated this deep into the caves, making even a vampire blind.

She could navigate the rest of this cave by memory and touch alone, but she much preferred to have a torch with her. For some reason, the idea of light made her feel not quite so alone.

"Please work," she whispered as she pulled a match from the box and struck it against a rock.

It took a few fumbling tries with her numb fingers, but eventually a flame sputtered to life at the end of the small head. She held it up to the cloth around the torch and watched as it blazed to life. Walking back, she replaced the matches in their hiding spot in case someone else, who had once lived and survived within these caves, might one day need them.

She adjusted Braith on her shoulders, before dashing down the cave. The flame of the torch flickered and danced over the walls as she held it before her. Shadows danced sinuously over the gray rock surrounding her. The crackling fire warmed her chilled cheeks, but it did nothing to warm the rest of her.

The next gate she came to was open; she closed it behind her. After traveling another quarter of a mile beneath the earth, she stepped into a large cavern and gazed at the small, smooth bottom of the cavern fifty feet below her.

Along the edges of the center, black and gray rocks rose up from it like seats in an auditorium. The jagged rock formations circled the flat center all the way around and offered more protection from anyone looking to enter. It was impossible for someone to descend the rocks quickly, and anyone in the center would have plenty of warning and time to getaway if someone entered from above.

The shadows created by the torch lengthened and swelled imposingly with each flicker. Sniffing at the air, she detected the feral, musky scent of wild animals within, but she didn't smell humans or vampires. No footprints could be seen in the dirt within the cave, only the paw prints of some fox, raccoon, and opossum showed.

Her head tilted back to take in the stalactites forming on the ceiling above her. No bats hung from the ceiling, something Ashby would appreciate, as she knew from past experience he hated bats.

That was *if* her brother-in-law made it here.

"Don't think it," she whispered to herself.

Turning her attention back to the chamber, she carefully picked her way down the rocks to the open space beneath her. Arriving at the bottom, she carried Braith into the center of the cavern. Gently, she set him on the ground and propped his side against a rock to keep him from falling back on those arrows.

She had to get the arrows out of him so he could begin the healing process, but first she had to make sure they were safe here. With the torch in hand, she ran down each of the three side tunnels branching off from the lower level. She checked for keys before shutting the gates behind her.

William, Daniel, Max, Timber, and Jack would know where to look for those keys if they made it here. The others wouldn't, but the others would never make it this far into the cave without someone to guide their way. Returning to the cavern, she raced up the rocks with far more ease than she'd descended them and closed off the gate in the one other tunnel up there.

Once they were secure within, she ran back to Braith's side and fell to her knees before him. She pulled her bow and quiver from her back and set them on the ground within easy reach. She couldn't look at the pallor of his skin or the way his cheeks had hollowed out, as she broke off the feathers of all the arrows going straight through his body.

Her fingers shook when she gripped his shoulder and wrapped her hand around the first arrow head protruding from his chest. With a swift jerk, she yanked it from his body. She cried out as if it had been torn from her flesh. He, however, showed no reaction to the arrow being pulled from his body. Fresh blood trickled out of the hole, down his pale skin and broad chest.

"Keep going," she whispered.

He showed as much reaction to the next arrow as he had the first one, but her entire body shook uncontrollably. With a bleeding bottom lip that she bit to stifle her cries, she removed the seven arrows going completely through him, except for one. She couldn't bring herself to pull that one yet.

By the time she was done with them, she couldn't stifle the flow of her tears. They slid down her cheeks and dripped off her chin as she stared at the six remaining arrows in him. These six still had the arrowhead embedded inside of him. She would have to pull those arrowheads out through his body from behind. It would tear at his flesh and bones, and it was going to hurt him far more than anything else she'd done so far.

Or at least it normally would have.

She wiped her tears on the end of her cloak and moved around to his broad back. More blood trickled from the holes of the arrows she'd already pulled out. Bending, she kissed his flesh and rested her cheek on his back as she took a minute to stabilize herself before going back to work on removing the rest of the arrows.

Grabbing the first arrow below the feathers, she bit her lip again as she pulled it out. Her body jerked as if it had been pulled from her and pain bloomed through her chest. Braith showed no reaction that the pointed end of an arrow had just been torn from his body.

With a surprisingly steady hand, she inspected the still intact arrow before slipping it into her quiver. At some point in time, she would put an arrow tainted with Braith's blood into that bitch claiming to be queen. The idea caused her fangs to prickle with anticipation as bloodlust rolled through her.

Aria gripped the five remaining arrows and pulled them free. She didn't realize she was crying again until her tears dripped off her chin to land on his back and trickle down his pale skin. Her tears mixed with his drying blood, creating pink rivulets over his battered flesh. She ran her fingers across his skin as she lifted him so his back rested against a rock.

Making her way around to his front on her knees, her gaze fell on the arrow she'd broken the flight off of and left within him. The head stuck an inch out of his chest, the shaft directly through his heart. She stroked her fingers over the metal before dropping her hand away. He wouldn't be able to heal if the arrow remained within him, but what if the arrow was all that kept him alive now? What if pulling it out killed him?

She crept closer to him and rested her cheek against his shoulder. Normally his arms would wrap around her, dragging her against him as he enfolded her in his warmth and love. Now his arms remained unmoving at his sides, his palms turned up as his chin rested against his chest.

"Braith," she whispered as she fought to keep from screaming and cursing anyone and everyone who had ever lived or died. "Can't fall apart now. Get it together."

However, she didn't know how to get it together right now. They were supposed to be living in peace, humans and vampires finally united and working together. Instead, their world had crumbled in the blink of an eye.

"And it has before," she said aloud and forced herself to sit back away from him. "It has before and we've gotten through it. We will get through it again."

She had to keep the faith that would happen this time too. The bloodlink was still between them, which meant he still lived. She would know the second it was severed.

Tilting her head to the side, she studied the arrow, her fingers rising to wrap around it again before falling back to her side. Once she pulled it free, she had no idea what would happen. Together, they may all be able to stop that woman without Braith, but he was the only one strong enough to go head to head with her and the only one Aria knew for sure the vampires and humans would follow without hesitation. If she removed the arrow and he died, the peace could be lost forever.

Or maybe not forever, she thought. *After what I saw today...*

A crunch behind her had her snatching her bow from the ground and spinning with an arrow nocked and ready to fire.

CHAPTER 5

Aria

Jack threw his hands up and stepped back. "Easy, Aria," he coaxed.

Aria stared at him as relief and love washed over her. They were alive; they had made it. Everything was still a mess, but they were *here*. Her tensed muscles held the bow for a minute more before she lowered it to her side. "I should have heard you," she berated herself.

"I think you have more to deal with right now." Jack's gaze flicked to Braith; his jaw clenched as his shoulders went back. Sorrow and anger caused his eyes to switch from gray to red and back again. The colors within his black, brown, and gold hair danced in the torchlight. He was shorter than Braith at six foot three and leaner, but there was still a great deal of power within him and there was no denying they were brothers.

William's shoulders were stooped and sadness radiated from him as he stepped toward her. Aria moved closer to Braith. She would have to leave him soon, but not yet.

"Aria, you can't stay with him," William said.

"He's not dead!" she retorted when she realized what William and Jack were thinking.

She slapped Jack's hand away and bared her fangs at him when he held it out to her. Hannah took a protective step forward, but Jack held out his arm to keep her back. "The arrow is through his heart," Jack said to her.

"I know where the arrow is, Jack!" she retorted. "I also know I'm as intricately bound to him as you are to Hannah, so I would know if he were dead. He's *not!*"

Aria's gaze fell to the arrow sticking out of Jack's right thigh and the broken arrow shaft protruding from his calf when he limped closer to his brother and knelt before him. Her fingers bit into her thighs as she resisted the urge to shove him away from Braith. Jack wouldn't harm him, but the idea of anyone touching Braith right now made her see red.

Jack gently clasped Braith's cheeks and lifted his head toward him. Vampires didn't have heartbeats and they didn't breathe, but Jack leaned toward him until their foreheads nearly touched.

Aria tore her gaze away to focus on the others. She couldn't watch someone touching Braith in such a vulnerable state and remain restrained. Melinda had her hand against her mouth to stifle her sobs. Xavier leaned against Ashby with his arm draped around Ashby's shoulders. Timber, Daniel, and Max had collapsed to the ground. If it wasn't for the bruises covering their faces, they would be as pale as Braith.

"Daniel—"

"I'm fine," he assured her and waved his hand dismissively.

"We all are," Max said. His sandy blond hair stuck up in spikes around his normally handsome face. Bruises marred his cheekbones and eyes; blood trickled from his nose and the bite marks on his neck. An arrow protruded through his side. Judging by the position of the arrow, it wasn't a mortal injury and would heal once the arrow was removed. His full lips were nearly white, but his blue eyes were steady when they met hers.

"He's alive," Jack murmured from beside her, and Aria's shoulders slumped.

She'd known that, but hearing Jack confirm it made it more real.

"The arrow isn't through his heart?" William inquired.

"It is," Jack confirmed. "Dead center."

"How is that possible?" Max asked.

Jack's eyes were gray once more when they met hers. "A bloodlink makes a vampire stronger," he said.

"Strong enough to defeat death?" Timber demanded.

"I don't know," Jack said. "But the arrow has to come out if the wound is to heal."

"Will that kill him?" Hannah whispered.

Aria tilted her head back to study her sister-in-law's beautiful features. Hannah's chocolate-colored hair tumbled over her shoulders and clung to her round face. Because she hadn't been able to go out in the sun before meeting Jack, Hannah's skin was normally alabaster, but now it was three shades paler. Her jade-colored eyes brimmed with tears as she stared at Aria.

Hannah went to kneel beside her, but Aria waved her away. She liked Hannah and loved how she'd finally made Jack happy, but she would completely fall apart if someone tried to comfort her right now, and there was no time to fall apart. "I can't," she whispered.

Hannah hesitated before taking a step away from her.

"I don't know if it will kill him or not," Jack said and looked to Aria again. "But it has to come out."

"I know it does," she whispered. Jack gripped the arrowhead. Aria seized his wrist before he could tear it free. "No."

"Aria—"

"It has to be me who removes it. If it's you, or anyone else, and he dies, I *will* kill you."

Jack didn't laugh off her words, didn't point out that he was over nine hundred years older than she was. A vampire severed from their bloodlink could be capable of almost anything afterward. His father had managed to destroy most of the world; she might be able to take down one of the most powerful vampires in existence.

Jack hesitated for a minute before his hand fell away. "Are you sure about this?"

"It has to be me. If he dies, I will follow him after she is made to pay. I can live with the guilt of this until then."

And if she couldn't, it would only fuel her desire for revenge until the day she destroyed that woman and could then die too. Jack stepped back and pushed Hannah protectively behind him before bracing his legs apart.

Wrapping her hand around the arrowhead, Aria leaned forward to kiss Braith's forehead and then his lips. Her mouth lingered against his as the scent of his blood filled her nostrils. How many times had she experienced the searing heat of his kiss before? Now there was only coldness.

She kissed him again before sitting back and tearing the arrow free with an anguished cry. The arrow fell from her numbed fingertips as she threw her arms around his shoulders and buried her face in his neck.

"Don't die. Don't die," she pleaded.

She'd said she could handle the guilt if he died, decided she would get her revenge no matter what, but she wasn't sure she could go on without him. Her fingers dug into his neck as she waited for the connection between them to waver and shatter apart. Waited for the beautiful link she'd never expected to have with him to disintegrate like snowflakes on the tongue, but though it was weak, the bond continued to shimmer between them.

Blood from the hole in his heart ran down to cover her thin shirt, but she didn't stop it. She would need his blood on her when she left here. Her fingers slid through his thick hair as she kissed his neck, then his cheek and temple. She had to pry herself away from him before she crawled into his lap and stayed there until he moved again.

She couldn't do that though; there were far too many lives counting on her, including Braith's. She knew her brothers would have been careful about entering the cave, and she had been too, but despite the traps and no matter how cautious they'd been, there was a chance they could be discovered.

Sitting back, Aria turned her wrist over and bit into it. Placing it against Braith's mouth, she tipped his head back so her blood flowed into his system. When she felt her bite healing, she bit her wrist again and again until she was sure she'd managed to get a fair amount of her blood into him.

Afterward, she kissed his lips and rose to her feet. Her legs wobbled, but she believed it was more from exhaustion than lack of blood. However, there was no time for rest right now. She gathered her bow and quiver and slid them onto her back.

When she was done, she knelt before Braith again and used the bottom of her undershirt to wipe the rest of the blood on him away. Most of his injuries had already closed, but she still managed to get a good coating of his blood on her clothing.

"What are you doing?" Jack inquired.

"Preparing to leave," she replied.

"What?" he demanded, grabbing her arms and spinning her toward him. "You cannot go back out there."

"I have to."

"You do *not!*"

Aria swallowed and couldn't resist looking to Braith again. So vulnerable, so unlike the powerful warrior she knew and loved. If their roles had been reversed, he would do what he had to in order to defend their people.

She would do the same.

"I was careful coming here," she said, unable to take her eyes away from Braith. "I know you were too, but they're going to search this area over and over again until they find us. The traps in this cave system will take out some of them and keep the rest busy for a couple of days, but they won't stop them."

"We'll be able to leave here before then," Jack replied.

"And go where? To another cave system only to be hunted again? You're barely walking. Are you up for another run right now? And if they corner us in here? What then?" she inquired.

"If they believe Braith is dead, they may not pursue us."

"Yes, they will. You heard her, she wants his head. She won't stop until she has it."

"You can't know that," Ashby reasoned.

Aria finally tore her gaze away from Braith to look between Ashby and Jack. "I *do* know that. She won't be satisfied with less."

"Aria—"

"Think, Jack!" she snapped. "Think of who that woman was!"

His forehead creased as his hands around her biceps tightened. "I don't know who she was."

"I've only ever seen eyes that color once before, on your father," she said quietly.

"My father had no other children," he said forcefully.

"She's not his child. *He* was *hers.*"

CHAPTER 6

Aria

Jack looked as if she'd punched him in the gut when his mouth fell open. It was a face she knew well as she'd managed to do so a few times when they were still rebels training in the woods together. She understood why he couldn't see who that woman was, knew why Braith probably hadn't realized who she was either. They had enough monsters in their family line, neither of them wanted to add another one to it, but they had to now.

William wouldn't have recognized the woman for who she was either. He hadn't spent as much time with the mad king as Aria had. William had recognized something familiar about her, but he wouldn't know the distinct shades of green in her eyes, or the depth of the cruelty within them, but Aria knew she was right about the woman's identity.

"Freaking vampires," Timber muttered and Max nodded in agreement.

"Sabine is dead," Jack said. "She was staked through the heart."

"And so was your father, but he came back to life," Aria said. "This would help explain *why* he did. It also explains her looks and her power. That woman is related to you, and I believe she is Atticus's mother. Your grandmother."

"You vampire families are so messed up," Max said and everyone gave him a look. He lifted his hands and shrugged. "Am I wrong?"

Jack's hands fell limply, and his skin took on a ghostly hue as he stepped away from her. His gaze fell to Braith. "Do you think they were like Braith, and they only looked dead when they were buried? Did we bury Atticus alive?"

There had been no love lost between Jack and his father, but she heard the note of anguish in his voice at the possibility. "No," Aria said. "I think they were both dead when they were buried."

"But how did they come back?" William demanded.

"I don't know," Aria replied. "But they are all a part of the one true vampire line, a line that can be traced all the way back to the original vampire Lucifer created. We have no idea what a vampire of that lineage could be capable of."

"It is the oldest and most powerful vampire line," Ashby said. "If there was a chance any vampire could beat death, it would be a vampire from that line. If they knew they were capable of surviving what would kill any other vampire, they would make sure there was no record of it. If they died in a public way, the survivor would have to go into hiding after rising."

"So she's been in hiding all this time?" Melinda asked. "Wouldn't someone have seen her at some point?"

"Not if she was careful and left Europe immediately after she woke again. She may have even been in this country all that time. Back then it was wild and secluded enough that she would have been able to lose herself completely," Ashby said. "Any who might have known her have perished over time."

Jack ran his hand through his hair, tugging at the ends of it as he paced about the cave. With every step he took, he limped more and more. Blood trickled from his wounds to stain the ground, but he didn't pay it any attention as he continued walking.

"Do you think Atticus knew about this?" he asked as he spun to face her again.

"No, I don't," Aria said. "All he wanted was death. If he'd known there was a chance he could come back, I think it would have driven him even more insane while he was still alive."

"Don't think that was possible," William muttered.

"Why would Sabine keep the knowledge from him?" Jack inquired.

"She may not have known about it either, or most likely she never got the chance to tell him," Ashby said. "A vampire that can't die by staking is something else entirely. There's a power involved that would be more than a little frightening to other vampires. They would have risked their entire line being destroyed if their secret ever got out. She may have been waiting until Atticus was old enough to keep the secret before telling him."

"Att...icus was only fi..." Xavier rested his hand against the closing hole in his throat. He winced with every word, but continued speaking. "Five when Sabine die...d."

"They die, but somehow they rejuvenate after death," Ashby said.

"Shit," Jack muttered.

"So that means Jack could withstand a staking?" Hannah asked.

"I don't think so," Aria replied. "Sabine only asked for Braith's head earlier. Jack may not be as old or as powerful as Braith, but he's still a *big* threat to her too. She'll want him eradicated as well." Aria turned to face Melinda. "And there's no reason she would know that you're not Atticus's child. She would have asked for your head too, if she believed you could come back."

Melinda clasped her hands before her, twisting them into her cloak when they began to tremble.

"She's right," Ashby said and Xavier nodded in agreement. "This is something to do with the first born in the line. Sabine, Atticus…" He glanced at Braith. "Even when he was young, there was always more power in Braith than in Caleb or you, Jack, or many of the vampires who were older than he was."

Jack pulled at his face, rubbing his hand over the stubble lining his jaw as he stared at his brother. "He's always been more powerful than most," Jack agreed before focusing on Aria again. "What if you're wrong and it's not Sabine?"

Aria couldn't stop her gaze from falling to Braith. "If I'm wrong and he dies, then he will remain dead, but either way, I have to leave here in order to keep him from being discovered."

"I'm not letting you leave here," Jack stated.

"I am *your* queen. You have no say in this."

"Aria—"

"Someone has to lead them away from Braith and the others from Badwin and Chippman who are still out there depending on us to get them to safety. If they're discovered, they will be slaughtered."

Hannah released a choked noise as her eyes darted toward Jack. Tempest stepped closer to William and gripped his arm. Many of Hannah's friends and family were with those waiting for them to return. The children Tempest had rescued from the orphanage, along with some other residents, and her best friend, Pallas, were also with them.

"We can't leave them out there alone," Aria continued. Her gaze ran over those gathered within before landing on Melinda and Ashby. They had faired pretty well during the battle and were well known and liked within the palace. "After I go out to lure Sabine's followers away, Ashby and Melinda can return for the survivors and lead them safely back to the palace."

"I will go out and lure the vampires who attacked us away," Jack said.

"You made it here, but you're limping badly. Hannah isn't going to stay here without you, and neither of you will be able to traverse the forest with the speed it will require. These are my woods—"

"I know these woods well too," he interrupted.

"Yes, but not as well as I do, and you know it."

"And if he wakes up while you're gone?" Jack demanded.

"If anyone will understand why this has to be done, it is Braith."

"What if you get killed and he wakes up? You think Atticus was vicious, do you know what Braith will do if he wakes up to discover you dead? How do you think he'll handle that?"

"He will do what he must," she replied. "He is not your father."

Jack and William exchanged a troubled look. "I'll go," William said. "I'm not as badly injured as everyone else, and I know these woods as well as you. You will stay here, Aria."

How entirely tempting that sounded. She could curl up in Braith's arms and simply wait. If he did wake, they could be together again. She would be here to kiss him, to hug him, to laugh and cry as he *finally* hugged her back and cradled her to his chest. If he didn't wake, then someone would have to take mercy on her and put her down.

A lump clogged her throat, and she turned away from them before they could see the tears burning her eyes again. She had to stay strong. She was a queen, and so many lives depended on her. She couldn't stay here and wait. She had to lead her people.

Right now, protecting the many who needed it and destroying Sabine were all she had to drive her onward. That and the possibility Braith would survive this and come back to her.

"They will not expect us to part," she whispered as she gazed at Braith's unmoving form. "They will believe he's with me, if I lead them away." She turned back to William and gestured down the front of her shirt. "His blood is all over me. It is *inside* of me. It will be *our* scents they trail from these caves. He is as much an intricate piece of me as I am of him. You can't say the same."

She recognized the stubborn set of his jaw. "Then I will come with you."

Tempest's hand trembled on his arm, but she didn't protest his words. Aria glanced between the two of them. "I'd prefer you stay," she replied.

"Since when have I cared what you prefer?" he retorted.

"What about what Tempest prefers?" she countered, knowing it was the one thing she could use to deter him from this decision.

Some of the fight went out of him as he took hold of Tempest's hand. Aria didn't blame him for staying behind; Tempest's life depended on his now. He had to protect what they shared between them.

Turning back, Aria knelt before Braith and cupped his chin in her hand. She couldn't stop the tears flowing down her face as she leaned forward to kiss him again before resting her lips against his ear. "I'm going to do everything I can to keep you safe. Please, come back to me. I love you."

Closing her eyes, she rose and stepped away from him again. She never thought she would be separated from him again in her lifetime. Now she didn't know if she would ever see him again at all. The bleak possibility shredded her heart. Her fingers bit into her palms, drawing blood as her nails tore into her skin.

She had to get moving. Those vampires would be swarming up there, lost in the woods, likely to stumble over the caves any minute now, but her feet wouldn't move. *Turn away. Do it. Now or he'll die!*

With a cry, she wrenched her gaze away from Braith and spun on her toes. "Take care of him, Jack," she choked out. "Make sure he stays safe."

She couldn't look at anyone in the room again as she made her way forward. "*I am co…* ming with ya," Xavier said, the words garbled and difficult to understand when he moved to block her.

Despite the blood covering him from head to toe, his face was resolute. Xavier had become more than her bodyguard over time; he was also her friend.

"No. You're barely standing and you'll leave a trail of blood behind you as you go. You won't be able to make it and I can't lose you," she told him.

"Yer not goin' a…lone."

"She's not," William said and stepped forward when Daniel tried to rise to his feet.

Daniel slumped against a rock but straightened himself and rose. He swayed for a second until Xavier's hand shot out to steady him. Xavier helped to guide Daniel down when his legs gave out on him and he slumped to the ground.

"William—" Aria started to protest.

"The peace must be protected at all costs," he said. "We have always known that."

"You have a choice," she said.

"We haven't had a choice since we were born, Aria."

"Tempest needs you."

"I'm coming with you," Tempest said. "I've maneuvered through mountains and caves silently before."

"We might be climbing through the trees too," William said to her.

"I'm not staying here without you, and if I can climb a mountain, I can climb a tree," Tempest insisted.

"It's not safe out there."

"It's not safe anywhere right now, but I'm safer with you than without you."

Her brother couldn't argue with that logic and he knew it. William turned helplessly back to Aria, but she couldn't help him on this one. She would have used the same reasoning with Braith if he'd tried to leave her behind. She didn't like the idea of being alone, but she also didn't want her brother or Tempest to think they *had* to do this.

"You can stay," Aria told him. "I can lead them away on my own."

"No," he said. "I can't stay. You need another set of eyes for your back, and if something happens…" His words trailed off as he glanced at Braith.

"There's no telling what I'll do," she finished for him when he couldn't.

"I *am* coming with you."

"You may not want to be there to see what happens to me if he dies," she said.

His blue eyes were steady when they met hers. "I wouldn't be anywhere else."

Aria's shoulders slumped as she realized there would be no deterring him. William wouldn't want her to see him if something were to happen to Tempest, but she wouldn't be anywhere else either.

He took hold of Tempest's hand and pulled her against his side. Aria turned away from them and squeezed Xavier's arm. "Heal friend," she said. "I'll need you to protect me in the future, I'm sure. Braith needs you now."

His brown eyes were unwavering as they held hers. "You can d-do this."

She bowed her head before rising on her toes to kiss his cheek. "Watch over them all for me," she whispered in his ear.

He placed his hand over hers. "I will. I think you're ri...ght. I thi... think it is Sabine."

Xavier was the wisest vampire she knew. If he believed she was right, it only further served to confirm her theory. She stepped away from him and hurried to Daniel next. Kneeling beside her brother, she took hold of his hands and squeezed them. "I love you," she said and kissed his cheek.

"I love you too. Keep yourselves alive."

"You do the same."

Rising, she said a good-bye to the others before walking over to Melinda and Ashby. "Wait at least an hour, preferably two, before trying to go for the refugees," she instructed.

"We will," Ashby said.

Melinda gripped Aria's hands within hers. "Braith will be fine, Aria, you'll see. It will take far more than this to destroy my brother."

"Yes," Aria murmured.

She released Melinda's hands and moved away from her. She didn't look back as she made her way up the rocks and away from all those gathered below. Behind her, she could hear William and Tempest's feet on the rocks as they followed her.

"Aria," Jack called to her when she arrived at the top. Setting her shoulders, she braced herself before looking back at him. "What do we do if you don't come back?"

"Keep him protected, even if he dies. Also, continue to give him blood even if he dies. It may help to keep him stronger or help him rise faster if he does come back."

"Don't let him awaken to discover you dead!"

"That will never happen," she replied and turned away.

CHAPTER 7

Aria

Aria bit her wrist again as she slipped through the trees. She kept her arm against her mouth before allowing it to fall to her side where drops of blood spilled onto the leaves beneath her feet. The thick canopy of the pine trees above them didn't allow for any of the moon or stars to shine through. Whatever snow had managed to fall to the ground during the last storm had already melted as winter gradually gave way to spring.

Beside her, William and Tempest did the same with their wrists, biting into them then letting their blood trickle to the ground. Aria paused to lean against a tree. She became completely still as she listened to the distant footfalls struggling to keep up with them. Curses and grunts sounded as their trackers became entangled in the thick briars they'd traversed a quarter mile back.

She'd had to take her cloak off in order to make her way through the thorny underbrush. Her thin undershirt had been sliced to shreds by the briars, but she barely felt the chilly air against her flesh. Every part of her not focused on leading these vamps away from everyone else without being caught was focused on her connection to Braith.

Still alive. For how long? She shuddered, but it had nothing to do with the February night and everything to do with the progressing weakness she felt in their bond.

Forcing herself away from the trunk of the pine, she continued onward. They moved swiftly over another mile of forest before coming to a stop near another familiar cave system.

"How far have we gone?" Tempest asked.

"About ten miles," William replied. "We have to go farther."

"Yes." Aria's gaze searched the woods before she tipped her head back to look at the trees above her. Interspersed with the pines were some smaller oak trees. Their branches creaked and swayed in the wind. "I'm going to see how many of them are following us and make sure they stay on our trail."

"And how do you plan to do that?" William demanded.

Aria shifted her gaze to look at her brother and gave him a sly grin. "I'll sneak up on them and piss them off."

"Aria—"

"We can't keep going if they're not coming with us. I'll stay to the trees. They'll never know I'm there until it's too late."

"We'll come with you," Tempest offered.

William shook his head at her when she stepped forward. "Just like I couldn't keep up with you climbing mountains, we can't keep up with her in the trees."

Aria pulled her cloak from where she'd tucked it in between her quiver and her back and handed it to him. "I'll be back."

Adjusting her quiver and bow, she grabbed hold of the branch above her head and swung herself into the oak tree. As a human, she'd been able to move fast from tree to tree, but as a vampire, she climbed with such speed that she made it to the middle of the tree in seconds. She rubbed her chilled hands together and studied the pine tree across from her before running across the limb and leaping onto the next one.

Normally, she felt a sense of flying and being free when running through the trees. Now, she only felt a need to move as fast as she could, to get answers, to draw their pursuers onward. She didn't think Sabine was with the group of their immediate trackers. She seemed like the type who didn't exert herself until it became absolutely necessary. Sabine would have herself in a position to move forward with her plan to destroy Braith as soon as she received word from her followers that they'd been caught.

Aria landed on the next limb and raced across it before dashing to another limb, around the trunk, and onto the next tree. The air tore at her braid, pulling strands of hair free to whip around her face as she leapt through the trees.

She'd been a queen for almost a year and a half now, but every time Braith took her to her treehouse, she spent time running through the trees, laughing as he looked on. The memory of him smiling while he watched her caused a tug at her heart that she ignored as she continued effortlessly onward.

She covered nearly a half a mile before settling onto a limb against the trunk of an oak. Her gaze ran over the woods and the shadows dancing as branches swayed around her. The cool air brushed over her skin as she drew on vampire senses that still felt new and foreign to her in many ways. She'd always been a part of the forest, but as a vampire, the woods came alive in a much more intense and vivid way.

She spotted a couple of field mice scooting into their den, a coyote slinking through the trees, and behind her she could hear an owl's claws clicking as it wrapped them around a branch. Her fingers rested against the rough bark beneath her, feeling every groove and hollow within it.

Muttered curses and the cracking of twigs drew her attention to the right as a couple dozen men and women emerged from the night. They swung their arms and hacked at sticks and thorns with their swords as they awkwardly made their way through the thicket.

It was a spectacle she would have found amusing, if she wasn't fighting against the urge to shoot an arrow into each and every one of them. The only thing holding her back was the fact that she didn't have enough arrows to kill them all, nor did she want to give away her location. Not yet anyway.

Didn't mean she couldn't take at least one out, pissing off the others and making them more cautious about following their trail. They wouldn't turn back; she had a feeling they dreaded Sabine's wrath if they disobeyed her far more than they dreaded being taken out by an arrow. An arrow would be quick. From what William had told her, Sabine's torment would not be.

Pulling her bow forward, she drew an arrow from her quiver and nocked it against the bow. She examined each of their hunters before settling on the largest man in the center of the pack. Taking aim, she released the arrow, tossed the bow over her back, and fled back through the trees. She didn't have to witness it; she knew her aim had been true and the arrow had struck him straight through his heart. The startled cries and barked commands accompanying her kill only confirmed it.

She smiled grimly as she returned to where she'd left William and Tempest. Slipping back down the tree, she dropped to the ground beside them. "One down," she said and reclaimed her cloak from her brother. "They'll keep following us, but they'll be more cautious about it from now on."

"You shouldn't have gotten so close," William scolded.

"I should have killed more of them," she replied. "Next time, I will."

She bit into her wrist again, leaving a few blood splatters on the leaves beneath her feet before continuing on once more.

***

Jack

"We shouldn't have let her go," Ashby said.

"We didn't have a choice," Jack replied.

He rested his fingers against Braith's cool cheek. He'd never seen his brother so still before, so weak, never believed it was possible for Braith to be categorized as either of those things. He'd known it was possible Braith could die, of course he'd known it, but he'd never believed it might actually happen. He'd always been so strong, so capable.

A bomb that would have destroyed any other, had only blinded him. Braith had mastered his blindness before Aria came along and had learned to use it to his advantage as he honed every one of his other senses until they made up for his lack of sight.

Not dead. Despite the pallor of his skin, his nearly white lips and completely unmoving body, Braith was not dead. Jack could feel life within him, but it was growing weaker by the second.

"What if Aria's wrong and that's not Sabine out there? Or what if it is her, and Sabine didn't actually die, but somehow faked her death? What happens if Braith doesn't survive this?" Ashby asked. "Are you ready to be King Jericho?"

Jack tore his gaze away from Braith to glower at Ashby. "Don't call me that."

He'd abandoned his birth name when he'd gone to live with the rebels. It wasn't a name he ever planned to use again. Ashby folded his arms over his chest as he gazed at him. Ashby was family, but there were times when Jack would like nothing more than to punch him in the face.

"Atticus didn't fake his death and he came back from the dead. There is something in their blood," he said to Ashby. "There has to be."

"Atticus was over a thousand years old when he came back. Maybe his rising from the grave was due more to his age than his heritage."

"Ashby," Melinda said and rested her hand on his arm when red flashed through his eyes.

Ashby's arms fell away from his chest. He took a minute to compose himself. "We let her go out there and we have no idea how she'll react to his loss if he dies."

"We had *no* choice," Jack growled. "Aria was right, most of us aren't up for travel right now and someone had to lead them away. Otherwise, we'd all be sitting ducks, trapped in this cave. We have to get the others to safety. We can't leave them out there. That woman will destroy them if she finds them. Aria will keep it together if we lose Braith."

"For how long?"

"For as long as she has to," Jack said and sniffed at the air. "I can smell animals in here, bring me some blood for Braith."

"What if he dies and she becomes like Atticus?" Ashby pressed.

"Aria will destroy herself before that ever happens!" Daniel snapped.

Ashby rolled his eyes at him. "I'm sure Atticus believed the same thing, before he went completely off the rails. He pretended to be sane for *centuries*. Many believed he *was* sane until he destroyed much of the world's population."

"There is no way to know the future. All we can hope to do is survive the now, and so far, we are," Hannah said. "We will take everything else as it comes at us."

"She's right," Max said and winced when he shifted his leg.

Ashby ran his fingers through his hair as he stared at the ground with a look of intense contemplation on his face. Jack winced, his shoulders hunched up when Ashby began to whistle a haunting tune. It was such a habit for him, that he knew Ashby probably wasn't aware he was doing it, but the sound set Jack's teeth on edge.

"Ashby, not now," he said.

Ashby looked up at him with his brow furrowed questioningly.

"You were whistling," Melinda told him.

"Oh," Ashby said and looked around the cave once more.

"There was often a store of supplies left within these caves for future humans to use when traveling through." The rebel's willingness to share and provide for others within their close knit community was one of the things Jack had always admired about them. Aria's father, David, had brought him into the rebellion and had been his first real friend. "We need to get these wounds cleaned and dressed. There may still be something we can use within these caves."

"There were supplies stored in that tunnel," Daniel said and pointed to the one behind him. "If you lift me, I can take you to them."

"I'm in better shape. I'll go," Max said and climbed to his feet.

"Hannah, stay with Braith," Jack said and rose. "I'm going to go with him. Ashby, catch me one of those animals."

Ashby smoothed his hair and rumpled clothes the best he could as his normally composed demeanor slid back over him. Max walked toward him with a slight limp, took hold of the torch Aria had left behind, and moved on toward the tunnel. Jack followed him. He'd come to know these woods and caves well over his years with the rebels, but he hadn't spent as much time within this cave system as he had some of the others.

Max dug the key out from a crevice in the rocks and unlocked the gate. Habit had Max returning to hide the key before closing the gate and continuing onward. Jack limped after Max as he made his way down the tunnel. The pierced skin and muscle in his thigh and calf knitted itself back together with every passing second, but he couldn't get rid of the limp, yet.

"What will happen if Braith doesn't wake up?" Max asked as he turned into another small tunnel. "If he does die?"

Jack watched the fire of the torch flickering over the cave wall as he debated this question. "I have no idea," he finally admitted.

"Will Aria really die without him?"

At one time, Max had harbored more than friendly feelings for Aria, and before she'd met Braith, she'd also had a crush on the young human, but Jack knew both of them had long since moved past those feelings. Now, Max was asking because he didn't want to lose his friend. Neither did Jack. He still wasn't over losing David. He was coping with it much better now, but to lose David's daughter, the woman who was a sister to him, *and* his brother...

He couldn't think about it. He would get through it if it happened, they all would, but the prospect of such a reality made the world a far sadder place in his mind.

"Maybe not right away, but she will want to die," Jack confirmed. He knew he would want to die if Hannah did.

Max stopped outside of a metal door. Unlike the gates, this one was a solid door with a small window in the center of it. The window was open to allow air to flow through. Max's eyes were haunted when he lifted his gaze to Jack. "I'm not ready for that."

"Neither am I," he admitted.

"Will you become king?"

Jack inwardly cringed at the thought. He wouldn't turn away from the responsibility, but it wasn't something he'd ever thought about before, or wanted. He'd been quite content to be third in line for the throne behind Braith and Caleb. He could do as he pleased, which is what he'd done throughout most of his life. "Since he has no children, I would be Braith's heir."

Max bent to dig out another key. "If it's not him or Aria ruling, then I'm glad it will be you."

"I think Sabine—"

"Do you really believe it's her?"

"Yes, I do," he admitted.

Jack recalled the woman's broad features, her blood-red lips, her *eyes*. When he'd first seen her, he'd felt as if he had seen her somewhere else before, but for the life of him he couldn't place where or *how* he could possibly know her. Once Aria had said Sabine's name and that she thought it was her, it had all made sense to him. He'd seen Sabine in Atticus's face every day. Seen those eyes, gleaming with malicious intent and those lips constantly curved into a mocking smile.

He now knew Atticus had not started out as a vicious bastard, but fate had twisted and molded him into one. Caleb, however, had always been vicious and so had Jack's other sister, Natasha before she'd been killed. There had never been any good within either of them, as children or as adults. Jack sensed the same kind of wrongness in Sabine, the same twisted compulsion for cruelty that had always resided in Caleb and Natasha.

Max slid the key into the lock and turned it. The door creaked as it swung open to reveal the nearly empty supply room beyond. A few bags of grain were stacked on top of each other against the back wall. Judging by the moldy scent wafting from them, they had gone bad long ago. A crate was tucked against the back wall and some clothes were draped over a rock in the back.

"Guess no one saw the need to restock it," Max said as he limped into the room toward the lone crate. He placed the torch against the wall, grasped the top of the crate, and pulled it off. He set it aside before exploring the contents of the crate. "Some bandages," he said and pulled out strips of cloth, laying them across a nearby rock. "Stakes, blankets, furs, and what looks like a jug of wine."

"I think we could all use some wine right now, and I'm not turning down any kind of weapon. I'll carry the crate. You carry the clothes."

Max walked over to the rock with the clothes on it and gathered them before heading for the door. Jack hefted the crate and followed him out of the room. Though there was nothing of use left within the store room, he closed the door behind him and listened as the lock clicked into place.

Max limped down the tunnel, placed the torch against the wall, and bent to retrieve the other key for the gate. He opened it up and stepped back to allow Jack to pass through first. Jack stepped into the cavern as Ashby descended the rocks with a fox in hand.

They wouldn't be able to stay here forever, but they could make a stand in these caves and keep Braith protected until he healed enough to wake again. Jack knew there was a possibility Braith still might die; he just wasn't ready to acknowledge it yet. Braith had made it this long after having an arrow pierce his heart. He'd make it longer.

Jack's gaze went to Hannah as she rose to her feet from beside his brother. Her lower lip trembled, and tears streamed from her eyes as she gazed at him. The desolate look on her face froze him in place. The crate fell from his hands to crash against the rock. He didn't recall covering the distance between them before he fell to his knees in front of Braith. Seizing his brother's chin, he turned his head toward him, but even before Braith's cloudy, open eyes met his, Jack knew his brother was gone.

CHAPTER 8

Aria

Aria's body bent and her head fell back as if she'd been hit by a bolt of lightning. A wail of sorrow caught on the lump in her throat, choking her. Her hands flew to her chest. Her fingers clawed at her flesh, raking her skin open with her fingernails. Tears spilled from her eyes. Sounds she'd never heard before came from within her when she fell to her knees.

Blood pooled from her sliced flesh as she sought to get to her heart, to tear the shattered and broken organ from her body as shards of pain sliced like glass over her skin. Broken. Gone. Braith was gone. The connection had been severed as cleanly as she'd severed tangled fishing line over the years.

Her hands touched upon bone before they were yanked away from her body. Words were shouted at her; she didn't hear them as someone hauled her to her feet and dragged her onward. She reached for her chest again. Those hands jerked her hands back, and more words were spoken, but she didn't think these ones were directed at her and she didn't care if they were.

She was dying. Nothing mattered anymore.

Somewhere in the back of her mind, she recalled that something did matter. There was something she was supposed to do, others she was supposed to help, but the sorrow and insanity swirling through her mind made it difficult to concentrate.

She collapsed against the arms holding her and was swung up off the ground. She could barely make out the blurry world around her. When she lifted her hands once more to her chest, they were slapped aside.

"No!" William's voice penetrated through her grief-stricken haze. "There are caves up here."

He wasn't speaking to her, and she dimly recalled Tempest was with them too. They'd been doing something...

They'd been drawing the vampires who had attacked them away. Fury burst over her like the sun rising over the mountains on a clear summer morning. It dried her tears as she balled her hands and resisted bellowing into the night sky. Squirming in William's arms, she shoved against her brother's chest.

"Kill them!" she hissed through her teeth.

His arms tightened around her, but on her next shove, she broke his hold on her. He grabbed for her as she tumbled from his arms. She hit the ground running, back toward where she'd last seen the white-cloaked troops following them. She made it only ten feet before arms enveloped her ankles. With her legs yanked out from under her, she slammed into the ground.

Her fingers tore at the earth. She kicked at whoever held her until she knocked their hold on her free. Red filled her vision, and a snarl tore from her as she became determined to kill whoever had tackled her. Flipping over, she hooked her fingers into claws and went for the eyes.

William ducked back in time to avoid having his skin torn from his face. The sight of her brother knocked some of the driving urge to kill from her. No matter how much she craved death right now, she would not hurt her brother, her twin. William clutched her arms, pinning them to her chest as he loomed over her.

"Listen to me!" he yelled. "Remember that you think there's a chance Braith can come back from this. That he can rise from the dead, like his father. If you die, there is *no* coming back for you, and he will rise only to want to die again."

Her struggles against him eased as his words sank in. "They have to pay."

"They will, but not tonight. You have to stay with me in order to get them."

Keeping hold of her forearms, he yanked her to her feet. He pulled the ruined remains of her shirt from her upper body, leaving her only in her bra, then wiped her blood away before tossing it on the ground. The frigid air caressing her skin had nothing on the icy tendrils encasing her heart.

He was dead, her Braith was dead.

He's coming back!

What if he doesn't? What If I'm wrong?

She wrapped her arms around her middle. Her fangs pricked her bottom lip when she drew it into her mouth. She hadn't realized they'd extended. She craved sinking them into someone's throat and tearing out their jugular to watch them bleed all over the place. To tear out that *bitch's* throat.

Oh yes, that was exactly whose blood she wanted sliding down her throat. She could keep it together until then; she had no other choice. The analytical, vengeful side of her brain slowly rose up to take over the weeping, shattered pieces of her mind.

If Braith didn't return, she would continue until Sabine, and anyone who aided her, was dead.

William pulled her cloak snuggly around her, lifted her up, and tossed her over his shoulder. "I can walk," she gasped when she found herself staring at his back.

"I don't trust you right now," he replied honestly and broke into a jog with Tempest by his side.

Aria had no idea where they were going; she didn't care. She had plans to make, and she knew exactly how to set those plans into motion.

***

Jack

Jack couldn't tear his gaze away from Braith's eyes. Open and unseeing, there was nothing there anymore. Even after Braith was blinded, he may not have been able to see anything, but his eyes had reflected life to the rare few who had seen him without his dark sunglasses on.

Anguish squeezed his chest. Behind him, Melinda sobbed openly as Ashby tried to comfort her. Tears pricked his eyes, burning and making him blink rapidly. Braith had been his older brother, at one time his enemy, then his friend. He'd expected that friendship to grow and deepen throughout the coming years.

A single tear slipped free. Braith would come back; he had to.

Until then, the kingdom had just fallen to him. He may not want it, but he would protect it and everyone in it.

Hannah knelt at his side, her arms wrapped around his shoulders. Her sweet scent filled his nose, and his arms encircled her waist as he pulled her closer. He took some comfort in her as he turned his head into her silken hair.

She'd been his redemption in a time when he hadn't felt as if he deserved it, or ever expected to find it. He'd sworn to protect her, to cherish her, yet their world was crumbling around his feet. Sabine had power and was growing a large army. They'd lost their king, and their queen was within the forest, probably losing her mind.

"Aria," he whispered. Wherever she was now, he knew his sister-in-law was aware of Braith's passing.

"What do we do, Jack?" Hannah whispered.

"We can't lea… ave him," Xavier croaked out. "It's not over, not yet."

Jack was glad the history keeper sounded so certain, because he wasn't. He believed Aria was right about that woman being Sabine; he just didn't know what to make of all of this right now.

"We have to do what we told Aria we would. The residents of Chippman and the survivors from Badwin must be taken to the palace," Jack said. Keeping his arm around Hannah, he rose to his feet and turned to Ashby. "Enough time has passed. It should be safe for the two of you to return to them and lead them the rest of the way."

Ashby lifted his head to look at him, the fox he'd caught lay where he'd forgotten it on the rocks. Tears swam in Ashby's eyes as Melinda sobbed against his shoulder. He held her closer before giving Jack a brisk nod. "You should come with us. They'll need a leader at the palace. One of your line."

Jack glanced over the others within the cave. They would all heal. They were all fighters, but they were in no shape to protect Braith from their attackers if their hiding place was discovered.

"I can't," he said. "If someone came for Braith now, they wouldn't be able to fend off an attack. Xavier may be able to carry him now, if it became necessary, but none of the others could. I know these caves and forests well. I'll be able to move Braith around much easier and into better hiding spots than Xavier would. There is also a chance we could end up having to separate if it becomes necessary."

In other words, the humans may have to be left behind in order to protect Braith's body. They all knew it, but they wouldn't argue the decision if it became necessary. If there was the smallest chance of Braith coming back, he had to be protected above all others.

He'd also promised Aria he would keep Braith safe no matter what, and he planned to uphold that promise.

"No one at the palace knows Melinda is not of our line. She will be there to rule with you, and Gideon will also be able to help you keep control. The humans like Melinda, the vampires will follow her, and she will be able to keep them calm until we are able to join you."

Melinda lifted her head from Ashby's shoulder. Tears continued to stream from her eyes as she stared at Jack. "But I'm not a leader," she whispered.

"Neither am I, but we're both about to learn how to be one, sis. I *know* you are capable of doing this."

She blinked at him, swallowed heavily, and wiped the tears from her eyes. "What should I tell them, about you and Braith?"

"Tell them we were attacked, that there is a new threat rising, but assure them they will be safe. Tell them Braith and I are recruiting more troops and securing the vulnerable border towns. I'm hoping Sabine holds off on attacking the palace in order to search for Braith, but start preparing them for an attack. If Aria was right, Sabine will be looking to behead him in order to ensure he really is out of her way."

Melinda turned a shade of green. "I think you're right."

"Mention nothing about Braith being shot or his... his..." Jack couldn't bring himself to say the word death. "This," he finished. "Tell only Gideon about this. There is no reason to create a possible panic or mutiny between The Council members if we can avoid it. Gideon will know how to handle them and will keep this quiet." He hugged Hannah closer to his side when her hands curled around his forearm. "You should go, now."

Melinda broke away from Ashby and made her way around the others to stand before him. They embraced each other before she knelt by Braith's side and leaned forward to kiss his cheek. "I *will* see you soon."

She said her good-byes to everyone else in the room before returning to him.

"Be careful," Jack said as he took hold of her hands. "You can do this and they *will* follow you."

She may have been removed from the palace by his father when she was a child, and she was far younger than him or any of his siblings, but he'd always liked and cared for Melinda. She was kind and she was far stronger than many gave her credit for, including herself. Even knowing her heritage, he didn't consider her a half-sister. She was his blood.

"Do I tell The Council that Atticus wasn't my father?" she asked.

"If you feel you must, but I wouldn't. There is no reason for them to know, and you are still our sister and, therefore, entitled to rule as I have instructed."

She tilted her chin up as pride blazed in her gray eyes. "You're right. I will see you soon."

"You will," he promised.

"I'll lead them to the surface," Max offered.

"Thank you," Jack said and turned to look at his brother again. They couldn't leave him there like this. "We have to get this cavern set up, weapons made, food and water found. We may be here for a bit."

CHAPTER 9

Aria

William finally set her down in another cave about ten miles from where she'd lost her mind. Aria still wasn't sure she had it back, but at least the desire to rip her own heart from her chest with her bare hands had passed. Her legs shook as she walked over to a boulder and sank down to sit on it.

William grabbed her hands when she lifted them to her chest again. She jerked them away from him. "I won't." Those two words were all she could manage to get out right now. Her hands fell into her lap as she bent forward. Tears burned her throat but refused to fall; there was no way to soothe the aching rawness of her emotions.

She would never be able to escape the emptiness coursing through her. The stark realization made her fingers curve with the urge to tear out her heart once more. Her fingers dug into her thighs as she resisted the impulse. The only thing that would ease this barren, hollow sensation was Braith's arms around her. Right now, all she felt was the absolute certainty that would never happen again.

"What do we do now?" Tempest asked.

"We wait here until we can return to the others," William replied. "We lost Sabine's followers about five miles back, but they'll still be in the area, fanning out and searching for us."

"We're not going back to the others," Aria grated.

"Why not?" William demanded.

Her body felt as if it were made of glass and would shatter apart at any second when she lifted her head to look at him. "Because we need to know more about that woman. We need to know her every weakness, and trust me when I say, she won't have many. We have to be prepared for her and we have to *destroy* her."

Her hand fluttered to her chest, and her fingers dug into her flesh once more as her heart clenched. She didn't understand how an organ that had ceased beating on the day Braith had changed her from human to vampire and granted her eternal life could hurt so badly.

Eternal life, without him.

Madness loomed before her, spiraling around like a whirlpool looking to suck her in and never let her go again. She gritted her teeth against it, tore her hand away from her chest, and gripped her thigh.

"I will not become Atticus," she grated.

William knelt before her and grabbed her hands. "We should go back, Aria."

"She has to die, William. We need to learn more about her. We need troops who will fight her and her followers, and we have to gather them now. She has to be squashed, *completely*."

"What if the troops we try to gather decide to follow her instead?" Tempest asked.

"There are many vampires and humans who want to keep the peace too. Things have been good between the species since Atticus was defeated," William said. "Humans don't have much of a chance against vampires if the vamps decide to turn them into slaves again. There are many cruel vampires out there, but there are more of them who aren't cruel. Many of Sabine's followers are scared, and that is why they've joined her. If they think she can be defeated, they'll turn on her or run."

"I saw what they did in Badwin, William. They destroyed my town and there were a lot of them who enjoyed doing it," Tempest replied.

"Yes, but I'm sure some of them didn't."

"I have to get close to her," Aria said. "Somehow."

"That's impossible," William said. "Believe me, I know. The only way I got close to her was to be captured by Kane and taken to her. If she captures *you*, she'll kill you."

"Not if Braith is still out there," Aria murmured. "She would keep me alive until she had his body. If she believes there's any chance he will rise again, she would use me to control him, but I can't let her capture me."

William gripped her chin and pulled her head toward him. "I won't let you sacrifice yourself."

She took hold of his hand, a hand she had known since their creation. Distress etched his features. She couldn't imagine the sorrow she would feel if their roles were reversed. She would have done everything she could to keep him safe, to stop him from destroying himself, but there were few other options for her anymore.

"If Braith doesn't wake, I have already been sacrificed. You must know that." Her brother winced at her words as his blue eyes glinted like steel. "Dying for this cause would be the way I'd want to go, but I won't willingly let her capture me. No, we have to learn more about her, but we also have to be able to relay whatever we discover about her to the others. Rotting in a prison cell would make that impossible. We also have to start quietly gathering recruits."

"How will we ever get close enough to learn anything about her?" Tempest asked.

Aria gazed out the cave and to the night beyond. "We've always been good at going unnoticed within these woods. She's in our territory now."

"True, but that can be discussed later." William rested his hands on his knees before rising to his feet once more. "First, let's hope there are some clothes in here, somewhere. And some sunglasses."

Aria glanced down at her dirty bra beneath her cloak. She didn't care if she wandered around like this for the rest of her days, but it wasn't exactly regal and many would be a little hesitant to follow the queen wearing a bra and looking as if she'd just rolled around in dirt. The Mad Queen; she almost laughed aloud at the realization they would call her that. Atticus had kept his insanity hidden; right now, she wore it for the world to see.

"Sunglasses?" she asked.

She lifted her head to look at William. Dirt streaked his rugged features, and his auburn hair stood out in a hundred different directions from the wind. He didn't look much better than she felt, but somehow she knew he appeared far more stable than her right now.

"Your eyes are redder than rubies," he said and clasped hold of her arm to help her rise. "I have a feeling they won't be changing back anytime soon either."

"Me too," she murmured as he took hold of Tempest's hand and led them deeper into the cave.

***

Melinda

"We have to be getting close to where we left them," Melinda whispered as they crept through the trees. They'd left the caves behind almost a half an hour ago.

Even though she was accustomed to moving quietly and undetected through the woods, the forest was not a place she enjoyed being right now. Not with the vampires who had attacked them earlier still out there.

She and her mother had lived in the forest after Atticus had banished them from the palace. After her mother's death, she'd spent a lot of time trying to remain hidden from Atticus's troops, until the day Jack discovered her. He'd promised to keep her safe and brought her back to the palace.

Then Ashby had been banished, and she'd often snuck out of the palace and into the woods to see him. She'd spent more of her life hiding within the forest than she'd spent living out of it.

Ashby took hold of her arm and drew her behind him when a twig snapped from somewhere ahead of them. The evergreens in this section of the forest were sparse enough to allow the moonlight to spill around them. The moon's rays created a pathway of glittering crystals across the snow-covered ground before them. A doe stepped out from behind a tree. Her tail swished, and her ears flicked toward them. The deer stepped carefully over the snow before fleeing into the woods.

"Come," Ashby said and released her.

She glanced up at him, love swelling her heart as tears burned her eyes. It easily could have been him who had died so many years ago, or again today. She'd never understood why Atticus had banished Ashby from the palace instead of adding him to his trophy room. Ashby always had been known for his refined taste and party lifestyle within the palace. A hundred years ago, he would have looked as out of place amongst these trees as a fawn in a bear den; relegating him to a life of no luxuries had been a harsh punishment for him.

However, that trophy room had been Atticus's pride and joy, and Ashby would have made a nice edition to it. She shuddered to think Ashby could have ended up seated beside her real father there. Ashby had been married to Atticus's daughter Natasha at the time of his banishment, but the couple's intense loathing of one another had been well known within the palace. A worse punishment for Ashby would have been to be locked in a room with Natasha or turned into her slave. Instead, Atticus had exiled him to a treehouse in the forest.

Sometimes Melinda wondered if Atticus had known about her relationship with Ashby and spared his life for her. Before reading his journals, she would have stated without a doubt Atticus had no heart, had been born a monster and would always be one. Now she wondered if there had still been a small sliver of the man he'd once been within him, and he'd taken pity on her and allowed Ashby to live.

She may not have been his daughter, Atticus had known that, but perhaps that's why he may have shown some kindness to her when he wouldn't have done so for his own children. He hadn't been forced to create her in order to keep up appearances as he had with her siblings.

She would never know the answer to the question, but she would never deny that a part of her had come to believe it to be true. Maybe she only hoped there had still been kindness in him, still been a piece of the man who had at one time existed in this world, before it had all been torn away from him. Melinda shivered and rubbed her hands over her arms.

Ashby swung his cloak off, but she waved it away when he went to drape it around her shoulders. "You're shivering," he whispered.

"I was thinking," she replied.

"About Braith."

It wasn't a question, but she answered him anyway. "Braith and other things."

She couldn't resist stepping closer to him. She'd never known it was possible to love someone as much as she loved him. Every day it grew stronger. The idea of losing him—

It was not one she would entertain.

"What other things?" he inquired as he returned his cloak to his shoulders and clasped her elbow.

"Do you ever think maybe Atticus knew about our relationship, and that's why he sent you away instead of adding you to his trophy room."

Ashby's handsome features hardened at the mention of Atticus, and his green eyes swung back to her. "Yes," he admitted.

"Do you believe it to be true?"

"I don't know." He pushed aside a branch for her so she could duck under it. "We will never truly know what he thought. His mind was rotten from years of a driving thirst for vengeance. Perhaps there was still some of the man he once was in there, but there wasn't much of him."

Melinda stopped when she came face to face with a massive boulder more than twenty feet tall and fifty feet wide. She frowned at it before beginning to make her way around the rock. "That's what I think too, but I like to believe he did have some kindness left in him."

Ashby drew back on her elbow, turning her to face him. Brushing back a strand of her hair, he bent to kiss her. Melinda had just relaxed against him when he pulled away and cupped her face. "Then I will believe it with you."

She smiled at him and rested her cheek against his chest. With everything that had been going on, Jack's wedding to Hannah, William's return with news of this rising threat, their rushed evacuation of Chippman, and now this attack, she hadn't had a chance to tell him about the baby. She hadn't wanted to take anything away from Jack and Hannah's day, and had planned to wait until they were back at the palace before revealing it to him, but now she knew there may be no returning to the palace.

Her brother was dead. Her heart clenched at the reminder, and fresh tears burned her eyes. She'd never been close to Braith after Jack had returned her to the palace. He was far older than she was, distant and reserved. He'd always been polite to her, but he'd been polite to everyone without ever getting close to them. Then, Ashby had accidentally blinded him in the rebellion of the aristocrats against Atticus. Afterwards, she'd stayed further away from Braith out of guilt over her relationship with Ashby and fear of their affair being discovered.

Since Braith had discovered Aria and broken out of the role Atticus had relegated him to, they had grown closer. She'd come to consider him her friend as well as her brother, and now he was gone. Aria was gone now too, not only to lead their new enemy away, but she would be lost to them if Braith didn't come back from death—a feat she would have believed impossible before Aria had stated that she believed the vampire threatening them to be Sabine. Now Melinda held out hope that Aria was right. She'd come to love Aria as a friend and sister; she would mourn her loss the same as the loss of Braith.

After the events of today, she knew they had no idea what awaited them in their future, and there would never be a perfect time to tell Ashby, at least not anytime soon.

Ashby went to turn away from her, but she took hold of his hand and drew him back. "What is it?" he inquired.

"I'm pregnant."

He couldn't have looked more shocked if she'd told him she'd grown a tail. His mouth parted, and his eyes held hers for a minute before falling to her still-flat stomach. His mouth closed, then opened again; his hand extended toward her stomach before dropping away. She clasped hold of his hand and pressed it against her belly.

"Are you sure?" he croaked out.

"Yes. I know this wasn't planned—"

She never got a chance to finish before he lifted her into the air. Melinda bit back a laugh as he spun her around. They couldn't draw attention to themselves, but the radiant smile on his face and the glow in his eyes made her almost scream with joy. He crushed her against his chest, his hands smoothing back her hair as he rained kisses across her face. She giggled as she hugged him close.

"How long have you known?" he inquired when he set her on the ground and clasped her cheeks.

"I've suspected for a couple of weeks now."

"Why didn't you tell me?" he demanded.

"I was waiting until after the wedding, until we were home, but now we may never make it home."

The growl rumbling through his chest surprised her. His good-natured ease, roguish charm, quirky smile, and whistling habit were some of the things she loved best about him, but he was not a willing fighter.

"We *will* make it home," he grated. "We will grow to see our child play in the gardens with his many cousins over the years to come."

The joyful image of such a thing filled her mind; she could practically hear the laughter of all the children, but as the image rose, it died away. There may never be cousins if something were to happen to Jack too.

"It could be a girl," she murmured instead of expressing her depressing thoughts.

"And I will spend many years fending off all the men sure to be chasing her around if she's half as beautiful as her mother."

Melinda wrapped her arms around his back. Her fingers dug into his flesh as she held him against her and simply allowed herself one second of serenity in a world that had become filled within nothing but grief.

"We must go," she whispered and turned her face into his neck to kiss him.

He took hold of her hand as they turned to finish making their way around the boulder. Stepping out from the back of the rock, Melinda gasped and took a startled step back when they came face to face with half a dozen bows and arrows pointed directly at them.

CHAPTER 10

William

"William." He turned to find Tempest standing in the doorway of the storage room established within the cave. She looked so small, so fragile with the dark circles under her eyes and her silvery hair falling around her shoulders. He drank in the sight of her slender body with its enticing curves.

Releasing the clothes he'd been gathering, he covered the ten feet separating them in an instant. Her hands fell on his shoulders when he lifted her up, clasped hold of her hair, and pulled her head back to claim her mouth with his. Her lips burned into his, heating the chill permeating his body since Aria, in her grief and despair, had collapsed into the snow to claw at herself like an animal trying to free itself from a trap.

Shoving the image out of his mind, he carried Tempest over to the wall and rested her against it as he released her mouth. He lowered his head and sank his fangs into her throat. Her sweet blood surged into his mouth, strengthening him as it flowed through his system. He growled low in his throat when he felt the scrape of her fangs over his flesh before they sank into him.

He was being too rough with her, but he couldn't get close enough to her right now. All reason vanished as the bond between them swelled and grew further. He could stay in here with her for the rest of their lives and be fine with it.

But he couldn't, and no matter how badly he desired her now, no matter how badly he *needed* her, he could not lose himself to her. He forced his fangs to retract and rested his head in the hollow of her throat. Her familiar and much-loved wintry scent assailed him.

He understood what Aria was going through. If someone took Tempest from him, he would tear the world apart, but he had to keep his twin from getting herself killed, and he had to keep Tempest protected.

"I lost control. I'm sorry," he said hoarsely against her throat.

"Don't be," she whispered as she threaded her fingers through his hair and pulled his head back to look at him. "I need you too, badly, but there are things we have to do first, and your sister..." Her voice trailed off. Her doe brown eyes darted away before settling on the clothes he'd been holding. "I think getting her cleaned up will help. I came to ask if there is water somewhere in these caves?"

William reluctantly released his hold on her and stepped away. "I'll get it if you'll take the clothes out to Aria."

Tempest walked over to retrieve the clothes he'd dropped. This store room had some provisions in it, but there was no human food remaining here, and there were no medical supplies or bandages. Thankfully, most of Aria's injuries would heal soon enough. As he turned to leave the room, he kissed Tempest again.

Taking one of the torches he'd lit, he didn't look back as he left her behind. He snaked through the tunnels before arriving at a locked gate; he dug out the key and slipped through to the other side. After they'd made it to the center cavern, they'd discovered two of the locked gates no longer had keys, which limited their options for fleeing if they had to, but they wouldn't be leaving here tonight anyway. They had to rest and get cleaned up before they could continue on.

He hoped in the morning Aria would agree to return to where they'd left the others, but he wouldn't bet on it. His sister was as stubborn as he was, and she was determined to seek her revenge. He understood what drove her now. It hadn't been that long ago that he'd been driven by his need to kill Kane. Tempest had helped to ease that driving thirst for vengeance in him, but Aria had no one to temper her, not anymore.

A chill ran down his spine as he recalled the night in Hannah's tavern when Aria had revealed Atticus's journals to him. Had it really only been days ago? He could never forget Aria's words to him, or the lifelessness within her when she'd spoken... *"So if he is taken from me, I need you to understand why I may have to be destroyed too. To really understand, William, and not just say you do."*

He'd wanted to blow her off at the time, to convince her nothing would happen to Braith, but he'd been unable to. Aria expected him to be able to destroy her if it became necessary. He would do it before he ever allowed her to become as malevolent and warped as Atticus had become, but he would also do *every*thing he could to save her before he ever considered the possibility of ending her life.

The trickling sound of water drew him to the spot in the caves where water from a stream above flowed down the rocks. He placed the torch beside the ice flow forming on the floor and over the wall of the cave before grabbing the pitcher sitting on a rock shelf beside the water. He filled it and made his way back to the main cavern.

Entering the cave, he found Aria sitting on one of the rocks, her head bowed and her shoulders hunched up around her ears. Over the years, he'd seen his sister boney from lack of food, withdrawn after being separated from Braith, and devastated by the loss of their father, but he'd never seen her look so small or broken before. Her torment made him feel more helpless than he'd ever felt in his life.

Tempest lifted her head from where she sat beside Aria, her hand resting on Aria's shoulder. It surprised him that Aria allowed Tempest to touch her right now, but he had a feeling she had little real acknowledgement of the world surrounding her anymore.

He walked across the room toward them and Tempest turned to pull a rag from a pile sitting beside the rock. "I'll take care of her," she said and took the pitcher from William's hands. "Can we build a fire in here or will the smell of it travel?"

"It will travel," he replied and walked away to inspect the gates they'd closed off upon entering. They'd lost their pursuers in the forest, but he couldn't let his guard down even a little right now.

"I can do it," Aria said to Tempest.

"Let me help," Tempest said, and though he'd expected her to protest, Aria didn't speak. "I couldn't gather all of the clothing, can you do it, William?" Tempest asked him.

He nodded and turned to leave. He froze when he heard the crunch of a footstep from within one of the tunnels. Aria was up and beside him in an instant, her bow raised and an arrow nocked as she took aim at whoever hid within the shadows beyond the closed gate.

"Who's there?" Aria demanded.

Silence met her question.

***

Melinda

"I'm sorry milady," one of the king's guard apologized and hastily lowered his bow.

Melinda's shoulders slumped in relief, but Ashby continued to scowl at all of the men and women who had pointed their weapons at them. Behind the king's guard, the residents of Chippman and the refugee survivors of Badwin were huddled close together. Their eyes were filled with alarm as they surveyed her and Ashby.

"Where is the king?" one of the king's men inquired.

"We were ambushed by the same group of people who devastated Badwin." Cries of alarm met her statement, and frightened murmurs raced through the crowd. "My brothers are working to try to keep everyone protected." Not entirely a lie. "We've been sent back to see you safely onto the palace, but we must move quickly."

"Is Hannah okay?" An older-looking vampire shoved his way to the front of the crowd to demand. Melinda recognized him as Hannah's uncle Abe.

Many of the residents of Chippman had some kind of genetic defect. Abe hadn't stopped aging until he was sixty-two. He was spry and healthy, and wouldn't age another day, but he looked older than most of the vampires surrounding him. Beside him stood his son, Lucas, and Hannah's best friend, Ellen. Their faces were filled with worry as they stared anxiously at her. Tempest's best friend, Pallas, and a few of the children she'd fled Badwin with also pushed their way to the front to stare at her.

"Hannah is fine. Everyone is fine," she assured them, or at least most of them had been fine the last time Melinda had seen them. "Now, we have to go."

They would be able to move faster now that the sun was down and the vampires from Chippman who were unable to stand its rays, like Lucas, could travel without the hindrance of the covered carriages built for them.

"Leave the carriages behind," Ashby said when some of the vampires started to ready the horses for them. "We will be returning to the palace tonight."

"What if we don't?" one of the vampires demanded anxiously.

Ashby's gaze didn't waver as he met and held the man's. "We have no choice but to reach it tonight."

Uneasy murmurs went through the crowd. "Then we will reach it tonight," Lucas declared. "Easy enough if we move out now. Let's go everyone."

Melinda took a minute to gather herself as she watched them all saddle their horses. They were doing as she and Ashby had instructed. Now they had to get them all to safety. Ashby claimed a horse from one of the king's men and lifted her into the saddle.

"I can get up on my own," she said.

"Nope," he said as he swung onto the saddle to settle himself behind her. "Get used to being pampered and not lifting a finger. I intend to spoil you."

"More than you already do?"

His smile was strained; his normally lively eyes didn't dance, but she still saw the joy in his gaze as he stared at her belly then her. "Far more."

She settled back against him when he nudged the horse in the side and they took off at a brisk trot through the woods. They weren't as familiar with this area of the forest as Aria and her brothers were, but Melinda had been through here enough to know at least three ways back to the palace.

"We can't take the main road," she said.

"No, we can't," Ashby agreed as he steered them toward a rocky ledge and two side roads.

One side road ran parallel to the main road, about three miles away from it, but still too close to the main for her liking. The other was a convoluted pathway that meandered through the woods, over a mountain and down into a valley. It was a little known road and rarely traveled, but it would add hours onto their trip, and if they were cornered in the valley, there would be no escape.

"We're going to have to stay in the woods," he said.

"Yes," she agreed and rested her hands on top of the lean muscles of his forearms. "Let's hope we don't get lost."

"I'm like a compass. I always know the way," he replied.

"I feel like your compass might have us going in circles."

"Then it's a good thing I have you to help guide the way."

"I hope so."

He led the horse down a steep embankment and into a gully; she didn't think it was the same gully from earlier today— had that really only been today? It felt as if days had passed since they'd first been attacked. Looking out at the landscape before them, her stomach turned at the reminder of her brother's death.

CHAPTER 11

Aria

"I know you're there! Show yourself!" Aria commanded.

"Don't shoot," a woman replied from the shadows. "I'm coming out now, and I mean no harm."

The woman stepped out of the tunnel where she'd been hiding. Her hands were raised in the air. Gray speckled the brown hair tumbling around her thin shoulders and weathered face. She was probably only in her late thirties, but life had etched lines around her brown eyes and mouth.

Something about the woman tugged at Aria's memory, but she didn't lower her bow. Even if this woman had known where the keys were and how to traverse these tunnels, she trusted no one right now.

"Your Highness," the woman said and kept her hands raised as she gave a small curtsy. "It has been a while."

That *voice*, she'd heard it before, but where? If her heart wasn't so badly shattered and her mind could grasp at anything other than death and destruction, she was sure she would know who this woman was, but the answer continued to elude her.

Her gaze ran over the woman again as her voice tickled at the back edges of Aria's mind. Then, recognition burst to life within her. "Mary?" she inquired.

Her voice hitched as the memory of being trapped within the king's dungeon slithered through her mind. Mary had been in the dungeon with her.

The woman smiled and dropped her hands to fold them into her skirt. "It is me," she confirmed.

Aria finally lowered her bow. She may not trust Mary completely yet, but she sensed no one else standing behind the woman, and she'd be able to kill a human easily enough if it became necessary. "What are you doing here?"

"My son, John, said he saw you coming into the caves," Mary said.

"You found him?"

"It took some time, but yes, I found him after I was set free of the dungeon."

John was the reason Aria had been captured and brought to the palace to be auctioned off to the highest vampire bidder in the first place. Braith had stepped forward to claim her from the man who had originally bought her and taken her with him to the palace. At the time, she hadn't known why Braith had done it, but eventually he'd told her it was because she was the first thing he'd actually been able to *see* in a hundred years.

Aria had sacrificed herself, allowed herself to be captured in place of John, and everything in her life had changed for the better. Even now, when she felt at her bleakest, she had to remember that. Mary had been taken with her on that long ago day, imprisoned in the dungeon and freed when Braith had come to rescue Aria. Mary had had no idea where her son was when she'd left the palace, but she'd found him once again. A small beacon of hope swelled within Aria at the realization.

Aria's capture had been the beginning for her and Braith, and they had already come to their end. No matter what happened from here on out, no matter the heartache she endured now, it had all been worth it.

"There is always good in the bad," Aria whispered.

Tempest squeezed her arm and William shot her a look, but she didn't acknowledge either of them.

"What are you doing here, Mary?" Aria inquired.

"John said it looked like you were in trouble when you came in." Her gaze ran over all of them, taking in their bloody and torn clothing. "Judging by the looks of you, I'd say he was right. You saved my child. I owe you much, and I'm here to help."

"There are vampires after us. This is not something you should be entangled with." Aria glanced at her brother. "Our guard was down if we didn't notice John out there."

"John would have made a fine rebel. He's nearly as silent as your family was in these woods," Mary said proudly.

William's face seemed to say exactly what she was thinking; *had they missed someone else?*

Mary's brow furrowed. "You are our queen and a vampire. Why would vampires be after you?"

"There is a new threat rising," William said.

"Get John somewhere safe, Mary," Aria said.

"Will this new threat hurt us if they uncover us?" Mary asked.

"Yes," Aria answered honestly.

"Then we are already in danger. Come with me. I know somewhere safe."

"Safer than these caves?"

"And warmer," Mary replied with a smile. "And there will be clothes. Come, Your Highness, I promise you will be safe with us."

"I'm just Aria. Please don't call me Your Highness." Mary blinked at her.

"Where is the king?" Mary inquired and Aria couldn't stop herself from flinching.

"Elsewhere," she replied crisply.

Mary frowned but didn't press it further. "Then come, let's get you clean and warmed up."

William glanced questioningly at Aria as she remained unmoving. Part of her plan had been to locate new recruits. Mary had been a rebel too. Aria was certain she still associated with many of the people who had once moved freely through these woods and caves. They would need vampires too, but humans could be almost as lethal as a vampire when properly armed and trained. After years of having to be stealthy, humans could often be quieter when necessary.

And if Sabine's soldiers followed them here, Mary and John would need help to stay safe. From what William and Tempest had told her, Sabine did not treat humans well.

"I promise you will be safe," Mary said.

Aria swung her bow over her back and returned the arrow to her quiver. "Lead the way then."

***

Melinda

Melinda had no idea where they were in the forest, only that they were going in the general direction of the palace, or at least she hoped they were. For all she knew, they could be heading back to Chippman, something that would prove lethal to all the vampires susceptible to the sun's rays.

She really didn't want to tell Hannah they'd been responsible for her cousin's horrific death by sunlight. At the edge of a stream, Ashby didn't hesitate before plunging the horse into it and guiding him through the flowing water. The animals had to be exhausted. Many of the vampires and humans surrounding her were slouched forward in their saddles and struggling to keep their eyes open, but they couldn't take a break and they couldn't let up on their relentless pace.

Every muscle in her body ached from sitting in the saddle for these past hours. Her ass had to be bruised, but she didn't utter a complaint and neither did any of those with them. Ashby's body thrummed with tension as he constantly surveyed their surroundings.

Splashing out of the stream, a flash of something on her right caught Melinda's attention and she sat up straighter in the saddle. Joy burst through her chest when she spotted the treehouse Braith had built for Aria nestled within the trees. They were going the right way, and what was more, she knew her way back from here!

"Look!" she slapped her hand against Ashby's arm and pointed to the treehouse. "We're almost home."

Ashby relaxed a little against her before going rigid once more. She didn't think he would relax again until Sabine was destroyed.

"We are," he said and kissed her cheek.

He turned their mount to the right and nudged him into another trot. *Lots of carrots for these horses when we get back*, she decided when the animal grudgingly resumed his pace. Ashby lifted his hand to push aside branches when they plunged back into the thick woods once more.

***

Jack

Jack finished helping to clean the blood from Xavier and sat back on his heels. He could bandage the wounds but saw no point. The blood had ceased flowing and the holes were closing. He'd already taken care of the humans who had fared better than Xavier. He was fairly certain Daniel had a concussion and suffered from blood loss and exhaustion, but their bruised bones and bodies would mend and none of their arrow wounds would be deadly if they were kept clean.

"I should have go… gone with her," Xavier said. His voice already sounding better, but it was still difficult for him to get words out.

"You would have only slowed them down," Jack replied.

Xavier gripped his wrist when he went to turn away. "I believe she is right, about Sabine and about Bra...ith."

"Believe or hope?" Jack inquired.

"Both."

"I hope you're right. I'm not ready to lose Braith and Aria, and I'm not meant to be king."

"No, but you would do well with it if it became necessary for you to assume the throne." Xavier released his hold on him. "You should ma... make sure Braith has blood."

Jack glanced at where they'd placed Braith's body in the shadows of the cave. They'd covered him in some of the furs and blankets from the store room, and Jack had tried to make sure his brother was as comfortable as possible, though he questioned if it mattered and doubted Braith could tell the difference.

"I don't know about that," he murmured.

"Your father was decaying when he rose from the earth, starv... ing and frail, most likely from lack of blood. If we can get some blood into Braith, he'll be strong... er when he rises."

Jack appreciated that Xavier said *when* instead of saying *if* Braith rose; he wished he could have Xavier's confidence in this matter.

Atticus returned.

He'd also been over a thousand years old at the time. Maybe there was an age someone had to reach for resurrection. At nine hundred fifty-four, Braith was pushing one thousand years old, but still shy of the millennial milestone. He may never get there now. Sabine hadn't been a thousand when she was killed, but did they really know if she had actually been killed and not faking her death?

Then he recalled Sabine's words, *"Kill them all, but bring me his head."* There had to be a reason for that specific command with Braith, there simply had to be, or was he grasping at straws in the hope Braith could return from the dead?

"How long do you think it will be before he comes back, if he does rise again?" he asked and saw the other's heads turn in their direction.

"I don't know," Xavier replied. "It was about a month before we saw Atticus, but in his weakened condition it could have… taken him a while to dig out of his grave. We ha… have no idea how much time he spent in the woods before he made it back to the palace. For all we know, he could have risen again two weeks after his death, but… I… I doubt it."

Jack rested his fingers on the cool stone beneath him. A month within these caves, trying to keep Braith protected. It could be done, it *would* be done, but it would be a month for Sabine to gather more troops and wreak more damage upon those who could, or did, stand in her way.

"When Aria returns—"

"I don't think she will return," Daniel interrupted Jack. "She'll lead Sabine and her followers as far from here as she can, but if she knows he's gone—"

"She knows," Hannah murmured and her gaze latched onto Jack. She ran her hands over her arms as she stared at him. "Believe me, Aria knows Braith is dead."

Daniel's fingers clenched around the rock he was resting his arm on. Anguish twisted his features as he turned his head briefly away from them. "Then she will go to work," he said.

"Doing what?" Hannah inquired.

"Raising an army, learning what she can about our newest enemy," Daniel replied. "She won't die without making that woman pay first."

Hannah glanced nervously at Jack and folded her hands before her. "I'd make her pay too."

Jack rose to his feet and stalked across the cavern to her. Wrapping his arms around her, he held her close against him.

"Won't she come back for Braith?" Hannah inquired.

"I know what she said about this woman being Sabine, about there being a chance Braith could rise again, but I imagine right now she doesn't believe in much," Jack said as he ran a hand over Hannah's silken. "And if Braith does rise again, instead of coming back here, she's going to do whatever she can to protect him, which means gathering an army."

"She'll be going back to our rebel roots," Daniel said. "I bet she's already formulating a plan. It's what we would have done before."

"Aria will go for the humans and she will try to get closer to Sabine, if that is who that woman is," Max said.

"What do you mean go for the humans?" Hannah inquired.

"Many of the rebels are still living within the forest," Max explained. "The rebel life is what we knew for so many years, so even after peace was achieved, many chose to stay. These woods are the home of the rebels and where we were always more comfortable, even Aria. We know how to avoid vampires. We may not have their strength, but we know how to hide, know how to sneak up on someone and how to set traps. We know how to take a vampire down. Outside of the palace walls, Aria will return to the rebels."

"And she's going to get closer to the palace walls," Daniel said. "She'll want to know what is going on there. We will find her somewhere in that area when we go to meet with her."

"You can barely walk," Jack said.

"Not now," Daniel replied. "But as soon as we're feeling up to it, we'll go for her. It has to be done."

"He's right," Timber agreed.

"Sabine has been gathering her troops. It's time to start gathering ours," Daniel said.

CHAPTER 12

Aria

Aria swung her bow onto her back again and adjusted her quiver. Though she'd recently washed herself off with a cloth, washed her hair in the basin, and wore the clean clothes Mary had given to her, she didn't feel any fresher. She didn't think she'd ever feel clean again.

She managed to keep her hands from shaking as she lifted them to pull her wet hair into a braid. She couldn't bring herself to look in the mirror above the washbasin until she'd finished. Her hands clamped onto the sink when her ruby-colored eyes greeted her in the mirror.

No matter what she did, no matter how badly she willed them to do so, she could not get her eyes to return to their normal blue hue. It was something she wouldn't care about if she wasn't going out amongst humans. She'd been a human, the daughter of their leader, they still trusted and liked her, but a vampire's red eyes signaled a loss of control. The humans would be apprehensive around her.

She couldn't let them know what a tumultuous mess she was right now. They'd flee from her, and if they fled from her, they could wind up in Sabine's clutches. All she wanted was to keep them safe, but if she couldn't keep up appearances, she may end up being the one to drive them to their deaths.

She had to be controlled, confident, and a leader; her eyes signaled she was anything but. Lifting her hand, she almost drove her fist into the mirror, but stopped herself from doing so. Destroying the hateful thing would only confirm to them her instability.

A knock on the door had her lowering her hand and clutching the basin once more. "Come in."

William opened the door and slipped inside. His eyes met hers in the glass. "I can't get them to change," she admitted.

"I know."

Walking forward, he handed her a pair of dark sunglasses. Her fingers shook when she took them from him and settled them onto her face. It may be nighttime, and they may be underground, but the glasses hid her eyes and she wouldn't be taking them off until she was able to get her eyes to return to normal, if they ever returned to normal again.

"Where is Tempest?" she inquired.

"Speaking with Mary and John. They've taken a liking to her."

"That's easy enough to do. This place, it's so like those drawings and plans Daniel did before the war with Atticus."

He grinned at her as he rested his hand on her shoulder. "The rebels discovered some of his plans in one of the caves. Either he forgot them there, or he never had the chance to return for them after everything unfolded. They used his designs and calculations to build a few of these, what they call, safe houses."

Aria glanced at the beams of wood in the ceiling above her head. Daniel would be happy to know his design had come to life in such a way, and the rebels had done an amazing job of it. William turned her away from the mirror and pulled her out of the small bathroom. A single lantern hanging on the wall cast shadows over the dirt floor and wooden walls.

Her gaze fell on the back door, one of the only two exits out of this place. However, she doubted anyone would ever find it. She followed William down the long hallway toward the main room. At least twenty doors lined the hall, most of which were open to reveal the small rooms and straw pallets stacked on the floor within. Another room held at least a month's worth of supplies for at least fifty people, and another had clothes and a large cache of weapons stashed within.

They entered the large main room where Mary, John, and Tempest sat around a table near the wall across from them. John's face lit up when he spotted her; he leapt from his seat and gestured for her to take it.

"Thank you," Aria said to him and slowly sat on the edge of the chair.

"Thank you," John said. "You saved my life and my mother's, Your Highness."

"Please, just call me Aria," she murmured as she kept her gaze focused on the windowless wall across from her.

Mary hadn't been kidding about taking them to a safe place. Aria never would have discovered this safe house buried beneath the earth. She had thought the walls of the caves pressed against her, they were nothing compared to the oppressive air encompassing this place.

Judging by the look on William's face, he felt much the same way as he paced from one wall to the other.

"You can wash up now, Tempest," Aria said.

Tempest glanced at her before her gaze went to William, who stretched his hand out to her. Aria didn't turn to watch them walk away, but she hoped they would stay gone for a while. They needed time alone, and she needed time to just *be*.

John settled into the chair across from her. In the time since she'd last seen him, he'd gone from a child to a young man. His brunet hair hung in waves around his narrow face and his brown eyes were eager. Brown peach fuzz dotted his upper lip, cheeks, and chin.

"I'm glad you are well," Aria said to him.

"What is life like in the palace?" he inquired.

"Manners, John," Mary scolded.

"When was this place built?" Aria inquired to distract the conversation from anything having to do with the palace or her life there.

"After the last war," Mary replied. "I know we were all supposed to be safe, there was a truce and things have actually been going extremely well, but..."

"But it is always better safe than sorry," Aria finished when Mary's voice trailed off.

"Yes, and it had become well known by the vampires that many of us resided within the caves, so we knew we had to do something different."

"So you built shelters beneath the ground," Aria said and forced herself not to shudder at the reminder that ultimately she was standing in a large coffin. If one of those beams in the ceiling gave out...

Stop it!

"Yes, and until now, we've never had a reason to use one. We keep them stocked, make sure the water supply and ventilation system is still operational at least once every two weeks, and we clear away any debris obstructing the peepholes. Your brother is a genius."

"He is," Aria agreed. "I wish there was no reason to have to use one of these safe houses now."

Rising to her feet, she paced over to the wall, feeling uncomfortable in her own skin as it seemed to tighten around her as much as these walls were. Her hand went to her heart, and she placed her palm over the deadened organ as she once again fought the impulse to tear it from her body. It was unnatural for a bloodlink to carry on without their love, and all of her instincts screamed at her to end it, while another sinister part of her hungered for blood and revenge.

"This new threat, is it bad?" Mary asked.

"Yes," Aria replied as she stared at the wall and tried to ignore the enticing rush of blood in their veins.

"Is it... is it the king?" Mary asked hesitantly and Aria couldn't help but wince as she kept her gaze locked on the wall. "Has he become like his father?"

"No, he hasn't," Aria replied. *His wife might though.* She took a minute to regain her composure and make sure her fangs weren't visible before facing Mary. "How many of these safe houses are there?"

"Five."

"Are there any closer to the palace?"

"One."

Aria turned to pace over to the other wall. Caged. It's what she felt right now and she needed free of these bars. *Easy, calm.* "How far is it from the palace?"

"About five miles."

"Close enough," she murmured as Tempest and William reappeared.

The scent of their mingled blood drifted to her, along with the fresh scent of the pine soap. William had his arm around Tempest's waist as she rested her head on his chest. Turning away, Aria paced over to the other wall and then around to the door they'd entered through. She almost grabbed the handle and fled into the hallway beyond, but she managed to keep herself restrained from doing so. If only there was a window. If only she could feel and smell fresh air instead of the musty air surrounding her.

"Close enough for what?" William inquired.

"I don't think Sabine will go for the palace, not yet," Aria replied. "She'll try to find Braith first, but she'll be in the area of the palace, getting ready for her next move. We have to be there too, if we're to learn anything about her and to corner her when she does finally attack."

"How do you know that is her next move?" Tempest asked.

"Because she left your town and headed toward the palace," Aria replied. "I don't think she planned to discover us in the woods earlier. She would have had more of her followers with her if she had. She probably didn't realize Braith was outside the palace walls. Once she was uncovered in Badwin and knew there was a chance you would get word to us, she decided to make a move to seize the palace before we could gather more troops to defend against her."

"How do you plan to get past her troops to the safe house closest to the palace?" William asked.

Aria finally turned to face him. "Quietly."

Despite the fact he looked tempted to throttle her, a smile curved his lips. He had Tempest to worry about now, a family to start, a woman to love, but her brother relished the thrill of a good challenge. They both did. Taking down Sabine may be the ultimate challenge.

His cocky grin widened as he ran a hand through his wet hair. "Quietly usually works."

"When it's us, it always works, but first we have to meet with more rebels." She looked to Mary. "Can you bring more here for us to talk with tomorrow? If they don't want to come, I understand, but this new vampire trying to take control has no sympathy for humans. She'll make Atticus look like he was a friend to them."

"She locked the humans away in Badwin," Tempest said. "After she arrived, we never saw them again."

"I don't think that will change as time goes on," Aria said.

Mary paled at their words; she took hold of John's hand. "We will all fight to keep the peace," she said. "We've worked our entire lives to build a future of peace and safety for our children. We won't let it be taken from us without a fight."

"We will also gather vampires as we go. I'm sure there are a fair amount of them who won't want to be enslaved to her, and some who have already escaped her clutches," Aria said.

"Will it really matter to them if she wins?" John asked.

"Yes. There are many vampires who only want to live in peace with the humans and who aren't cruel. Also, she killed the vampire children in the other towns she took over. Maybe she'll stop doing that now, instead of taking the risk of turning some of the vamps against her by continuing to kill them, but I'm not sure she will," William said.

"Why would she do that to the children?" Mary gasped.

"Because the children can't fight for her," William answered. "They are a hindrance, and she couldn't allow one of them to get free and warn someone of what she was trying to do. She slaughtered or imprisoned any who disagreed with her. The vampires she doesn't kill outright for standing against her, she imprisons and starves until they become mindless killing machines. She didn't bother to do that with the children."

"Monster," Mary whispered.

Aren't we all? Aria's gaze went to the wall once more. She certainly no longer knew of what she was capable. She felt as if she were unraveling, becoming completely unbound from all the rules once governing her, from everything she'd always known and believed. Now she was adrift in a world she could barely make sense of, but she would protect it.

"She is," Tempest confirmed.

"How will we know which vampires we can trust and which have already been turned to her side?" Mary asked.

"We will have to be cautious," Aria replied. "But we always have been, and I'm sure the rebels already have some they trust. After we speak with the rebels here, we will move onto the next safe house and talk with the ones there."

"I will bring as many rebels as I can to you tomorrow."

"Thank you," Aria said and settled onto the chair once more.

"You can use one of the rooms to sleep," Mary offered her.

Aria focused on the wall across from her once more. "I'm fine here, but please, all of you, rest."

She required sleep in order to be at her best, but the idea of sleeping without Braith beside her wasn't something she could handle right now. She didn't think she'd ever be able to sleep again. Mary and John rose from the table; they spoke with William and Tempest before their footsteps retreated down the hall. Two doors opened and closed and she knew only William remained behind with her.

"Go, Tempest needs you," Aria said without turning to look at her brother.

He didn't say anything, just walked over to the table and pulled out another chair. He settled into it and folded his arms over his chest as he stared at the wall across from him. "I hate walls. They make me feel trapped," he murmured.

"I know. Tempest has made it better for you though."

"She has," he admitted.

Aria bowed her head and stared at her hands clasped before her. Her beautiful, delicate emerald ring and her simple white gold wedding band mocked her with the broken promise of eternity. She grabbed the bands with the fingers of her right hand, intending to rip them off and heave them across the room, but instead she brought her hands together and clasped them tightly to her chest.

She bit her lip and struggled to regain her composure before she did something she would regret. Lifting her head, she found William's gaze upon her. There was no sympathy in his eyes. He knew she'd hate to see that from him as much as he would hate to see it from her. Instead, there was only understanding.

"Things were so simple before I was captured," she said. "They were hard, but they were simple. Father loved us, we hunted, we avoided vampires, when we couldn't avoid them, we killed them, and we had our woods."

"Then it all changed."

"Then it all changed, yet now I feel as if we've returned to the beginning. We're without Dad, but back to avoiding vampires and hiding out within our woods once more. Actually, beneath our woods."

He glanced at the ceiling. "We survived then."

"Yes."

"We'll survive now."

"I will make sure of it."

Her head bowed again, her gaze focusing on her rings. The flickering light of the lantern caused shadows to dance over her hands. The wood creaked and groaned every once in a while, but otherwise silence filled the safe house beneath the earth.

CHAPTER 13

Melinda

"Close the gates!" Ashby yelled to the guards in the turrets on the wall surrounding the palace.

Melinda craned her head back to look at the guards peering down at them from atop the wall. Voices and footsteps echoed on the stone above them as more of the king's guard came out to look down at them. The horse's hooves rang out on the cobblestone roads within the castle walls as everyone accompanying them crowded into the bailey.

"Did you say *close* the gates?" one of the guards called down. It was an order that hadn't been given in some time.

"Yes!" Ashby slid from the saddle and turned to pull Melinda into his arms. "Close them now!"

Around them the survivors of Badwin and the residents of Chippman fanned out into the massive courtyard. Their eyes were wide as they took in their surroundings and murmured with awe to each other. Melinda adjusted her skirt as the gates swung closed and the large wooden drawbridge Braith had ordered built rose into the air.

No moat surrounded the palace, but the heavy piece of wood was extra protection against any possible, future attack. At the time, her brother had believed he was being overly cautious by building it. She'd never been more thankful for that caution as the heavy wood settled into place against the metal gates, blocking out the homes beyond the gates.

"What about the residents of the outer town?" she asked Ashby.

"We'll have them awakened and brought in now," Ashby replied. "But those gates will remain closed until the residents are ready to enter and we have more guards to defend these walls." He thrust his reins at a passing stable boy.

"Make sure all of the animals are well taken care of," Melinda said to the stable boy before turning to face the palace.

Set into the mountain above them, the palace rose high into the night. Its golden spires gleamed in the moonlight shining down on them. Lanterns flickered in the windows of the main areas within, but many of the rooms were dark. Some of The Council members still resided within, but most of them had moved out of the palace and settled into the bailey town or the outer town.

It was as beautiful as she remembered and as imposing. Atticus had made it a formidable place he could readily defend against his many enemies. The enormous stone walls surrounding the palace enclosed nearly four square miles of land around it.

Aria and Braith had made the palace more inviting since they'd taken over and settled within. There had been no laughter within its walls or in the surrounding town before their rule, but now there were parties and dancing; there was happiness between the humans and vampires who coincided in peace. There was still the occasional disagreement, but more often than not it was solved without the authorities having to get involved. It was a life she'd never pictured having; secure, fun, and full of love, and now it may be coming to an end.

She hugged her arms around herself as she stared at the serene streets. Lanterns came to life in some of the homes closest to them. Doors opened as humans and vampires curiously peered out of the two and three story buildings lining the street.

"Where is Gideon?" Ashby demanded of the head guard on shift who came down from the wall to meet them.

"He is within the palace," the man replied.

"Have some troops readied to go out and bring in the residents of the town. Bring as many of them to the palace for shelter as possible. Find homes for the rest within the walls," Ashby instructed. "More of the king's guard is to be awakened and brought down to defend the wall until there is a guard standing every ten feet around the entire wall. Alert them that we could be facing a possible attack soon and to be on the alert for anything unusual, no matter how small it is."

"What of the king, will he be returning?" the guard inquired.

"Not tonight."

The guard's eyes widened, but he didn't question Ashby's statement or orders. The guard nodded briskly before turning away. Melinda watched him vanish into the growing crowd filling the street. Ashby gripped her elbow and led her forward. Her legs felt wooden as she walked beside him toward the palace.

More lanterns blazed to life in the houses surrounding them and residents spilled into the street to see what was going on. The growing voices rang off the buildings until they echoed all around her. Even the animals were roused as a pair of spooked chickens ran across the road before them.

Melinda kept her chin raised and displayed an air of calm she didn't feel as they hurried up the hill toward the front door of the palace. Before Ashby could grab the handle, the door swung open and the vampire within stepped aside to give them entrance.

"Is Gideon in his rooms?" Ashby demanded.

"Why, yes... milord," the guard stammered out, his eyes raking over their torn and bloodied clothes. "I believe he is sleeping, but I'll wake him for you if you would like?"

"No, I will get him."

Ashby kept his hold on her elbow as they strode across the glistening marble floor and beneath the chandelier to the stairs at the far end of the hall. They ascended to the second floor, where the remaining members of The Council still living in the palace resided. Gideon's rooms were at the end of the hall, the largest and most lavish of all the rooms in this section. Ashby knocked loudly on the door, but he didn't wait for a response before opening it.

"Gideon!" he called into the dark sitting room they entered. "Gideon! Get up!"

A woman's startled cry came from the adjoining bedroom and curses sounded as feet hit the floor.

"Get out!" Gideon barked from the other room and a young vampire scurried out from the bedroom with her clothes still in hand. Melinda lifted an eyebrow at the unfamiliar girl, but Gideon wasn't known for his lasting relationships.

"What is the meaning of this, Ash?" Gideon demanded as he strode into the sitting room, tying the belt on his red robe as he walked.

Ashby stiffened at the much hated nickname; the two men glowered at each other. Before they could really start going at each other, Melinda stepped forward to end any further bickering between them. Gideon's hazel eyes narrowed on her over the bridge of his hawkish nose. His straight brown hair was tussled around his face.

"We have a problem, Giddy," Ashby said and Gideon's eyes shot toward him. Ashby smirked in return.

"Enough!" Melinda snapped. "Now is *not* the time."

Gideon's eyes came back to her. "What is going on?"

Melinda walked back to close and lock the door of Gideon's apartment. "Is there anyone else in here?" she asked, well aware there could be a few more women lingering about.

Gideon frowned at her. "No, we are alone now."

She glanced at Ashby who took hold of her hand for support. "Braith is dead," she said bluntly, but she had no idea how she could sugarcoat the news.

The color drained from Gideon's face. He took a startled step back, his knees connecting with the sofa behind him. He sank onto it before rising again. "You're joking!" he blurted.

"I'm not. We were ambushed. He saved the rest of us, but was shot through the heart with an arrow. He's dead, Gideon."

"Ambushed by who?" Gideon demanded.

"We believe it was Sabine, Atticus's mother," she replied.

"She's dead."

"And so was Atticus, but he came back."

Gideon blinked at them before spinning away. He stalked over to the sideboard and the cluster of liquors set up on top of it. He poured himself a generous glass of whiskey before turning to face them again. With a trembling hand, he lifted the glass to his lips and drank it all in one gulp. He ran the back of his hand across his mouth before staring at the empty glass as if it had somehow betrayed him.

"Where is Braith's body? If they came back, he could too," Gideon finally said.

"Safe, hidden with Jack," Ashby replied.

Gideon lowered the glass and poured himself another drink. "Where is Aria?"

"Aria, William, and his bloodlink, Tempest, led our attackers away from where Braith is hidden," Melinda said. "He died shortly after they left us."

"Shit," Gideon muttered.

"There's more," Melinda said and proceeded to fill him in on everything that had happened with Tempest and William, the new residents they now had within the palace walls, and the ones who would soon be joining them from the outer town, if all went well. "If it really is Sabine, and we all believe or want to believe Aria is right about her, she's most likely going to come here."

"Most likely," Gideon agreed.

"She looks like Atticus," Ashby said, and Gideon lifted his eyes from his whiskey glass to Ashby. "And the amount of power coming off of her, it was like nothing I've ever experienced before."

"Nothing like either of us have ever experienced," Melinda replied.

"No one, outside of this room, can know Braith is dead, not yet," Ashby said.

Gideon poured himself another whiskey and sipped it as he contemplated Ashby's words. "I agree. I trust the members of The Council, but the death of a king will cause chaos, and the more who know about it, the more likely panic will spread through the masses. Many might turn to who they feel is the strongest leader in order to survive. If this woman is who you believe she is and is as powerful as you say, they could turn to *her*. That cannot be allowed. Braith's death will be kept from everyone else, and if he does manage to rise again, no one else will ever have to know it occurred."

"What if he doesn't awaken?" she asked.

"Then we will let the others know, when Jack is here and can help to keep everyone calm. As the next oldest of the royal line, they will look to him for guidance," Gideon replied and finished his whiskey.

Jack was currently the only living member of the line, but Melinda kept that information to herself.

"Jesus, not Braith." Gideon set his glass down on the sidebar. "We must prepare for an attack."

"I've already ordered more guards on the wall, and to have the residents of the outer town brought inside. I don't know what to do about the border towns. Sending more of the king's guard out there for them will only weaken our forces if they are attacked too," Ashby said.

"We'll send out a few to tell the border townspeople to come in, and let them know their safety is in peril, but we can't risk many soldiers," Gideon agreed. "We will do what Jack said and tell The Council that Braith, Jack, and the others are recruiting more soldiers as we speak," Gideon replied.

Melinda squeezed Ashby's hand. Exhaustion tugged at her eyelids. She felt like she could sleep for a week, but there would be no rest, not for a while. "We must wake the rest of The Council and gather them together," she said.

"Yes," Gideon agreed as he poured himself another whiskey. "I'll get dressed and join you in the private solar where we hold Council meetings."

"Very well," Ashby said and turned her away.

"Melinda." She turned back to find Gideon watching her. "Your brother is the strongest vampire I know. If his ancestors came back, he will too."

She couldn't help the hot wash of tears flooding her eyes. How badly she wanted those words to be true.

"We will defeat this woman just as we defeated Atticus," Gideon assured her.

"You didn't see her, Gideon. She was terrifying."

"And from what you said, she had you greatly outnumbered, yet only one of you fell. Next time, if he is prepared for her, and with a bloodlink to fuel him, Braith will be more than a match for her."

"You're right," Melinda agreed.

She thought she heard Gideon whisper, "He has to come back. He's the only friend I have," as she walked out the door, but she couldn't be sure.

CHAPTER 14

Aria

After a week, Aria still couldn't get her eyes to return to normal, but at least no one questioned her about the ever-present sunglasses she wore, or her short periods of sleep. The only time she slept was when exhaustion took over and her body gave her no other choice but to rest. Often times that happened when she was sitting in a chair, but then her chin would hit her chest and she'd jerk awake again.

She hated sleeping for any length of time as she always dreamed, and *all* of her dreams were of Braith and what they had once shared. Most times, she woke crying from the dreams of Braith holding her.

Either from lack of sleep, or because she so badly wanted him back, she would often think she saw him somewhere too. When she turned to look, he would be gone and she would once again be left with her emptiness. Sometimes, she would smell him and the scent would be so vivid she could almost believe he was there. Then the smell would fade away to be replaced with whatever surrounded her.

Madness threatened to consume her in those moments when reality became almost too much to bear. It took a concentrated effort for her to wrap her mind around her mission to destroy Sabine.

Now, she stood within another one of the safe houses, talking with the humans who had been brought in to hear what was going on and what they should prepare for. This was the fourth safe house they'd been to, the next one would be the last one, and the one closest to the palace. Those gathered within listened raptly as she outlined the new threat they faced. Many of the faces paled, but all of them assumed a resolute expression. They would fight; there had never been any doubt in Aria's mind about it.

"Do you plan for all of us to go to the palace now?" a man inquired.

"No," Aria replied. "Weapons must be gathered or forged first."

"We already have many weapons stored away, Your Highness," a woman said to her.

"Please just call me Aria," she said for what felt like the thousandth time. "I am simply Aria." *Now.* But she always kept that word to herself. "We also need time to recruit more fighters for our cause, and to learn more about this woman and her troops. We have to be careful about gathering so many in one place right now. We can't take the risk of our forces being slaughtered because we don't fully know what we're up against yet."

They nodded enthusiastically as they looked around the room at each other. Aria pulled on the collar of her shirt as sweat slid down her back. Despite the cool dirt pressing against the walls, the heat of so many bodies within made it nearly unbearable to stand in here. Not to mention all of those annoyingly alluring heartbeats and the blood pulsing through their little blue veins.

Saliva rushed into her mouth, her fangs tingled with the need to sink them into someone and ease this turmoil inside her. Blood, it would center her, it would make her forget if only for a minute everything her world had become.

Atticus killed, and when he did, it eased the agony.

She craved a *second* of peace from her reality, and often wondered how long she could hold out for. How long could she keep going when the only thing driving her was death and vengeance?

For as long as it takes! I will not harm another!

Before, she'd only fed from Braith. Now she fed from animals, but the lure of human blood was becoming more and more enticing with each passing day.

Though it was tempting, she couldn't retreat further into the shadows of the room in order to put some distance between her and the heartbeats calling out to her. She had to be strong, had to present an impeccable façade of leadership and stability no matter how volatile she felt.

William glanced over at her as she rubbed her forehead. She was keeping it together, but she feared her brother sensed her unraveling. Of course he did. She would sense it in him as well, even if he acted as if nothing was wrong.

"How will we know when it is time to gather and move?" another man inquired.

"We will be sending runners out to the safe houses when it is time to move," William answered. "Most likely it will be in seven days."

"Plenty of time for us to recruit more to the fight," a woman said and everyone in the room gave a brisk, decisive nod.

"I know of some vampires we can bring in," a man near the back of the room declared. "Ones who can be trusted."

"I don't expect you to bring them here, but I would like to speak with them," Aria said. "Soon."

The rebels at the other safe houses had been willing to bring vampires in too, but none had offered to divulge their newest locations. Aria didn't blame them for keeping the safe houses a secret. If she hadn't once been human, the daughter of the fallen rebel leader and the sister of their representative on The Council, they most likely wouldn't have revealed the locations to her either. The title of queen didn't matter to these humans; it hadn't mattered to her either.

"I will get them and bring them to the waterfall in an hour," the man replied.

"We can bring you there," a young woman at the front offered.

"Thank you," Aria replied and the man left the room.

"What if something happens before the week is over? If this woman attacks the palace or the nearby towns?" a man at the back of the room asked.

"There is nothing we can do about that," Aria replied. "The palace will be able to fend off any attackers for a time, and I'm sure the towns closest to it have either been evacuated or informed of the risk to them."

"If this woman has more vampires on her side, how will we ever be able to defeat them?" the woman before her inquired.

Don't look at her neck. Don't look at her neck.

"The vampires may be stronger than humans," Aria said as her fingers dug into her palms. "But we rebels survived in these woods for a century. We are lethal, fast, and best of all, we know these woods better than they do. She, and many of the vampires following her, underestimate humans, and we're going to show them how wrong they are to do so."

An excited murmur ran through the crowd. "Damn right we will," the woman beside her said.

Despite her every intention not to look, Aria's gaze fell to the woman's neck. *Thump. Thump. Thump.* Every beat of the woman's heart pulsed within her vein.

She had to get out of this place, soon.

"We will gather many others," another man said, "and be ready to go within a week. The peace will be protected."

"Thank you," Aria said.

They all came forward, taking hold of her hands as they spoke to her. She couldn't move as each one of them squeezed her outstretched hands. If she moved, she'd break, but she couldn't turn them away right now.

Every single one of them would fight. She knew they were doing it to give themselves and their children better lives. However, they were also doing it because she and William would be leading them into battle, and because they had loved her father.

It was nearly an hour before the last one filed out the door, leaving her unmoving at the edge of the room as she worked to calm herself.

"Are you okay?" William inquired.

"I need a minute before we go to meet with the vampires," she replied.

He walked over to lead Mary and John from the room. She hadn't wanted the two of them to come with them to the other safe houses, but Mary had insisted she be the one to lead them and introduce them to the rebels at each one.

Four safe houses down, one more to go. Then she would find Sabine and learn everything she could about her.

The sound of someone entering the room caused her to turn toward the doorway. William gave her a questioning look from the doorway, but didn't say a word.

"I'm ready," she told him and pushed her braid over her shoulder.

She shifted her bow on her back and followed him into one of the narrow hallways to the door at the end. Tempest stood by the doorway with Mary and John. Tempest dropped her hand away from her mouth when they approached. Aria's gaze fell to Tempest's fingers; she'd bitten one of her nails low enough to draw blood.

William took hold of Tempest's hand and wiped away the blood beading there. "Everything will be okay," he said.

"I know," Tempest replied. "Habit."

Aria turned away when Mary opened the door. She drew her cloak tighter around her before striding forward to climb the stairs that ascended a good twenty feet to the earth above. The other three safe houses had all been hidden beneath a different entrance.

The first one they'd visited had been in the floor of an old home. The door had been intricately carved to blend in seamlessly with the wood around it. The second was behind a boulder in the forest floor. The third had been in an old, abandoned church on the outskirts of a rebel town. This one though, had been the most carefully hidden, and she couldn't help but think of how much Daniel would appreciate it as she stopped at the top of the stairs and looked out the tiny peephole to the forest beyond.

Her gaze scanned over the woods, and she scented the air as a pair of squirrels raced through the tree across the way. She checked the other small peepholes surrounding her before pushing the button to release the lock keeping the door secured. The door swung open and she stepped from the center of the hollowed out tree.

Turning, she stared up at the towering maple. The tree's thick branches showed no signs of rot as they stretched high into the sky. Carving a hole into its foundation, in order to hide the entrance to the safe house, might eventually kill the tree, but then again, it might be strong enough to withstand the injury. So far, she was surviving having had a piece of her carved away, just like this tree.

Aria rubbed at her cheeks while she inspected the woods around her. Even with knowing where some of the air vents were located for the safe house, they were so cleverly hidden within the forest, she could barely detect them amongst the trees and forest floor.

The sun filtered through the empty branches surrounding her to dance across the fallen leaves and dead branches littering the forest floor. February had given way to March a few days ago and already signs of spring were becoming evident. The sun was in the sky longer, the animals were more active, the snow that had lined most of the forest floor had melted.

She turned toward where she'd left Braith and the others. For a second, an image of Braith shimmered within the trees before her. His gray eyes surveyed her, and a smile curved the edges of his full lips as he extended a hand to her.

In her chest, her deadened heart lurched and she took an involuntary step toward the mirage before it vanished. A scream welled in her throat. If there hadn't been humans nearby waiting to take her to the waterfall, she would have bellowed her despair to the sky before sinking to her knees and sobbing out her misery.

Instead, she remained completely still. If she moved at all, what thin control she had of her shredding sanity and composure would crumble around her. She could return to the cave, to check on them, but she didn't think she'd be able to leave Braith, not again.

If Braith came back, he would find her.

***

Daniel

Daniel poked his head out of the cave and examined the forest surrounding him. A week within the musty, gloomy confines of the cave had him blinking against the sun. He inhaled a big breath of fresh air and closed his eyes to savor it. Being within the caves, trapped with the melancholy and death, had worn on his soul more than he'd realized. Now he couldn't get enough of the warmth of the sun and the cool air brushing over his face.

Xavier rested his hand on his arm, holding him back from stepping out of the cave. Determination was etched onto Xavier's handsome features as he searched the forest around them and scented at the air.

"I sense no one nearby," Xavier said after a minute.

"Are you sure you want to do this?" Jack inquired.

Daniel turned toward him. "We have to know what is going on by the palace, and we have to try to find Aria."

Jack turned to gaze at the woods. "You could return to the palace and the protection of the walls."

"I'm sure Melinda and Ashby have things covered in there," Daniel replied. "We'll be needed outside the walls to report back to you what we find."

Jack took hold of Hannah's hand when she stepped into the sunlight. Her head tipped back and her eyes closed as the rays played over her delicate face. Having been denied the sun for most of her life, Daniel hated to think of her locked within the caves again. However, Jack wouldn't leave here, not until they had their answer about Braith, and Daniel couldn't stay anymore.

Their injuries were healed well enough for them to move on. He focused on the forest around him once more before stepping from the cave beside Xavier with Timber and Max close on his heels.

"Be careful," Hannah said from behind them.

"Always," Max replied and Daniel turned back to wave at the couple before slipping into the trees.

"Where do you think Aria is?" Xavier asked after they had covered a couple of miles and paused to rest beside a lake.

"Most likely near the palace," Max replied as he rose from the edge of the lake and tossed back his wet hair.

There had been a small water supply in the cave they'd used to wash themselves with, but Daniel had still felt rank and dirty until he'd scrubbed his flesh with the lake water. His relief over finally having washed the scent of mildew and dead animals off his body far outweighed any chill he might have felt from the freezing cold water.

Daniel rose from where he'd knelt beside the lake and flicked away a few of the beads of water still trickling down his face. Xavier had always been a calming presence, a wealth of knowledge Aria loved to question and learn more from. Now, Daniel sensed the stoic vampire was about to explode.

Xavier had been tense and restless for the last week within the cave. The more he healed, the more he paced like a caged tiger. They were finally out and Xavier was more on edge than ever as he stalked through the trees, his gaze constantly searching the shadows.

Daniel couldn't help but admire the flex and bunch of Xavier's powerful muscles as he moved, but then it was impossible not to notice how attractive Xavier was. He'd certainly noticed it long ago. Throughout his life, Daniel had always been attracted to those he had a connection with regardless of what sex they were. He enjoyed someone who appreciated beauty and art, and could talk for hours. Someone who didn't have reservations and judgments of others.

It was a rare combination to find in a man or woman, which was why he spent more time alone than with another. He required an emotional connection to anyone before he climbed into bed with them. He liked Xavier, and couldn't deny his brown eyes and skin, intelligence, and unwavering loyalty had intrigued him for some time, but Xavier took his role as Aria's guard seriously and allowed little room for distractions, especially of the romantic sort.

Besides, despite the fact Xavier was one of the wisest and most knowledgeable men Daniel knew, he felt no emotional connection to him, only desire. He'd never been with someone he didn't have a bond with before, and had never considered a vampire partner as he planned to leave this world the way he'd come into it, human.

However, life was short. Even for an immortal, he realized as he recalled Braith lying dead in that cave. It may be getting a whole lot shorter for more of them, if not *all* of them, by the time this thing with Sabine was done.

Daniel's head tilted to the side as he watched Xavier pace from one tree to another. He didn't kid himself into thinking they would all make it out of this alive. Maybe it was time to start taking what he desired now; there may not be many more tomorrows. Nothing could ever come of the two of them, but nothing had ever come of his past relationships either, as both parties had agreed to go their separate ways, and he did like Xavier after all.

Xavier rubbed at his stubble-lined cheeks as he met Daniel's gaze and held it. "I'm going to scout ahead," Xavier said and slipped into the trees.

"What is with your family and vampires. Can't you guys lust after someone with a heartbeat?" Max inquired of him after Xavier vanished.

Daniel scowled at him. Max may be his best friend, but he was tempted to plant his foot in his ass and shove him into the water. William and Aria would have. Sometimes he hated being the sensible one of the three.

"I'm not lusting after anyone," Daniel replied.

"Sure, I see you staring after every vamp and human you meet like that," Max said and knelt at the edge of the lake again. "I don't remember the last time I saw you staring at anyone with any interest."

Neither could he, but Daniel didn't exactly feel like talking about his relationships right now.

"You and that one?" Timber stopped scrubbing his arms in the lake and thrust his thumb at the woods where Xavier had disappeared. "Good luck, I was beginning to suspect he may be asexual."

"He's not," Daniel said and Max laughed.

Screw being sensible. Grasping the back of Max's head, he dunked it into the lake. Max came up sputtering and pushed his streaming hair from his eyes with his hands. "You only get to do that once," Max said as he wiped the water away from his mouth.

"Once was more than enough," Daniel replied with a smile, and Timber shook his head.

Max gave him the finger and rose to his feet. "So can we expect the entire family to become vamps?" he inquired.

"No," Daniel said.

"But if he's your bloodlink or something—"

"He's not," Daniel interrupted.

"How do you know?"

"I just do. It's not the same as what I see with Jack and Hannah or William and Tempest." He didn't say Aria and Braith; he couldn't. They may never be again. Daniel couldn't stop his hand from rubbing over his heart at the idea of losing his little sister. Max's eyes softened as he noted the absence of their names. "He's attractive, and he's fascinating, but no more than that," Daniel finished.

He turned to gaze at the lake as the sun shone over its surface, creating a pathway across the ripples fluttering outward. "I won't become a vampire. I was born a human and I will die a human. When it is my time to go, I will meet it without hesitation," he said.

"What if you fall for a vamp?" Max inquired. "Which, with your family's track record, may be a good possibility."

Daniel turned away from the lake to face him. "I will die a human. If something happens to me, make sure of that. I don't want to be a vampire. I don't hate them anymore; I understand there is good and bad in both humans and vampires, but being a human is my natural course in life. Make sure of it."

"I will." Max rubbed at his neck as he turned to face the lake. "Aria and I spent a lot of time here after Jack took us from the palace. Fishing, always with the fishing," he murmured.

"I remember," Daniel said.

Aria had been heartbroken over learning Braith had a fiancée and having left him behind in the palace. Max had been so angry, so lost after what he'd endured as a blood slave. At the time, Daniel had believed Aria and Max both lost. He'd expected them to turn to each other for comfort, and they had, but not in the way Max or any of the rest of them had expected. Aria would not move on from Braith and Max hadn't known what to do about it.

To this day, Max rarely spoke of his time as a blood slave and had never revealed what had been done to him, but Daniel had a good idea about it. Max would never be the same as he was before he became a blood slave, but he'd become better at handling his anger. He seemed to have times when he was truly at peace again, or at least relaxed in a way he hadn't been for a long time after his capture.

Daniel rested his hand on Max's shoulder, squeezing it as a deer approached the lake and dipped its head to take a drink. There had been a time, after being a blood slave, Max would have shrugged him off, unwilling to allow many to touch him. Now he stood for a minute before turning to Daniel.

"Where do you think Sabine is?" Max asked.

Daniel studied the mountains surrounding them. Tempest's town of Badwin had been far to the north, nestled in a remote mountain range, but Sabine had made her way there. "I think she has a lot of knowledge of this country," Daniel said. "She could be anywhere."

The subtlest shift in the air around them, not so much a sound but something else, had them all turning toward the woods. Max was the only one of them who had managed to keep his bow and arrows after the attack, and he slipped them from his back to aim at the woods. Daniel rested his hand on Max's arm, pushing it gently down when he spotted Xavier emerging from the trees.

He really was a magnificent man to behold, Daniel decided as he watched the sun dancing over the tribal tattoos on Xavier's hands, arms, and neck.

"What makes you think she has knowledge of this country?" Timber asked as he rose to stand beside them.

"If she was able to gather the amount of troops William and Tempest said she had, then she's been moving around this land undetected for quite some time," Daniel replied.

"Most likely," Xavier agreed. "There's at least three clear miles ahead of us."

"Let's go then," Max said and slid his bow around to his back again. "The sooner this is over, the happier we'll all be."

Daniel followed his friend into the forest. It had been over a year since it had been necessary for him to remain hidden within the woods, but his instinctive ways fell easily back over him as he searched for any hint of a change in the woods around them. They moved so noiselessly that the birds roosting above them never took flight.

Until ahead, and no more than fifty feet away, a dozen or more sparrows shot into the air like they'd been shot out of a cannon. Before he heard the crack of a branch, Daniel knew they were no longer alone.

CHAPTER 15

Aria

Aria froze, her foot stopped in midair when the sparrows burst into the air. Her hand tightened on her bow as she studied the woods around them. William grabbed her forearm and tried to pull her back.

"It's *her*," Aria hissed as she resisted his impatient tugging on her arm.

"If it is, we're not ready for her," he hissed back at her. "Aria, we can't face her now."

She surveyed the trees above her. "I can get closer."

"It's daytime and there are no leaves to hide you. We must go."

"William, *I* can get closer." She turned to face her brother. Behind him, Tempest, Mary, and John stood near the edge of the thicket they were working their way around. They'd arrived at the final safe house last night and were only a hundred yards away from it. They had left it a little bit ago to inspect the area.

"Take them back to the safe house," Aria told him and slipped her cloak from her shoulders. She couldn't have the material hindering her movements or flapping and drawing attention to her. "I will meet you there."

"No. I forbid it."

"Yeah, that's going to work for you," she muttered and pulled her glasses off. She felt exposed without them, but she couldn't take the risk of them falling off. She kept her head averted from Mary and John so they couldn't see her eyes as she handed the cloak and glasses to him. "I won't do anything reckless."

"And the sky is green," he bit out from between his teeth.

She lifted her head so her gaze bore into his. "*I* plan to kill *her* not the other way around. I won't do anything reckless."

Before he could argue with her further, she tugged her arm free and leapt up to snag hold of a branch above her head. She threw her legs around it and pulled herself around so she sat on the branch. She rested her fingers on the rigid bark before rising to her feet and leaping for the next branch above her.

She worked her way through the tree until she was hidden within the middle of the limbs. The borrowed pants and shirt she wore were a plain brown hue and made of flax. They were the clothes of those who lived within the woods, the clothes she still felt most comfortable in. They weren't the same color as the trees, but she'd be able to blend in with her environment well enough to go unnoticed. She pulled the hood on the shirt over her hair and tucked away any loose strands.

When she was certain there was nothing that could give her away, she rubbed her hands together and ran across the limb before leaping for the next branch. Wind whipped at her hair and tugged at her clothing as for a minute she actually felt like she flew. She landed on the next limb, nimbly running across the branch as she raced through the trees.

She didn't look back as she moved so swiftly and with such a buoyant step, the branches didn't even bow beneath her weight. Nearing the area where the birds had been scared from their perches, she moved more cautiously through the trees as she examined the forest floor.

The whisper of words caused her to flatten herself against the trunk of an oak as she strained to hear more. A branch snapped from below. She bit her bottom lip as excitement and adrenaline coursed through her. She searched over the woods, waiting for whoever was out there to move into view, and then a dozen or so vampires emerged beneath her.

They didn't wear the white cloaks she'd seen on them before, but deep brown cloaks that caused them to blend in better with their environment. *Clever girl,* Aria thought as she studied each of the vampires. Sabine kept her troops in whatever clothes best suited their environment. With the snow gone and no leaves on the trees, the brown was perfect for this time of year.

Watching them, Aria knew they were not part of the king's guard. They would be wearing the wolf patch if they were, and they were not simply nomadic vampires either. They were too alert for that and moving with trained precision.

She doubted any of them would think to look into the trees, but she didn't dare move as she watched more and more emerge below. They moved quietly, but they were still louder than any rebel would ever be. They broke branches as they walked, stepped on the smaller pines, and crushed the saplings fighting for survival on the forest floor. Leaves and pine needles were kicked up by their passing, making it entirely possible to track their every movement by scent as well as sight.

Watching them made her cringe. No rebel would have done such a thing. The world would look as untouched after their passing as it had beforehand.

She steadily counted each vampire as they moved past. She was up to over two hundred when the woman she believed to be Sabine rode into view on the back of a large bay.

For a second, Aria thought the branch she stood on had broken as the world lurched out from under her. Then she realized that she remained standing against the tree, but she'd wrapped her arms around it in an attempt to keep herself anchored. Her fingers dug into the bark as she imagined tearing into the woman's throat, feasting on her blood, and pummeling her body until she was nothing more than broken bones and battered flesh.

Red flooded her vision, and her body quaked with the need to maim and kill. Bloodlust like she'd never experienced before filled every fiber of her being. She could dive from the trees right now, land on top of that woman...

Be on her in an instant! Then Sabine's followers would take her. They would capture her before she could succeed in killing Sabine and it would all be over.

Right then, she didn't much care about that.

Her hands dug deeper into the bark. A large piece of it broke off beneath her fingers and fell into the air. *No!* She bent and caught the piece before it could fall past her and hit the ground, or one of the passing vamps. Kneeling on the branch, she remained tensed to spring, to flee into the trees if someone had witnessed her stupidity.

Get it together or end up dead before you can be of any use to anyone.

Closing her eyes, she took a moment to steady herself. She felt a little more stable when she opened her eyes again. Movement to her right drew her attention; her eyes widened when she spotted Xavier, Daniel, Max, and Timber crouching in the entrance of a small cave fifty yards away from her. A cave she knew dead-ended twenty feet behind them. They would be trapped if they were spotted.

Daniel had his hand on Xavier's forearm to hold him back; she realized it had been Xavier who had drawn her eye to them. She was certain he'd moved when he'd witnessed her foolish, beginner mistake with the bark. Xavier relaxed slightly and knelt between her brother and Max once more.

She was not worried that the vampires walking beneath her would see her in the tree as the four of them had. They knew her preferred way to travel through the woods and would have looked for her where no one else would have.

Aria turned her attention back to the woman with her black hair trailing over the horse's rump behind her. Now that she wasn't consumed with the urge to bathe in the woman's putrid blood, she was able to take note of more details about her. The potency of her power electrified Aria's skin.

She was beautiful and as sickly twisted as her son had been. Unlike Atticus, Aria had a feeling this woman's maliciousness was something she'd been born with, like Caleb, who was the sickest individual she'd ever had the displeasure of dealing with.

The strange, almost albino-looking man was the only other one on a horse as he rode beside Sabine. All of those around them were dressed in brown cloaks, yet the two of them arrogantly wore deep red cloaks that stood out like beacons. The ruby rings on the man's right hand caught and reflected the sun, causing waves of red to dance over the trees around them.

That arrogance was the first chink in Sabine's armor, and one of the things that would lead to her downfall. No matter how many more vamps continued to emerge from the woods, Aria knew this to be true.

Aria's eyes lifted to where the palace lay beyond the woods.

They're steadily moving closer.

Should she step up their plan with those they'd already recruited? Aria's hand clenched around the bark in her palm as she debated this. Sabine would most likely try to go through the villages near the palace—if they hadn't already been evacuated—to gather as many troops as she could and slaughter those who might stand against her.

If the towns had already been evacuated, Sabine would probably find a village to settle in for a bit as she worked out the final stages of her plan. The woman was ruthless, but she wasn't stupid; she wouldn't rush through this, and she was arrogant enough to believe she'd be able to take the palace with ease. Sabine would never expect rebels and vampires to close in on her from behind when she did go for the palace.

Aria couldn't rush things either. They needed time to gather more of their own troops and weapons first. They needed more time for the rebels and vamps to spread the word to be prepared for something lethal coming their way. Time to get as many children as they could to safety before they entered into war, again. It would be best if they stuck to their original plan, no matter what Sabine tried now.

Aria had lost count of the troops beneath her as the number swelled to well over a thousand. *So many, and what if there are more elsewhere?*

Then they would fight them all.

Her heart plummeted into her boots when the last of Sabine's entourage came into view. Except these were no longer vampires, but at least a hundred humans tied together like cattle and being led through the woods by the dozens of vampires surrounding them.

When a dirty, pale woman fell, one of the vampires snapped her neck and cut her loose from the others without so much as a second glance. Aria's hand flew to her mouth. The humans around the woman cried out and scurried away from her body. This time it was Max's rising that drew her attention back to her friends, and Timber who pulled him back.

Her gaze latched onto Max as he shook within Timber's grasp. His cheeks were tinged red with fury and his lips clamped so firmly together they turned white. Aria couldn't look at the abused humans again; she wouldn't be able to stop herself from attacking if she did.

It's all going backwards, returning to the beginning, she thought.

We will fix it! They had to; there were no other options.

She remained in the tree for well over an hour after the last of the vampires and humans vanished from view. Her ears strained to pick up any noise within the woods, but it remained silent and still. Her cramped muscles protested when she rose from her crouched position and climbed down the tree.

Her feet had barely touched the ground when Daniel wrapped his arms around her and embraced her. She'd barely been able to stand the touch of anyone all week, but she lifted her arms to hug him back. He needed this hug, and she needed him. The piece of bark digging into her palm fell from her hand as she clung to her brother. So like their father, he was a source of calm in a world that had become utter chaos for her.

"You're safe," he whispered.

"So are you," she breathed. "It's so good to see you."

"You also."

"Braith?" she choked out through the lump in her throat.

His arms tightened around her. "He was still unresponsive when we left the cave."

"And dead."

"Yes."

Aria slumped against him, somehow managing to stem the flow of tears burning her eyes and clogging her throat. If she started crying now, she'd never stop, and they had to get out of here before one of Sabine's followers returned.

CHAPTER 16

Daniel

"Amazing," Daniel murmured as he watched the door hidden perfectly in the floor of the old barn swing open to reveal a set of stairs leading into the darkness below. Aria had filled them in on everything they'd gone through this past week and all they'd achieved with the rebels. He still couldn't help but be impressed with what the rebels had accomplished here.

"You should have seen the one in the tree," Aria said to him over her shoulder; her ruby-colored eyes briefly met his before flitting away. "You would have really appreciated it."

"I do just hearing about it," he assured her as she stepped onto the first stair.

The set of her shoulders and the color of her eyes belied the aura of calm she tried to project. His heart ached as he watched his little sister. He would do anything to take away her suffering, to protect her from what was to come, but he was helpless to do either of those things. All he could do was protect her as much as possible.

No matter what unfolded, he would keep her safe if it was the last thing he did.

"I will go first," Xavier said and rested his hand on her arm to pull her back.

She gave him an exasperated look and blew a loose strand of hair out of her face. "It's safe, Xavier. I've been here before."

"I will still go first."

Aria hesitated before moving aside to let him lead the way below. The door at the bottom of the stairs opened before they reached it to reveal William. Daniel breathed a sigh of relief. Aria had told him they'd split up and that William and Tempest would be here, but he'd been afraid to believe her, until now. William gawked at them all for a minute before breaking into a grin.

"You always did like to rescue the strays, Aria," he said as he slapped Xavier on the back. He hugged Aria before turning to embrace Daniel. "You have no idea how good it is to see you," he whispered in Daniel's ear.

"I can imagine it's been a fun-filled week," Daniel replied as Timber closed the door behind them.

"Oh yes, death, mayhem, and trying to keep that one from getting herself killed."

"I can hear you," Aria grated and flashed them both a fulminating glare as William stepped away from him to shake hands with Max and Timber. "My glasses?"

Tempest walked forward to hand them to her. "How did you find them?" she asked.

"They had themselves cornered in a cave," Aria replied.

"Not cornered," Max replied defensively.

"Were you going to dig your way through the solid rock at your back if you were spotted?" Aria demanded.

Max grinned at her as he folded his arms over his chest. "But we weren't spotted, and if I recall, you're the one who almost gave away your position by nearly dropping bark on their heads."

Aria scowled at him but refrained from commenting.

"Really?" William asked, unable to keep the disbelief from his voice.

"Sabine was there," Aria muttered. "I should have better anticipated my reaction to being so near her. I won't underestimate it again."

Daniel stepped away from them to examine the small room they'd entered. Beams ran across the ceiling, not more than three inches separating them as they kept the earth above them from caving in. The beams were at least a foot wide and thick; the wood they'd used to create the ceiling looked to be a good six inches thick. He spotted a small vent in the side of the wall and itched to trace its pathway to the earth above, to see how they had created the ventilation system.

He'd designed a concept extremely similar to this one when they'd still been rebels hiding from vampires. At the time, the caves were being raided, and though they were taking out vampires in those raids, they were also losing fighters. *No* one would think to look for them under the earth.

With the war and the events that had transpired after Aria and Braith had gotten together, he'd never had a chance to start the underground buildings, but these rebels had. He would have loved to watch the building process take place. He enjoyed being on The Council, keeping the peace and working with the vampires for that peace, but he missed building and his designs. He still sketched often, but it wasn't the same as seeing his sketches come to life before him as they once had. When all of this was over, if he survived, he would make time to design and build more often, to enjoy doing something he loved so dearly once again.

"Who came up with the plans for this?" he inquired.

"You did," Aria replied, drawing his attention away from the thick walls.

"They found your designs within one of the caves and used them," William expounded when Daniel frowned questioningly at his sister. "Your plans are the foundation for all of the safe houses."

"They used my designs?" he said in awe as his gaze ran over the beams again and the pipes he now saw running in between them. "Do they have functioning plumbing and a water supply?"

"They do. The water is piped in from the nearby lake," William replied.

Daniel's chest swelled with pride. "They did a great job here."

"You're a talented man," Aria said.

He didn't deny it; there was no reason to. He felt Xavier's eyes on him and turned to meet the man's steady, inquisitive gaze.

"Did you learn anything about Sabine?" Tempest asked.

"She's arrogant," Aria said as she exited the entry room and started to make her way down the hall. The walls brushed against her arms as she walked. "It will be her downfall."

Daniel continued to study the structure around him, taking more note of the detail and care the rebels had taken to fortify it. There was no sign of bending or bowing in the wood used in the construction. Great effort had gone into making sure this underground fortress stayed sturdy and strong. He knew the calculations and supplies he'd made and listed in his design in order to keep the walls and ceiling this solid, and they had followed them perfectly.

Aria came to an abrupt halt at the end of the hall, causing him to crash into her back as his attention was still on the ceiling. Her shoulders became rigid, as if she were preparing for a blow, before she opened the door and stepped into the room. He followed behind her to discover nearly fifty humans gathered within.

"They weren't here before?" he whispered to her when he guessed at what had caused her to tense. She was trying to cover it up, but he had read Atticus's journals too and suspected she was battling her vampire instincts to kill with every passing second. Having so many humans in one place wouldn't help her.

"No," she replied crisply.

Xavier muscled his way forward to stand beside her. "I will ask them to leave."

"No, they are safe here. We need as many of them safe as we can get. Otherwise they could become like the humans we saw earlier."

"What humans?" William inquired.

"We will fill everyone in at once," Aria told him and gestured toward a table in the center of the main room.

Someone thrust a drink into Daniel's hand when he passed and slapped him on the back as they greeted him. He took a sip of the hard liquor. It made his eyes water and his throat burn, but it hit the spot. He watched his sister settle onto a chair and hold herself as if it pained her to move even a centimeter.

He'd almost hoped there would be some way to save her if Braith remained dead, but as he watched her now, he realized it was more than the humans around her that had her so on edge. She was in pain, and it was a pain so deep it had become physical as well as emotional.

***

Aria

Aria held herself stiffly in the chair to face the person who had said her name. *Won't break. Won't break.* She kept telling herself this, but her body felt as if it would fracture and fall apart at any second. Seeing Sabine, or whoever the hell she was, earlier in the forest had rattled the walls she'd worked so carefully to craft this past week.

It didn't help that she hadn't expected all of these humans to arrive while she was gone. Their hearts thumped and their pulses raced as drinks were passed around the room and Daniel explained to the group what they'd seen in the forest with Sabine and her followers.

"How can we ever expect to withstand so many?" a man inquired. "We will surprise them, yes, but that surprise won't last long."

"They'll be focused on the palace," Aria forced herself to say. She had to respond, had to be normal and in control. They were wavering; they needed a leader. Rising to her feet, she kept her head held high and her glasses in place, as she turned to face the room. "They'll have their backs to us when we attack them. When they turn to come at us, they'll make themselves vulnerable to the palace guards and they will panic. The surprise won't last long, but we can drastically cull their numbers before they get over their panic, and by then, it will be too late."

Aria paced over to stand in the doorway leading out and turned to face them with her hands clasped behind her back. She couldn't allow them to see that her clenched fingers wouldn't open.

"She is *arrogant*," Aria said. "So arrogant she has her followers dressed in brown cloaks now, to blend in, while she strolls about in a vivid red one. It marks her for all to see because she believes there are none who can beat her. The mad king, Atticus, believed the same thing, yet he is no more. This threat will be met the same way as we met him, and she will be taken down with the same ruthlessness, because she has underestimated her enemies."

"And the king, when will he be joining us?" a woman asked, and Aria somehow managed to keep herself from flinching as if she'd been slapped. A fresh knife drove through her heart and twisted there at the reminder of Braith.

"When he is able to," Aria managed to get out.

"Will it be before we approach the palace?" another asked.

Daniel stepped forward. "We will be leaving soon to carry word back to the king about the advancements we have made in gathering troops. We will have a better idea of what will happen then."

Aria cast him a grateful look; she'd had no other answer for them. Technically, Jack was the king now, so Daniel hadn't lied to them. If Braith wasn't awake by the time they returned to tell Jack about what was going on, Jack would have to leave him in the cave. She may be the queen, but a member of the royal family had to be there when this fight started. One who could assume the rightful role of king if they defeated their enemy and Braith didn't rise, because she wouldn't be here to do it.

She fought the urge to rub at her temples in frustration. It could be construed as a sign of weakness or stress. Right now, she couldn't afford the smallest chink in her armor to show through. Not when they were asking these humans to follow her into battle, to lay down their lives. Everything they'd worked for would vanish like dust in the wind if she did.

Murmurs ran through the crowded room. "We can defeat her," Aria said loud enough for her voice to carry over theirs. "We *will* defeat her. I will not let my father's death be in vain—" *or Braith's* "—and I will not allow us to be returned to a time when humans lived in fear and violence was an everyday way of life. William and I may be vampires now, but we have never forgotten our roots, nor will we ever forget them, and we will fight for *every one* of your lives. I will die to give your children the better lives they deserve."

The crowd nodded excitedly as they talked eagerly with one another. They were going to touch her again; she knew it before the first woman stepped forward to approach her. Xavier made a move to block the woman from coming closer. Aria subtly waved him away before she forced her hands out from behind her back to take hold of the woman's hands.

Won't break. Won't break. Then why did she feel as if she would shatter into a million pieces right now?

Person after person came forward to clutch her hands and thank her for standing by them, for protecting them. Aria almost laughed out loud. If they knew what she was truly thinking, how she was battling back the impulse to tear every one of their throats out and drown all of her misery in their blood, they would run screaming.

Instead, they saw her as a savior.

She'd never felt like more of a fraud in her life.

CHAPTER 17

William

"It's bad, isn't it, with Aria?"

William adjusted his hold on Tempest, settling her deeper into his lap as Daniel leaned across the table toward them. Tempest's lashes tickled his neck when her eyes fluttered open.

"I don't know how she's still going," William admitted honestly. "I'm not sure I could, but revenge is a powerful motivator."

"You would know," Tempest murmured.

"No, not like this. I sought revenge on Kane, yes. I would have died to get it, but that was a drop in the bucket compared to what is driving her." Tempest leaned back to stare up at him. "I understand that only because I have you now. If it had been you who had been taken from me…" The concept of such a thing caused his fangs to lengthen. "I would have destroyed everything in my path."

Tempest's fingers played with the hair at his nape as she leaned forward to kiss him. "It's not me," she murmured.

"But it is *Aria.*" His gaze went to the room Aria had disappeared into hours ago. "I shared a womb with her. We hid together and listened while our mother was killed. She's always been stubborn and strong, but I can feel her slipping further away from us. She didn't go in there to sleep. She doesn't sleep more than a few minutes at a time anymore. She went in there to get away from the humans."

"I'm sure it's overwhelming for her," Max said as he leaned across the table toward them.

William glanced around the room before moving closer to them. They were the only ones still within the main room. The rest of those staying here had retreated into the rooms lining the hall, but he still didn't like saying this out loud. "She's fighting not to kill the humans."

"Don't think that," Tempest said.

"I don't think it," he replied and clutched her to his chest. "I *know* it. I feel the insanity creeping closer around her, feel the emptiness engulfing her, and there's nothing she can do to get away from it. I'm not sure how long she can keep going before she cracks just like Atticus did."

Tempest shuddered against him. Max and Daniel leaned away from him while Timber and Xavier remained staring at the wall across from them. "Atticus kept it together long enough to complete his goal," Xavier finally said.

"How many did he slaughter before that happened?" William asked. "How many did he slaughter because that *was* his goal?"

"Too many," Daniel said.

"She'll keep it together until Sabine is defeated, or at least I think she will, but as soon as this is done..." William's voice trailed off, and his gaze returned to the closed door Aria was behind once more. "She's my twin. I feel her anguish here"— he rested his hand over his heart—"and anguish is such a completely inadequate word for what she is experiencing. It's deeper than that. It's a complete twisting and destruction of the soul. She'll die when this is done, or she'll lose her mind."

Tempest pressed closer against him as his own raw sorrow slipped through. He kissed her forehead, taking in her scent as he tried to ease his growing distress. With every day that passed, Aria slipped further away and he felt their chances of Braith rising growing slimmer. It had taken time for Atticus to return, he tried to remind himself of this, but he couldn't help but feel as if their time was rapidly running out.

Xavier rose from the table, the chair skidding out behind him as he paced away from them. He stalked toward Aria's closed door and stood there. Finally, the vampire came back to the table and rested his fingers on it.

"As she always has, Aria will accomplish what she must," Xavier said. "Have faith Braith will return to us soon, because if we have to destroy her, we will have to destroy him too if he rises. If you think Aria is falling apart, imagine what he'll be like when he realizes he rose from the dead only to learn that those he trusted the most destroyed his wife. If we must, we will find a way to restrain or imprison her—"

"We can't do that to my sister!" William snapped.

"You think I like the idea?" Xavier snarled. "She is my friend, one of the few I have in this world. I would have taken every one of those arrows Braith received for her, but I failed in my duty."

So that was the source of all of Xavier's pent-up frustration, William realized. The vampire believed he'd failed Aria.

"We were all supposed to protect them. We all failed," Daniel said.

Xavier's gaze shot to Daniel, but he didn't acknowledge his words as he started to speak again. "What Atticus did to this world will look like child's play compared to what Braith would unleash on all of us if Aria is dead when he awakens. He stayed alive for *hours* after having his heart pierced with an arrow. Not even Atticus managed that feat, and I'm betting Sabine didn't either. Braith did that for *Aria*. He knew what his loss would do to her, but even sheer strength of will and the bloodlink could not deny the course nature has set for all of us."

"And what will he do if he wakes to find we've imprisoned her?" Timber asked.

"He might still kill us all, but at least he won't burn what remains of the world down too," Xavier replied and paced away once more.

William stared across the table at his brother. "You will return to the cave and Jack?" he inquired of Daniel.

Daniel tore his gaze away from Xavier to focus on him. William lifted an eyebrow at the brief look of yearning that had crossed Daniel's face while watching the vampire. His brother composed his expression into a mask of indifference as he stared blandly back at William.

"We told Jack we would report back. He has to have some idea of what is going on outside of those caves," Daniel replied. "Braith can track Aria if he wakes."

"When will you return to him?"

"We'll wait a couple of days, help gather as much information about this woman and help as much as we can here before we return. I think it will be best if Jack comes back with me. Someone has to be able to lead if Braith never awakens and Aria is locked in a cell, again."

"She's going to lose her mind," Max muttered as he gazed at the scarred table before him.

"She already is," William replied.

Xavier walked back over to them and sat in the chair for a minute before rising and walking away again. "Perhaps you should feed," William suggested to him.

"I fed earlier," Xavier replied, his gaze focused on the door once more.

"Okay, but—"

"I will be fine when she comes back out," he interjected.

William rolled his eyes, took a deep breath, and bit back his next words. Xavier had been composed when Aria was out here earlier; he would be so again when she emerged.

"Where do we sleep in this place?" Timber asked.

"With everyone else," William replied. "Yesterday we had plenty of room in here. Now, not so much." He glanced at Tempest. No damn privacy at all. "There are numerous straw-filled mattresses in every room."

Timber clasped his hands behind his head as he stretched his long legs before him. "So right here then."

"That's what I planned," William said.

Timber kicked off his boots and tilted his head back to stare at the ceiling above him. "You did some good planning, Daniel," he said. He closed his eyes and released a snore on his next breath.

"Amazing," Tempest muttered as she gazed at Timber's slumbering form before resting her head on William's chest once more.

Everyone within the room froze when the door of the room across from them opened and Aria padded out. Her loose braid dangled over her shoulder. The shadows around her eyes formed dark circles beneath the rim of her thick glasses. Without a word, she settled into one of the empty chairs and lifted her head to gaze around the room. Xavier had stopped moving the second she'd emerged. He stood guard beside the door leading out as he watched her.

Her head turned toward Xavier. "You should get some rest," she said to him.

"I will watch over you," Xavier replied.

"There are plenty here to watch over me," she replied. "And it's not like you'll be far." Xavier folded his arms over his chest but made no move to leave. Aria stared at him before turning to Daniel. "Take him somewhere. His pacing is driving me nuts. I could hear him prowling back and forth from the other room."

"I will not move again," Xavier vowed.

Aria rested her forehead in her hands as she rubbed at her temples. "Xavier, please, get some rest. If only for an hour or two, it would make me feel a lot better."

He stood for a minute, seemingly torn between staying to protect her and obeying her request. In the end, he bowed his head and turned to open the door behind him.

"Go with him," Aria said to Daniel, who frowned at her. "Watch over him. He's coiled tighter than a spring and needs someone calming around."

Daniel rose to his feet. William watched as his older brother strode out the door behind Xavier. He remained casual in appearance, but William could hear the increased beat of his heart as he closed the door behind them. Aria slumped in her chair.

"I couldn't take one more second of his pacing and blaming himself," she murmured. "Daniel will keep him distracted for a bit."

"You know they're attracted to each other?" Max inquired of her.

"I'm not blind."

"I didn't know you were aware of Daniel's interest in, ah… men as well as women." Max turned as red as an apple as he said this to her.

"I wasn't for a long time, but I've noticed the two of them watching each other for a while now," she replied. "

"You sacrificed your brother for some peace and quiet," Max said with a snort. "I like the way you think."

The corner of Aria's mouth quirked. It was the closest she'd come to a smile in a week. "I don't think either one of them will consider it a sacrifice."

William glanced over at Max who smirked at him as he placed his folded hands behind his head. Tempest lifted her head to look at the door they'd left through. "Xavier is so much bigger. I hope he doesn't break him," she murmured.

William and Max both roared with laughter until tears streamed down Max's face and even Aria gave a small chuckle.

CHAPTER 18

Aria

Aria checked to make sure her glasses were safely in place and inched open the door to the room she'd been given by the rebels the next morning. Beside the door, Xavier settled the chair he'd been leaning against the wall on the ground. He and Daniel had come back in after she'd retreated to the room again, but she didn't know if her attempt at drawing them closer together had worked or not, until she smelled Daniel on him. Not in him, they had not shared blood, but they had gotten close to each other.

Good. Her heart was shattered around her, but she would do everything she could to make sure those she loved found happiness in this world. Found someone to help them move on and thrive after she was gone.

William rose from his chair with Tempest cradled against his chest. He went to set her down on the chair, but Aria pushed the door to her room open and gestured for him to enter. Requiring some time alone with his bloodlink, William didn't argue with her, but strode forward to stop beside her. She ducked her head and stepped out of the way when he went to touch her shoulder.

Her skin felt more sensitive today than it ever had. Every time she moved, her normally lightweight clothes scraped against her flesh.

Insanity looms, she realized grimly.

William stared down at her, but she couldn't meet his gaze.

Six more days. Hold it together for six more days.

She could do that. Somehow. At the end of those six days, if she needed more time to ensure that Sabine's head rolled from her shoulders, she would hold it together for that time too.

She waited until William closed the door before moving further into the room and toward the door leading out. Opening it, she walked down the hall to the stairs at the end. She needed to feel fresh air on her face, and she needed to feed.

She checked the peepholes before turning the heavy metal latch and pushing the door open. Cool air caressed her cheeks when she stepped into the barn with Xavier close on her heels. Though there were no animals within anymore, the familiar scents of straw, hay, and horse tickled her nose. For a moment, she recalled what her life had been like in those simple, early days before she'd been captured and taken to the palace.

She'd loved the forest, her family, her friends, and the animals she'd cared for. It hadn't been an easy life. There had been many nights she'd fallen asleep cold and hungry, many nights she'd prayed not to be discovered or doubted she would live to see the next day, but it had been her life. Then it had all been thrown into a whirlwind never to be the same again.

She'd never trade one day of her life with Braith, even if this was the way their love ended, but she had let her guard down. She'd been unprepared for the bad she'd always been prepared for as a human.

In her days as a rebel, she'd accepted that she would most likely have a short life and meet a brutal end at the hands of a vampire. With Braith, she'd had an eternity of love and laughter laid out before her like a never-ending road. Now the road smashed into a brick wall, and she found herself lying awake every night, once again feeling cold and hungry, but this cold and hunger was unlike anything she'd ever experienced as a human.

Footsteps sounded behind her as Daniel made his way up from below. Over the years, she'd seen her brother with women, but then she'd also seen him sitting close to men. She'd never really thought much about it. Daniel had always been more private about his love life than most of the other men and women in the forest. However, Daniel had always been more private and introverted than most anyone she knew.

He was often busy with his sketches and designs. He looked at the world and saw things entirely different than anyone else did. Her vision had been enhanced when she'd become a vampire, but she knew Daniel still saw more detail in their environment than she did.

She'd noticed Xavier's growing interest in her brother when they'd traveled back to Chippman for Jack's wedding, and started to notice the way her brother watched him too. They were an odd pairing, but then she and Braith hadn't exactly been normal. Odd pairings could work well and she thought the two of them balanced each other nicely; Daniel with his dreamer ways and Xavier with his fiercely loyal heart.

"How are you feeling today?" Daniel asked her.

"Fine," she replied and lifted her hand to her forehead in an attempt to further shade the rays of sun filtering through the rafters and causing the dust motes to dance in the air around them.

Daniel went to pull her hand from her forehead, but stopped himself. "We'll find you something to eat and you'll feel better," he said.

"Yes, that will help," she lied and really hoped he bought it.

Xavier slid the barn door open and stepped outside. "Stay here," he said crisply over his shoulder to them.

"I'm happy for the two of you," she whispered when Xavier disappeared. "You both deserve happiness, someone to love."

"It's not like that, Aria," Daniel reluctantly said, as if he didn't want to burst her bubble. "Not everything is a love connection. Sometimes two people, or beings, or whatever they are, simply need each other."

"Could it become more?" she asked, unwilling to give up on her hope for the two of them finding love together.

"Perhaps."

Having just lied to him, she recognized one when she heard it. "Liar."

He went to take hold of her elbow, but she moved away from him before he could touch her raw skin. Sighing in frustration, he lowered his hand. "I care for Xavier. He is honorable and confident..."

"But?" she prodded when he trailed off.

"I have no intention of ever becoming a vampire or settling down with one. It's not something I want, and to be honest, neither is a relationship. Not at this time in my life."

"But one day you might want a relationship with a man?"

"Or a woman. One cannot help who they love after all."

She knew that better than anyone. She'd fallen in love with a vampire after all, her greatest enemy at the time. "No, they can't."

"The day for a relationship may not even come for me."

She recoiled from his words. "That day *will* come! I'll make sure of it."

"Aria, you more than anyone, know you cannot will something into being. Whatever unfolds along the way is the course we are to follow."

"I will not lose any more of those I love."

He opened his mouth to respond then clamped it shut once more. He was right, they both knew it, but he also knew it would be pointless to argue with her right now. Secretly, she'd always hoped Daniel would choose to become a vampire too, if he survived the transformation. Maybe one day he would change his mind and join her and William, but Daniel had always stayed on his course once he chose it, and she doubted that one day would occur.

Max stepped out of the doorway behind them. His sandy hair stood out in spikes around his face as he rubbed at his swollen eyes. "Did I miss anything?" he asked as he stretched his back.

"No," Daniel replied

Xavier stepped back into the doorway. "It's clear and I spotted some deer by the lake."

Aria's mouth watered, and her fangs tingled as she hurried out the door. They moved quickly through the woods until they arrived at the lake. She separated from Max and Daniel to hunt with Xavier.

When she'd glutted herself on deer blood, she sat back on her heels and wiped her mouth. Xavier stood beside her, his gaze incessantly scanning the trees for any hint of danger. Aria rested her hands on her knees as she surveyed the woods. Satisfied they were still alone, she rose to her feet and returned with Xavier to where Daniel and Max remained hidden within the forest.

"I think we should try to get closer to Sabine again," she said.

Xavier shot her a dark look. "No. We have a plan. We stick with it."

"We have to know more about her. Arrogance can't be her only weakness."

"Beheading is another," Max said.

"We're not 100 percent sure who she is. If it's not Sabine, we could be walking into something worse than what we're preparing for. We need more information," Aria insisted.

Daniel and Max exchanged a look before Daniel spoke, "We can't risk people."

"Not people, me."

"Absolutely not," Xavier said.

"I don't have a suicide wish. I can get close to her without her knowing I'm there, and if by some miracle she catches me, she won't kill me. She'll slaughter or enslave anyone else, but not me. Not right away anyway, she'll use me as leverage."

"If Braith awakens—" Max broke off when her jaw locked.

"And you have been caught, then what?" Xavier demanded, finishing what Max had been unwilling to say.

Aria took a minute to gather herself before speaking again. "The three of you have this wrong. I'm not suggesting this. I'm not asking for permission. I'm *telling* you I intend to get closer to her."

Silence met her statement. Xavier opened his mouth then closed it again.

"William will want to go with you," Daniel finally said.

"No, I'm going alone. I can get closer to her by myself, and William has Tempest. He has to protect her. I won't risk something happening to either one of them. They can never know what *this* is like." Her hand rested over her heart. "I won't do that to them."

"That's why you want to go now," Max deduced. "Because William's not here to stop you or go with you."

"Yes," she admitted.

"I will come with you," Xavier said.

"You're fast, but I'm faster and quieter when it comes to these woods."

"It doesn't matter. I am coming with you. You don't know where she is."

"Believe me, the trail she left will be impossible to miss," Aria replied. Max and Daniel nodded their agreement.

"We're coming with you," Daniel said. He held his hand up when she opened her mouth to protest. "Extra eyes are *never* a bad thing."

"And if you take off without us, we'll just follow the trail too," Max said and smiled at her when she frowned at him. "It will simply take us longer, and put us more at risk by not traveling together, but we can follow her as easily as you can."

"Fine," she relented, "but someone has to tell William and the others where we've gone. They'll send out search parties if they're not informed, and someone could get killed because of it. The humans follow you, Daniel. You're their representative on The Council and they look to you for guidance as much as they look to me. I think you should stay."

His arms folded over his chest, but whereas she and William were hotheaded and impulsive, Daniel was practical. He couldn't deny the truth of her words. "What do I tell them?" he inquired.

"The truth," she replied and shifted her bow and quiver on her back. "I'll only be two days. If I don't find her, or I'm unable to get close to her, I'll return. That will still give you enough time to return to Jack and let him know what is going on. If I'm not back, you or William have to return for him no matter what."

Daniel took a deep breath and dropped his arms to his sides. He stepped forward to hug her before stopping himself. Aria braced herself for the discomfort she knew would come from touching another and stepped forward to kiss his cheek. "I love you, and tell William that for me too."

"He's going to be irate."

"Yeah, well, he's pissed me off a time or two before himself."

Daniel smiled before stepping away. "Good luck and be safe." His gaze went to Xavier who bowed his head to him and turned away.

"We always are," Max replied.

Aria didn't look back as they slipped into the trees.

CHAPTER 19

Daniel

"Are you kidding me! What were you thinking to let her go and do something so foolish!" William exploded.

Accustomed to his brother's temper, Daniel simply ignored him as he walked over to the door of the barn and peered out at the woods surrounding them before closing the door.

"Damn it, Daniel, she'll get herself killed!"

"No, she won't," he replied calmly, something that only irritated William further as his eyes flashed red.

"You have no idea what the bloodlink bond is like, or what she is going through—"

"And neither do you," Daniel interjected. His gaze flicked to Tempest who remained unmoving beside Timber near the entrance of the safe house. "You think you know how you would react, what it would feel like to lose Tempest, but you don't, not really. Aria is doing everything she can to make sure you *never* know. It's why she went without telling you."

"I'm going after her."

"No, you're not."

The look on William's face caused Daniel to roll his eyes at the nearly identical expressions of defiance the twins had. He loved his younger siblings, he'd lay down his life for either one of them, but half the time, he'd also love to choke them.

"Are you going to stop me?" William demanded.

"You're not going to take Tempest into those woods, and you're not going to leave her behind," Daniel replied.

With a volatile curse, William spun away from him and stalked over to the closed barn door. Tempest's eyes filled with worry as she watched him. Daniel gave a subtle shake of his head at her when she looked like she would go after him, and she remained where she was.

William swung back toward them. "Max and Xavier are with her?"

"They are," Daniel said.

"When she gets back, I'm going to kill her."

"I'm sure she felt the same way when you took off after Kane."

"You followed me, if I remember correctly!" William retorted.

"Things are different now, William. Many lives hang in the balance here. As much as I *don't* like it, Aria is right. We have to know everything we can about this woman before we make a move against her."

"Aria will go for her if she gets close."

"She's not going to do anything reckless, not this time."

"How can you be so sure?" William inquired.

"Because she knows she's needed here, and no matter how much trouble Aria has gotten herself into in the past, she's *never* done anything to hurt the ones she loves. She's doing this for us, not for her revenge. She'll try to kill that woman when she thinks the time is right."

"I hope you're right."

"I know I am." *Mostly.*

William's gaze swung to Tempest who stood watching their interaction, waiting to see what he would do. Finally, his shoulders sagged and he walked over to her. Daniel focused his attention elsewhere when William wrapped his arms around

Tempest and drew her against his chest. That had gone as well as he'd thought it would. Thankfully, Tempest calmed his brother; otherwise, he had no doubt William would have charged out of here after Aria.

Daniel froze, his head tilting to the side when he heard voices coming closer. Humans wouldn't have approached so brazenly or with so much noise, as twigs and leaves crunched. Daniel's heart leapt into his throat. He pulled the bow he'd taken from the weapons room of the safe house below from his back.

William spun Tempest around and almost shoved her down the stairs. He closed the door as the barn door slid open to reveal the three vampires standing there.

***

Aria

Aria settled at the edge of the small town they'd arrived at. The trail Sabine and her followers had left ended here. Max knelt beside her; his hair was damp with sweat and stuck to his face. His breath came in short pants, but he hadn't argued with her brisk pace or asked to take a break. Beside him, Xavier surveyed the vampires moving throughout the town.

Aria dimly recognized it as a border town she'd seen a couple of times as a rebel. It was one of the places where rebels sometimes interacted with humans who hadn't sided with the vampires in order to have a better life, but who hadn't fully committed to the rebellion either. The people in those towns were often helpful and protective of the rebels, but she'd never fully trusted anyone who wasn't willing to risk it all.

Her father would sometimes use towns like this when he was bringing in new recruits. These towns were a helpful way to keep the rebel locations hidden, but still offered some measure of protection for him.

"Qualdon," Max said.

"Is that what this place is?" Aria asked.

"Yes. I spent a few nights in the tavern over there," he said and pointed at the small, gray shingled building. "Before I was captured. That's also where your father first met with Jack."

So long ago. Their lives had started to change that day, when their father had unwittingly brought a vampire into their midst. A fact he would later discover and keep to himself, as Jack became one of their strongest allies and her father's close friend.

Aria turned her attention back to the town again. Like William and Tempest had said about Badwin, she saw no humans in the streets with the vamps. At the end of the street, a wire had been stretched across the road. Something dangling from the wire turned slowly in the wind blowing down the street. Horror curdled through her when she recognized it was people hanging from the wire by a chain around their throats.

No, not people, she realized when one of them kicked a leg out at a passing, brown-cloaked vampire. *They're vampires.*

Tempest had said the influential vampires and the ones loyal to Braith were imprisoned, put into stocks and burned alive in Badwin. Apparently, they'd figured out a new way to restrain and torture vampires since then. It took everything she had not to storm down the street and slaughter every brown-cloaked vampire who tried to stop her from freeing the vampires spinning at the ends of their chains.

"Come on. Let's circle around and see if we can figure out where she's holed up," Aria finally managed to get out.

She remained crouched as they made their way through the woods enshrouding the back of the buildings lining the main street. It took them almost an hour, but eventually they located a large building surrounded by a heavy contingent of vamps. The windows of the home were all covered with thick drapes, making it impossible to see any movement within.

Aria studied the back of the faded blue home. There were ten windows on the wall, but no way to get to any of them with all the vampires standing guard. Even if she could somehow lead them away, the five bottom windows were covered with bars. She may be able to tear the bars free, but not without alerting someone to her presence. There was no way to get to the windows on the top floor, no trees near them or any sort of vine climbing the house. Her eyes settled on the two chimneys on the roof.

The entire building was surrounded by vampires on the ground, but no one was on the roof. Her eyes darted to the buildings on each side of the home. One was too short, she'd never be able to get from that roof to this one, but the building next door was a little higher. The only problem was the pitch of the roof on the house before her.

She bit her lip as she studied the rooftop. It was one thing to hop between trees; it was another thing to run up and across such steep angles. She could do it if she could find some nails or tacks to stick through the soles of her boots; she would have an easier time gripping the shingles then and wouldn't alert anyone to her presence. If someone did hear her, they'd most likely think she was a raccoon or a squirrel.

"You can't seriously be considering that," Max said when he caught the direction of her gaze.

"If she's in there, I can do it," Aria replied. "Tacks will help me grip the roof."

"Let me pull those out of my ass for you," he retorted and she glared at him though he couldn't see it from behind her glasses. "You said nothing reckless."

"It's not reckless, not if I plan it right. Now shush, we have to keep watch."

"You'll break your neck," Max pressed.

"Good thing that won't kill me anymore."

Now he scowled at her as his hands fisted. "*I* might."

"Get in line," Xavier muttered under his breath and Aria glowered at him. He didn't look at all repentant as he glowered back at her.

Aria turned away to study the vampires surrounding the building. This home was the only one with such a large number of vamps outside of it. It had to be where Sabine, or whoever she was, was staying, but she couldn't do anything until she knew for sure. "I have to know if she's in there first," she murmured.

***

Daniel

Daniel watched the vampires in the doorway as the first one broke into a grin and stepped inside. "Three trapped little piggy's," he said.

Behind him, William adjusted his stance to keep the door beneath him from opening again if Tempest should try to come back out. The other two vamps stepped into the barn as Timber pulled the staff from his back and brought it before him, to hold it there. He grinned back at the vamps beckoning the first one forward with a wave of his fingers.

The vamps hesitated when confronted with Timber's eagerness for a fight. They exchanged a look. "Easy prey," one of them said to the others, and Daniel nearly laughed out loud.

Behind him, William chuckled, drawing the vamp's attention to him. "Vampire," one of them said to the others.

"Give this guy a cookie. You're pretty observant, aren't you?" William inquired of the vampire as he nocked his arrow against his bow.

The vampire's lips skimmed back to bare his lethal fangs at William.

"About as observant as a rock," Timber replied.

Daniel remained unmoving, studying his opponents as they fanned out farther. Judging by their lumbering gait, their lack of weapons, and the way they all moved separately from each other, they had no formal training in weapons or defense. They also hadn't been working together for long. Otherwise, they would know not to let the one with the blond hair go to the right. He had a barely noticeable limp, but he would be slower to move off his right foot and was a weakness to their line.

They relied on their vampire strength to carry them through any battle they encountered with a human, but they were awkward for vampires. Strength meant nothing if they couldn't catch their opponent. Even Timber, for all of his lumbering size, was quick from years of having to be. He could pick a pocket before anyone ever noticed him in a crowd, a seemingly unattainable feat considering he was impossible *not* to notice, but Daniel had seen him do it many times before.

These three vampires would tear someone's jacket off while trying to shake their hand. Daniel couldn't help but smile at the men. This was going to be a good time.

He pulled an arrow from his quiver as William released his string. His arrow pierced through the shoulder of the first vamp, who yelped as he stumbled into the wall. Daniel released his arrow, effectively silencing the vamp when his arrowhead pierced through his heart and pinned him to the wall. The vamp's legs kicked against the wall before going completely still.

The one with the limp and the other vamp exchanged a frightened look before Timber leapt forward and swung his staff out, taking out the legs of the other vamp. The vamp spun away, scrambling to get back up. Timber spun the staff around and lifted it over his head. Like he was cutting wood, he swung it down and smashed it off the back of the vamp's head, shattering his skull.

The vamp howled as he threw his hands over the back of his head, trying to protect himself from any further blows.

"Shut up!" William leapt onto the back of the vampire, slicing his neck open in one clean stroke with the knife he wore at his side.

Limpy was trying to make it to the door, but Daniel followed his every move, stalking him like a cat after a mouse as he kept his arrow aimed at the vamp. He would be fast enough to dodge the arrow if Daniel shot it straight at him but not if he...

Daniel released the arrow. It thudded into the wall of the barn, one foot away from the door. He grabbed another arrow as the vamp leapt back, like he'd anticipated, and fired again. The arrow pierced straight through the vamp's side, pinning his right arm to his chest and coming to a stop in the center of his heart. The vamp lurched awkwardly, thrown off balance by his pinned appendage. Blood gurgled from his lips before he slammed face first into the ground.

"Nice shot," William commented as he walked over to retrieve the arrows they could use again. "Now let's get this garbage out of here."

CHAPTER 20

Aria

"I love this place," Aria whispered as she settled on the bench before the fountain. The couple within the center of the fountain, forever gazed yearningly at each other, but they would never be able to touch. Braith had once told her that in the beginning of their relationship, he'd thought of the couple in the fountain as them and had understood the torment on the faces of the couple as he'd been afraid to get too close to her.

She'd later learned Atticus had built the fountain because of Genny.

How fitting now.

"I know you do."

She tilted her head back as Braith settled onto the bench beside her. This close, she could clearly see the beautiful blue of the band encircling his iris. Black stubble lined his square jaw as his eyes held hers. The heat of his body warmed hers, the love in his gaze making her sigh as she leaned against him.

"I love you," she whispered.

His fingers slid over her hair, lifting it up and letting it fall back down. "And I you, more than you could ever know."

"Oh, I know."

Releasing her hair, his fingers stroked over her cheek, turning her head toward him. Behind his back, hundreds of red roses climbed the trellises and spilled over the walkways of the garden. She didn't recall there being so many roses before, but now they were everywhere she looked. Their heady fragrance tickled her nostrils, but his scent enveloped her when he leaned down to kiss her. Her hands encircled his forearms as something tugged at the back of her mind.

She couldn't let him go. She could never let him go. If she did...

What? What would happen? She should know the answer to that, but she didn't, and right now she didn't care. Not when his tongue was moving over her lips in that demanding way. She opened her mouth to his heady invasion, her toes curling and a moan escaping her when she felt his fangs against her lips.

Need the connection.

Her fangs lengthened, and she bit down on his lip, but no blood filled her mouth. Pulling away, she gazed up at him as he cradled her cheeks within his hands. "Why can't I taste you?" she asked.

Sadness filled his eyes as he bent to rest his forehead against hers. For a minute, she simply savored their closeness before his hands lessened their grip on her face. "You know why," he whispered.

Over his shoulder, the roses drooped. The edges of their petals wrinkled as the vibrant red color darkened in hue. She couldn't bring herself to look at him as the once vibrant red roses became the color of midnight. Blood pooled in their centers before sliding down to drip off of their black petals. The pristine, white rocks of the garden pathway turned crimson with the blood spilling over them.

"Don't make me leave here," she pleaded.

"You can't stay here, Aria. You have to go back."

Her hands flew up to cover his on her face. She tried to press them closer again, but they were fading away as his appearance wavered before her. "Braith," she choked out.

"I'm always with you," he said, and she felt the feathery caress of his ghost lips against her forehead. "Always a piece of you, and I will come back for you, not even death will keep us apart."

Tears dripped off her chin as he shimmered before her and vanished.

***

Aria

Stars twinkled against the midnight backdrop of the sky as Aria lay on her back, staring up at them. She propped her hands behind her head while she tried not to recall the dream that had woken her over an hour ago. She cursed herself again for falling asleep, but exhaustion had drawn her under.

Not even death will keep us apart.

How desperately she wished those words were true, but the emptiness inside her made believing in anything nearly impossible right now. She watched as the stars changed position in the sky and tried not to think of the many times she and Braith had lain out beneath the stars together. It was impossible not to recall those nights, his kisses, the scrape of his fangs against her skin, his body moving over hers...

Aria rolled over and shoved herself into a seated position. She shook her head to clear it of the memories. Recalling happier times did not make things better; they made it far worse. Lifting her head, her gaze fell on the trees. From within their dark depths, Braith stood staring at her, watching her in that fascinated way he had so often since she'd met him.

For a second, she swore her deadened heart gave a lumbering beat once more. She rose to her knees and almost leapt to her feet to run to him. Then the image faded away, as it had in her dream. She was left with nothing but the shadows of the trees and her encroaching insanity.

Her fingers dug into the earth, tearing away pine needles and leaves as dirt embedded beneath her fingernails and the world became filled with a reddish haze. Her fangs lengthened when bloodlust surged to life within her.

He could still be coming back for me.

Don't think it. Don't get your hopes up. You won't survive the loss of those hopes.

That little inner voice was right and she immediately shut down any belief of Braith's return.

Xavier lifted his head from where he sat against the trunk of an oak when she took a ragged breath, then another. She hadn't required air in some time, yet she kept trying to draw it into her lungs now as her gaze remained riveted on where she thought she'd seen Braith standing.

Xavier rose and walked over to kneel beside her; he rested his hand on her back. She wanted to shy away from his touch, but she found herself unable to move enough to do so.

"Easy," he soothed.

She took another rattling breath before closing her eyes and carefully reining in all of her unstable emotions. Lifting her glasses, she rubbed at her swollen and gritty eyes.

"I'm okay," she whispered when she had herself back under control.

"If you're not, that's okay too," he said.

She lifted her head to look at him. They'd come from two completely different worlds, yet he was her friend and protector. "No," she said. "It's not, and we both know it. Queens are not allowed to fall apart."

He rested his cheek against her hair and rubbed her back. "That is not always true."

"It is now."

He kept his hand on her back as she rose to her feet and carefully made her way toward where Max was keeping watch over the house. He turned toward her when she knelt at his side. "Anything new?" she whispered.

"I haven't seen her and none of the guards have changed," he replied.

Aria settled in beside him. "If you want to sleep, I'll watch."

"I'm fine," he replied as Xavier sat on his other side.

Aria peered through the thick underbrush before her. Thirty feet of bushes, vines, and trees separated them and the vampires who were most likely guarding the evil woman inside. If the vampires did smell them, there was little difference between their scent and the other vampires of their town. They were too far away for Max's heartbeat to be detected.

Her gaze drifted around the woods behind them. She cautiously scented the air as she searched for any hint of a shift in their environment, but she detected nothing. Turning her attention back to the house, she carefully watched everything as the moon crept higher into the sky. She lifted her glasses to rub at her eyes again when a curtain above pulled back to reveal the white-haired vampire often at Sabine's side.

"Goran," she murmured as she recalled what William had said his name was.

Xavier and Max followed her gaze to the window. The man stared out it for a minute more before settling the curtain back into place. Aria restrained herself from jumping up and running to the building next door to climb to the roof.

If Goran was in there, then that bitch was too.

***

Aria

The next day, Aria stood sixty feet back in the woods, staring through the trees and brush to the house next to the one Sabine was in. They'd spent all last night and most of today trying to learn as much as they could of the vampires who had invaded the town. There were thousands of vampires, far more than they'd seen in the woods before. It was one more bit of information to file away, one more piece of the puzzle they hadn't had before.

To get inside the house with Sabine and Goran could be the best way to get more information, but how was she going to land safely on the roof and then climb up it? The roof was nearly a ninety-degree pitch in some places. Even if she could find tacks or nails or something to stick through the soles of her boots, there was no guarantee she wouldn't be spotted or wouldn't plummet onto the vampires standing guard below.

Death was not an option for her, not right now, and neither was being caught. They had to get closer, but how? By going inside?

Even she had to admit it was one of the craziest ideas she'd ever had, but Sabine had yet to leave the residence and Tempest and William had said she'd rarely been seen outside while in Badwin.

"Crap," she hissed between her teeth.

"I second that," Max said.

"The reasons to go inside are sound."

"Many things are sound and still stupid," Max replied, and she had to agree with him. "What are you going to do once you're in there? What if she smells you? You're going down a chimney so you're going to have soot all over you. You'll never be able to leave the chimney with soot all over you, because you'll leave a trail bigger than the one they left that led us here. Staying inside the chimney isn't an option either as you won't be able to hear anything inside the stone walls."

"What do we do then?" she asked. "We risked our lives to come here. We need more information than they have *bigger* numbers than we first thought. Not exactly morale boosting."

Max lifted his hand to rub at his temples. The sleeve of his too big shirt fell down to reveal the bites and burn scars marring his wrists. He'd obtained those scars during his days as a blood slave. It had been well over a year since Aria had seen his scars. He usually kept them covered up, but wearing borrowed clothes instead of having his own, had made that impossible for him.

She was glad she wore the glasses. If he'd seen the direction of her eyes, he would have covered the scars back up and shut himself off from her. Max had come a long way since he'd been freed from his captivity as a blood slave, but any reminder of it still caused him to withdraw.

"I have an idea," Xavier said from behind her, and she turned to look at him as he unfolded himself from the tree he'd been leaning against and walked toward them. His eyes focused on Aria when he stopped beside her. "You're not going to like it."

"I don't like many things, but I'm willing to do anything to stop her," she replied.

"Those soldiers, not all of them are overly loyal to her. I'd bet at least half of them, if not more, are following her out of fear and because of the vast amount of power she has."

"True," Max said.

Xavier's gaze went past them to the vampires gathered around the building and patrolling the streets. "We capture one of them and make them tell us what they know about her."

The blood drained from Aria's face. She knew Xavier; if he got a hold of one of Sabine's followers, he would do anything necessary to make them talk. Yes, she'd just told them she would do anything to stop Sabine, but could she condone this action? Could she help carry it out?

Max clasped her arms, drawing her attention to him. Her skin bristled against being touched, but for some reason she could withstand it better today than she could yesterday. Every day brought something new now; it wouldn't surprise her if being touched tomorrow brought pain again.

"Doing this is far better than risking you," he said. "We have a better idea of how many followers she has now. We know she has continued her campaign of punishing vampires who go against her, and you saw what she did with those humans in the woods. *One* of her followers is a small sacrifice to make in the grand scheme of things."

"Wouldn't we be sacrificing a piece of ourselves too by doing this?" she inquired.

A muscle in his jaw twitched, his gaze went beyond her to the town. "It's a piece of myself I'm willing to lose if it helps us stop her."

"Max…"

His eyes were like chips of blue ice when they came back to hers. She swallowed heavily as she was once again confronted with the man who had been set free from the palace, angry and capable of doing anything to make the vampires pay for what had been done to him.

"I learned long ago we all must do things we don't want to do in order to survive," he said.

She knew those words were only a hint of what he'd been through, of what it had taken for him to live through his time in captivity. Resting her palm against his cheek, she sought to give him some comfort. It would be easier for all of them if she closed herself off to those she loved before she died, but she couldn't. Beneath his words, she sensed the wealth of suffering in Max's heart. Their experiences as blood slaves had been completely different from each other. Braith had treated her kindly. Katrina, the vampire who had bought Max, had not been so kind.

He placed his hand over the top of hers and gave it a squeeze.

"Yes, we must," she agreed. She was willing to sacrifice anything to ensure her loved ones, and those who followed her, had some peace in their lives again. She looked to Xavier. "How do we lure one of them away?"

Xavier turned to look at the vampires guarding the house again. "It won't be one of them. They've been trained to protect her, and they won't leave there one at a time. We have to lure one away from somewhere else."

"Let's go then," Aria said. She slid her hand away from Max's cheek. He kept hold of it for a minute more before releasing her to follow them through the woods.

***

Aria

They settled in to watch the stables at the edge of town as a handful of vampires exited and entered. It only took an hour to determine that the small, redheaded vampire who remained standing in the doorway of the stables was the one in charge. The only time he left the doorway was when someone brought in a horse.

"What if he doesn't know anything?" Aria asked as she studied the stocky man with a bulbous nose and eyes that looked about to pop out of his head.

"If he provides care to the horses, then he probably knows more than most in this town," Xavier said. "There tends to be talk in a stable."

She'd spent a fair amount of time in the stables in the palace to know that was true. "What if he's new to her group?"

"He's not new. So far, he's known every vampire who has walked into the stable. He's been with this group for a while."

Aria's eyes narrowed on the ugly vampire. What had he seen and done during his time with these vampires? She recalled the parade of humans being dragged around with them and the way that vamp had broken the poor woman's neck.

Keep remembering that later when you have him, she told herself. She hated them all and wanted them all dead, but there was a big difference between murdering someone and torturing them.

"We'll need somewhere discreet," Xavier said.

"There are caves about five miles from here we can take him to," Max replied.

"That will work."

They waited until the vampire was alone, standing in the doorway and chewing on a piece of straw before Max took a knife and drew the blade across his palm. Aria noticed Xavier staring at the scars once again visible on Max's wrist before he turned away. A muscle twitched in the corner of his eye. Xavier could be ruthless and cruel when necessary, but he would never allow another to be hurt for pleasure as Max had been.

The stable vampire's head turned, and his nostrils flared as he scented Max's blood on the air. Max walked into the woods with Aria and Xavier flanking him about thirty feet out on each side while Max lured the vampire deeper and deeper into the forest.

When the vamp went to leap on Max, Xavier pounced and brought him down beneath his weight. He shoved a piece of cloth into the vampire's mouth and jerked his arms behind his back with one hand to pin his wrists there. He balled his other hand and drove his fist into the vampire's temple. The man's eyes rolled up in his head, and he went limp.

Xavier lifted him and tossed him over his shoulder. "Lead the way."

Aria broke into a brisk jog through the woods with Max by her side. She kept alert for any hint of danger within the forest as they ran over the rough terrain. After three miles, they had to stop so Xavier could knock the man out again and Max could take a break to drink some water, but they made it to the cave in less than an hour.

The vamp was starting to regain consciousness again when they entered into the cool rock walls of the cave system. Max lifted a stick from the ground and ripped off a piece of the vampire's shirt. He wrapped the cloth around the stick before following them into the caves. The vamp kicked his feet in the air as his hands beat against Xavier's hold, but Xavier didn't ease his grip on him.

They were almost to the center of the cave when she heard the strike of a match and light burst forth as Max set the piece of vampire's shirt on fire. Aria stopped at the entrance to a small cavern. These were not caves that they had once resided in. There were no booby traps and no gates, but she'd hidden here before and knew they were well out of sight and no one would hear them down here.

They may not be as protected here as they were in some of the other caves, but it was sheltered. Searching the rocks above them, she saw no bats that would be scared by their presence and possibly alert others to their location if they decided to take flight. Xavier walked over to a large rock in the middle of the cavern and dumped the vampire unceremoniously on the ground.

Stepping away from the vamp, Xavier grabbed the ends of his shirt and pulled it over his head. He tossed it to Max. "For the torch," he said. "And for other things," he added ominously and Aria shuddered.

Max caught hold of the shirt and tucked it into his waistband for later use. The vamp's brown eyes nervously took them all in before settling on Aria. His mouth parted as his eyebrows shot into his hairline.

"I think he recognizes you," Max said.

"Can't say the same," she murmured.

His already buggy eyes bugged out more when Xavier took the torch from Max and walked over to stand before the vamp.

"Aria, go back into the cave and wait for us there," Xavier said.

"No."

Xavier's face was merciless when he turned to face her. "There is no reason for you to see this."

"I suggested going after her. I agreed to this. I am condoning it. I will not walk away and let you bear this on your own. Whatever happens here is mine to bear also, and I will stay here until it's over." She turned to Max and rested her hand briefly against his arm. "I understand if you don't wish to see this."

"I'm not leaving," he replied.

"Max—"

"I intend to help with this. I'm not leaving."

"There are some things that can never be unseen," Xavier said to her.

"I would hate myself more if I walked away to leave you both to this. I'm not going anywhere."

Xavier turned away from her. The firelight danced over his brown skin and the tattoos covering his chest and back. It was the first time Aria had seen all of the markings etched onto his chiseled muscles. The smaller vamp at his feet made a strangled sound and tried to squirm away, but Xavier rested his foot against the man's shoulder and pinned him in place.

"I'm going to pull out that gag and you're going to answer my questions," Xavier said to him. "Otherwise, I'm going to make your insides your outsides."

Sing like a canary, Aria silently pleaded as Xavier pulled the gag from the man's mouth.

CHAPTER 21

Aria

"I *cannot* believe you took off like that!"

"Not now, William," Aria replied as she stepped off the bottom step, through the doorway, and into the safe house. The walls pressing against her made her almost turn around and flee back outside.

"You should have waited. You shouldn't have gone at all!"

Aria spun on him. "I said *not now!*"

Her brother gave her a 'huh?' look, and took a step back as Max and Xavier stepped off the stairs behind her. Max held himself rigidly, his jaw clenched as he stared at William. Blood still splattered the bottom of Xavier's and Max's pants, but there had been no help for it as they'd kept them on throughout...

Aria abruptly cut off the memory of what had occurred.

"What happened?" William inquired, his tone much softer than it had been.

"We can discuss it later," Aria replied and forced one foot in front of the other down the hall.

She froze at the entrance to the main room. At least a hundred and fifty faces turned in her direction. All of them looked tired and frightened, but she also saw the hope blooming in their eyes as smiles curved their mouths. A few of the children released delighted cries and clapped their hands together.

"They've returned!" a young boy, no older than five, said as he bounced on his mother's lap.

"There's so many," she whispered.

"They've brought word that our troop numbers have grown rapidly. We're over twenty-five hundred now," William replied.

Tears burned Aria's eyes. The memory of what she'd witnessed today, what she'd condoned would forever be burned into her mind, but staring at everyone gathered within, she knew they'd done the right thing.

After a few hours, they'd finally gotten the vampire to spill what he knew; they had answers to many of the questions they'd sought, and one *big* possible weakness. They'd done something terrible to get those answers, but they were better prepared to defend those surrounding them now.

She would do what she'd done today again if it meant protecting these innocents. This time, when the first one took a step toward her, she welcomed it as each of their touches was a reminder of why she stood here and of who would really suffer if they lost this battle to Sabine.

She'd be dead, her misery over with if Sabine won, but the vampires wouldn't kill off their human food supply. No, what they would do to the humans would be far worse.

***

Max

Max kept his hands clasped before him as he stared at the numerous scars marking them. His neck had started to ache an hour ago from his forward, hunched over position, but he didn't dare move. What had happened in that cave had triggered memories he'd been trying to bury since he'd escaped his vampire captor, Katrina.

But now the memories were there again, teasing at his mind. Screams echoed in his head, but they weren't the screams of the vamp from today. They were his own. The fangs sinking into his flesh over and over again, burying deep into the same places until his skin was so raw he felt as if it had been flayed from his body. Katrina's cruel laughter echoed in his ears as she ran her fingers over his bare flesh while he remained tied up and helpless to resist anything she did to him.

Breathe.

Sometimes, when the memories came to him, he forgot to breathe. He would find himself gasping for the air he'd unconsciously denied his lungs while waves of loathing for the vampires and himself swamped him. What had been done to him hadn't been his fault, he'd always known that, but knowing it didn't always make it any better. He'd physically responded to Katrina, his body reacting on its own even as he cursed himself and she laughed.

She'd always laughed too. Every time, she had laughed while destroying him one more small piece at a time. Plans of escaping her had been all that kept him going. Of escaping, rescuing Aria, and taking her far away. She'd always been Daniel's kid sister to him, but he'd started to look at her differently before their capture.

Aria had grown to become a very pretty woman, but she'd been a scrawny teen. However, she had more spirit than anyone he knew, and he admired the strength of her love for her family and her rebellious nature. When she'd sacrificed herself to save John from the vampires, he hadn't been able to let her go to the palace alone. He'd been convinced he could free her.

How incredibly wrong he'd been. If it hadn't been for Jack rescuing them, he would be dead by now. Sometimes he wondered if he would have been better off never being saved as parts of him already felt dead.

Once they'd been set free and were no longer at the palace, he'd seen Aria as someone who could understand what he'd endured. He'd clung to the hope that her understanding would somehow be his salvation. No matter how often she'd told him her time as a blood slave hadn't been the same as his, he didn't believe her. He'd believed she couldn't admit what had been done to her while she was imprisoned, that she'd been warped to have feelings for the vampire who had claimed her as his, but he'd been wrong.

He'd been livid with her afterward; she'd betrayed him and all of her loved ones for a monster. A monster who had loved her more than Max had ever seen anyone love another, a monster who had fought alongside all of them to bring freedom to humans. Somewhere along the way, Max had stopped seeing Braith as a monster and Aria as a traitor. He'd started seeing the good and bad in vampires as well as the good and bad in humans. He'd started to heal.

And now that healing was falling apart around him. Braith, the monster who had become his friend, was dead. Aria was barely holding herself together. The freedom they'd attained was fracturing around them, and his memories had been set free by a vampire who had deserved everything he'd gotten today, probably more.

He kept that thought firmly in mind as he finally lifted his head to look at those surrounding him. Most of the humans had retreated to bed hours ago, leaving only him and his friends behind. The flame from a lantern behind William's shoulder caused his hair to shine like blood. Max turned his head away as images of his own blood streaming down from his wrists, tied above his head, filled his mind.

Closing his eyes against the memory, he rubbed at his wrists before rising to his feet and walking over to the jugs of wine stashed on another table.

"Do you think that's a good idea?" Daniel asked in a low voice as Max poured himself a large glass of wine.

"Yes, I do," he said as he drank all the dark liquid he'd just poured before refilling the glass. The wine was bitter on his tongue, but it warmed him all the way down. He looked to Aria and tipped the glass in a questioning gesture.

She nibbled at her lip. "No, I can't."

Lifting her glasses, she briefly revealed her blood-colored eyes as she rubbed at them before settling the glasses back into place. William glanced questioningly between Max and Aria before turning to watch while Xavier paced the room. Tempest sat in his lap, her gaze also focused on Xavier as he turned and walked back to the other side of the room.

"What happened out there?" William inquired.

"We found where they are right now," Aria replied.

"Did you learn anything?" Timber asked.

"Yes," Aria said.

Max drank down the rest of his wine and scowled at his wrist when his sleeve fell back to reveal his scars; the ever-present reminder of Katrina. She was dead, but he would forever bear her marks. Whatever Hell she was in now, he knew she was laughing over that knowledge. He poured himself another glass despite Daniel's disapproving look. Maybe it wasn't the best time to get sloshed, but he really couldn't think of a more appropriate one.

Daniel, Timber, and William exchanged looks but no one prodded him further. Aria's nails dug into her thighs as she gazed at him. Xavier stopped pacing to stare at Daniel for a minute before resuming his stalking movements.

Lord help Daniel tonight, Max thought and couldn't stop himself from chuckling as he drank the wine and poured himself another glass. At least the wine made Katrina's laughter in his head die down some.

"Is it helpful information?" Daniel prodded.

"It's helpful," Max replied.

"Well…?" William inquired.

"It is Sabine," Aria confirmed, drawing all of their attention to her. "Whether she did die and rose again or not, we don't know, but that *is* the woman's name. I'm sure there have been many Sabine's over the years, but judging by her vast amount of power and her looks, she *has* to be Atticus's mother."

"You're sure that's her name?" William inquired.

In his head, Max could hear them repeatedly asking the vamp for the woman's name. In the beginning, the vamp had claimed not to know it. Then he'd claimed he'd never reveal it. In the end, he had sobbed Sabine's name repeatedly. Never once had they suggested the name to him before he confessed it on his own.

"We're sure," Max replied when Aria remained silent, probably recalling the man's cries too. "She has about ten to fifteen thousand troops." The vamp had told them twelve thousand. They'd agreed he was most likely exaggerating, but it was better to be safe than sorry. "Right now, they're divided into three different towns until they're ready to go after the palace. She has some of her followers traveling in smaller groups, circulating through areas and acting as scouts who report back to her. She moves often, sometimes in extremely large groups, sometimes in smaller groups as she always deviates her patterns. We were lucky she was in a smaller group the night they discovered us."

"There's easily ten thousand within the palace walls right now. If Melinda was able to evacuate the border towns before Sabine got to them, there will be more," Daniel said.

"Including those we are gathering, our numbers are about equal with hers," Xavier said. "Our source could have been lying about their numbers, most likely was, but it will be close."

"You have a source?" Tempest asked.

"We did," Aria confirmed. "He no longer lives."

Max drank another glass.

"She'll be ready for the palace soon," Daniel said.

"She's moving on the palace within the week," Aria replied.

"Your source told you this?" William asked.

"No, he said they wouldn't be moving until next week. We believe he lied."

"Won't she seek out more followers first?" Tempest asked.

"Arrogance is one of her biggest weaknesses," Aria murmured. "I think she believes she can turn some of those within the palace to her side."

"She may be able to," Xavier said as he stopped his pacing. "Fear is a powerful motivator."

"Are we going to warn them?" William asked.

"We'll figure out a way to do so," Aria said.

"Should we bring our troops in sooner than planned?" Timber inquired.

"No," Aria replied. "The palace is going to have to defend itself for a few days if she moves before we're ready. The Council will be able to keep it together for a few days, especially if they have the better position and the walls to defend from. It will also take time to bring Jack here."

Blood spilled from Aria's palms as her fingers tore into her flesh with those words. It dripped onto her pants, but she didn't notice it and no one commented.

"I don't think we can get Jack here before she marches on the palace. There simply isn't enough time," Aria continued. "When he does get here, we'll send the runners to the safe houses to start gathering our troops."

"We will return for Jack tomorrow," Daniel said. "If all goes well, it will only take us a day to get there."

"Yes," Aria said.

"Did you learn anything else?" William inquired.

"Goran may be her other big weakness," Max said. Their informant had let that one spill in order to keep his other eye. "They're rarely apart."

"Is that it?" Timber asked.

"It's more than we had before," Aria said defensively as more blood fell onto her pants. "And we also learned that Goran is her son."

A pin dropping would have been heard from a mile away. The chair Timber had been leaning back in hit the floor to finally break the silence. "You're kidding!" Timber blurted.

"No," Aria said. "I'm not sure when he was born, it must have been while she was in hiding, but he is her son."

"Judging by the power I sensed in him, I would say he is younger than Braith and Jack, but not by much," Xavier said.

"Holy..." Timber's words trailed off. "This just gets more and more messed up."

"Yes," Xavier said. "She has also been in this country for at least five hundred years, possibly longer."

"How do you know that?" Daniel inquired, his face paler than normal.

"Our informant told us she *is* Croatoan," Xavier answered.

"What the hell is Croatoan?" William demanded.

"Croatoan was once associated with a colony of humans who came to settle this land in the fifteen hundreds. They disappeared, but left the word croatoan behind. Many believed the settlers were trying to say that they'd gone to live with the Native American tribe in the area, also of the same name, but they were never sure. Our informant told us Sabine was responsible for those settler's disappearances and deaths. Why the settlers called her this, I don't know, perhaps they believed she was one of the Native Americans. Sabine has been responsible for many mass disappearances over the years that have gone unsolved."

"And after seeing her parade of humans in the woods, I think we know what she does with those people," Aria said.

Max placed his glass down and walked over to her. She tried to jerk away when he clasped her hands, but he kept a firm hold on them as he lifted them and uncurled her fingers from where they'd torn her flesh back on her palms. Her forehead furrowed at the blood flowing from the large gashes, and he realized she hadn't known what she was doing.

Daniel rose and entered the room the humans had left open for Aria to sleep in. He returned with a towel and handed it to Max who wrapped it around her hands. The cuts would heal quickly, but he didn't want her to get any more blood on her pants.

"Are you going to tell us what happened out there?" Daniel inquired.

"There are some things that can never be unheard," Aria murmured.

"No," Max said.

She tugged on her hands again, and this time, Max released them to her before returning for his glass of wine. He stared at the wall as Xavier resumed his pacing.

"Would you please get him out of here? His pacing is driving me nuts," Aria said to Daniel.

"Not leaving you," Xavier said flatly.

"I'll be fine. There are plenty of guards, and I know you'll stay close. I need a moment of stillness."

Xavier went completely still, but the tension radiating from him made him feel like a bomb about ready to explode as sweat beaded across his forehead and trickled down his temple.

"Xavier, please go," she said. He made a disgruntled sound before turning on his heel and stalking over to the door. He opened it and walked into the hallway. Aria turned toward Daniel. "I don't think he should be alone right now."

Daniel rose to his feet. "Are you sure?"

"Yes."

Daniel bent to kiss the top of her head. "I don't know what happened out there, but you did good, you all did. This is all useful information."

Before she could respond, he turned and followed Xavier into the hall. "You two can have the room," Aria said to William. "I won't be sleeping tonight."

"I'll stay up with you," William offered.

"No, rest. You look tired."

"Someone took off and left me behind to worry about them."

The corner of Aria's mouth quirked into the faintest hint of a smile. She removed the towel from her hands and set it in her lap. "Serves you right for taking off after Kane."

"At least I said good-bye."

"Only because I stopped you before you could leave town."

"I didn't take two others with me."

"Only because you insisted upon going alone. Go, get some rest."

William hesitated, but when he glanced down at Tempest, Max knew he had lost the battle before he rose to his feet and walked out of the room with her cradled against his chest. Max filled two glasses of wine and returned to his seat.

"You know," Timber said quietly, "ugliness is a way of the world. You have to accept that, but it's when you let the ugliness eat at you until it makes you ugly too, that you truly lose a piece of yourself."

Aria's mouth parted as she turned toward him, but before she could respond, Timber's chin fell onto his chest and he released a loud snore. "How does he *do* that?" she asked in awe.

Max stretched his legs out before him. "I wish I knew."

Aria stared at him with her head tilted to the side. "Today made you think of your time with *her* again, didn't it?"

He knew she'd avoided saying the name to try to spare him some distress, but there was none to be spared, not tonight. "With Katrina, yes."

Aria's mouth pursed, a muscle in her jaw twitched. "If she hadn't already been put to death, I'd kill her again for you."

Max smiled as he stared into his glass of wine. "I know you would."

"You never talk of what happened there. Would you like to now? I'll listen to anything you're willing to tell me."

"There are some things that can never be unheard," he reminded her.

She removed her glasses to reveal her reddened eyes and set them in her lap. "I think we've all gone beyond the point of being sheltered in our lives."

"Then why not tell them what we did today?"

"Because it's not necessary for them to know. They shouldn't have to carry that burden too."

"And hearing my horror stories are necessary to know?" He couldn't keep the sharp edge from his tone.

"I think it would be better if you let it all out instead of continuing to keep it in, you know, like that whole ugliness thing Timber said."

"And when are you going to let it all out?" he inquired. "Your eyes have yet to go back to their normal color."

"That's entirely different and you know it. I'm a dead woman walking without Braith," she reminded him. "I'm barely keeping it going until all of this is over. You're twenty-three years old and you have your whole life ahead of you. You deserve love and happiness, more than the rest of us probably."

"Not true," he said.

"You sacrificed yourself and became a blood slave because of *me*. What was done to you should never have been done to another. You *deserve* some peace, and I will do anything I can to help you find it."

"You sacrificed yourself and became a blood slave because of John. If not for Braith, your experience would have been as bad as mine, if not more so. I am happy now." At her raised eyebrow and disbelieving look, he continued. "Happier than I've been in a long time. Well, before everything went to shit anyway. I was healing. I'd found my place at Daniel's side, helping him to rule and make decisions with The Council. I may not have been in charge, but I was still doing good, for all of us, and I enjoyed it."

"And how do you feel after today?"

"Today broke me again a little," he admitted. "But I'll figure out how to put myself back together. I did before."

"I can help with that, or I can try to anyway."

"Sometimes, just sitting with someone helps."

"Like when we used to sit together and fish without speaking?"

He smiled at the memory of those early days after they'd both been freed. They'd been such somber days, but the two of them sitting together had helped. "Yes, like that."

"I can do that."

"Are you sure you wouldn't like some wine?"

"I'd like nothing more than to be drunk right now, but I'm afraid if I let my guard down even a little, I'll snap. I might even eat you."

"I would have accepted no for an answer."

She gave him a small smile as she leaned back in the chair, her reddened eyes surveying him. He missed their crystalline blue color, and he missed her full smile, the one that lit her face and radiated her joy. They didn't speak for half an hour before he rose to his feet and poured himself two more glasses of wine.

Walking over, he sat in the chair across from her once more. "Do you remember when we were younger and used to play hide and seek in the caves?" he asked.

"I do," she replied.

"How about the time William put a snake in your blanket?"

Her gaze flicked toward the closed door William and Tempest had gone through. "I'd forgotten about that. I *never* should have given him my room tonight."

Max laughed and took a sip of wine. "What about the time you dove off the waterfall?"

"And my pants came off?"

"That's the time."

"I'd never been more embarrassed in my life, and all you guys did was point and laugh as my pants were swept downstream."

"You were so mad."

"You would have been mad too. The water was freezing."

He smiled at the memory of Aria, sopping wet as she stomped her way out of the river after reclaiming her pants. "You didn't speak to any of us for the rest of the day."

"But you all brought me flowers the next day and said you were sorry."

"None of us ever liked it when you were mad at us."

"I know," she said. "It was always the same way when one of you were mad at me. You weren't as easily bought off with a bouquet though."

"You always brought us a new fur."

"I did."

He thought he saw a flash of blue in her eyes, but it was gone before he could be sure. He'd once believed he was in love with her; he now knew he'd been lost and looking for someone to care for him when he'd never felt more dirty and unlovable in his life. The thing was, Aria had always loved him, just as he would always love her.

"I'm not ready to lose you," he said honestly.

Her eyes darted toward the door to the hall, her fingers fidgeting in her lap. "I'm not ready to lose any of you, but without Braith—"

"I understand," he interrupted. "No explanations. I don't think either of us need to hear what we've experienced and are experiencing. I think we both *know*."

Her gaze came back to him. Tears glistened briefly in her eyes before she wiped them away. "You're right. Those kind of revelations aren't necessary."

He sipped at his wine, but he found that this time he far preferred talking with her to the silence. He didn't know if he would ever get this chance with her again. "Remember when we all covered ourselves in mud along the riverbank and jumped out of it to scare your father?"

This time Aria actually did give a real laugh; it was short, but it was there. "Not even as a vampire have I ever run as fast as I did when he chased after us."

"Neither have I," he admitted.

CHAPTER 22

William

"Is she asleep?" William whispered in disbelief when he stepped out of the room and spotted Aria in the chair she'd been sitting in last night. He assumed it was morning because he'd awoken and felt somewhat rested, but couldn't be sure of the exact time of day.

Max lifted bloodshot and bleary eyes to him. "She is," Max whispered back.

"How did that happen?"

"We were up talking until late. She fell asleep about an hour ago."

As far as he knew, that was the most she'd slept since Braith died. "Hopefully it will last longer than that," William said as he soundlessly closed the door behind him. If he didn't think it would wake her, he'd carry Aria in to sleep with Tempest, but there was no way she would sleep through being relocated. She couldn't possibly be comfortable sitting in the chair with her chin on her chest, but he would leave her be. "How much did you drink last night?"

"Enough to kill my liver, but not enough to get me drunk," Max replied.

"Will you be going with Daniel to retrieve Jack?"

"Yeah."

William eyed the two empty jugs of wine and then Max. Despite the red veins encircling his blue eyes, he looked entirely alert as he watched William. "I think you definitely killed your liver."

"Believe me, I know," Max replied.

"What were you talking about all night?"

"Old times in the forest. I wouldn't mind an hour or two of sleep myself."

William knew when he'd been asked to shove off. "If Tempest wakes, tell her I'm in the barn."

"Will do," Max replied.

William made his way out the door, down the hall, and up the stairs. He checked through the peepholes, spotting Xavier, Daniel, and Timber standing with a group of humans from the safe house, talking amongst themselves. Undoing the lock, he shoved the door open and stepped into the early morning rays of sun filtering through the cracks in the roof above.

Daniel turned toward him as he emerged and closed the door behind him. William walked over to join them.

"How are Aria and Max?" Daniel asked.

William glanced at Xavier, wondering if he'd told Daniel what had happened while the three of them were out there. He seriously doubted it. If Aria and Max weren't talking, the normally stoic vampire wasn't about to either.

"Aria is actually sleeping and Max is trying to get some sleep now," William replied.

"Will Max be ready to leave soon?"

"He drank two jugs of wine, looks like he's been awake for two weeks straight, and smells like a brewery, but I'm pretty sure he's good to go."

"Good. The sooner we get this journey over with, the better," Daniel replied.

The creak of the door drew their heads around as Aria pushed it open and entered the barn. Her glasses were back in place, but she still lifted her hand to rest it against her forehead to shade her eyes from the sun.

"At least she got a little rest," William said as Max exited behind her and turned to offer his hand to someone else.

Tempest's crisp, wintry scent reached him before he caught sight of her. William hurried forward to take her hand from Max and help her out of the safe house. She was still annoyed with him for pushing her back down into the stairwell when those vampires found them the other day, but she took his hand and gave it a little squeeze. The smile she gave him melted his non-beating heart and let him know the rest of her annoyance with him had faded away.

Leaning forward, he kissed her forehead. "What is going on?" she asked.

"They're getting ready to go back for Jack," he replied.

A small shudder went through her and he knew she was thinking the same as him. *What would happen with Braith?* They couldn't bring him here, others couldn't know he was dead, but to leave him alone in the caves would be to leave him vulnerable. No matter how much Jack loved his brother, he wouldn't agree to leave Hannah behind so she could watch over him, and Daniel, Timber, and Max may not be enough to keep Braith protected. He highly doubted Xavier would agree to remain in the caves with Aria here.

"Are you ready?" Daniel asked Max.

"I have to gather some things," Max replied and smoothed down his spiky hair. "But I'll be ready in ten minutes."

"Are you sure you don't want some of us to go with you?" one of the humans asked.

"We'll only be a couple of days," Daniel replied. "And we need as many people here as possible."

All of the humans and vampires they'd encountered had been told Braith and Jack were out on a mission of their own, and in a way, they were. Jack was on a mission to protect his brother, and William really hoped Braith was working on a way to make it back to them. Somehow.

The knowledge it *was* Sabine trying to destroy them all had helped to bolster his hopes that Braith would come back, but it could still be impossible. Had Sabine died like originally believed, or had she faked her death? He felt there would have been a body for her family to have believed her dead, but what did he know about something that occurred over a thousand years ago?

He vaguely recalled something in Atticus's journals about her being buried in the family plot in a place called Traslania? Trasylvia? *Transylvania,* he finally remembered. If there was a burial plot, there had to have been a body, or at least he really hoped there was.

Sabine had come back, so had Atticus, and so would Braith, but would it be in time?

It may not be, and there was nothing they could do about that, except carry on with their plan. If they didn't stop Sabine, they would lose everything and Braith would awaken to find his world burned to the ground by a member of his family, again. He may wake to find all of his loved ones gone, lost to the war, including Aria.

William shut the thought off and drew Tempest closer against his chest. He would do everything he could to get them both through this. He'd vowed to give her a better life than the one she'd known in Badwin. Now he wasn't sure any of them would still be here next week.

Resting his hands flat against her belly, he drew her back so she fit snug against his chest. He planned to ask her to marry him when all of this was settled, but it may never be settled, and he didn't want her to have any doubt about his feelings for her, or the integral part she played in his life. If something were to happen to them, she needed to know exactly how he felt about her.

This place wouldn't be romantic, and he didn't have a ring, but he would figure something out that would make it special for her.

"Gather what you need," Daniel said to Max.

Max retreated back into the safe house. Aria opened her mouth to say something then closed it again. They waited until Max returned with a full quiver of arrows and a bow slung over his shoulder before heading outside, leaving the humans from the safe house behind.

"Braith," Aria said and winced as if the name had torn her open anew.

Max steadied her when she briefly swayed on her feet. William resisted knocking her hand away when it rested over her heart again. For as long as he lived, he would never forget the image of his sister trying to tear her heart from her chest.

"Someone must stay with him," she managed to croak out.

"I will," Max offered.

William's eyebrows shot up at this statement. They definitely got along better than they had in the beginning, but Max and Braith had never been close.

"You will need help," Aria said. "Just in case."

"You know how much I love a good fight, but I will stay with him too," Timber offered. "Daniel and his brain will be needed here, to help guide and lead the humans."

Daniel planted his staff into the ground and leaned against it. "Everyone wants me for my brains. What about my beauty?"

"Get better looking," William said to him, and Daniel's smile grew.

Aria smiled wider than he'd seen in over a week. He didn't know what Max had done to her last night, but he almost hugged the guy. For the first time, he had hope that maybe his sister would get through all of this and be okay, even if Braith didn't come back.

Then his gaze fell to Tempest and his hope deflated. No, Aria may be showing signs of life because she loved them all, but no one came back from that kind of loss. No matter how much he loved everyone gathered around him, he could not continue on without Tempest. He pulled her closer against him, a possessive rumble working its way through his chest as he kissed her temple. She turned to look at him, her doe eyes full of understanding as she rested her hand against his cheek.

Aria turned to Xavier. "I know you won't want to stay with Braith—"

"I am not going with them to get Jack, Aria."

Daniel didn't look at all stunned by Xavier's words, but Aria's mouth dropped. "You must," she said.

"They can detect someone else's passing through the forest and know when someone is closing in on them. They read these woods better than I read the history scrolls. My duty is to you first."

"And to Braith," she protested.

Xavier clasped his hands before him. "No, it is to *you*. Braith knows that. I am to guard you, to defend *you* with my life. It is what I have *chosen* to do until the day I die."

"But Braith will need a vampire to watch over him too."

"There is nothing one vampire can do against Sabine's troops that the humans can't do."

"They can't carry him," she protested.

"Timber can."

"We've discussed it already and it has been decided," Daniel said before Aria could argue with them further.

"What if I asked you to go?" Aria inquired of Xavier.

"You could command me to go and I would not. You are the one I protect. I couldn't come with you when you left the cave before, but I will not leave you now," Xavier replied.

"We'll be fine," Daniel said. "Xavier is right. We know these woods better than anyone, and it's time for us to get going. We're wasting time discussing this. Hopefully, I'll be back with Jack by sundown tomorrow."

William glanced between them and then to Xavier and Aria. The last thing he wanted was to leave Aria alone. She had Xavier here to watch over her, but she could decide to do something crazy in a split second. However, he didn't want his brother and his friends out there alone.

Aria's been good so far.

"I'll go with them," William said and Tempest stiffened in his arms.

"Then I'm coming with you," Tempest said.

"We'll move faster if it's just us. We have more knowledge of the woods," William said gently. "And I will move faster knowing you are safe here."

"If I can climb a mountain in a blizzard, I can find my way through these woods. I'm not staying here without you. You can't expect me to when you wouldn't."

She had him there, but the idea of her in those woods again made him consider changing his mind about offering to go with them.

"You both forget you were once human too, and would have felt secure doing this without a vampire as added protection," Daniel said and looked sternly between him and Aria.

With that look on his face and his mouth curved into a disapproving line, he looked so much like their father that William heard the, *I'm so disappointed in you,* in his head without Daniel having to say it. Aria must have felt the same way as she bowed her head and folded her hands before her.

"Sorry," she and William muttered at the same time.

Daniel gave a brisk nod before turning to William. "Unless you're willing to stay with Braith also, then it's best you stay here." He gave a pointed look at Aria before continuing. "They need your skill with a bow here. We need as many vampires as we can get on this side of the palace walls, and Jack will want you here."

William had to agree that Jack *would* want him here. They'd been friendly when Jack had been in the forest, pretending to be a rebel, before Jack had actually *become* one, but after his father had died, the two of them had become much closer. During the time after his death, they'd leaned on each other, traveled together and fought together. Jack trusted his opinion as much as William trusted Jack's. William knew being king was not a role Jack wanted. He would do well with it as he was kind, fair, and likeable, but Jack would chafe against the bonds being king would put him in. He would look to his friends for advice and to help keep him sane.

"You're right," William finally agreed, and the rigid set of Daniel's shoulders eased.

"Good, we'll see you soon," Daniel said briskly.

They said good-bye to everyone before disappearing into the woods as if they'd never been there to begin with. The only sign of their passing was the still shaking pine needles, which were barely noticeable to the naked eye.

"We have to notify the palace about Sabine's impending attack," Aria said.

"How?" William inquired.

"We'll fire an arrow at them," Aria said and walked back toward the barn.

"Is she kidding?" Tempest asked.

"No, she's not," William replied.

CHAPTER 23

Aria

Aria drove the head of her arrow through the note she'd written onto a piece of white shirt. They'd torn the shirt into sections of rags. It was the best they could do as all of Daniel's sketchpads were in the palace and paper wasn't exactly the easiest thing to come across in the forest unless they made it themselves. Since she had no idea how to do that, they'd sacrificed a shirt.

She'd carefully folded the clothing into something resembling an envelope and written Melinda's name on it with some coal dust they'd scrounged from one of the nearby caves. She was counting on Ashby and Melinda having made it safely back to the palace. On the cloth, she'd written a simple message: *Attack coming to you soon from confirmed Sab. Help comes end of week, A.*

She would have said less in the note, in case someone got ahold of it, read it, and later turned to Sabine's side. However, she had to give Melinda and the others some hope that, if they held their ground, they would have help. If they didn't have hope, they may fall to Sabine before Aria could ever do anything to help them. She also had to let them know exactly who they would be dealing with.

Beside her, William stabbed an arrow through another piece of cloth. They'd written three identical messages, one each to Melinda, Ashby, and Gideon. Hopefully at least one of the messages would be taken to the rightful addressee, and not taken as a sign of war and destroyed immediately.

Lifting a rock, she filed down the lethal point of the arrowhead. It would not fly as true, but it wouldn't accidentally kill a bystander on the other side of the wall either. Beside her, William did the same as she prepped the note meant for Gideon.

Aria slipped from the shadows of the home they'd been hiding behind. It was situated about a hundred feet outside of the palace walls. She'd never seen the town so calm before; the stillness unnerved her almost as much as the hundreds of troops spread out across the top of the wall. However, the sight of all those men and women standing guard also heartened her. If the town was empty and the guards were more than tripled on the wall, Ashby and Melinda had definitely made it back with word of what had happened to all of them.

Aria steadied her hand as she aimed her arrow over the wall. With a twang, she released her bowstring and let it fly.

Shouts rose from the wall as the arrow cleared over the top of it. Bows spun in their direction, but she and William had already released the next two arrows and were fading into the shadows when arrows from the wall thudded into the ground where they'd been standing.

Aria pushed back the hood on her cloak and listened as more shouts echoed from the wall, but the drawbridge did not come down and the gates didn't open. *Good.* She needed those within the palace to be overly cautious right now, and not looking to charge into a war when they didn't know what awaited them.

Xavier and Tempest slipped from the shadows to join her and Willian as they gathered their things and left the town.

***

Melinda

"Milady."

Melinda lifted her head to stare at the young king's man hovering in the doorway of the meeting room she sat in with the members of The Council. They hadn't told The Council about Braith, but they all knew an attack was most likely imminent and from whom. There had been no point in trying to hide it. If The Council members ever saw that woman, they would know of her power and be enraged over not being informed about the force of the threat. They may mutiny, and she couldn't risk that happening.

The look on the man's face had Melinda rising from her chair. "What is it?" she demanded.

"Someone fired three arrows over the wall," the man replied.

Ashby rose beside her, his fingers resting on the table as he leaned forward. "Only three?"

"Yes and that is not the weirdest part."

"What is?" Melinda asked.

The man approached the table with an arrow in hand. He extended it to her. Melinda took the arrow, turning it over in her hands as she studied the blunted end and the piece of cloth stuck to it with her name written on it. *Aria*. It had to be.

She tugged the cloth free and read the simple note scrawled on it before passing it to Ashby. She stood for a minute, digesting the words on the note. Aria had confirmed it was Sabine who would be coming after them, which meant there really was a chance Braith could rise again. Hope leapt in her chest, but she shoved it back. There was too much to do now to count on Braith rising again in time, or at all.

"You said there were three. Where are the other two arrows?" she asked the man.

"We believed it was an attack. The other two were trampled before we could get to them."

"Were there notes attached to them too?"

"I believe so, milady."

She had no doubt the other two notes had been addressed to someone else in this room, most likely Ashby and Gideon, if they both hadn't also been addressed to her.

"What does it say?" Calista demanded and rose from her seat as Gideon read the message. Her close-cropped black hair emphasized her beautiful features and mocha skin. Her brown eyes pinned Gideon as he handed the cloth over to her.

Gideon turned toward the king's man. "Have more guards put on the wall. Tell them an attack is coming soon and to be prepared."

"Yes, sir," the king's man said and left the room.

"A?" Saul, another member of The Council, inquired as he stared at the note.

"Aria," Melinda replied. "She's letting us know they're gathering troops on the other side and to hold the wall until they're ready to make a move to help us."

"Then we will do just that," Calista said firmly.

"Why has Braith not returned here, and why didn't he send the note?" Saul demanded, his gray eyes surveying her.

"We all know Aria is far better with a bow and arrow than Braith, so of course she sent the notes," Gideon lied with ease as he strolled around the table. "We have to make sure we are completely ready for this threat. We must go out and be with the residents now, assure them we have this under control and that we will win this fight. If they're fearful, it will make them weak and in turn make us all weak. We will bolster their confidence!"

Melinda stared after him as he exited the room with those words floating almost cheerfully behind him.

"What about the other two arrows? What if those notes said something more?" Adam, another member of The Council, inquired.

"There is nothing we can do about that, but there is something we can do about this," Melinda replied. "Gideon is right. We have to get out and assure everyone that this threat will be handled. Let's go."

Ashby slipped his arm through hers and led her out of the room. Gideon was at the end of the hall waiting for them. "If Braith was awake, she would have signed it B, or he would have written the note," Gideon said when they joined him.

"I know," Melinda replied, "but Aria has warned us, and we will be prepared. I have a feeling Jack will be there for this battle. He is liked enough that everyone will follow him."

"He hasn't been here in over a year," Gideon reminded her.

"He'll return and prove he'll fight for them. It will mean something to them," Ashby said.

"I hope you're right," Gideon said and turned away. "None of us will survive if you're wrong."

***

Daniel

They had about ten more miles to cover when the sun dipped behind the trees. Daniel stopped to wipe the sweat from his brow, cursing the short days even as his fingers itched to paint the pinks, reds, and oranges spreading across the blue sky and illuminating the mountains.

It would be best to take a break now, drink some water, and hunt for their dinner while there was still enough daylight left to do so. They continued on for a half a mile before coming across a set of caves and slipping inside. Daniel rushed through the twisting tunnels winding deeper into the earth, until he was sure they were far enough away from the outside that it would be safe to build a fire.

Timber worked on gathering the wood while Max went out to hunt for their dinner. Daniel ignored the grumbling of his belly as he set up two sticks beside the firewood to hold the spit and started a small fire. Max returned with a rabbit and sat to skin it. The meat wouldn't go far between the three of them, but it was something, and he'd definitely done with far less in his lifetime.

When he was done preparing the rabbit, Max stuck another stick through it and set it over the fire. "We should make it to Jack tonight," Max said as he turned the spit.

"I hope so," Timber muttered as he eyed the rabbit with a ravenous gleam in his eyes.

The scent of the cooking rabbit caused Daniel's stomach to rumble again as he hungrily watched its meat brown. Finally, Max deemed the rabbit done and pulled it from the flames. They split the meat between them, giving Timber a slightly larger portion. When he was done eating, Daniel licked the juices from his fingers before rising.

He studied the walls surrounding them; this hadn't been one of the caves they'd resided in over the years. He was sure he'd probably been inside here a time or two, but he'd designed no traps or gates within these tunnels and it wasn't as secure as some of the other caves. The sooner they were out of here, the happier he would be.

When Max and Timber finished eating and rose to their feet, Daniel kicked the fire out before leading the way back through the dark tunnels to the night that had descended while they'd been eating.

Stepping out of the cave, he tilted his head to the sky as the first star blinked to life. The smallest crinkle of a leaf whipped his head around as a young woman darted around a tree and raced toward them with the ease of someone who knew these woods well. Her eyes widened when she spotted them and ran over the weapons they carried, marking them as most likely human instead of vampire. She didn't slow her frantic rush toward them.

She all but barreled into Max, knocking him back a step as she lowered her shoulder and sprinted into the cave. "They're coming!" she panted over her shoulder at them.

"Who?" Max demanded as she fled down the tunnel.

"Vampires."

Daniel barely heard the word before the woman vanished into the cave. He tore his attention away from her to search the woods, but he didn't see or hear anything unusual out there. Then, the scent of pine reached him and a stick cracked loudly. She was right, something was coming, and judging by the scent and sound, there were more than a few somethings. They couldn't risk making a stand against numbers that could more than double their own.

Daniel didn't wait to see what would emerge from the forest. He turned and fled into the cave behind the woman. From up ahead, he heard her curse and the clattering of sticks as she ran into the remains of their fire.

CHAPTER 24

Max

From behind them, the skittering of rocks across rocks resonated through the cave. Max kept his breathing and steps as quiet as possible while they felt their way steadily on through the darkness blanketing them. They'd caught up with the girl. The only reason he knew that was because he'd felt the brush of her breasts against his arm when she'd stepped into him a few hundred feet back.

No light pierced this deep into the caves, and to start a torch may be guaranteed death, but to continue blindly feeling their way along could also get them killed or, at the very least, lost. His heart pounded in his chest as he tried not to think about the possibility there might be a sudden drop off somewhere ahead. The cool rocks were rough beneath his fingers as he felt along their surface. He edged his foot cautiously forward as he felt ahead of him in the hopes he would feel a drop off before plummeting to his death.

Sweat beaded his brow, but he kept himself outwardly as composed as possible. Years of training had taught him that remaining calm was the only way to survive, while inwardly he fought the instinct to run. Death lay in running blindly ahead.

The girl's small hand touched his forearm when she leaned into him. The warmth of her breath tickled his ear and neck when she spoke, "This way."

She gave a subtle tug on his hand. He grasped hold of Daniel on his right before seizing Timber before him. It was only their shallow breaths and their body heat that let him know where they were.

They followed his movement down a side tunnel. After a hundred feet, Max couldn't walk straight anymore and had to turn sideways in order to continue. Never one for claustrophobia, he couldn't help but feel a little squished as the jagged rocks scraped against his chest and back. He had no idea how Timber was making it through this crevice without becoming wedged between the walls, but the heat of his friend's arm remained against his side. Daniel brought up the rear of the pack.

Not being able to see the rock brushing against his nose only made him want to run more. The blood rushed through his ears as he strained to hear anything of their hunters over his heartbeat, but the cave they'd left behind remained undisturbed.

Then, the walls gave way and a rush of cool, fresh air wafted around him. Max inhaled a gulping breath when he was able to walk straight again. Specks of light filtered through here and there, illuminating the walls around him and the woman before him.

Tipping his head back, he realized they had left the caves behind and were now in a hollow beneath the earth. Massive tree roots intertwined through the ground above them, holding the trees up despite the lack of dirt beneath them, but it was only a matter of time before nature took over and the trees lost their battle for life.

Glancing behind him, he strained to hear any sign of pursuit, but slipping into that narrow passageway seemed to have thrown the vamps off their trail. The girl continued onward, leading them further beneath more tree roots until they arrived at a rounded hollow created by water that had worn away the dirt over the years. It only went three feet beneath the earth before dead-ending.

She crept to the end and turned to settle in the shadows. Max frowned as he searched their surroundings. He ran his hands over the cool dirt, inhaling its rich scent as he sought some other way out, but he found nothing within the roots and earth surrounding him.

Kneeling beside the girl, he hissed in her ear, "It's a dead end."

In the light filtering through the roots, her cerulean blue eyes stood out starkly against her pale skin and black hair. "I know," she whispered.

"Why would you bring us into a dead end?" he demanded as Timber and Daniel crept closer.

"Because the cave dead-ends too, or at least the direction we were going dead-ends," she replied. "At least here we will hear and see them coming. We will be able to attack them before they can enter here and we can climb out through the roots if we must. Besides, the chances of them finding the crevice to lead them here are slim to none. I've hidden here before."

Max's teeth ground together. If she was telling the truth, she'd been right to bring them here. *If?* He saw no reason why she would lie to him, but he hadn't lived this long by not being cautious.

Daniel stepped forward and craned his neck to peer up at the thick roots twining down from above. "We can make it through them if we must," he agreed. "Timber, come with me. We'll listen for the vampires if they come this way. Max stay here and watch above."

Daniel and Timber cautiously crept back across the cavern beneath the roots and to the jagged crevice in the wall. They took a position along the sides of the rock walls to wait for any possible attack.

ERICA STEVENS

"What are you doing here?" the girl inquired, drawing Max's attention back to her.

She'd pulled her legs up against her chest and hugged them to her slim frame. He guessed her to be no more than five feet tall. She was delicate looking with her slender hands, a ski-slope nose, and pouty lips. When she turned to face him completely, he saw a scar running down the right side of her face, but he couldn't see the extent of it through the dark.

"We are meeting with some friends," he replied. "What are you doing here?"

She shrugged and rested her chin on her knees. "I live here."

"In this cave?"

"Sometimes. Sometimes I live in the forest."

"Who do you live with?"

"Friends."

Her words made him take a closer look at her. She knew the caves well. She was elusive and had been nearly silent when she'd run at them from the woods. "You were a rebel," he guessed.

"Aren't we all a little bit of a rebel?"

He couldn't stop himself from smiling at her. "Some are. Some are simply surviving."

"And which are you?" she inquired.

"I've rebelled every step of the way."

"There's something coming again with the vampires. Something's not right. That's why they chased me in here. They're hunting humans again."

"I know. We're preparing for it."

Her head tilted as she studied him, seeming to try to decide if she could trust him or not. He glanced toward Daniel, knowing that he could gain the woman's trust by revealing who Daniel was, but he wasn't certain if he could trust *her* with the

204

knowledge yet. She had been fleeing from the vamps, but he wasn't taking any chances with his best friend's life.

"Have you been to one of the new locations?" she inquired nonchalantly.

Max's eyes slid back to her. "Yes. Have you?"

Her eyes ran over him again. "Perhaps."

Smart, cautious girl.

"Then you will know how much airier they are than these caves," he replied. Her lips clamped together. Max watched her closely but no emotion played over her pretty, dirt-streaked face.

"Very airy," she said and turned away from him.

Were they both playing with each other, or had she really not been to one of the safe houses?

Before he could try and figure out the answer to that question, the earth around them began to shake. Bits of dirt and debris rained down from above. Darkness and moonlight flickered through the holes in the roots when figures moved over them from above. The jingle of saddles drifted through the air as horse's hooves thudded over the ground.

Max snatched hold of the girl's arm, holding her back when she craned her head to peer up. She shot him an irritated look and tried to jerk her arm free, but he kept hold of her. He couldn't take the risk of her accidentally giving away their location. Beneath his hand, her wiry muscles bunched and flexed, but she remained unmoving.

He held his breath as more dirt fell through the holes and the ground around them vibrated with every step the horse's took. Across the way, Daniel and Timber flattened themselves against the rock wall and watched as shadows danced over the holes in the trees above them.

Then, light slid back through the holes as the horses rode on. "The vampires after you, were they on horseback?" Max inquired of the girl when he was certain it was safe to talk again.

"No," she whispered.

He looked across the way to Timber and Daniel. They wouldn't be able to move on now, not until they had an idea of where the vamps who had chased them in here were.

"There have been a lot of vampires in this area recently. Far more than usual," she said.

Max looked back to her. "Do you know why?"

"No."

They were close to the cave where they had left Jack and Braith. Had the vampires realized Braith was somewhere in the area and were searching for him? The possibility chilled him. They had to get out of here and get to Jack as soon as they could—if it wasn't already too late for Jack, Braith, and Hannah.

***

Jack

Jack let the blood from the coyote he'd caught drip into Braith's mouth, which he'd propped open for this purpose. To him, it was such a morbid thing to do, yet everyday he caught more animals and brought them to his brother. He was feeding him more than Braith would have required if he were still alive, but he figured it took a lot to come back from the dead.

He had to leave the caves to hunt the animals now as the ones within had either already been captured or they'd fled. He hated going above and taking the risk of exposing them, but there was no other choice.

As he fed Braith the blood, he studied his brother. Despite the passing of time, Braith looked no different than he had over a week ago. His body wasn't decomposing as their father's had, or as any other normal vampire would be by now. His skin was still as pale as snow and his lips colorless, but they were the same hue they'd been when he'd first died. Jack didn't know if Braith's eyes were still cloudy; he'd finally gotten them to stay closed. He couldn't bring himself to look into their unseeing depths anymore.

Maybe this lack of decomposition would happen with every vampire who died and was given blood afterward, but he doubted it. This was something more than normal; he just wasn't sure what yet, and he refused to get his hopes up.

Jack didn't like doing this, but he wouldn't stop until he knew for certain if Braith would rise again or not. Draining the last drop from the animal, he rose back to his feet.

Hannah watched him as he walked across the cavern and into one of the tunnels. She remained behind when he opened the gate and returned to the surface with the animal carcass. Running through the woods, he traveled a mile before discarding the remains. His gaze lifted to the sky and the fading stars as the night crept toward dawn. The fresh air felt good against his skin, but he couldn't remain here.

Turning away, he sped back to the dank tunnels and plunged inside, eager to return to Hannah and assure himself she was safe. If he never set foot in a cave again for the rest of his life when this was over, he would be perfectly content with that. He'd done fine amongst these caves when he'd been a renegade from his father's rule. Now, he despised every dark turn, mineral scent, and rock in the damn thing.

He opened the gate again and closed it behind him before rejoining Hannah in the main cavern. As the days wore on, her skin became paler, more like the ivory complexion it had been when he'd first met her, and less of the golden hue it had become since she'd started venturing into the sun.

She'd also taken to staying further and further away from Braith's body. She didn't complain about their conditions or their current situation, but he could tell that it wore on her. He'd promised her a better life, and so far, he was failing her. She'd been kept away from the sun that would destroy her without his blood for most of her life. She'd finally found a measure of freedom, and now she was being locked away again.

Walking across the cavern, he wrapped his arms around her waist and lifted her into his arms. She kissed his neck as he carried her up the rocks to one of the tunnels above. "We'll leave here soon," he promised her.

"Will we be able to?" she asked. "We can't leave Braith here, and it seems nothing is safe anymore."

"Nothing is right now, but it will be again," he promised.

She rested her hand against his cheek. He found himself mesmerized by her jade eyes as she studied him. "If it's not, I want you to know these months with you have been the best of my life."

"There *will* be many more," he grated through his teeth, refusing to think of the possibility that there may not be much time left for them.

She smiled, but it didn't reach her eyes. "There will be."

He placed her on the thick furs and blankets he'd set out as bedding for them. Kicking off his shoes, he crawled onto the furs to join her. He'd gotten little sleep over the past week and would get little again now, but she had to rest and she was unable to do so without him beside her.

Running his hands over her back, he massaged the tight muscles he uncovered there until he worked them loose and she released a blissful sigh. Jack brushed her silken hair back from her neck to expose the bite marks he'd left on her this morning. A thrill of possession went through him as he pulled her closer against his chest.

She was settling against him when he heard the faintest click from one of the tunnels below. He rolled Hannah to the side before leaping to his feet. Snatching two of the stakes from the supply he kept stashed near their bedding, he hurried to the end of the tunnel and looked out on the cavern below him. From here he couldn't see Braith's body, but he had a good view of the rest of the cavern. Nothing moved and the only sound he heard was the crackling fire on the torch he'd left below.

"Stay here," he said to Hannah sharply when she came up behind him.

"Jack…"

He didn't wait to hear what she had to say as he rested his hand on the rock closest to him and leapt over it. He scurried over and around the rocks as he made his way steadily downward, his gaze constantly darting over the cave around him while he listened for another sound. Moving around another set of rocks, he spotted Braith where he had left him.

Another sound brought his attention to the tunnel beyond Braith, the one *he* had just used to return to the caves. Something clicked before scraping across rock. Jack's lips skimmed back to reveal his fangs as he made his way toward the tunnel.

His gaze went to where Hannah was making her way toward him. He held his hand up and shook his head at her. *Stay,* he mouthed and she glared at him.

Poking his head around the corner and into the tunnel, he listened for more noise. Nothing sounded within the shadows, but he could feel something in the darkness, waiting for him. He glanced back at Hannah to make sure she remained a safe distance from the tunnel.

He wouldn't allow anything to happen to her. He didn't care who, or how many beings he had to destroy to keep her safe, he would do it. Ducking around the corner, he steadily crept toward the closed gate. Little light penetrated this area, but he didn't return for the torch, it would only give him away to whoever remained hidden beyond the gate.

Had he missed something when he'd gone above again? Had there been a spy somewhere that he hadn't seen or scented? It would be possible if they were good and stayed downwind of him, but he'd been so careful with every move he'd made in and out of these caves.

Jack reached the bend in the tunnel. Pressing his back against the wall, he slid down until he was sitting on his haunches. Another click caused him to freeze as he strained to hear anything more.

Have the others returned? Even as he thought it, he knew they hadn't. They would have opened the gate and come in.

No, it was not his friends in the shadows beyond, hunting them.

He poked his head around the corner, careful to expose as little of himself as he could to any arrows that might come his way.

He froze, and his hands tightened on the stakes when he saw what waited for him there.

CHAPTER 25

Max

Daniel slept with his chin on his chest while Timber kept watch over the crevice. Beside Max, the girl had fallen asleep an hour ago. Her knees were against her chest as she slept with her back to the wall. Many rebels slept with their backs to a wall, but he'd never seen any who slept in a ball before. She was tiny enough as it was. This position made her appear like a fox trying to hide from a coyote.

In her hands, she clenched a small knife before her nose. He knew it had to be a weapon she slept with often if she felt comfortable enough not to accidentally stab herself with it in her sleep. In the early morning sun filtering through the roots, he could see that the scar on her face started at her hairline above her right eye. It trailed all the way down the center of her right cheek to curve around to the middle of her chin before stopping.

The scar was white in color and he saw no evidence of stitches on her skin. The knife she held had not created it. She would have woken long before she could have cut herself like that, but a blade had left the mark upon her.

Max's hands balled at his sides as the desire to destroy whoever had done that to her slid through him. *No* one should ever be abused in such a way.

The scar could not deter from her prettiness though. His fingers itched to brush back the black hair falling around her face, but he kept himself restrained from touching her. It had taken hours of her eyes falling closed then opening again to stare at him warily before sleep had finally succeeded in dragging her under. If he touched her while she slept and woke her, she might stab him, and she would never come close to him again. For some reason, he wanted her to trust him, even if he didn't entirely trust *her*.

Across the way, Timber shifted and sat with his back against the wall. Sleep tugged at Max's eyelids, but he wouldn't give into it, not until she woke again. He had to guard over her.

The girl never moved, but he sensed her eyes on him. He turned his head to find her watching him as one would watch a wolf circling them. She kept her back pinned against the wall when she pushed herself into a sitting position. Anger filled her eyes, but he had a feeling she was angrier at herself for falling asleep than she was with him.

She slipped the knife into her ankle holster and tugged her pants back into place over the weapon. "Have you heard anything from them?" she whispered.

"Nothing," he replied.

"We can't move until we know they're gone."

"We may not have a choice."

She scowled at him. The expression pulled on her scar, causing it to become whiter against her flesh. She looked to be about his age. Though the knowledge in her eyes gave her an air of someone far beyond her early twenties.

"I don't like it either," he said to her.

They had to get to Jack *soon*, hiding in the shadows of a cave had never been part of the plan. Every passing day was one day closer to when they would have to call all those they'd been gathering to move against Sabine. They couldn't delay their plan for more than a day, maybe two. The people and vampires they'd recruited would get nervous if they did, and the fear within the palace would grow. Aria would have to move without Jack; she would have no choice but to go on without him.

No, they had to get out of here, preferably today. Max's head tipped back as he examined the roots above his head snaking through the earth to create a spotty dome above. Lowering his head, he found her gaze still on him.

"I'm Max," he said and extended his hand to her. "The tall guy over there is Timber and the one sleeping is Daniel."

"The queen's brother is named Daniel, and from what I've heard, he has a friend named Max."

Max kept his hand extended to her. "Hmm," he replied.

Her gaze went to Daniel, and her head tilted as she studied him before she looked to Max again. "He does look a little familiar, but then it's been a while since I saw the queen's brother, and it was only briefly."

Another minute ticked by before she extended her hand toward him. The sleeve of her shirt pulled slightly back to reveal the scars marring her wrist, scars he knew well. She jerked her hand back before he could take hold of it. Tugging at the sleeves of her shirt, she pulled it back into place while she glowered at him.

Max sat back on his heels as she lifted her chin. He didn't know what to make of this woman, but beneath her obstinate stare, he sensed her vulnerability. Her eyes followed his movements when he grasped the edge of his shirtsleeve. For the first time since he'd been freed of the palace, he willingly pulled his shirt back to reveal the bite marks and burns marring his flesh.

A muscle twitched in the corner of her eye as she gazed at his scars before looking back to where Timber and Daniel were now watching them both. "My name is Maeve," she said without glancing at him again.

Max settled his sleeve back into place and leaned against the dirt wall. "It's a pleasure to meet you, Maeve."

When those entrancing blue eyes again met his, he realized he'd actually meant it. Since his time as a blood slave, there were few people in this world he wanted to meet. He never knew who to trust, but he was glad this girl had stumbled across them.

His attention was pulled away from her when shadows danced across the holes in the roots once more, blocking the flow of light into their small cavern as someone passed above. Max held his breath when one of the figures walking above stopped directly over their small cavern.

***

Melinda

"I don't like how quiet it's been," Melinda said as she surveyed the empty town sprawled out before them from the top of the wall. "When will she make her move?"

"Soon, but she may still be looking for Braith," Ashby said from beside her.

Gideon grunted in response as a cat ran out from between two of the homes and into the woods. A scrap of garbage, caught up in the wind, danced down the street before going still.

They'd managed to evacuate some of the surrounding towns; unfortunately, they'd also uncovered a few towns like William had discovered when he'd been hunting for Kane. The vampires in the town, who weren't killed outright, had been locked into cells where they'd been starved until they'd become nothing but mindless monsters who were incapable of being saved and had to be put down.

There were no signs of any humans in the towns. The bodies of the vampire children the king's guard discovered had left them with a thirst for revenge against those who had killed the children.

Unfortunately, they didn't know where Sabine's vampires were, as they'd shown no sign of themselves in the two days since Aria's message had sailed over the wall. There were no nearby towns for Sabine to go through and rampage anymore. It was only a matter of time before the woman made it here.

"She's going to eventually give up her search for him and come for us," Gideon said. "Probably sooner rather than later. We're still weakened without him and she knows it. Now is the prime time for her to pounce."

Melinda's hand instinctively fell to her belly at his words. It was still too soon for her to be showing, but every day she fell deeper in love with the child growing within her, and she would do everything she could to keep it safe. Catching her protective movement, Ashby rested his hand over the top of hers.

"We will get through this," he vowed.

Gideon glanced between them before his gaze fell to her stomach. "Congratulations."

"I bet that hurt, didn't it?" Ashby asked.

Gideon actually chuckled. "A little."

A flash of movement drew Melinda's attention back to the street. She tensed, her fangs tingling as she watched shadows slipping through the trees.

"I don't think that's the cavalry," Ashby said.

"Our quiet is about to end," Gideon said.

A rock lodged in her throat as she watched the vampires cloaked in brown slipping from the trees. They moved with the determined step of those who believed they had a right to be here and believed they couldn't lose.

"What if she's found Braith?" Melinda whispered.

"The men and women gathered within here have all seen, or at least heard, what she's done to those other towns. They will fight her no matter what," Gideon replied with far more confidence than she felt right now.

Melinda tried to believe him. However, the vamps here may not like what had been done to those towns, they may resist Sabine, but *no* one wanted to die. When they got a sense of Sabine's power, they may well think they had no chance of defeating her.

All around the wall, the king's guard raised their bows in preparation of a fight, but the vamps entering the town stopped before they could be within easy striking range of the walls. The rock in her throat grew into a boulder as the intruders split to each side of the road in one fluid motion.

"Well trained," Ashby murmured.

"Ours are better trained," Gideon replied.

From the edge of the forest, Melinda watched as the striking woman they'd seen once before, stepped out of the woods to walk through the vampires who had split apart to create an aisle for her. Her vivid red cloak was as bright as blood on snow against the gray, overcast day as she moved toward them.

Gideon's nostrils flared. "Power," he said.

"A lot of it," Melinda replied. "Enough that those in here may follow her if they think we will lose."

"We need Braith."

"In case you forgot, there is a bit of a problem with that right now," Ashby said.

Gideon cast him a scathing look. "Then we will hold her off until the problem is resolved."

"I'm sure it's not all that easy to pull a Lazarus, and it might have been as long as a month before Atticus rose again!" Ashby retorted.

"Stop it!" Melinda interrupted harshly. "There is nothing we can do but defend ourselves and those fighting with us. Fighting with each other is not going to help! Braith has a bloodlink. He will rise sooner than Atticus did. Aria is plotting something. We have help out there, and Jack will come. All we have to do is hold them off until they are ready to make their move."

"How do you know Braith will rise sooner?" Gideon inquired.

Melinda bit her bottom lip before turning to face him. "He stayed alive with an arrow through his heart for *hours*, and it was for Aria. Because of her blood within him making him stronger and their link, he'll come back earlier than Atticus did and he'll do it *for her*. If he doesn't, we are all doomed."

Sabine stopped at the edge of her followers and lifted her hands into the air to command everyone's attention. All around Melinda, a ripple of shock ran through the guards on the wall as Sabine's gesture held each of them riveted upon her. Even from this distance, the pull of the woman's power could not be denied.

"I am not here to fight!" Sabine called in a clear, girlish voice that floated to the residents gathering nervously near the gates to hear what was about to unfold. "I am your rightful queen! Your *true* ruler. I am of the royal line, older than your king, or I should say, your *ex*-king. I'm also more powerful as I'm sure you can tell."

More murmurs went through the crowd; Ashby took hold of her hand, squeezing it as her skin became clammy and sweat beaded across her brow. The breeze blowing down the mountains and causing tendrils of hair to tickle her face should have cooled her. It didn't.

"I say *ex*-king because I have killed him," Sabine continued.

Melinda's heart plummeted into her shoes as cries of distress echoed throughout the town below them and sobs filled the air. The king's guard dipped their bows down, their gazes darting nervously to the three of them as the other members of The Council shoved their way through the crowd to the gates. Melinda couldn't meet The Council's gazes when they made it to the front of the crowd and stared up at them with distrust in their eyes.

"Maybe we should have told them," she whispered.

"No, we shouldn't have," Gideon said. "They have no idea when he was supposedly killed."

Gideon turned away from her and thrust his shoulders back as he faced Sabine. "Anyone can claim to have killed the king. Do you have proof of this?"

Sabine's smile grew as her eyes narrowed on Gideon. Melinda was certain he'd just signed his death certificate, but if these walls were breached, none of them would be walking out of here alive anyway.

"I do," she replied and turned away. Her blood-red, pointed nails shone in the sun when she waved her hand toward someone at the back of her following.

Melinda took an involuntary step forward to watch as the white haired vampire made his way down the street toward Sabine.

***

Aria

From her vantage point in the tree, Aria's fingers dug into the bark, tearing it away beneath her nails. Her fangs pierced her bottom lip as she leaned forward to watch Goran making his way past the rows of vampires who had spread out to allow Sabine to pass. It had been over a day since Daniel and the others had left. They should be returning tonight if all had gone well, but what if something had gone wrong?

Proof! Sabine had proof of Braith's death. How? When?

Oh, Aria knew when he'd died, she could still feel that wrenching of her soul deep within her, but when had Sabine

gotten proof of such a thing? What *was* the proof? Had Jack
and Braith been discovered?

Please no.

William rested his hand on her shoulder, drawing her back
when she perilously leaned too far over the limb. Her stomach
pressed flat against the branch, and her arms and legs were
twined securely around it as she tried to make herself as small
as possible. William clung to the branch above her, his knuckles
white from his grip. He'd always been able to move through
the trees, never with her ease, and it had never been his favorite
thing to do, but since he'd fallen over the cliff in Badwin, his
dislike of heights had grown. He'd followed her into the
branches of this tree to keep watch over the palace with her.

"Maybe you should go down," he suggested.

"I have to see," she whispered.

"It might be best if you didn't. I'll let you know."

Cold seeped through her body as her fingers dug deeper
into the bark. "I *have* to see. I'd know if she'd found him." She
turned to him, her tone more pleading than she would have
expected. "Wouldn't I?"

In his eyes, she saw the truth she felt within herself. She'd
already *known* the second Braith had left her; there was nothing
else for her to know anymore.

Terror rolled so rapidly through her mind that it caused
her head to spin, and for one disconcerting moment, she
thought she might actually fall out of the tree.

A sob lodged in her throat as Goran stopped at Sabine's
side and handed her something. Aria couldn't tear her gaze
away as Sabine turned back to the palace walls and lifted
something in the air. It took her a minute to realize that Sabine
held a brown cloak. On the back of it was the golden wolf
insignia of the king that the king's guard wore, but this one also
had a crown above the wolf's head. Aria didn't have to see it up
close to know it had belonged to Braith.

"Braith lost it in the battle when they attacked us," she murmured.

"Come on, let's get out of here," William said and tugged at her shoulder again.

She refused to move until she knew what was going to happen next. "Not yet."

"A cloak is no proof!" Gideon called from the wall.

"It is the king's cloak," Sabine said with a smirk. "I can have it brought to you if you would like."

"I can see it's the king's cloak, but it's easy enough to lose one of those in a fight or to simply leave one behind!" Gideon replied with a laugh. "I, myself, have done that a few times after spending some time with a lady!"

Beside him on the wall, the king's guard all nodded enthusiastically and a few chuckled. Aria admired Gideon's unruffled and brazen demeanor. Sabine would make him pay for it if she ever got her hands on him, but he would not back down from her, no matter what happened.

Sabine's fingers went to her lips as a smile curved them. An uneasy feeling settled in Aria's stomach. Sabine was too smug right now, too sure of herself. There was more; there had to be. She should get out of this tree, *right now*.

She found herself unable to move.

"Then I will show you more proof," Sabine said in a nearly singsong voice.

"William," Aria whispered as the hair on her arms stood up.

His hand constricted on her shoulder as Sabine turned to Goran. From within his cloak, Goran removed something, but Aria couldn't see what it was from her angle. Atop the wall, a murmur ran through the crowd as those closest to Sabine and Goran got a glimpse of what it was. More than few of the king's guard took a startled step back.

"Aria, come with me, *now*," William commanded and pulled more firmly on her shoulder.

She was unable to move even a centimeter, never mind the fifty feet or so it would take to get out of this tree. Sabine turned back to the wall, her smile so big, Aria could see the glistening points of her fangs as she lifted something into the air.

"How about his head?" Sabine taunted as she lifted a head high into the air. She had her fingers entwined into its thick black hair as she proudly displayed it for everyone to see.

Aria's vision blurred. Black hair and the open eyes of the head were all she saw before the world plummeted out from under her.

CHAPTER 26

Melinda

All around them, sobs erupted. Melinda remained unmoving as she gazed at the head in Sabine's hand.

"Holy shit," Gideon whispered from beside her.

Chaos erupted in the courtyard. Those gathered below couldn't see what Sabine held, but they had heard her proud declaration and seen the reaction of the king's guard on the wall. She could taste the metallic hint of their terror on her tongue, hear the increased pounding of all the human's hearts.

Her hands pressed against her stomach as she stared at the head swaying in the breeze. The face was distorted, the color off, but then it had been cut from his body and Braith had been dead the last time she'd seen him. She didn't want to believe it was him, but she couldn't deny what her eyes were telling her as she gawked at all of that black hair and the swollen, broad cheekbones.

"Oh no," she moaned.

Before this, there had been hope that Braith would rise again. She hadn't realized how much she'd been counting on that happening, until the shattered pieces of all that hope scattered about her feet like broken glass. Her brother was dead.

Tears burned her eyes, but she kept them suppressed. Despite this new revelation, they had to put on a brave front, had to act as if they could still defeat Sabine without their king.

His black hair glinted in the light filtering down around Sabine as she continued to hold the battered head high in the air. Melinda tore her gaze away, unable to look anymore. He hadn't known he was going to be an uncle. She choked back a sob as she wrapped her arms around her belly. Braith had sought to protect all of them, and they had all failed to protect him.

Her gaze went toward the town. "Aria," she whispered.

Odds were her sister-in-law was close by, watching to see how everything and everyone here fared. She had probably heard this, had probably *seen* this announcement.

Calista shoved her way through the dumbfounded king's guard on the wall to stand beside Gideon. "Did you know about this?" she demanded.

"How was I ever supposed to know about this?" Gideon retorted.

Calista bared her teeth at him. "Did you know Braith was dead?"

"No," Melinda said. It wasn't a lie; they hadn't known for sure. Braith had passed, they had known that, but there had still been a chance he'd return. "We didn't know."

"That means we have lost our queen too," Calista said. "She won't survive without him. The humans will panic."

"Not necessarily," Gideon replied. "Aria will hold on and do what must be done."

"Even if she doesn't, Jack is now the king. Tell that to the people in the crowd," Ashby said to Calista. "Make sure they know we still have a member of the royal line, and a rebel to lead us."

"You want me to tell them the *youngest* of the three brothers, the one who left out of here over a year ago and hasn't returned since, the one who was *never* supposed to rule is now their king?" Calista demanded. "We don't know where Jack is! She could have killed him too."

"No, she would have said that, and she would have brought his head as well," Ashby replied. "Whatever happened, Jack managed to get away. I want you to tell the crowd that and tell them the man who went against his insane, brutal father and aided the rebels, *became* a rebel and fought side by side with the humans for years, is now their king."

Her eyes narrowed on him. "The vampires will love that."

"They'll like it better than the alternative!" he spat. "You're a politician, Calista, put a *fucking* spin on it."

Melinda squeezed his hand. He was normally so calm and unruffled, but he'd been rattled by this development. Struggling to calm down, he ran his hand through his hair and tugged at the ends of it. He looked at her before lowering his hand and focusing on Calista once more.

"Every vampire in here has unfailingly followed Braith. If they think Sabine is going to let them out of here alive, they're delusional and we have to make sure they know that. We have these walls. We have the advantage right now," Ashby said more calmly.

"We will be right down to help you with everything," Melinda said.

Calista cast Ashby and Gideon a scathing look before turning away from them. Melinda watched her walk away before focusing on Gideon. "Despite what Ashby said, there is a good chance Jack is dead too if she found Braith."

"I know," Gideon replied. "But they can't know that, and unless Sabine brings out Jack's head, there's no reason for anyone here to suspect that possibility, and don't forget, there's always Aria."

"A bloodlink does not survive without their other half," Ashby replied.

"And a blood slave does not become a queen, but it happened. If anyone can pull it together to do what must be done, it is Aria. Everyone loves her. She may not remain a queen without Braith, but she will lead and they *will* follow."

"You're right," Melinda agreed.

"You two must go down and calm the crowd. They'll want to see a royal face amongst them. I will stay here to get the guards rallied and prepared for battle," Gideon said. "We will fight until the end."

Melinda placed her hand on her stomach again. She would do everything she could to keep her child safe. "We will fight until they're dead," she said and strode away from Gideon with every bit of confidence she possessed. She may not actually be a descendent of the pure vampire line, but she was a royal and she would be everything they needed her to be right now.

***

William

William caught hold of Aria's arm when she toppled from the tree. His gaze returned to the town as Sabine and her soldiers moved further down the road, spreading out through the buildings. They had to get out of this tree *now*.

Aria stirred in his grasp; she jolted when she saw her feet dangling above the earth. Then she went completely still. Her head tilted back to look at him as her feet touched down on a branch beneath her. Behind the black lenses of her glasses, her eyes burned like hot coals as they met his. William swallowed the lump in his throat at the sight of those volatile eyes.

"Let me go," she said, and he barely recognized the flatness of her voice.

"No."

"We have to get out of the tree. Let me go."

"You'll go after her."

"No, I won't."

He glanced back at the vampires coming closer and closer to them. Right now, he didn't have much of a choice. She stood below him. He couldn't get her up here to throw her over his shoulder, and even if he could, she would never allow him to carry her from the tree.

"Let me go."

"Stay with me?" He'd meant it to be an order; it came out as a question.

"I will."

He could feel the riot of her emotions as she held his gaze, but Aria had never lied to him before. He had to trust she wouldn't start now. However, he wasn't entirely sure about anything she would do from here on out. She'd been broken again. There was only so much a battered spirit could take before it fell apart completely, and she was on the edge, if she hadn't already been pushed over.

Opening his hand, he released her shirt. The second he let her go, she scurried down the tree. Forgetting all about the fact that, even if the fall didn't kill him, it would hurt like hell, he followed her down the tree so fast he was on her heels when they both hit the ground. He lunged for her, wrapping his arms around her waist before realizing she hadn't tried to take off toward the palace.

Her lip skimmed back to reveal her fangs, and her eyes burned hotter when she turned to look at him. Tempest's brown eyes stood starkly out against the pallor of her skin when she met his gaze over the top of Aria's head. Xavier moved closer to box Aria in if necessary. Tempest and Xavier may not have seen Braith's head dangling from Sabine's hand, but they'd heard her proud declaration, and they knew Aria was a powder keg waiting to go off.

"Must go," Aria said in a clipped tone. "Now."

William reluctantly released her, took hold of Tempest's hand, and fell in beside Aria as Xavier remained close against her other side. They moved through the woods, briskly eating away the ground between them and the safe house. Aria abruptly drew up outside of the barn. Turning away, she walked deeper into the woods before sinking onto a rock out of view of any of the peepholes.

"What are you doing?" William inquired.

"I can't go in there," she murmured.

"Aria—"

"I can't go in there, not now. I'll kill them all!" Aria spat.

There it was. He'd sensed the savagery in her, sensed her unraveling, but she'd been keeping it restrained and hidden from them. Now, it was on full display.

"Death. Blood. They're the only things that will make the pain stop," she murmured.

William turned to Tempest and took hold of her shoulders. "Go inside."

"No," she said.

"I have to know you're safe. Please, go in."

"None of us are safe anymore, William. I'm not leaving any of you out here." She stepped closer to him. "Aria needs those who love her right now."

He couldn't argue with that, but how did he tell her he wanted her safe *from* Aria right now. Atticus had lost his mind and Aria was coming apart before his eyes. She was a new vampire, a turned vampire, but he didn't think it would matter. If she attacked, she would be lethal and only death would stop her.

"We sent Daniel, Max, and Timber back to that cave," Aria said. She tilted her head back to look up at him. "We sent them to their deaths."

Xavier knelt before her. "You do not know that."

"She had his head, Xavier," she whispered. "She held it so... so proudly." Her voice broke on a sob before she straightened up and dried her tears. "If it's the last thing I do, I will cut that *bitch's* head from her neck."

The unpredictable sway of emotions had William protectively stepping in front of Tempest. Xavier rested his hands over Aria's. She jerked her hands away with a hiss that caused the hair on William's nape to rise. He'd never seen her like this before, not even when her bond with Braith had first been severed had she been like this.

"Easy," Xavier murmured. "I won't touch you again, but let us be here for you."

"For me? Who am I anymore?" A strange laugh escaped her as she bowed her head and placed her hand against her forehead. "I'd really expected him to come back to me. I didn't dare to hope it was possible, but I *did* hope, more than I'd realized, and now..."

Her shoulders shook with her sobs as she released a sound that tore at his heart and reminded him of a wild animal. William stepped toward her, but she recoiled as if he were going to strike her. Her hands flew up in front of her face to ward him off.

"What am I? *Who* am I?" In the next instant, she once again stopped crying. "Sabine will *die*."

Madness, William could feel it seeping out from her as her thoughts became more jumbled and her emotions more chaotic. Xavier's head bowed; he reached for her again before lowering his hands.

Releasing Tempest, William knelt before Aria. He didn't rest his hands on hers as he wanted to, but kept his fingers on the ground before him. "You are a rebel, who became a blood slave, who became a queen. That's who you are."

Aria's fingers rubbed at her temples, her nails scratching her skin until she drew blood. William grasped her hands, ignoring her snapping fangs as he held them firmly in her lap. "I won't let you hurt yourself."

Tears spilled from her eyes again. "There is nothing left of me to hurt. Don't you understand that?"

"Yes, I do." Sitting on the rock beside her, William draped his arms around her and pulled her close.

Aria stiffened in his hold, and her tears once again ceased as her fangs sliced into her bottom lip. His heart felt as if it were being squeezed in his chest. Aria hadn't been the only one who believed Braith would come back to them. They'd all been trying to get her through the days until he returned, and now there was no more getting through, no more waiting. He was gone. It was over.

"I also understand that you want your revenge, and we will help you get it," William vowed.

"Now, I want it *now*," she said and began to laugh again.

CHAPTER 27

Max

Max's stomach rumbled as the fading daylight filtered through the roots above them. They'd remained as unmoving as possible within the hollow throughout the day. Only rising to ease their bodily needs while they patiently listened for more sounds outside.

He didn't speak with Maeve again, but when she drifted asleep a few hours later, she did so without the knife in her hand, though she remained tucked into a protective ball. She was a fellow blood slave, one who had also had it pretty bad judging by her scars and current sleeping position.

When she woke again after an hour of sleep, she blinked up at him and jerked back against the wall.

"Easy," he soothed when she glanced wildly around the hollow. "You're safe."

"I've never been safe," he thought she murmured, but couldn't be sure as she'd spoken so low. "Any hint of them?"

"No. We may be able to make a move at nightfall."

She brushed back a strand of her black hair. "Where will you go?" she inquired.

"We have a friend we must meet with."

Her eyes slid toward him. "Sounds important."

"It is, and judging by the vamps around here, we may already be too late."

"Then why not turn back?"

"There is no turning back, not for us, and not for this."

"Is this about the upcoming threat the queen has been gathering humans and vampires to defend against?"

"You know about that?" he asked.

"I know where the safe houses are, so of course I know about that. It's all anyone can talk about. That and the growing rumors of humans vanishing and vampires being destroyed in nearby towns."

"And are you planning to fight?"

"I'm always planning to fight," she replied. "It is the only way to survive."

"For a while it wasn't."

"Maybe not for you, but in these woods, we've always known we would have to return to what we once were."

"No," Max said firmly. "If we win this, there will never be the need to return to fighting. We will know freedom."

"Until the next threat."

"There will be no more."

"How can you be so certain?" she inquired.

"I have to be."

"How do you have so much faith after what you've been through?"

"Because I have faith in Braith and Aria to do what must be done."

"You know them so well then?"

"Yes."

She sighed as she drew her knees against her chest. "I hope you're right."

"I know I am. How long were you a blood slave?"

"I'd been bought two weeks before the last war," she replied. "I was freed when the mad king was killed. You?"

"About a month."

Her tiny fingers played with the stitching on the bottom of her pants. "I'll die before I ever go through something like that again, and I'll do anything to stop it from becoming a common practice once more."

"That is the way I feel. It is the way many feel, even those who were never enslaved."

She didn't speak again as the sun crept lower in the sky and neither did he. Daniel rose and walked toward them with his bow in hand. Kneeling beside Max, he lowered his bow to the ground and rested his hand on it. "I think we should go at nightfall," he said.

"What if they're waiting for us out there?" Maeve asked. "They know we have to come out at some point."

"They only know of you for certain. They won't stick around for one human," Daniel replied.

"You *think* they won't you mean."

"We have no choice," Daniel said. "We can't stay here anymore."

"We can go another day without water. They'll be more likely to move away by then."

"*We* have to go," Max said. "Staying here isn't an option for us, but we can go back through the cave. They'll never have to know where you are and we'll lead them away from you, if they're still out there."

She gave him a scathing look. "I'm not going to stay hidden in the shadows while others risk their lives."

"Well then, be prepared to climb through those roots," Daniel replied. "I'm guessing we're at least two hundred yards from the entrance to the cave. If they are still waiting around, they'll be closer to the cave entrance than us."

"You're right. We are about two hundred yards from the entrance," Maeve confirmed.

"We'll leave in an hour, before the moon can rise too high." Daniel turned and walked back across to Timber.

"I don't know what you're doing, but I'm coming with you," Maeve said.

Max was surprised to realize he wanted her to come along. He wanted to know where she was and help keep her safe, but no one else could know where Braith was, or what condition he was in. "You can't."

"I can do anything I choose to do." Her gaze slid over to Daniel before coming back to him. "I can help."

"You can't help with this. If you follow us, then know you'll be staying with me until *I* am able to leave, and I have no idea how long that could be. You will essentially be a prisoner again. None of us will allow you to be free until we're certain it won't endanger anyone else. Go back to your people, Maeve, and prepare to go to war again."

"I have no people anymore. My family is dead. They either died as blood slaves or were killed during the war. I have no one, and I'm fine with that. It makes things easier. I'm prepared for a new war, but I think I can be of more help to you."

A pang of sympathy stabbed at him. He had no blood family of his own anymore either, but Daniel, William, and Aria had always been there for him, and their father, David, had taken care of him. They had all become his family. Maeve said she was fine with having no one, but she wouldn't be trying to come with them if she really was. She put on a brave front, but he sensed her fear and vulnerability beneath it.

He hated the idea of turning her away, but countless lives depended on them now. "You can't," he said. A flinch so small he nearly missed it was the only indication his words had stung her. "I'm sorry."

She tossed her hair over her shoulder. "It doesn't matter," she replied flippantly, but she wouldn't meet his gaze again.

"Where will you go?" he asked.

"That's none of your concern."

He opened his mouth to respond, but Daniel and Timber rose across the way and Maeve hastily climbed to her feet. She didn't look back at him as she strode into the middle of the hollow to meet the others. Reluctantly, Max rose to his feet and stretched his back. The sooner they left here, the sooner he would leave her, and that was the last thing he wanted to do right now.

It couldn't be helped though. He walked over to stand beside her; she was so small her head barely reached his chest. She moved her arm away from him when he rested his hand on her elbow. "If the vampires are still out there—"

"I can take care of myself," she interrupted.

With that, she leapt up and grabbed one of the thick roots hanging over her head. She shimmied up so fast that Max barely had time to grab another root before she arrived at the top. He'd half expected her to shove her way out of one of the holes, but she waited for them to make it to the top before she rested her hands on a couple of roots and pulled them back.

"Good luck to you," she said.

He didn't have a chance to respond before she slipped through the hole. He followed behind her. The second he broke free of the hollow and set his hands on the ground, he pulled his bow from his back and nocked an arrow against it. His gaze ran over the shadowed forest surrounding them.

Tree branches clicked and swayed in the wind blowing through the woods. The scent of rain hanging heavily on the air and the clouds filling the sky alerted him there was a storm coming as Daniel came to stand beside him.

Maeve had already vanished, not even a whisper of movement revealed where she'd gone. Disappointment filled him at her departure.

***

Aria

Aria stood in the barn, listening to the rain pelting the roof. Wind howled through the rafters, slicing through the holes and cracks in the boards and blowing across her chilled skin. She sensed William's presence before he draped the cloak around her shoulders.

She almost threw it off. Her skin may be numb, but nothing could melt the ice encasing her heart and soul right now. However, after her breakdown earlier, she knew she couldn't do anything to cause him more unease so she left it on.

Act normally, or as normally as you can. Give them this much of you before it's gone.

"Thank you," she murmured and pulled it snuggly around her shoulders.

William walked around her and pinned the cloak together with her silver horse broach. Her fingers brushed over the weight of it against her throat. What would her father have done if he were in her shoes?

The answer to that came quickly to her; he would have continued on, he would have done what had to be done, even after Sabine was defeated. The death of her mother devastated him. They may not have shared the same bond she had with Braith, but their love had been deep and true. He'd continued to fight on after she'd been murdered by vampires, and he would expect her to do the same.

She'd just completely fallen apart, had felt insanity looming within her in a way she never had before, yet she'd never seen anything clearer than the pathway she saw opening before her now. This whole time she'd expected Braith to come back to her, or for her life to end, but neither of those options would be for her, not anymore.

"You should come inside," William said.

"They should be back by now, or soon," she replied. They had to come back. She couldn't have sent her brother and friends to their death. She did all of this for them, so they could lead happy and full lives, and she may have been the one who had taken that away from them.

"They could have gotten delayed by something, and this weather will certainly slow them down," William replied.

"Yes."

She hated the worry in his gaze when he surveyed her from head to toe, but she was acting as normally as she could right now. She didn't know what else to do. Didn't know how to make the emptiness in her heart stop. Didn't know how to get that image of Sabine lifting Braith's head into the air...

Her fingers clenched on the cloak as she broke the thought off. *No more!* No more could she think of that and not expect to fall apart again. Shame filled her as she recalled her incoherent babbling earlier because her mind had been firing in a million different directions at once. Death, insanity, murder, blood, desolation, agony, sorrow; the emotions had battered her so fiercely she hadn't been able to process any of them.

At least she hadn't tried to tear her heart out again. No, her heart would remain where it was. Seeing Braith's head like that had broken her again. He never should have been put on display and treated that way, and she would make Sabine pay for it, but she felt stronger now, resolved. There was much that still had to be done in this world, and she would do it.

"I think it would be best if you came down, at least to warm up a little," William said.

"My eyes," she said and her fingers went to the glasses covering them. William had told her earlier he could see the red of them through the lenses. She'd terrify everyone below if they saw her, and she wouldn't blame them if they all fled from here.

"I'm sure they're still red, but you can't see them through the glasses anymore."

"Good. I'm going to do this," she said to him. "I'm going to fight her and I'm going to win. When that is done, I am not going to give up on this world. I'll find a way to continue, somehow, without Braith. It's what my dad and Braith would want me to do."

She didn't know how she would do it, but she would find a way. When she'd first seen Braith's head, she hadn't thought she would be able to make it through the next minute. Then she'd made it through the one after that, until the minutes had become hours. One second to the next was how she would have to live from now on, while being ever vigilant that she didn't slip away into the beckoning madness.

"Aria—"

"I'm not like Atticus. Well, maybe I am a little. I want her dead, but after her death, there will be so many who will still count on me. They won't let me remain queen without Braith, and while knowing what a broken bloodlink can do to a vampire. I understand that, but I can be of help in other ways until…"

"Until what?" Xavier prompted when her voice trailed off.

"Until my time is up. I helped to start all of this, and I will see it through to the end and not just *her* end. If I die in battle against her, then so be it, but I'll do everything I can to see peace and freedom restored to everyone."

William squeezed her shoulder. "And we'll all be here to help you do that."

She turned with William to the doorway. Xavier and Tempest stood beside it. Xavier bent and pulled it open for her to descend. She hadn't been able to go back inside yet. She still wasn't sure she was ready for this, but she had to be. The humans knew what had happened at the palace earlier; there would be no keeping that revelation from them.

The door at the end of the hall was open, the people within abnormally subdued as they huddled close together.

There were well over two hundred of them in the safe house now, and none of them had any idea of what to expect anymore. Their voices stopped when she stepped inside. Aria clasped her hands before her as the others entered the room to fan out beside her.

The straggling vampires they'd gathered along the way were all hiding in one of the nearby caves. Preferring not to stay in the safe house, some of the humans were also in the caves with the vamps. The humans here were willing to work with the vampires, but they weren't willing to reveal all of their secrets by letting them know the locations of the safe houses. Aria didn't blame them. If she hadn't once been human and a rebel, she knew they wouldn't want her standing here either. Xavier and Tempest were allowed in here because the humans had no other choice in the matter.

"Your Highness, is there anything we can get for you?" a young woman inquired.

"My name is Aria." She struggled to keep the irritation from her voice as her fangs pricked and the beat of their hearts sounded like drums in her ears. The tingling in her skin now had nothing to do with the cold, and everything to do with all of the warm blood surrounding her. She didn't recall the last time she'd fed, but even if it had been an hour ago, it wouldn't have been enough to douse *this* hunger. "And no, thank you. Have the people we sent to spy on the palace returned?"

She'd been in the barn for the past hour, but before that, she'd stayed as far from the safe house as she could. The shifts of people and vampires they had keeping watch over the palace were supposed to switch; she wasn't sure if that time had come and gone already or not.

"They have, Your... Aria," a man replied.

"What did they learn?"

The man glanced nervously around the room. Her reddened eyes couldn't be seen behind the lenses anymore, but sweat beaded their brows and their hearts beat faster than normal around her.

Act the same. Be normal. They're uneasy because they think you're just learning of Braith's death. Keep it together and they will relax around you once more. Give them stability and they will continue to follow.

"The palace is under attack." The man stepped back and gestured at the large, round table in the room. "They have surrounded the walls."

Aria moved closer to discover they had created a crude drawing of the palace's walls with coal on the table. Daniel could have made it a masterpiece; this one consisted of stick figures, x's, and squiggly lines, but she understood it. She'd drawn enough plans of her own like this to be able to read this one.

"They're attacking mostly in this area." The man used a stick to point to where most of the x's were clustered by the front gate. "But they've spread out and are attacking various places along the wall."

"Looking for weaknesses in it," Aria murmured.

"I believe so," the man replied. He moved the stick to point toward more x's positioned within the crudely drawn buildings representing the town. "They have more soldiers watching their backs throughout the homes here. Our men guess there to be about a hundred of them, but they'll be able to get a better number tomorrow, if the storm clears, and once Sabine has her troops officially positioned."

"A hundred will be easy enough to take out quietly," William said. "We'll have them down and be at Sabine's back before she knows what happened."

"And Sabine, where is she?" Aria inquired.

"Here." The man moved his stick to a building near the end of the street. "It's a brick home, no trees around it, at least forty guards, and it's far enough away from the palace that she can avoid anything they might shoot at her."

"But not what we can," Aria said. "We'll take out her men and set that house on fire, flushing her out like the rat she is. Once she's out in the open, we'll have her."

"We have to get close enough to the house," William said.

Aria lifted her head to look at him. "I'll get so close I could knock on her back door."

Around her, the people nervously shuffled their feet, but grins spread across their faces as they nodded enthusiastically. A man entered into the room from the hallway leading out to the barn. "We have a problem," he said.

Aria turned toward him, her nostrils flaring at the potent aroma of fear wafting from him. "What is it?" she inquired.

"Vampires. They're in the barn, and judging by the brown cloaks on them, they're not our allies."

Aria stepped away from the table and followed him down the hall to one of the peepholes near the exit. She pressed her eye to the hole, and her hands balled at her sides when she spotted the ten vampires mulling around inside the barn.

They were probably only trying to get out of the storm, but more than a few of them were examining every inch of the building. As she watched, one knelt by the doorway in the floor.

CHAPTER 28

Daniel

Daniel's feet slipped in the wet leaves and pine needles beneath him. The rain came down so hard it didn't sink into the ground, but slid over it in torrents that poured down the embankment they were trying to scale. For every two steps forward, he took one step back. Water sluiced over his hair, pouring down his face and into his eyes. He wiped it away, but it did little good as more ran over his eyes and his hair was plastered to his skin.

They were only a mile away from the caves where they'd left Jack, yet with the way they were going, it may take them hours to get there. His soaked clothes pulled heavily on his body, weighing him down. He wouldn't be surprised if an icicle formed on his skin. No matter how badly his legs ached and shook from exertion, he continued stalwartly onward.

They didn't try to be as quiet as they normally would have been as the storm covered any noises they made and masked their smell, but it would also do the same for anyone pursuing them. However, he didn't think their enemies would be crazy enough to be out in this; no one with any sense would, unless they had to be.

Max grunted beside him as he lost his footing and fell onto the side of the embankment. He lay for a minute, panting on the ground with mud splattering his face. Daniel held out his hand to him. After a minute, Max took hold of it and climbed back to his feet.

Timber made it to the top of the embankment first, his eyes scanning the forest before he turned back to wave them onward. Daniel gritted his teeth and leapt toward the top. Timber took hold of his arm and helped to haul him the rest of the way over.

Daniel bent over, resting his hands on his knees as he inhaled gulping breaths of air and searched the forest. Water slid off his lips and into his mouth. He greedily drank it down as he tried to ease the burning in his lungs.

They desperately needed a break, but couldn't stand here; they'd freeze in the icy rain if they did. Rising, he broke into a brisk jog as he led the way through the woods. Despite the fact the rain and wind made it difficult for him to see more than ten feet ahead of him, he didn't ease his pace. They were already behind; they had to make it there tonight and get Jack back tomorrow, assuming they would still find Jack still alive and in the same cave where they'd left him.

The rain may have driven Sabine's vamps to seek shelter tonight, but there had been a fair amount of them moving around the caves they'd left behind. Had Jack and Hannah been found?

They had to have answers tonight.

With every step he took, his heart pounded more and more with excitement and dread. *Nearly there. Nearly there.*

They were almost a hundred feet from the cave when a flash of movement on his right caught his attention. Daniel spun, swinging his bow off his back and nocking an arrow against it in one swift movement. His fingers were numb, but he'd still hit his target.

He went completely still as he controlled his frantic urge to gasp for breath. The hair on his nape rose as he felt eyes on him. Someone was out there watching them, stalking them.

***

Aria

Aria stood at the bottom of the stairs, staring at the doorway above her head. William and Tempest remained unmoving beside her. Xavier stood resolutely on her other side. The vampires were still up there; she could hear them moving about the barn, their feet stomping over its surface. The lingering scent of animals in the barn and the thick wood would cover their scent, but they couldn't allow them to remain above.

She didn't think the vampires would find the door, but if they did…

She'd put an arrow straight through the heart of the first one who entered. "We'll go out the back way and circle around to the front of the barn," she said.

"Or we could wait for them to pass on," William said. "Which they'll probably do when the storm breaks."

"And if they don't? We're close enough to the palace that they could be considering using the barn as part of their base. With the storm, we can sneak up on them a lot easier. The rain and wind will mask any scent or noise we may make," Aria said. "We'll also be taking out some of Sabine's numbers."

"And if she notices them missing?" William asked.

"Do you really think she will?"

"I don't know," he reluctantly admitted.

"She knows we're still out here, she has to expect that we'll still be looking to fight her. She might even think they fled," Tempest said.

"If they were smart they would," Xavier replied.

"They would," Aria agreed. "Come on, let's get this over with."

She turned and walked back to the main room. Everyone within remained eerily silent as she strode into the center of the room. "We're going to go after them," she whispered. "We can't take the chance they'll remain after the storm. We'll take at least twenty with us."

Men and women rose to gather their weapons as they worked it out between them who would go and who would remain. Aria waited for them to decide, before striding down the back hallway, passed the rooms lining it to the door at the end of the hall. The humans who would be coming with them, followed her.

William opened the door and peered into the hallway beyond before entering it. She followed him down the dank-smelling, ten-foot long hall to the wall beyond. William's fingers searched over the wood before he pushed on something and the door swung inward to reveal the root cellar beyond.

The sharp scent of mildew and dirt wafted over her as she stepped into the abandoned cellar. The wood over her head sagged beneath the weight of the earth trying to reclaim it. She warily examined the bowing beams as she walked over to another small door, sagging on its hinges and splintering down the middle.

She waited for everyone else to fill the room. The last woman in closed the door behind her, briefly plunging them into complete darkness until Aria turned the rotten handle and cautiously pulled the door open. Rain lashed against her, stinging her face and numbing her skin as she stepped into the storm.

The wind howled through the trees. From somewhere deep in the forest, a branch cracked and plunged to the ground, taking more branches with it in a cascading, thundering crash as it fell. She wiped the water from her eyes to focus on the barn a hundred feet away from them. Behind her, the others filtered out into the storm.

She gazed over the humans and vampires surrounding her before jerking her head toward the barn. They moved silently across the muddy, slippery ground, or at least they couldn't be heard over the whipping wind and pelting rain. As Aria gripped the handle of the barn door, she held up a finger to halt everyone before putting it down and sliding the door open in one fluid motion.

She pulled her bow from her back and grabbed an arrow as five of the vamps within leapt to their feet. The other five remained asleep, for now. Shock registered on the vampire's faces before William's arrow struck the first one and sent him reeling backward. Aria unleashed three arrows in rapid succession, killing two vamps and catching a third in his shoulder.

More arrows whistled around her as the humans fired at the vampires. The other five vamps woke and leapt to their feet. The vamp's confusion didn't last long as they took in the dead bodies surrounding them and the group standing in the doorway.

They charged toward them with murderous expressions on their faces. Aria aimed at the one barreling toward Tempest. Before she could fire, William swung his arm out, catching the vamp in the back of his head and sending him spiraling to the ground.

He pounced on the vamp, jerking his head back and to the side before wrenching it from the vamp's shoulders. One of them leapt at her, but Xavier dove at him. His arms encircled the vampire's waist as Xavier slammed the vamp into the ground with enough force to shake the building.

Three left. Aria released another arrow, taking down one of the three.

"You!" the word was spat at her from her left.

Turning to face the new threat, she didn't get a chance to fire before something crashed against her temple and the side of her face. Her head spun as she took a stumbling step to the side and swung out with her bow at the same time something else cracked against the back of her head. Blackness swirled up around her. She tried not to lose consciousness, but her vision was becoming smaller and smaller as it crept down to a single bead of light in a world of shadows. She tasted blood in her mouth, *her* blood.

"Aria!" William bellowed as something else hit her and she saw no more.

***

Jack

The low growl on his left caused Jack's lip to curl back and his hand to tighten around the rabbit he'd caught to feed to Braith. Blood dripped from the rabbit and into Braith's mouth as claws clicked across the rock floor toward them.

"Enough already," Jack grated and tossed the bloodless remains of the rabbit to Keegan.

Despite his new meal, the wolf glowered at Jack as he settled in at Braith's side and rabbit bones crunched within his jaws. Ever since the wolf had arrived the other night, apparently drawn into the cave by the scent of his former master and Jack, Keegan had refused to go far from Braith's side. Jack hadn't seen Keegan since he'd returned to the wild after the war with Atticus. The wolf's loyalty to Braith remained as true as ever though.

Jack could still recall the disbelief that had run down his spine when he'd poked his head around the corner of the cave wall to find Keegan's emerald eyes blazing at him through the darkness. The wolf's hackles had been raised, his head bent low as he eyed Jack like a meal. If he hadn't recognized him as Braith's wolf, he would have killed him before the wolf could try to feast on them.

Instead, he'd opened the gate for him. Keegan had given him a disgruntled look as he'd trotted by, his claws clicking over the rocks until he'd arrived at Braith's side. The wolf had settled beside Braith and only left him to go to the bathroom in one of the other side tunnels or to eat.

Keegan barely tolerated Jack's presence around Braith's body. The wolf allowed him to feed Braith blood, but watched his every move and emanated a series of growls the entire time Jack knelt at his side. Despite his dislike of the animal, Jack wouldn't turn away the added protection for Braith. Keegan also now disposed of the remains of the animals, and he only had to leave the cave once a day to hunt for them.

Jack wiped off his knees and rose to his feet. Keegan lifted his head, his lips skimmed back to bare his fangs. Jack gave him the finger before turning away.

Hannah's lips clamped together as she resisted laughing at him. "He's only an animal."

"He's a dick."

"There's certainly no love lost between you two."

Jack shrugged as he climbed the rocks to sit beside her. "He doesn't know me. When Braith got him, he was only a puppy, and I was getting ready to leave the palace to infiltrate the rebels. Keegan was ever-present at Braith's side and served as Braith's eyes while he was blind."

Hannah rested her hand on his knee as she gazed across the cavern at Keegan. The wolf finished off his rabbit and rested his head on Braith's stomach. His emerald eyes glistened as he focused on Jack and Hannah. His thick gray coat shone with health in the torchlight playing over it. He released a yawn that revealed all of his lethal teeth.

The wolf *was* a dick, but he was an extremely protective one and Jack admired him for it.

"He's beautiful," Hannah said. "I wish he would let me pet him."

"Maybe when Braith wakes," he replied.

"I like it when you're optimistic."

"One of us has to be," he teased and nudged her side.

She tilted her head back to smile at him. "I always try to see the bright side of things."

"That is one of the many reasons why I love you."

The light in her jade eyes was irresistible and he bent his head to kiss her. Her hands twisted into his shirt to drag him closer. Her mouth opened to the gentle prodding of his tongue. Lifting her from the rocks, he climbed easily over them as he made his way toward their sleeping area. After spending a week and a half in this cave, he knew every inch and crevice of it, so he didn't have to look to see where he placed his feet as he climbed.

Leading her into their side tunnel above, Jack laid her down on the blankets and furs. She lifted her arms to him and he eagerly went into them. He lost himself to her in only the way Hannah could make him lose himself. For a period of time, he was able to forget his brother was dead, their world was coming apart, and the future he'd planned and hoped for them was unraveling.

When he separated himself from her again, he cradled her against his chest as he listened to the distant drip of water sliding over rock and the crackle of the torch flame. Earlier, rain had been pelting the ground when he'd gone to hunt for Braith, but deep beneath the earth there was no indication of that. It remained calm, almost peaceful in this fortress of rock.

He stared at the ceiling over his head, watching the distant flickering of the torch playing across the rock and listening to Keegan's claws clicking over the rock. The wolf had probably gotten up to go to the bathroom again. Jack ran his fingers over Hannah's silken flesh, inhaling her tantalizing scent and the scent of the two of them together. Their blood mingled and flowed strongly as one, binding them for an eternity.

His hand stilled on her when Keegan's claws stopped clicking somewhere in the middle of the cavern.

Hannah murmured something; her hair fell away from his shoulder when he abruptly sat up. He heard no other noise within the cave, but Keegan never just stood somewhere. "Get dressed," he whispered in Hannah's ear.

He tugged on his pants and reached for his shirt. His hands wrapped around his stakes as the torch he'd left below suddenly went out, plunging the cave into a darkness so complete that even his vampire eyes couldn't see his hand in front of his face.

Hannah's shirt settled into place over her with a rustle of material. Her hand encircled his arm, her nails biting into his flesh. "Jack," she murmured.

Turning his head into Hannah's hair, he rested his lips against her ear. "Stay here." She shook her head and he took hold of her chin, running his fingers over her face as he tried to memorize her features through touch. "There is a storm outside. A gust of wind probably came down one of the tunnels and caught the torch, putting it out. I'll be fine, but stay here."

Her chin trembled in his grasp. He knew she didn't entirely buy his theory, but it was a good possibility. He kissed her quickly before rising into a low crouch to make his way toward the end of the tunnel. His ears strained to hear anything within the cavern, but silence hung thickly in the air.

Too silent. He now understood what it was like to be in a tomb.

The torch had been newly lit a short while ago, but a downdraft from the storm outside could have caught it and put it out. That would also explain why Keegan had risen if the air in the cave had changed and carried a new scent with it.

But why hadn't Keegan returned to Braith's side?

Jack remained low as he rested his hand on the first of the jagged rocks at the top of the cavern and crept his way forward. Memory and the feel of the rocks guided him onward as his eyes remained completely ineffective. He was almost tempted to start swinging out with his hands, but he couldn't take the risk of hitting something and making noise.

He should have kept two torches lit, but he hadn't wanted to waste materials in case they were here for longer than they expected. However, if he'd had two torches going, in two separate areas, he would know if it had been a downdraft or if someone had entered the cavern with them. It couldn't be Braith; his brother would have alerted him to his presence. He would have known Jack was in the cave with him, would have scented him.

Jack paused near the bottom of the cavern, his hand resting on a rock as he perched three feet away from the cave floor. He crouched lower, his head canting to the side as he scented the air. He caught no hint of anything else with them, sensed no movement within, but the hair on his nape rose as he got the overwhelming sensation something hunted him from the shadows.

He turned to look behind him, but there was nothing to see there either. It couldn't be Hannah watching him; he knew the weight of her gaze. Still, he couldn't lose the feeling that something tracked him.

Follow your instincts.

His instincts told him to go back, to take Hannah to safety, but he couldn't leave here without Braith's body. No matter how much he loved her, no matter that he would sacrifice his life for hers, he couldn't put their safety over the thousands upon thousands of lives counting on them.

Every part of him screamed to return to her, but he took another step forward. He moved over the last three feet of rock before stepping onto the smooth surface of the cavern. Remaining low, his useless gaze swung back and forth, his ears straining to hear the slightest step. Keegan released a small breath from somewhere on his right. The wolf was still alive, but he had yet to move again.

Was Keegan hunting him? No, the wolf may not like him, but Keegan wouldn't attack him unless he was threatening Braith. No matter how much the wolf growled at him, he had to know Jack was only trying to protect and help his brother. Besides, if Keegan wanted to attack him, he would have by now.

Jack changed his grip on his stakes, pointing them to the sides so he could swing them at anything coming at him. He was ten feet away from where he'd left Braith's body when a hint of movement had him spinning to the right. Before he could attempt to defend himself, something smashed against his arm with the force of a battering ram, causing it to go numb instantly. Unwillingly, his hand opened and the stake fell from his grasp. The clattering of the wood against the rock floor battered his eardrums after the hush that had enveloped the cavern.

He swung his other arm up, but the stake was yanked from his grasp as if he were no stronger than a five-year-old human child who'd just had their lollipop ripped away. A part of him marveled over the power sizzling over his skin and the strength of his opponent even as a hand enveloped his throat. Lifted effortlessly from the ground, he was slammed into the cave wall with enough force to indent the wall and shatter the rock.

CHAPTER 29

Daniel

Daniel kept his gaze focused on the woods. Beside him, Max swung his bow in an angle, searching for any more movement. Timber lifted his staff and smacked the head of it against his palm in a skull-bashing gesture.

"Vampires?" Max inquired.

"Don't know," Daniel said. "But we can't go on until we do know." He felt exposed, but there would be no retreat from here until they'd flushed out whatever was stalking them. "Stay here and watch my back."

He crept forward, keeping his bow and arrow raised as he went. With the clouds in the sky obscuring any light, he moved mostly on instinct as he slid around the trunk of a maple tree before resting against an oak. If vampires were here, it meant they wouldn't be able to go for Jack right now.

The only problem was they had nowhere to fall back to. The caves in this area all led to the same thing, Jack and Braith. He blew out a breath as rain poured over his forehead and into his eyes. He didn't dare wipe the water away now. A second of distraction could spell his death.

Turning, he surveyed the woods behind him. Nothing stirred there, but he felt someone watching him, felt eyes boring into the back of his head. He kept his gaze focused away from where his instincts were telling him the threat lay. If whoever was watching him believed he didn't suspect where they were, they could grow careless and possibly reveal themselves.

Leaning around the tree, he caught Max's gaze. He gave a subtle quirk of his left eyebrow. Max stood for a minute before speaking with Timber and slipping to the side. Daniel kept his gaze focused ahead, straining to hear anything over the pelting rain and the wind howling through the mountains and battering the trees.

A small squeak had him jerking around, his fingers prepared to release his arrow. Nothing stirred behind him, and then, through the rain, he saw Max stalking forward with a squirming bundle locked against his side. Daniel lowered his bow when he recognized the girl trapped against Max's side.

Max set the girl on her feet before him. Her chin tilted up as she gazed defiantly between the two of them. The rain had soaked her hair to her face and her clothes to her body. He was astonished to find Max's eyes running over her appreciatively. Anger didn't shimmer in Max's eyes; instead, he looked almost... relieved?

That made no sense. Why would Max be relieved? She'd put them all at risk by following them here. Timber gave the girl a scathing look when he walked over to join them. Max had told them her name, but Daniel couldn't recall it right now. He was too pissed off, an emotion he was nowhere near as familiar with as Max, yet Max was starting to look... amused?

He contemplated smacking both of them with Timber's staff.

"What the hell are you doing here?" Daniel demanded.

The girl didn't look the least bit intimidated by the fact she was surrounded by three men all easily twice her size. Instead, her chin tilted higher up.

She and Aria would get along wonderfully, Daniel thought bitterly.

"It's a free forest," the girl replied, and Daniel resisted the impulse to shake her.

"Not for you, not anymore," Daniel replied. "Max told you not to follow us, told you if you came with us you wouldn't be able to leave. I don't know what made you think this was acceptable, but you'll be staying with us."

"What are you going to do, imprison me?" she retorted.

"Yes. Timber, carry her."

Max moved between her and Timber. "I'll do it," he said.

Timber stared at him for a minute before bowing his head and stepping back.

"Wait!" the girl—*Maeve*, Daniel finally recalled—sputtered. "You can't do this."

"I'm sorry, but we must," Max said, and he actually sounded regretful.

Despite wanting to hit them both, Daniel found himself intrigued by Max's reaction to the girl. Max hadn't been remorseful or sympathetic to anyone outside of their close circle since he'd been freed from captivity. Bending down, Max wrapped his arms around her waist as she spun to flee. With one swift motion, he tossed her over his shoulder.

"You can't do this!" she cried and beat at his back.

"Be quiet before you get us all killed," Timber grated at her and smacked his staff against his palm.

Maeve settled down, but Daniel believed it was due more to Timber's words than his implied threat. "Are you alone?" Daniel demanded of her.

Her mouth clamped shut, her lips becoming a thin line. It was obvious she had no intention of answering him.

"Stay here," he said to the others before walking away to search the woods.

Daniel worked through the area, making sure no one else hid nearby. The storm had covered Maeve following them; it could easily have covered someone else within the woods. He searched carefully, but detected no sign of anyone else as he made his way back to the others.

"She's alone," he said to them. "We have to go."

She scowled at Daniel over Max's shoulder as they closed the distance to the entrance of the cave. Daniel stepped into the shadows of the cave and hurried forward until he could find a torch and matches.

He lit the torch before turning back to Max. "We should probably tie her up."

Max paled as Maeve cried, "No!" The fear in her voice was the first she'd shown of the emotion.

"Not unless it becomes necessary," Max replied. "And then I'll do it."

Daniel heaved a sigh before walking around to look at Maeve lying against Max's back. She lifted her head to gaze at him. "You have no idea what you've stepped into, but I assure you, if you say one word about this to *any*one, I won't be the only one looking to kill you," Daniel said to her.

Her eyes narrowed minutely, but she wisely chose not to speak as Daniel walked away from her. "Let's go," he said and led the way into the caves, praying with every step he took that they weren't already too late.

***

Jack

Jack's fingers tore at the hand squeezing into his neck. His feet kicked against the wall and the imposing figure before him as he sought to dislodge the grip tearing into his skin any way he could. The hand only squeezed to the point where blood trickled from his wounds and he was certain his windpipe was about to be crushed. Red eyes blazed at him, but those impossibly glowing ruby eyes were all he could make out of his enemy.

Hannah!

Fresh strength surged through him; he smashed his fist down on the arm before him, earning him a low growl of warning, but no other reaction to the blow. He'd hit the vampire hard enough that he should have fractured a bone, but the hold on him didn't ease.

Son of a bitch!

Something clattered. Was it another vampire creeping up on him, coming for him? Were some of Sabine's guards nearly as old as she was? It was the only explanation for the strength of the vampire holding him and the power making his skin feel as if electricity danced over it. The sharp scent of ozone filled the air as the power amped up another level. If it weren't for the bristly hairs on the arm holding him, he would believe it was Sabine holding him, but maybe it was her follower, Goran.

A second of satisfaction filled him when his foot connected with a shin. His legs flopped in the air as he was dragged away from the wall before being bashed back into it. More blood spilled from the shredded skin of his throat. Another low growl sounded before he was thrust into the wall once more. His skull cracked off stone and pain burst through his head. Pulled away from the wall again, those reddened eyes filled his blurry vision as his nose nearly touched against the nose of the vamp holding him.

"Where. Is. She?" the words were bit out at him in a raspy voice.

Jack froze, his hands clamped around the one clutching his throat. Confusion swam through his rattled brain as he tried to understand the question and place the voice. The sound of stone clattering against stone pierced the darkness.

Was that a footstep? A creak followed. The faintest hint of light pierced the tunnel leading in. The tunnel Jack had been using the most.

Before he could process what was going on, he was jerked away from the wall and spun around. His feet dangled over the ground as he was carried relentlessly toward the tunnel. The faintest beat of hearts thudded in his ears as whoever had entered the cave steadily approached. It had to be friends, most likely Daniel returning to report what was going on. Jack opened his mouth to call out a warning, but he couldn't get any sound out through his constricted throat.

CHAPTER 30

Daniel

Daniel hesitated a few feet away from the main cavern and placed his torch against the wall. The flames danced over the walls and lit the first few feet of the cavern within. *Why is it dark in there?*

He exchanged a glance with Max and Timber. Max lowered Maeve from his shoulder. The gate was closed. She may know where the other key was to escape, but they would be able to catch her again if it became necessary. Right now, Max needed his hands free in case something came at them.

Daniel and Max pulled their bows forward again and each drew an arrow. Timber stepped behind Maeve and nudged her forward as they cautiously approached the cavern. No noise came from within. Jack had to know they were coming by now; he would give them some indication it was safe to proceed. All Daniel heard was silence.

Too late. We're too late. What do I tell Aria?

He swallowed at the prospect of having to deliver another devastating blow to his sister, but it may be inevitable. Stopping at the edge of the cavern, he nodded to Max and they both slipped out at the same time. Daniel didn't have a chance to look around before the bow was wrenched from his hands and a solid blow to his chest knocked him off his feet.

The arrow that had fallen from his hand when he'd been hit spun across the ground, causing Max to swing in his direction and fire his arrow. A savage snarl came from someone or something. The arrow was snatched out of the air and a body was heaved at Max. Darting to the side, Max wasn't fast enough to avoid Jack being thrown against him.

They both tumbled into the wall, falling over top of one another. Jack scrambled to get back to his feet, but tripped and fell when Max's legs got caught up in his. Timber stumbled back when his staff was torn away from him and heaved across the room. Hannah scrambled down the last few feet of rocks and snatched the staff from the floor to hold it before her.

A small clicking noise drew Daniel's attention to the wolf pacing back and forth across from him. Its hackles were raised and its head hung low as it watched them all with a look that said it was waiting for one of them to make a move. He blinked when recognition of the wolf descended over him, but though he'd once known the wolf, he had no doubt Keegan would tear his throat out if he deemed him a threat.

"*Where is she?*" Bellowed so loudly, the words vibrated the entire cavern.

Daniel turned to scramble away when someone stalked toward him from the shadows, but a hand seized his ankle and dragged him back. His fingernails scraped against the rocks, trying to find purchase on them, but all he left were white gouges on their surface.

He barely had time to process being lifted before he hung upside down. Blood rushed into his head, and his rain-soaked shirt fell about his face. With one swift motion, he was spun right side up and shoved into a wall. Ruby eyes filled his hazy vision.

"Where. Is. She?"

The lethal quiet of the words spoken to him were more frightening than when they'd been bellowed at him. Daniel blinked as he tried to bring his captor into focus. The second his eyes cleared, he wished they hadn't. He gulped as he found himself face to face with the most vicious, infuriated vampire he'd ever seen before.

In that instant, he knew two things. One, his brother-in-law had risen from the dead. Two, Braith was going to kill him.

***

Max

Max shoved Jack off him and scrambled for his bow again. His hand had almost closed around it when Jack seized hold of his wrist and jerked it back. "What are you doing?" Max hissed.

Jack didn't reply as he remained kneeling on the cave floor, his mouth ajar. Max followed his gaze to where Daniel was pinned against the wall, his hands encircling the wrist of the man holding him. Max took in the back of the vampire holding Daniel. It had to be a vampire with the flash of those red eyes he'd seen before Jack's body had hit his.

Gradually, Max's mind picked out the details of the vamp as the dim torchlight within the cave flickered over the cavern. The shadows seemed to cling to the vamp's bare, broad back and the black hair curling against his nape. Thick muscles bulged in the vamp's biceps and forearms as Daniel's feet kicked against the rocks.

"Easy, Braith," Jack coaxed.

Max's jaw dropped. He was sure his stunned expression mirrored Jack's as realization hit him between the eyes. They'd hoped Braith would rise, they'd been *counting* on it, but a part of him had been too afraid to believe he would miraculously return from the dead. Yet, there he was, standing before them and looking as if he had every intention of killing Daniel, of killing every *one* of them.

Max's gaze went to Maeve, standing beside Timber in the mouth of the cave. She gawked at the spectacle, but showed no sign of running away from what was unfolding before her.

"Where. Is. She?" Braith demanded again, and Daniel's feet kicked more firmly against the wall as his face turned red.

"She's safe!" Max blurted. "If you mean Aria, she's safe!"

For all he knew, Braith meant someone else entirely, or he meant a freaking horse or something. Atticus had been completely demented when he'd risen from the dead. Maybe they all came back broken and twisted, maybe that's why Sabine was the way she was now. Had they protected Braith and sheltered him only to have him rise from the dead as a monster they would end up having to destroy anyway?

If so, Max didn't think they had much of a shot at taking Braith down considering he'd just tossed them all around like rag dolls. Max's breath caught, and he resisted creeping backward when Braith's head turned toward him. He'd never seen eyes so red before. The savage expression on Braith's face made his bladder clench as those eyes bore into his.

Had Braith gotten *bigger*?

He'd always been massive, always been powerful, but now he seemed more so. Had dying not only twisted him in some way, but also strengthened him? They were so screwed if he decided to squash them, and he could. With a simple swing of his hand, he could knock Daniel's head from his body.

"Where is she?" Braith demanded.

"You can track her, Braith," Jack said, looking to soothe him, but though Max never would have believed it possible, Braith's eyes became a more vivid red. "Through your blood in her, you can track her."

Max's fingers twitched toward his bow again as Daniel choked and clawed at Braith's hand when it compressed around his neck.

"There's nothing there." Braith's lips skimmed back to reveal his fangs. The light of the torch glistened off the lethal points. "I feel no connection to her."

Oh, shit. Max didn't dare make another move toward his bow. He'd be headless if he did.

"We'll take you to her. Right now, we'll leave here and take you to her!" he blurted. "But first you have to let go of Daniel. I won't take you to her if you hurt him."

Jack gave him a look that said he clearly believed Max had lost his mind to give such an ultimatum. Max held his breath as he waited to see what Braith would do, and if he'd live to see the next minute. Finally, Braith set Daniel on his feet. He didn't release his throat, but his grip eased on him.

"Why can't I feel her?" Braith demanded, and his fingers minutely tightened on Daniel's throat again, causing him to choke and his eyes to bug out. "Why is there no connection between us?"

Max could feel Jack's searching gaze on him as he tried to come up with an answer for that.

"I don't know," Max finally admitted. "When you died, Aria felt the severing of your bond." William had told them she'd tried to tear her heart from her chest, that she'd known the instant Braith ceased living. "It will probably remain severed until the two of you can renew it."

Braith stared at him as if he were the bird the cat was about to swat out of the air. Max gulped, and his eyes fell to his bow once more, but he'd never get to it in time to stop Braith from attacking him.

"When I *died?*" Braith asked, and beside him, Jack went still as stone.

"Braith, you've been dead for nearly two weeks," Jack said.

***

Jack

His brother continued to stare at Jack as if Braith didn't know who he was. Jack saw Max's fingers twitch out of the corner of his eye, but he knew Max wasn't dumb enough to try to go for the bow. He would never make it in time. Daniel had gone completely limp in Braith's grip, his eyes riveted to him while he made as little movement as possible.

Atticus had been weakened and rotten when he'd returned from the dead. Braith was stronger, and Jack thought it was more than the blood of the animals he'd supplied fueling his brother now. No, more power radiated from him than ever had before, and Jack realized this was what had caused the waves of power emanating from Sabine; it had been more than her age strengthening her, but also her death.

If Atticus hadn't returned a half-rotten corpse and out of his mind, what would he have become after feeding well again? It had taken both him and Braith to kill Atticus in the end. He didn't know what could possibly take down Braith if he lost complete control now.

Braith couldn't feel the connection to Aria, which was making him unstable. Not to mention the rising from the dead thing. That had to be confusing as hell, and apparently Braith didn't remember the fight or dying. Max had said Aria felt the severing of their bond when Braith had died. It was possible the link wouldn't be there until they were reconnected. It was also possible she'd died since Max had last seen her.

Jack shuddered at the idea, his gaze moving to Hannah standing near the bottom of the cavern. She was paler than normal, but she held the staff against her chest and eyed Braith as if she couldn't decide if she wanted to beat him with it or not. Never had Jack considered his brother would harm her, but Braith wasn't in control of himself right now.

He understood the rage and anguish his disconnection from Aria would cause, but that didn't matter, not if Braith went after Hannah. Jack would still try to take him down, if he could, which he was pretty sure he couldn't. He went to move closer to Hannah, to put himself in between her and Braith, but Braith spoke before he could edge toward her.

"Dead," Braith muttered.

"Yes," Jack said.

"How?"

"Arrow through the back," Jack replied and took a couple of steps toward Hannah. Braith closed his eyes as his head fell into his hand and he briefly rubbed at his forehead. Confusion and distress radiated from him. Jack had to help ease some of that confusion, somehow. "Braith—"

When Braith lifted his head, his face was composed into a mask of stone as he focused on Max, but a muscle near the corner of his eye twitched. Jack froze when he realized the scars that had been etched around Braith's eyes were gone. Not only had he come back stronger, but he'd come back healed, completely.

"You can see," Jack whispered. In the beginning of their relationship, Braith had needed to be near Aria in order to see, but as he'd grown stronger and the bond between them had deepened, he'd been able to be further and further away from her. Now Braith didn't feel their link, yet he could still see. Jack had no idea what to make of this development, but he knew his brother had risen from the dead something *more*.

What that something more was though, he didn't know. Would Braith be twisted like Atticus and Sabine now, or would he calm when he understood better what had happened and he was reunited with Aria?

Jack's fingers twitched on the rock at the possibility his brother would never be the man he had been. That he may be as much of a threat to them as Sabine. The idea of killing his brother had never cross his mind, until now.

"Yes, I can see," Braith said to him before his attention returned to Max. "Where is she?"

"She's somewhere safe, about thirty miles from here," Max answered.

"When did you last see her?"

"Two days ago."

Braith went completely still before all of his muscles rippled and a snarl erupted from him. He dropped Daniel as if he was nothing more than a sack of grain. Daniel stumbled to the side, his hand on his bruised throat as he watched Braith stalk toward them. Jack tensed, his muscles bunching in preparation of getting Hannah out of harm's way when Braith stopped before them. He and Max tipped back their heads to take him in.

"So she could be dead and you don't know it," Braith grated.

Jack rose to his feet, holding his hands out in a pacifying gesture when he suspected Braith was about to snag hold of Max. He edged closer so that he was somewhat in between them, but Braith didn't so much as glance at him.

Because he knows I can't stop him.

"She is in an extremely safe place, Braith. Safer than these caves," Max replied.

"She could be dead and you don't know!" Braith roared and Max flinched.

"Yes," Daniel said from behind him, his voice raw from being choked. Red marks marred his fair skin. Some of them were already starting to darken into bruises. "But she's not. William and Xavier will make sure she stays safe."

"Take me to her, now," Braith commanded.

"It will take us some time to get there and with the storm—" Daniel broke off when Braith swung toward him again. "We'll go now."

Braith didn't acknowledge any of them when he turned away and walked into the tunnel the others had entered through. Timber hastily stepped out of his way. Keegan trotted passed them and down the tunnel behind Braith. A young human Jack had never seen before casually stepped aside to let Braith go by before turning to follow him. The girl had to be nuts if she wanted to be anywhere near him right now.

"Who is that and why is she here?" Jack asked.

"Maeve and she followed us," Max said as he rose to his feet and gathered his bow. "What do we do if something did happen to Aria after we left?"

Jack stared at the tunnel as Hannah walked over to join him. "Pray. Atticus destroyed much of the world. Braith will level what remains of it."

"Did he come back stronger?" Timber asked.

"Yes," Daniel croaked out and rubbed at his throat.

They all took a step back when red eyes blazed at them from the darkness of the tunnel before Braith emerged from the shadows once more. "Now," he growled at them.

Jack took hold of Hannah's hand and, keeping her securely behind him, he walked toward the tunnel. A tremor went through her and into him when they slipped passed Braith. Maeve stood by the gate, her arms folded over her chest while she watched them.

"I really hope Aria is still alive," Maeve whispered to Max when he bent to retrieve the key.

"We all do," he replied and unlocked the gate.

CHAPTER 31

Braith

The icy rain beating against Braith's skin did nothing to cool the wrath and terror clawing at his chest. *Dead.* He'd been dead for nearly two weeks. Aria had been out here, alone, in danger.

She is alive.

He kept telling himself this, but with the emptiness stretching out before him and the hole the breaking of their bond had created in him, he couldn't quite believe it. She *felt* dead. *He* felt dead. His fingernails tore into the palms of his hands. Blood dripped from the wounds, but he found himself clenching tighter and tighter, regardless of the pain. He'd thought the pain would help to ground him, help him to feel alive in some small way again, it didn't.

Would he become his father? At one time, he'd have said no, without a doubt, that could never happen. Now madness slithered through his mind, creeping deeper and deeper until all he craved was sinking his fangs into someone and tearing them to shreds. He'd thought he understood what had caused his father to snap and become the man he had. He'd believed he'd understood it, but had *known* it could never be him.

No, *now* he understood. Now, he felt the complete disconnect of his soul from his body. For the first time in his life, he completely comprehended what his father had gone through and why he became the way he did. He would not become like his father, he couldn't, but right now the temptation was nearly as tantalizing to him as Aria.

Blood and death, he wanted it so badly he could taste it. He'd once told Aria he'd go on without her, he would rule and he would make sure her loved ones were safe. He intended to uphold those words to her the best he could, but how long that would be or how well, he had no way of knowing. He could barely think straight right now; he couldn't think about what years of this emptiness would do to him.

Nor could he entirely process all of the changes he felt in his body now.

He could *see*. Somehow, while he'd been dead, he'd healed. He had no idea what to make of that, or the increased power he felt flowing through his veins. It felt as if something deep inside of him had been tapped, as if some well of strength had been loosed when the arrow had sliced through his heart, and now it would never be stemmed again.

His gaze slid to Jack at his side as he stood protectively in front of Hannah. He should feel bad for what he'd done to his brother, for what he'd done to Daniel. He felt nothing beyond this yawning desolation and impending insanity.

Brushing back the wet hair and rain streaming down his face, he turned to look at Daniel, Max, and Timber. He had no idea who the girl was, but the three of them kept her between them.

"Aria, is she… how was she when you last saw her?" He nearly had to shout to be heard over the storm.

Did she feel this hollow and this looming insanity? Had she been suffering through this clawing sensation in his chest for almost two weeks? The idea caused fresh fury to swell through him and the four humans came to an abrupt halt. Braith stopped, his head bowing and his shoulders heaving as he tried to maintain control.

"She is... coping," Daniel replied hesitantly.

More blood spilled from his palms as he heard the doubt in Daniel's words. Aria was in pain. He'd caused that pain; he'd left her. He'd been *dead!* And now very much alive again and stronger, but *she* could be dead. She could have been killed since they'd last seen her. He shook his head to clear it of the disconcerting thoughts filling his head.

Keep it together until you know for sure.

When he'd first woken, he couldn't remember anything. He'd felt empty; all he'd wanted was Aria, and she wasn't there. His passing had fractured their link. Now, as he struggled to piece together what had occurred, more and more of the events leading up to his death started to come back to him.

"And the woman who attacked us, where is she?" he demanded.

"We have confirmed that her name is Sabine," Max said. "And we believe she is your grandmother. Apparently, the first born in your line make it a habit to come back from the dead even if you're pierced through the heart." His gaze ran pointedly over Braith's healed flesh before landing on where his heart would be located in his chest. "Before we left the others, Sabine was planning to make a move against the palace."

"And Aria is near the palace?"

"Yes, we have been gathering forces and making plans to fight Sabine. Aria will wait for us to return before she carries out our part of the plan."

Braith's lips skimmed back. "Aria doesn't wait."

"For this, she will. She knows we only have one chance at this woman, and believe me, she is not going to blow it, not after what happened. She'll have her revenge."

Then there was a chance she was still alive, that she was okay and this emptiness within him could be eased. It *had* to be eased. Braith stared at Max as he tried to assimilate everything they were telling him into his chaotic mind. His gaze fell to the woman before Max. She didn't take a step away from him as she held his gaze.

Max rested his hand on her shoulder. "She won't tell anyone what she's learned."

"I won't," the woman said.

Braith turned away from them and broke into a loping run through the trees once more. He had to move, had to get to Aria. The ground slipped and slid beneath his feet as he pushed onward through the driving rain and whipping wind.

"We have to take a break," Daniel panted from behind him after they'd covered a few more miles.

Braith spun toward them once more, causing them all to take a stumbling step back from him. "Tell me where she is. How do I get there?" he commanded.

"In a barn... about fifteen miles away... near the palace," Max gasped loudly as he bent over to rest his hands on his knees.

"There are many barns near the palace!" he yelled. "I need more than that."

"Easy, Braith," Jack advised. Braith shot him a withering look that caused his brother to raise his hands in a conciliatory gesture. "I know you're eager to get to her. Believe me, I know." He looked at Hannah, standing by his side and shivering in the rain. "We will make it there, but they're doing the best they can, and it's better if we all stay together. If we can't find the barn, or them again, we'll be screwed."

Braith stalked into the forest with Keegan at his heels as on the horizon the night's black sky gave way to the slate gray color of a stormy dawn. He stared at the changing color as he tried to rein in his emotions. Jack was right, he knew that, but the clawing in his chest increased with every passing minute.

With a curse, he drove his fist into a tree. The bark and wood gave way until his arm burst free on the other side. The broken bones in his knuckles and his sliced-open skin were already repairing themselves when he pulled his hand free. Lifting his hand before him, he couldn't help the wonder filling him as he examined the already healed flesh and bones. Pink rivulets ran over his skin as the rain washed away the remaining blood. Never before had he healed so quickly; he never would have believed it possible.

When he turned away from the tree, all of them were staring at him with the same mixture of fear and awe that he'd often seen on those who had been in the presence of his father.

That realization rattled him more than his accelerated healing ability.

"I will not be like him," he vowed. "I will destroy Sabine. I will make her pay, but I will not become my father."

When their eyes lifted to his, he saw the uncertainty in their gazes. Unable to stand the sight of that uncertainty, he turned away from them. He blinked and wiped the rain away from his eyes when, through the trees, he spotted figures slipping through the woods. He took an abrupt step forward, his lips curling away from his fangs as he watched those figures closing in on them.

"We're not alone," he said over his shoulder to the others.

Jack came to stand beside him, his brow furrowing as he searched the woods. "I don't see anyone."

"They're there, and they're coming," Braith replied. "They're wearing brown cloaks, not white though."

"Those could be Sabine's followers," Max said from behind him. "They gave up their white cloaks when the snow melted, but many of the rebels also wear brown cloaks in order to blend in."

"Then we'll make sure that they deserve to die before they do," Braith replied. Bloodlust surged through him, and he nearly licked his lips at the possibility of a fight. It would take more time to kill them all than he wanted to spend right now, but he'd gladly tear into the throat of any who dared to stand against him, or who could be a threat to Aria.

Another flicker of motion drew his eyes to the right as a woman ducked low in the brush. "No heartbeats," he said.

"They could still be on our side," Daniel said. "We have vampires working with us too."

"If they come at us, we're going to fight."

"How many are there?" Timber inquired.

"A dozen or so," Braith replied when he spotted more of them within the trees.

The vision that had once been taken from him had become sharper during the time when he had been dead. His eyes were more than making up for the time they hadn't seen anything by picking out every minute detail within the woods. Right down to the vamp nearly buried in mud behind the oak tree to his right.

"Be prepared," he said to them as the first one moved to the edge of the clearing. The tip of an arrowhead swung toward them. "Not on our side," he hissed.

Malicious joy filled him as he realized he would get a chance to unleash the savagery building within him.

The vampire didn't have a chance to fire the arrow before Braith swooped down on him like a hawk on its prey. Braith yanked the vampire out from behind the tree and had his heart in his hand before he even realized he'd covered the distance between them with such rapid speed.

A grim smile spread across his mouth as the coppery tang of blood filled his nose and for a second the clawing sensation in his chest eased. As he turned to take on the next vampire stalking them, death became all he craved.

***

Jack

Braith moved so fast through the woods that he became a blur as he uncovered and slaughtered vampires Jack hadn't even known were there. Some of the vamps turned to flee from him, but they were nowhere near fast enough to escape the wrath descending on them.

Jack swallowed as his hand tightened on the stake he'd pulled free, but he realized he wouldn't be using it. He wouldn't get the chance to. Beside him, Daniel lowered his bow and returned his arrow to his quiver.

As Braith disappeared behind a tree, a startled yelp abruptly cut off and then a head came rolling out to rest against Max's feet. Max took a step away from the head, but he didn't truly seem to see it as his gaze remained riveted on the macabre scene unfolding before them.

In all of his many years, Jack had never seen anything like the savagery Braith unleashed. He was like a ghost, disappearing in and out of the trees. Despite the pounding rain washing away the smells of the forest, the scent of blood permeated the air. The screams of the dying were briefly heard over the howling wind and the clacking of the tree branches.

Beside him, Hannah began to shake and she moved closer to press her body against his. "What have we done, Jack?" she whispered. "What did we help to unleash? *Who* did we unleash on this world?"

"It's Braith," he said.

"Is it?" Daniel inquired.

He'd been in many fights with Daniel over the years, but never had he seen the stark terror on his friend's face that was there now. He had no idea how to answer that question. He wanted to insist it was his brother, that beneath the increased power, speed, and healing ability it was still Braith with them, but was it?

Braith had always been ruthless when he needed to be and stronger than most other vampires. He'd seen Braith kill without remorse before, but he'd never seen the eager gleam in his brother's eyes that had been there before Braith had gone after his prey. And he knew that Braith had thought of these vampires as nothing more than prey before he'd attacked.

Still, he wasn't ready to give up on his brother. He *wouldn't* give up on him.

"Yes, it's Braith," he said.

"But is it the Braith we all knew, or is it someone else entirely?" Max asked and brushed back the hair sticking wetly to his forehead.

"He's different." Jack couldn't deny it. They had eyes and ears too; they could see him and hear the screams of those falling within the woods.

"He's terrifying," Hannah whispered. "How will any of us ever stop him if he loses himself to the blood and to the killing?"

"Aria will stabilize him. He just woke from the dead, their link was severed by his death, and he has grown vastly stronger in a short period of time. He's understandably out of sorts right now, but she *will* help him to regain control."

Jack had to believe that as another scream abruptly cut off. When he'd agreed to help protect Braith, he'd done it because he thought it would be the best thing for all of them. Now, he was beginning to fear that it may have been the worst thing.

Braith said he wouldn't become like Atticus, but what if there was no help for it? What if it became inevitable the minute the bloodlink was severed or the second he rose from the dead again? What if their keeping him alive had sentenced Braith to this uncontrollable need for death?

Jack could feel Daniel's gaze boring into him, but he couldn't tear his attention away from the woods as Braith emerged from between the trees. He didn't appear the least bit fazed or worn down from having just slaughtered a dozen or so vampires as he strode purposely toward them.

Braith's reddened eyes were stark against the blood coating his face and chest. The rain washed the blood from his hair and down his cheeks in red rivulets. The torrential downpour should have cleaned the blood quickly from him; instead there was so much of it that it continued to streak over his body.

Jack reached for Hannah's hand, and he enclosed it tightly within his grasp as Braith stopped ten feet away from them. Behind him, the others drew in sharp breaths when Braith's gaze flicked over them and he wiped away some of the blood on his face.

"Let's go," Braith said crisply. He turned on his heel and slipped into the woods without looking back at them.

"What if Aria is dead?" Daniel asked in a choked voice. "What if her death, and not his, is the reason he can no longer feel their bond?"

Jack tore his attention away from where his brother had vanished to focus on Daniel. His mind spun as he tried to process the death Braith had just unleashed with such casual ease and in a matter of mere minutes.

He had no answer for any of them, but one, "Then God help us all."

He didn't wait to hear what they had to say; there was nothing they could say. Tugging on Hannah's hand, he followed Braith into the forest.

CHAPTER 32

Braith

The blood coating him had completely washed away by the time Braith opened the door to the barn. However, he detected the scent of blood the second he stepped inside the building.

Aria's blood.

He'd know its aroma anywhere. His gaze darted over the barn. He didn't see any blood on the floor or walls, but the scent of it was sharp in his nostrils. He'd butcher any who had dared to hurt her.

"I smell her blood," he snarled. "It's been spilled here."

The others exchanged frightened looks before Max closed the barn door, drowning out the sound of the rain beating against the earth. Keegan padded over to some bales of straw where he settled in with his head on his paws.

"Everything looks the same," Daniel said in a calming tone. "I'm sure there is a reason you smell her blood."

Braith just stared at him. His fingers had left perfect bruises around his throat, but Daniel didn't cower away from him.

"Where is she?" he demanded.

Max slipped passed him and over to a board in the floor. Braith watched as he knelt and his fingers felt around something before a click sounded. A perfectly concealed door swung up to reveal the space below. Body odor and sweat wafted into his nostrils, but beneath it all, he scented *her*.

His feet didn't touch a step as he jumped into the pit below. The man that had been standing at the bottom of the stairs, probably to keep watch, took a staggering step back. Braith strode forward, uncaring about what might await him as he followed Aria's scent through the dank hallway.

She would hate it in here, but there was no doubt she'd been here. Was she still here? It was possible she wasn't. Her blood had flowed above, and her soul no longer brushed against his as it had since the moment they'd completed their bloodlink. Had she been killed?

What would happen when he got the answer, he didn't know. He'd never dreamed he could become like his father, but he couldn't deny that killing those vampires in the forest had been the only release he'd been able to find from the insanity that had swirled within him since he'd risen from the dead. For one brief moment, the flow of their blood had filled the empty hole within him. Now that hole was wide open again, and he was about to learn if it would forever be a part of him or not.

The others descended the stairs behind him. The door clicked shut as he arrived at the end of the hall and pulled open the door there.

Hundreds of humans were gathered within, all of them had their backs to him as they listened to someone speaking at the center of the pack. A few glanced over their shoulders at him. They were turning back toward the center when they froze and their heads spun toward him once more. He could smell Aria in this place, but he couldn't see her and he couldn't tell how long it had been since she'd been here.

The ones closest to him took a couple of stumbling steps back. Their mouths opened and closed. A few rubbed at their eyes like they couldn't believe what they were seeing. He ignored all of them as he strode forward. More of them turned toward him as he approached and fell back to stare at him with incredulous expressions.

"She's sent more troops back here," a man said from somewhere in the center of the pack. "To attack this area of the wall."

More of the humans stepped away to finally reveal a table in the center of the room and a man standing beside it with a stick. Xavier stood next to the man and William on the other side of him.

William's head was bowed as he watched the man point to something with the stick while he continued speaking, "And here is where we believe she is keeping some of the humans."

William leaned forward and Braith froze as William's movement revealed Aria standing between him and Xavier. His deadened heart leapt in his chest. He almost lunged for her, but found himself rooted where he stood as he drank in the sight of her.

He'd never seen her so still, so rigid. Her hands were clasped before her, and her head was bent as she stared at the table. Dark glasses shaded eyes he instinctively knew were red. Her thick auburn hair hung in a braid over her shoulder. The cheekbones and figure that had filled out since she'd become his wife were gaunt and lean once more. She looked as if she weighed less now than when she'd first stepped onto that stage and into his life.

Yet, to him, she was still the most beautiful woman in the world. Love swelled within his chest. He yearned to touch her, to feel her skin against his, but he remained unmoving as he watched her. She didn't interact with the others while she watched them.

She's barely in control, he realized and had no idea how she'd managed to hang on for this long. Revenge was a strong motivator.

Her nostrils flared, and her head lifted in such a way that the movement seemed to pain her as her head slowly turned toward him. He felt as if he'd been punched in the gut when the left side of her face came into view. A black bruise marred the whole side of her face and a scratch sliced across her cheek; the scratch had once been deep enough to bleed. The dark color of the bruise stood out starkly against the pallor of her skin. A visible tremor went through her; it was the only movement she made.

"Not real," she whispered and turned away from him once more. Her head bowed as another tremor went through her.

Anguish twisted through him. *What has she been through?*

William shot his sister a curious glance before his head lifted and he noticed Braith standing there. His jaw dropped so fast, Braith thought he might have dislocated it. The man who had been pointing to something on the table lifted his head. He stopped speaking mid-sentence and the stick fell from his hand to clatter against the ground. Xavier took a step toward Braith before stopping to gaze down at Aria.

Her shaking increased as she whispered. "Not real, not real, not real."

She flinched away from Xavier when he rested his hand on her shoulder. Unable to stand her torment, or being apart from her for a second more, Braith closed the distance between them. William gawked at him as leaned back against the table to get out of his way and slid around it.

Aria whimpered when Braith stopped beside her. His hand trembled when he reached out to stroke his knuckles over her cheek. Her skin was chilled beneath his touch, but it sent a current of pleasure through him as the clawing in his chest finally eased. It didn't go away completely. It probably wouldn't until they were bonded once more, but he could at least think clearly again.

Bending, he kissed the top of her head, causing her to shudder as tears spilled down her cheeks. "I'm real, love," he whispered while he nuzzled her ear with his lips.

She whimpered again and flinched away from him as more tears spilled from her eyes. He wiped her tears away when she turned toward him and her head tipped back to look at him. Her fingers stretched toward his cheek before she pulled them away.

He grabbed her hand and pressed it to his face. Her lips parted, and her fingers curled into his skin as her other hand came up to grip him. He caught her against him when her knees gave out. She clutched at his back and buried her face in his neck.

Her tears wet his skin as he held her closer, savoring the scent and feel of her against him once more. Encircling her nape, he pinned her against him as he swung to meet Xavier's eyes. The man didn't say a word, only nodded his head to the right.

Braith didn't pay attention to anyone in the crowd that quickly moved out of his way as he carried her by them all. Xavier led them to a door and opened it. He stepped aside to allow them to pass. Braith kicked the door shut with the back of his foot and stopped to survey the small room with the straw mattresses lining the walls.

Aria's lips skimmed back. Her fangs pricked his skin before they pierced his flesh. His body reacted as if he'd been hit by lightning. He jerked against her, his hand clenching her neck tighter as her fingers dug into his flesh. She tried to get closer to him while she drank from him in deep, satisfying pulls.

Easy, she's been through so much.

Yet he found himself unable to restrain himself when she bit deeper. He pulled back her braid and sank his fangs into her throat, a groan of bliss escaping him as the hot wash of her blood filled his mouth and body. It seeped into his cells, warming him from the inside out. Adjusting his hold on her, he kicked one of the mattresses off the wall and onto the floor.

Renewed.

He could feel the bond reconnecting between them while he laid her onto the bed and followed her down. Power swelled within him as her blood flooded his system. The bloodlink had always made him stronger, but this was a whole new level of strength.

When he'd first seen Sabine, he'd wondered if he'd be able to match her power. When he'd risen from the dead, he'd known he was stronger than he'd been before, but he now knew he would *exceed* her.

Reluctantly, he released his bite on Aria's neck and leaned back until her fangs retracted from him. He stared down at her, absorbing every exquisite detail of her as she lay beneath him. The clamoring madness that had been ever-present in him since he'd woken in that cave eased within him. He no longer craved blood and death; all he craved was her.

Taking hold of her glasses, he eased them from her face to peer down into her crystalline blue eyes. His fangs throbbed when he saw that the bruise on her face also encircled her eye. His fingers hovered above it as he fought to contain his urge to kill.

"Who did this?" he growled.

"You're here," she breathed. "You're really here. Not a dream. Not an illusion."

"I'm really here, love," he replied and rested his fingers against her cheek as he gazed down at her. "Who did this to you?"

"They're dead. William took out the one who did this."

***

Aria

Aria couldn't understand what had happened. One minute she'd been standing at the table, trying to ignore the pounding in her head, and the next, she was lying here beneath him. The heat of his body against hers and the feel of his hands on her were all so familiar yet so *unreal*. Her eyes continued to run over him as her hands felt over his body. She touched him, but she couldn't get herself to believe it was really him.

However, those were his chiseled abs with the indent running down the middle, and those were his broad shoulders. Shoulders she'd clung to more times than she could count. That was his black hair and those were his beautiful gray eyes with the blue band around the iris, before they'd turned red at the sight of the bruise on her face. His blood stained her lips and infused her body, strengthening her in a way she'd never experienced before. The power of his blood awed her, but not nearly as much as touching him did.

Icy water dripped from his hair and onto her, making this moment all the more real. Her fingers stilled on his cheeks, and her gaze ran over his eyes as she realized the scars around them had vanished completely. She found she missed them even as she realized their disappearance was due to the wealth of power emanating from him. He'd come back different, but he was still *hers*.

"Braith," she whispered.

His hands tenderly clasped her cheeks as he bent to kiss her trembling lips. His mouth slanted over hers as his tongue slipped in to stroke over hers, tasting her until she quivered beneath him.

His hands worked to pull her shirt and pants from her as his kiss became more demanding. Clutching at the smooth, flexing muscles of his back, she eagerly met every hungry thrust of his tongue. She gripped him against her as he tossed aside his own pants and settled on top of her. The familiar weight and feel of his body against hers made her skin come alive. He pulled her firmly against his chest as his body joined with hers.

"Home," she whispered against his neck before sinking her fangs into his flesh once more.

The intricate, soul-deep bond between them, which she'd missed so much since he'd been taken from her, consumed her once again, dragging her into its fathomless depths. He smoothed her hair back from her forehead when she released her bite on him, and bent to claim her mouth again with his.

Her nails dug into his back when his tongue thrust into her mouth in the same demanding rhythm as his powerful body moving within hers. Aria gave herself over to the passion he so easily stoked to life within her, and to the pleasure only he could give her.

CHAPTER 33

Braith

Braith cradled Aria against him, her back pressed to his chest as she ran her fingers over and through his. "I did something," she whispered. "Or I allowed it to happen."

He propped his head on his hand and gazed down at the unmarked side of her face. Color had crept back into her cheeks and her skin glowed with vitality once more, but she was still far thinner than he liked seeing her. Shadows circled her eyes and the knowledge of things one shouldn't know shimmered in their depths.

He didn't care what it took, he would do everything he could to make it better for her again.

"What did you allow to happen?" he inquired.

Her hands stilled on his. "We had to learn more about Sabine. Had to know her plan and who she was. Had to know if she had any weaknesses. Xavier, Max, and I tracked her to another town and a house there. I was going to try to get into the house with her, but I didn't think I could do it without being caught. And I couldn't get caught," she grated through her teeth.

His hands clamped on hers at the possibility of such a thing. She wouldn't be here now if she'd been caught. She wouldn't be in his arms again, and the clawing sensation would still be tearing at his insides, driving him mad. Now, finally, it had been silenced by the renewal of their bloodlink.

"So instead of trying to get into the house, we lured away the vampire who worked in her stables there." She rolled over to look up at him; her haunted eyes searched his face. "What I allowed them to do to that vampire was cruel. It was brutal…" Her words trailed off as her gaze slid passed him to the ceiling.

"You watched this."

Her eyes were defiant when they came back to his. "I couldn't condone it then walk away and leave them to bear the burden of carrying it out. I would never do that to Xavier and Max."

Despite her show of defiance, he sensed the sorrow within her. "We do what we must in war," he told her.

"I'd do it again."

He traced his finger over her lips before kissing where he'd touched. "What did you learn from the vampire?"

She told him everything they had learned, the amount of recruiting they'd been able to do, and the plan to move in on Sabine in the next couple of days. He'd always been proud of her, always admired her strength and determination, but as he listened to her now, he realized she truly had grown to become a queen. A leader who did what was necessary despite her anguish, her struggle to keep from going insane, and her reservations about certain things that had to be done in order to protect her people.

He, personally, would have done to the vampire the same things she revealed Xavier and Max had done to him in order to learn more. "I tried to warn the palace about Sabine. I can only hope someone received one of the messages we sent them," she said.

"I'm sure someone did," he replied. He gently grasped her chin. "I've never been prouder to call you my wife, never been happier to have you as my queen. You are my everything, Arianna."

"Even with knowing what I allowed Xavier and Max to do?" she whispered.

"You are fierce, loyal, proud, and do what is necessary to protect those you love and our followers. You're more than I ever could have hoped for in my life."

She rested her hand against his cheek. "She had your head, Braith. Or at least I thought it was your head, and I'm sure those in the palace believed the same thing."

"Someone else's head, someone who looked like me."

"When she lifted it…" Aria broke off when her voice hitched. "Until then, I'd been trying not to, but I'd secretly hoped you would come back to me. That somehow you would find a way. When she revealed the head, it all fell apart. *I* fell apart. It was worse than when I felt the severing of our bond."

She rested her hand over her heart. "Then, I tried to tear my heart from my chest. When she held up what I thought was your head, I thought I would go insane. All I wanted was to die. Then all I wanted was to kill, and I didn't care who I killed in order to make it all just *stop*, if only for a second. I wasn't sure I could make it back from that madness or control myself. I didn't know how to at first, but I knew the others still deserved happiness and peace and I had to get it for them. It's the only thing that has kept me going since then."

His fangs slid free at the image of her consumed by a suffering so extreme that all she wanted was to destroy herself by tearing her heart from her chest. "I know the disconnect you felt, the emptiness. I felt it too when I first woke to find you gone."

"I had to go! I couldn't stay in that cave no matter how much I didn't want to leave you!"

He grasped her chin. "I know. I didn't mean gone from there. I meant from inside of me. You were no longer within me. Our bond no longer existed. I would have destroyed everyone around me if Max hadn't told me you were safe. I did destroy some of Sabine's vampires in the forest when we came across them on our way here. What I did to them was something that should never have been done to another. I was out of control. I craved their blood and relished killing them. I didn't think I'd ever come back from the bloodlust engulfing me while I tore them apart."

Her head tilted back so she could gaze at him. He'd half expected to see fear or condemnation in her eyes, but he saw only love and understanding there. "And now what do you think?"

"Now, I *can* think again. The insanity has been eased, the emptiness filled with the renewal of our bloodlink. We will defeat Sabine, but I will be in control when it happens. I won't be a monster again, not like that."

"You're not a monster."

"Yes, I was with those vampires. If you hadn't been here when we arrived, I have no idea what I would have done. I may have slaughtered everyone here before regaining control of myself, if I ever regained control of myself."

"You think that now, but you would have kept control and not hurt them. You would have done what needed to be done to protect your loved ones and your followers."

His fingers worked through the ends of her braid, unraveling it to spread her hair around them. The golden and blood-red strands in her deep-auburn hair shimmered in the dim light filtering around the edges of the door. "How can you have so much faith in me?"

"Because I know you and your heart." She rested her palm over it and shuddered. "Even when it was pierced, you still protected and fought for everyone else, and *me*. You would have done the same for all of those in this place who need you."

He wasn't so sure she was right, but he would never argue with her unwavering confidence in him. Lowering his head, he kissed her chest over where her heart had once beat so strongly within her. "I much prefer your heart where it is," he said against her skin and she actually chuckled.

"Tearing it out was all I could think to do when I felt you die, but William stopped me until I could regain control of myself."

"I understand," he said as he smoothed the lose strands of her hair back from her face. "When I first woke, I nearly killed Daniel and Jack."

"Are they all right?" she demanded.

"Yes, but I do owe them an apology."

She smiled at him as she cuddled closer. "That might shock them more than you rising from the dead did."

"I think you're right."

"Braith, how is it possible you and your family are able to do such a thing?"

"I don't know. I'm sure Sabine has some knowledge of it, but I don't think Atticus had any."

"I don't either," she said. "Goran is your uncle, but he's not as powerful as you."

She'd already revealed that to him, but a small kick of shock still went through him when she said it again. He had an uncle, who was just as malicious as many of his other family members had been.

"No, he's not," Braith replied. "He may be around my age, as I feel he is old, but whatever is in Sabine, was in Atticus, and is in me, is not in Goran or Jack. I think that whatever it is that makes the three of us different than other vampires, is why I was able to see you that day on the stage without having tasted your blood first."

"Hannah can't walk in the sun without sharing Jack's blood on a regular basis," she said.

UNBOUND

"Exactly, but something in my blood allowed me to see you, and to regain my vision without your blood."

"It's because you are the first born of your line," she murmured and stifled a yawn.

"You have to rest."

"I'm afraid if I close my eyes, I'll wake to find this really was all only another dream of you."

"It's not," he promised.

"You came back stronger," she said as she curled up on her side again and her eyes drifted closed. Her lids popped back open at once and her hand clenched around his as if it were a lifeline. "I can taste it in your blood. It is more powerful. Your vision and scars are completely healed."

"Yes. I also heal faster and move a lot faster. There were fourteen vampires in the woods. I killed them all."

She burrowed closer against him. "They couldn't have been allowed to live."

"No, they couldn't."

When you d-died," her voice broke on the word. "Did you know?"

"I knew I was dying," he said as he recalled those last moments of coherency before he'd woken again in the cave. His hand rested on her shoulder, and his fingers slid over her silken skin as she rolled over to look at him. "I tried so hard to stay with you, to not go, but I couldn't stop it."

"You lived for a while after you were shot. I had to take out the arrow that was in your heart."

"You will never have to do something like that again."

"We don't know what the future holds."

"I will do everything I can to make sure you never go through such a thing again. No matter what happens, not even death will keep us apart."

She started beneath him, her eyes widening as she gazed at him. "I had a dream about us in the garden, all the roses turned black around us, and you said those words to me then too."

"I am wise even in death," he whispered and bent to taste her lips once more.

She smiled at him when he pulled away. Her fingers ran over the stubble lining his cheek as he watched her. "You are."

"Rest, love," he whispered and kissed her nose.

She rolled over to stare at the wall for a minute before closing her eyes again. This time, they didn't reopen as sleep finally claimed her.

***

Braith

Braith closed the door behind him as he stepped from the room and into the main area once more. There were far less humans in here now; in fact, the only ones remaining were Daniel, Timber, Max, and the girl.

He didn't know who she was, but he may have to kill her, he realized as he studied her pale face. The knowledge of him being able to rise from the dead was best kept under wraps. There was no way of knowing how others would react to it, how many would try to kill him because of it, or worse, how many would go after his and Aria's child while they were still young and vulnerable.

They all knew Atticus had come back, but many believed Atticus hadn't actually been dead when they'd placed him in the ground.

Jack lifted his head from Hannah's hair as she slept against his chest. Tempest sat up in William's lap, her brown eyes following his every move when he walked over to the table to stare down at the crude drawing on it. Xavier watched him with his arms folded over his chest and the light of the lantern behind his shoulder flickering over him.

"I am sorry about your throat and what happened in the cave," Braith said to Daniel as he lifted his gaze from the table. "I didn't mean to hurt you, or you," he said to Jack.

"Nothing I couldn't handle," Jack replied.

"The bruises will fade," Daniel said.

"Aria informed me of everything that has been going on here," he said.

"Hopefully the storm breaks soon," William said. "It will slow down the runners we send to gather the troops and we have to send them soon. We can't take the risk of the palace walls being breached and those within being unable to protect themselves from Sabine."

There had been many times Braith had envisioned throttling William over the past couple of years, but staring at him now, he knew William was a big part of the reason Aria still lived. He could never again imagine thrashing his brother-in-law.

"We'll send the runners tomorrow and make our move against her to end this soon." Braith glanced around the mostly empty room. "Where has everyone gone?"

"There are fifteen rooms down here. The humans spilt off into them, and some have gone to keep watch in the woods. Aria has rarely slept in the room you were just in, but they continue to let her have it to herself," William replied.

"Has she slept at all?" Braith asked.

"Here and there, but not much."

Braith's teeth ground together as he contemplated what he would do to Sabine once he got his hands on her. He would thoroughly enjoy destroying the woman for what she'd put them all through.

Tilting his head back, he gazed at the beams running across the ceiling. "Ingenious place this is," he commented.

"Daniel designed it years ago," William said. "We never had the chance to implement these safe houses before the war, but the rebels did after the war was over. Good thing they did too."

"Why did they build them?"

"There may have been peace, but for a people who have been abused and mistreated by vampires for a hundred years, distrust isn't easily buried. They felt they were better safe than sorry, and if Sabine wins, they'll have been right."

"She won't win," Braith said. He focused on the girl between Daniel and Max. "What do we do with you?" he inquired, and she lifted her chin.

"Nothing," she replied. "Your secrets are my secrets."

"Is that so?"

"Yes."

Braith continued to gaze at her as Max rose to his feet. "I'll keep an eye on Maeve, but I do believe we can trust her."

"What makes you say that?" Braith asked.

"She hasn't told anyone what she's seen and heard yet, and it's not like she couldn't blurt it out before any of us could stop her."

"They'd all think I was crazy anyway," she said. "Who would believe me?"

"There are those who would," Braith replied.

"Perhaps, but you have all worked to give us freedom. Why would I betray that? I'm a rebel."

"Hmm," Braith murmured. "We shall see."

"You *will* see."

He wanted to believe her. He admired her spirit, but he'd break her neck at the first sign she might betray them. Maeve held his gaze unwaveringly, refusing to back down at the same time she tried to convey she spoke the truth.

Braith turned from her. Only time would tell with her, and for now, he intended to trust Max. Max had helped to keep both him and Aria safe; he'd more than earned that trust. "Aria told me about what happened with Sabine's stable man," he said to Max and Xavier.

"The man was very stubborn," Xavier replied, and Max paled.

So it was bad then. Braith rested his fingertips on the table as he rubbed his neck with his other hand. They'd done what was necessary; he just wished Aria hadn't been a part of it. "It needed to be done," he said.

"It did," Xavier agreed.

The others all exchanged looks and he got the impression they didn't know the extent of what had happened. Even with everything Aria had revealed to him, he wasn't sure he knew the full extent of it.

"You appear more in control," Jack said quietly.

"I am," he replied crisply.

"I've been informed we have an uncle too," Jack said, seeming to realize he was walking into treacherous territory and deciding to steer the conversation elsewhere.

"We'll welcome him to the family by killing him," Braith replied.

"Killing family members *has* become a tradition."

"That it has. How many troops have been recruited?" he asked.

"There are well over twenty-five hundred now," Daniel said. "There will most likely be more as those people are also recruiting others, and by now word has spread of the missing humans and the villages where vampires are brutalized and tortured. Where the *children* are murdered in cold blood. More will join the fight."

"They will," Braith murmured as he studied the x's on the map.

They'd all been busy while he'd been dead. Fury slid through him at the reminder of all he'd missed and all they'd been left behind to try to accomplish.

So many things could have happened to Aria while he'd been gone. So many things *had* happened to her while he'd been dead. She'd been beaten and her soul battered, yet she'd also been steadily working to create an army.

"Easy, Braith," Jack said.

His head shot up; he stared at his brother as his muscles flexed and his fangs pricked. He was far more in control of himself now that their bloodlink was reestablished, but the reminder of what Aria had endured rattled him. However, he hadn't realized his control had slipped to the point where they would notice it. They all looked between him and the door to where Aria slept as if they were debating on waking her.

"If anyone wakes her, I'll kill them," he promised and their eyes shot back to him. He removed his hand from the table and stepped back. "Who is going to gather the rest of the troops here?"

They glanced nervously at each other. "Timber, Max, and Daniel will go," William answered.

"I'll go too," Maeve said.

"We're not giving you a chance to escape," Daniel said.

She gave him a scathing glance. "I am a fighter. I don't back down from that, ever."

"Take her with you," Braith said. "Give her a chance to further prove herself, and kill her if she tries anything."

Maeve gave a brisk nod. "Fair enough."

"Will the humans be ready for this fight?" he asked.

"We never stopped being ready," Maeve replied. "We always suspected one day we'd have to fight again. It's all we've ever done."

"That's true," Timber said as he rocked back in his chair.

"They follow Aria. They like and trust her. She was once one of them, and even when she was teetering on the edge, she managed to put up a strong front for all of them," William said. "They'll fight for her, for themselves, and for their children."

A shimmer of distress radiated over him. He turned toward the room where he'd left Aria as the door opened. Her reddened eyes turned blue when they latched onto him, and she took a step forward.

"Even if the storm is still raging, leave at dawn," he said to them over his shoulder as he strode over to her, lifted her up, and carried her back into the room.

CHAPTER 34

Max

The rain pelted Max's skin as they made their way through the trees toward the last safe house location. He felt as if he'd been out in the rain for weeks instead of the two days it had taken them to traverse the distance to all of the safe houses. They would have made much better time, but the storm continued to lash the earth.

At his side, Maeve shivered and pulled the hood of her cloak closer around her face. Despite their brutal pace and the punishing weather, she continued onward without once complaining about the travel conditions. One of them had always stayed by her when they arrived somewhere new, but never once had she attempted to tell anyone else what she knew. Timber and Daniel were beginning to trust her more, and Max firmly believed she would not betray them.

He stopped outside the tree hiding the final safe house and pushed the button, opening it up and slipping inside behind the others. Within, they discovered well over three hundred people gathered and waiting for word it was time to move on. Max accepted the food and ale as well as the dry clothes offered to him.

The occupants of the safe house informed them there were more humans and vampires waiting in some nearby caves. At every safe house they'd gone to, they'd been told the same thing. Their numbers were more than they'd hoped for, and their recruits were ready to wage a war.

He would have given anything to be able to spend the night here, but they had to return to let Aria and Braith know they'd succeeded in making the rounds and that everyone should be arriving by tomorrow night.

With dry clothes and a full belly, he stepped back into the rain and in minutes his clothes were plastered to his skin. Maeve shivered again and he had to resist the impulse to drape his arm around her shoulders and draw her close to give her some of his body heat. He knew she would only draw away from him if he tried. They moved swiftly through the trees and back toward the safe house closest to the palace.

No one spoke as they walked and jogged over the sodden terrain. They were only five miles away from the barn when Daniel came to an abrupt halt. He ran a hand through his blond hair, shaking the rain from it as he tilted his head to the side. Max took hold of Maeve's arm, drawing her back to stand beside him while Daniel surveyed the woods.

"What is it?" Timber asked.

"I don't know," Daniel said. "But I don't like it."

Max's gaze ran over the trees and woods as he searched for anything out of the ordinary. As the hair on his nape stood up, he turned to look behind him, but still saw nothing there. "I think we need to get out of the open," he said.

"Yes," Daniel agreed.

Daniel turned and jogged up a steep hillside. Max followed closely behind him with Maeve, while Timber brought up the rear. At the top of the cliff, Max turned to look back down the rocky face as Daniel and Timber slipped into the small cave created by an outcropping of rocks. Maeve stood at his side, her arm trembling in his grasp. He knew the tremor was from the cold instead of fear; she had little fear of most things.

A flash of movement within the trees drew his attention to the right as a dozen vampires rode into view. The two of them slipped back, creeping into the small cave. Daniel and Timber were twenty feet away, examining the back wall. "Any way out?" Max inquired.

"No," Timber said.

"There's at least a dozen of them down there."

"I don't think they'll come up here," Daniel murmured as he turned toward them. "At least I hope not."

Max crept back toward the opening of the cave and crouched at the entrance. He rested his fingers on the stone as he gazed down at the vampires clustered below. "What are they doing?" Maeve whispered from behind him.

"I think they caught our scent, but with the storm they can't pinpoint us," he replied.

"Wonderful," she murmured.

Max remained kneeling, keeping watch as the vampires mulled about for a few minutes more before slipping into the woods. He didn't trust them not to be somewhere down there, waiting to ambush them, and neither did the others as no one suggested continuing on right now.

A shiver worked its way over his chilled skin. Goose bumps covered his skin as night descended. Daniel and Timber were sleeping when Maeve knelt at his side again and handed him a piece of soggy bread from the last safe house.

"When can we leave?" she asked him.

"Not until morning, at least."

She sat next to him and pressed her back against the wall. She'd pulled her wet cloak off earlier and set it with the others in the back of the cave. The thin shirt she wore underneath stuck to her petite frame as it dried. She had to be freezing, he certainly was, but still she didn't complain, and he couldn't build a fire to warm her.

Her black hair tumbled in waves around her shoulders as she picked at her piece of bread. The sleeves of her shirt had been pinned into place, hiding the scars there. Her arm brushed against his as her fingers pulled at the bread. He sensed she had something to say, but he waited until she was ready to speak instead of questioning her.

"Do you still have nightmares?" she inquired after a few minutes.

Though they had only briefly discussed it before, he knew she was talking about his time as a blood slave. "Yes, do you?"

"Yes." She stuck a piece of bread in her mouth and chewed on it. "Almost every night." Her fingers went to the scar on her face and traced over it.

"How did you get that?" he asked.

Her hand fell away, and her gaze focused on the opposite wall. "My captor sometimes thought it was more fun to cut me open to drink my blood. It's not the only one I have."

Max clamped his teeth together, barely containing his need to slam his fist into the cave wall. He took a steadying breath. She was a fighter, but she wouldn't handle seeing that kind of unprovoked violence from him, not after what she'd experienced.

"I see," he said when he could trust himself to speak again. He knew he couldn't show her pity; she would turn away from him if he did.

She continued to stare ahead, her fingers fiddling with the bread in her hand. "I survived at least, many didn't."

"Very true," he replied, though he knew a part of him had died in Katrina's hands.

Feeling more in control of himself again, he brushed a strand of her hair from her cheek. She flinched away when he traced over her scar. "Don't pull away from me," he said and rested his hand against her cheek. "I won't hurt you."

"I'm not afraid of being hurt," she retorted. "The scar reminds me to never be weak again, and I don't like anyone touching it."

"What happened to you doesn't mean you were weak."

"Doesn't it?"

"No."

For a second, she turned into his palm before looking away once more. "Then what does it mean?"

"That sometimes shit happens, and there is nothing you can do about it. That doesn't mean you're weak. It simply means you're alive."

She placed the loaf of bread on the ground and pulled at the edges of her sleeves, though they already covered her scars. Moving away from the wall, she turned to face him as she knelt before him. He watched in fascination as she took hold of his hand before she slowly worked the sleeve of his shirt up.

Normally, he pulled away from people, ashamed for them to see the burns and bite marks encircling his wrists and rising up his forearms, but he allowed her to explore them. She also tried to keep most of her scars hidden, but she had to bare the one on her face for the world to see, and he wanted to give this baring of himself to her.

He welcomed her delicate, chilled fingers running over his skin. He saw only understanding in her eyes as she uncovered more of his scars. She knew how he'd acquired every one of those marks and the degradation that had come with each one of them.

She drew her bottom lip into her mouth as she continued to stroke him with fascination. It had been years since he'd allowed anyone to look at him so openly, to touch him in such a way. He hadn't realized how much he'd missed and craved it until her skin warmed his.

His gaze fell to her tempting mouth. He'd give anything to be able to taste her. Her hands stilled on him and he lifted his eyes to hers.

"Did your captor do other things to you?" she asked. "Besides the feeding and the torture?"

He knew she spoke of the sexual abuse, but she couldn't bring herself to ask the question. "Yes."

Her head bowed, her black hair falling forward to shield her face. Tears brimmed in her eyes and one slid down her cheek. "Mine too," she whispered.

He smothered the burning rage that burst through his chest. "Is he still alive?" Max grated through his teeth. Because if he was, Max was going to make it a point to remedy that.

"No. He was killed during the war. What of yours?"

"She's also dead."

"Good."

Leaning forward, he encircled his hand around the back of her head and drew her toward him. She flinched then melted against him when he placed the lightest of kisses to her lips before sitting back. She sighed when he pulled her against him and settled her within his lap. Like a kitten, she nestled against his chest.

He'd never felt needed before, but he felt it now. She needed him, and he needed her. She understood what few in this world could, understood him and what he lived with every day, just as he understood her. Turning his head into her hair, he inhaled the scent of the rain clinging to her skin.

"No one will ever hurt you again," he murmured.

She tipped her head back, her cerulean eyes searching his before she leaned up and tentatively kissed his lips again. Forcing himself to go slowly, he threaded his fingers through her damp hair, holding her against him as he brushed his tongue over her lips. She stiffened for a second before relaxing in his hold and opening her mouth to his.

Her fingers clenched in his shirt while he tasted her. His heart raced in his chest as his hands gripped her tighter. She was so small and she was his; in that instant, he knew it was true. He would do everything he could to keep her safe because she belonged with him.

She broke the kiss off, her breath coming in small pants as she rested her forehead against the bridge of his nose. "I'm sorry," she whispered. "I can't... I don't... I'm broken."

"No," he said and kissed her forehead. "You're not broken."

"How can you know that?" she whispered.

"Because I have felt broken before too, but not now."

"And how do you feel now?"

He cupped her cheek in his hand. "Whole."

Her gaze traveled over his face before falling to his mouth again. "Whole," she murmured and lifted her fingers to run them over his lips. "What if I can never feel that way again?"

"You can."

She pulled her fingers away from his lips and rested them against her own. Max could still feel the heat of her against his mouth. He wanted nothing more than to replace her fingers with his lips, but he didn't make a move toward her again. She'd let him know when she was ready for that.

"Whole," she said again and nestled against his chest once more. "Have you ever told anyone about what you went through in there?"

"No, have you?"

"No," she said and touched the scar on her face once more.

Max rested his hand over hers. "The vampire who bought me was named Katrina," he said as he leaned against the rocks and stared at the wall across from him.

Memories he'd worked so hard to bury surged to the forefront of his mind as he recalled those early days in Katrina's hold, when he'd still been certain he would be able to break free. Then the later days, when he'd been certain he would die. He'd pleaded for death many times, but his request was never granted. Instead, Jack had arrived one day and released him from his prison. He'd been set free, yet there were times he still felt imprisoned by his memories and the nightmares.

For the first time, he set all of those memories free and told someone what he'd endured at Katrina's brutal hands. He didn't hold any of it back; there was no reason to, Maeve understood. When he finished, her hand spread out to slip between the buttons of his wet shirt. His breath sucked in when she placed her palm flat against his chest, over where his heart beat faster for her.

"The vampire who bought me was named Byron," she whispered, and he listened as she revealed the torture and torment she had withstood.

He drew her closer, holding her against him in an attempt to shelter her from the memories, but there was no sheltering her from what she'd suffered. "I wanted to hate them all for what happened to me," she said at the end.

"So did I," he admitted. "But humans had a hand in it too. Some of our own kind turned their backs on us long ago and allowed the vampires to become what they were."

"I know, but in the beginning, I hated everyone."

"Me too."

She lifted her head from his chest. Her hand rested against his cheek as she rose up to kiss him once more.

CHAPTER 35

Braith

"Where are they?" Aria murmured while she paced from one end of the barn to the other.

"They'll be back soon," Braith said as he followed her restless movements. He'd finally gotten her to get some sleep, easing the shadows under her eyes, and she was already putting weight back on again from drinking his blood, but she was still on edge.

She spun and stalked back toward the other side with Keegan trotting beside her. Xavier stood with William and Tempest near the barn door, watching her. Aria stopped pacing and spun toward the door as a new scent floated on the air.

"They're back," William said and opened the door.

On the other side stood Daniel, Timber, Max, and Maeve. Their hair hung in straggles about their faces, their clothes were wrinkled and wet, but they were unharmed as they hurried into the barn and Max closed the door. Braith lifted an eyebrow when Max slid his hand into Maeve's, drawing her closer against him. Aria's head cocked to the side, and he realized she had no idea who the girl was.

Taking a few steps toward them, Aria held her hand out to the tiny woman standing by Max's side. Braith studied the scar on Maeve's face and the proud set of her shoulders. She was willful, but there was also a vulnerable air about her. His gaze slid to Max as he recognized the same air about him.

She was a blood slave, Braith realized as Maeve took hold of Aria's hand. The sleeve of her shirt had been pinned, allowing no skin to be exposed. It was something Max had done often enough since he'd been taken from the palace.

"I'm Aria," she said and shook the woman's hand.

"Maeve."

"It's a pleasure to meet you, Maeve," she said before stepping forward to hug Max. "I'm glad you're back."

He patted her back before she turned away from him to embrace Daniel. "I was worried about you," she said.

"We ran into some company in the woods, had to take shelter until we were sure they'd moved on," Daniel told her.

"Did you make it to all of the safe houses?"

"We did. There are more fighters than we expected, close to three thousand, maybe more."

"Good." Braith walked forward to slide his arm around Aria's waist and draw her against his side. "When will they be arriving?"

"They should all be here by nightfall," Daniel answered and pulled his cloak off.

"That will be a good time to move," Braith said. "They won't expect a nighttime attack."

Daniel sank onto a bale of straw. He dropped his head into his hand and rubbed tiredly at his temples. Aria pulled away from Braith and walked over to sit beside her brother. "Are you okay?" she inquired.

Daniel gave her a wan smile as he lowered his hand. "I'm tired, but okay."

"You should go rest. We'll get everything set up," she told him.

"I think I'm going to take you up on that one, but I'll be in the back of the barn. I've had enough of being underground for a bit."

Braith watched him as he rose and walked to the shadows at the back of the barn. Aria remained seated on the bale, nervously watching her brother.

"We had better prepare the ones below and all those hiding nearby in the caves," Braith said, and Aria rose to her feet.

She took hold of his hand and followed him underground once more.

***

William

"It's so pretty," Tempest said, drawing William's gaze away from the glittering blue lake before them and to her.

He couldn't resist brushing back a strand of her silvery hair from her cheek. "Nowhere near as pretty as you," he said honestly.

Color crept through her face, and her gaze flitted away as she smiled. "You're a flatterer."

"Just calling it like I see it," he replied and enfolded his hand around her neck to draw her closer. He kissed her forehead and inhaled her wintry scent. "I love you."

"I love you too. We're going to get through this."

"Yes," he said and kissed her again. Though he knew there was a good possibility not all of them would make it through the coming battle. "We are. Sabine isn't going to know what hit her when she sees Braith, and she won't be prepared for the forces we've managed to gather."

Tempest's gaze went back to the lake and the sun reflecting across its smooth, blue surface. He took hold of her hand, marveling at how small it was as he ran his fingers over the back of it.

"I want to spend the rest of my life with you, Tempest."

A playful smile curved her mouth as she turned her head to the side. "I certainly hope so. You're stuck with me."

"I can't think of anyone I'd want to be stuck with more."

"You're such a romantic."

He grinned at her as he went down to his knee before her. Her mouth parted as he pulled a simple wooden ring from his pocket. With no jewelry nearby, or any way to get it right now, he'd made the ring from a small branch and etched a Celtic knot onto its surface.

"Will you be my wife?" he asked and held it up before her.

Tears filled her eyes and spilled down her cheeks as she gazed at it in awe. She opened her mouth to respond, but no words came out. William gazed up at her, his heart in his throat as he waited for her to say or do something.

"Yes," she finally croaked out. "Yes!"

William slid the wooden band onto her finger before launching himself to his feet. He wrapped his arms around her waist and lifted her into the air. Pulling her head back, he claimed her mouth in a kiss that left her shaking against him when he broke it off.

Her eyes were dazed when they met his, her lips swollen. Lifting her hand, she wiggled her fingers before her. "It's beautiful."

"When this is over, I will get you any ring you desire," he vowed.

"Absolutely not," she said. "*This* is my ring. It's the only one I want."

He grinned at her before kissing her again.

***

Aria

Aria gazed over all of the people crowding within the barn. There were easily over a few thousand individuals converging inside and flowing out the doorway beyond. Some men and women would be staying behind to protect and watch over the children who would remain below, but most would be coming with them.

Her fingers fidgeted at her sides as she struggled to appear calm and determined. They were going to war, *again*. Braith stood proudly by her side, his gaze surveying everyone within and those beyond the doors who wouldn't fit inside. The feel of his arm against hers electrified her skin as the hard edge of his power caressed her. She didn't think he was even aware of it seeping out of his pores right now, but the others were as they admiringly surveyed him while remaining a good five feet back.

What would happen if he died again? She didn't want to find out, but would he come back *stronger*? Or did he only get one chance to cheat death and the next time would be the last? Aria shuddered at the possibility.

Keegan brushed against her side, his large head rubbing her thigh. She smiled before resting her hand on his head. It had been so long since she'd seen the wolf and she'd missed him. White hairs speckled his muzzle now, but he was still formidable and protective as he circled around the two of them.

Her head tilted back when she felt Braith's gaze boring into her. "You did something amazing here, Arianna."

"They're always prepared to fight," she replied dismissively.

"It's more than that. You brought them all together during a time when many in your shoes would have fallen apart."

She glanced away from him, uncomfortable with the reminder of those dismal days. Their bond had been renewed, but she could still feel the madness dancing at the edges of her mind. She'd never forget what the impending insanity had felt like. If something happened to him again, she would snap in a way that would make Atticus look like he'd been a completely rational, caring man.

"I couldn't have done it alone," she said, uncomfortable with his praise when she'd spent a lot of that time trying not kill anyone who walked by her. "And I didn't. This never could have been accomplished without the others."

"No it couldn't have, but one could ever doubt you are meant to be a queen," he said.

The hungry look in his eyes caused her toes to curl as heat crept through her body. "You keep looking at me like that, and I'm going to jump you in a completely unqueenly way."

He laughed as he rested his hand on her shoulder and drew her against him. The heat of his body warmed hers and made her sigh in relief and joy. She still couldn't believe he really was back from the dead, standing beside her. She kept expecting to wake from a dream, but with every passing second she became increasingly convinced he was with her again.

Across the way, she spotted William and Tempest slipping through the crowd to enter the barn. Tempest had a leaf sticking out of her disheveled hair. William pulled the leaf away and tossed it aside as his gaze scanned the barn. He stopped searching when his eyes fell on her and Braith.

Taking hold of Tempest's hand, he led her through the crowd toward them, a big grin on his face. Aria couldn't stop herself from smiling at the joy radiating from him. "What is it?" she asked when they reached them.

"I asked Tempest to marry me and she accepted," he said proudly.

Aria did a double take. She'd known this was coming, but still she couldn't quite picture her brother proposing. She released a delighted cry as she threw her arms around him before turning to embrace Tempest. "Welcome to the family!"

Tempest hugged her back. "Thank you," she said as Aria released her.

Braith clasped William's hand and shook it before turning to Tempest. "It's not too late to change your mind and run," he told her when he took hold of her hand.

William scowled at him, Aria elbowed him, and Tempest laughed. "I have no plans of running," she said.

Braith released her hand as Jack, Hannah, Daniel, Timber, Max, and Maeve walked over to join them. For a minute, Aria could almost pretend she stood with her family, celebrating William's good news and simply being happy. Then, she glanced at the growing crowd around her and reality returned. They could celebrate now, but some of them would not survive the night.

CHAPTER 36

Braith

Braith kept Aria close to his side as they crept through the woods toward the palace. Despite the large number following behind them, he barely heard any movement within the trees. These people had been born into a world where stealth was their main mode of survival, and they were good at it.

Although they were natural predators, the vampires were louder than the humans, but their movements were still barely discernible amongst the creaking of the trees and the reverberating crashes resonating from the direction of the palace. He slowed as they neared the town bordering the palace walls. Flames flickered from the torches lining the walls and within the town itself. The storm had finally broken late last night, but clouds still obscured the stars and moon, helping to keep them hidden.

There were a hundred of Sabine's vampires positioned to watch the woods. The humans who had scouted the area had reported their locations. Their plan wouldn't work unless all of Sabine's followers watching the woods were taken out at the same time.

Braith stopped when he spotted some of Sabine's followers through the trees. All down the line, the vampires and humans with him also halted. Through the flickering shadows of the torches, Braith studied the vamps fifteen feet ahead of him. They were completely unaware of how close they were to the end of their lives.

Lifting his hand into the air, he made a fist that he pulled down toward his side. The gesture was taken up by others within the woods, spreading all the way down the line before Braith raced forward.

The three vamps closest to him spun toward him with their bows raised, but it was already too late for them. He had the one by the throat and the heart of the other within his hand before they could do more than squeak. He drove the last one into the ground and dispatched him quickly.

The bloodlust pulsing through his veins was stronger than it had ever been before he'd died. He struggled to keep himself from rushing through the trees to slaughter more of Sabine's followers. He couldn't leave Aria unprotected though. That thought helped to calm him enough to keep him where he was, but his body still thrummed with the need to kill.

Lifting his head, Braith looked through the underbrush to the walls of the palace and Sabine's troops still fighting to breach them, but no alarm had been raised. The humans and vampires around him had successfully dispatched Sabine's early warning system.

Some vamps loaded a large stone into a catapult positioned before the palace gate. The wooden drawbridge he'd ordered built was splintering and falling apart, he had no idea how many hits it had already taken, but it wouldn't take many more. Guards lined the palace walls, firing arrows onto their enemies below, but Sabine's followers still managed to fire the catapult sending the rock soaring through the air.

It smashed into the drawbridge with a resounding crash that echoed through the forest. Wood splintered and a piece of the bridge flew into the air to hit a house fifty feet away. However, the drawbridge remained intact, for now. If the palace walls or gates were breached, there would be a slaughter as Sabine's followers outnumbered those within. They had to take her down early, cut the head off the snake before dismantling every last one of her troops.

Aria crept forward to kneel beside him with her hand resting in the dirt. Streaks of black coal had been painted down both of her cheeks from temple to chin, another streak went straight down the middle of her nose. He had the same streaks on his face. The markings had been used so they could differentiate those who were on their side, from those who weren't. They had also forgone wearing any cloaks.

She leaned against his side, needing to feel his body against hers as much as he needed to feel hers against his. He wiped the blood off of his hand in the dirt before taking hold of hers and pressing it to his chest. Her fingers entwined with his as Keegan padded forward to sit at her side.

Shifting her stance, Aria released his hand to take another step forward. He placed his hand on her shoulder, drawing her back when she craned her head to look up and down the street. She leaned closer to him and rested her mouth against his ear. "She's down there," she said and pointed toward the brick house at the end of the road.

Braith nodded as around him more humans and vampires fanned out through the woods, creeping toward the town. Sabine's fighters outnumbered them, but with the element of surprise on their side and the guards on the palace walls, they could take her followers down, and they would. His gaze fell on Aria as she stared at him with apprehension in her crystalline blue eyes.

He would *not* lose her again, and he wouldn't allow her to go through what she'd endured when she thought he was dead again. No matter what happened, he would keep her safe and keep her from any more hurt.

He turned to Jack who knelt by his other side. "We'll move now. Make sure everyone waits until Sabine's house is on fire before they make a move."

"We will," Jack replied and took hold of Hannah's hand. Jack rested his other hand on Braith's arm, stopping him when he turned away. "Be careful."

"You also," Braith replied.

Braith took hold of Aria's hand again as they made their way through the woods toward the back of the house Sabine had taken up residence in. Keegan, William, Tempest, Max, Maeve, Daniel, and Xavier stayed close behind them along with half a dozen other humans. He glanced back to find Jack, Hannah, and Timber watching them as they moved away.

Fifty feet away from the house, Aria pulled on his hand, drawing him to a stop. He peered through the underbrush and trees to the fifty or so vampires spread around the house, keeping guard. Braith's fangs throbbed with the compulsion to destroy. They were so close to ending the woman who had tried to end him.

He would make her pay.

Aria released him to remove two arrows from her quiver. She wrapped the ends with a cloth as around her the others did the same thing. Her face was composed as she worked, her eyes steady and focused, but the small tremor in her fingers was something only he would notice. No matter how resolute she acted, she was still rattled by the events that had transpired over these past couple of weeks.

Braith rested his hand over hers, drawing her eyes to him. "I'm never leaving you again, Aria."

Her hand went completely still beneath his. "I know."

He couldn't help but smile at her as she thrust her shoulders back and pulled her hand away from his. Her hand remained steady as she finished wrapping the cloth around the arrow. The others finished tying off their arrows as matches and fuel were passed around to douse the rags.

Aria held one of her arrows out to him. "I love you," she said.

"I love you too."

With that, he struck the match and placed the flame to her rag. There would be no more hiding within the woods for them. Flames blazed to life all around them as Aria turned away from him, raised her bow and let the arrow fly. With her lethal aim, the arrow embedded into one of the shutters covering the back windows of the home. More arrows filled the sky, their flames lighting the night as the sparks trailing behind them danced through the air like fireflies in July.

Yells of alarm erupted from the vampires guarding the house and rang throughout the street. He lit Aria's next arrow and watched as she released it with the same deadly accuracy. This one embedded into the shingles on the roof.

Shouts sounded from the walls of the palace as the resonating twang of bowstrings resounded from the woods and arrows whistled through the air. Screams echoed through the night, more arrows were loosed in a deadly torrent as some of Sabine's vampires turned to face the attack coming from behind them while others tried to flee down the road.

Before they'd left the barn, he'd given the order that none of her followers were to survive this night. They had chosen their course when they'd decided to join her. He understood some had been forced into it, but there was no way for him to know which vampires those were, not for certain, and he wouldn't take the chance of any future rebellions. He was tired of war and fighting and death. Tonight would be the end of it all.

Their troops spilled from the woods and into the street to block Sabine's followers from retreating. The ones who tried to escape into the woods were pushed back by the humans and vampires waiting for them there.

Around the house Sabine resided in, many of the guards charged toward the woods, looking to take out whoever was trying to attack their queen. They fell back, screaming, when more arrows were unleashed upon them.

The flames from the arrows on the house caught on the shutters and spread across the roof. Braith remained unmoving, watching, waiting for Sabine to emerge. She would be *his*.

Five vampires managed to escape the arrows and barreled into the woods toward them. Braith rose, his lips skimming back to reveal his fangs. Bloodlust raced through his body, but unlike the uncontrollable urge to kill that had driven him in the woods after rising, he was far more in control of himself. He would slaughter these vampires, and any others who stood in his way of destroying Sabine, but this would not be a mindless, compulsive destruction.

One of them was nearly on top of Aria when he swung out with the back of his hand. The blow caved the vamp's skull in. He lunged forward and grabbed another vampire by his shoulders. Swinging him out, he bashed him into a tree, snapping his back.

He spun to the next vamp coming at them, but Aria released an arrow that pierced his heart and knocked him back. Another vampire rose up behind her, looming over top of her. Braith bellowed when one of the vamp's hands skimmed over her shoulder. Grabbing hold of the hand that had dared to touch her, Braith yanked it back and slammed it into the man's face, breaking his nose upon impact. He twisted the vamp's head on his shoulders and wrenched it free.

The body dropped from his hands as he lifted his gaze to meet Aria's. Firelight danced in her eyes as the roof of the house became engulfed by the flames eating away its surface. The crackle of wood and smoke filled the air; a beam within the house gave way with a loud crack. Cries of panic echoed through the town as the last of their army flooded from the woods at the end of the street, effectively blocking it off.

The potent scent of blood and the acrid aroma of the fire filled the air. He took hold of Aria, drawing her back as more vampires came at them. He punched one in the cheek before throwing an upper cut at another. The vampire launched ten feet into the air and crashed into a tree. Aria fired three arrows, taking out the rest of the vampires rushing at them.

Daniel and William were illuminated by the fire as Daniel released an arrow into the vampire William was fighting. Max and Maeve fired arrows at anyone trying to flee through the woods while Tempest and Xavier beat back some of the others.

At the front of the house, a flurry of movement caught his attention. "She's going," he growled.

He tore the arrow from the chest of the one Daniel had shot before he wrapped his arm around Aria's waist and lifted her against his side. Her fingers gripped his shoulders as she clung to him. He ran through the woods, battering back the branches slapping and tearing at her. The others followed them through the trees as the roof of the house collapsed beneath the flames engulfing it.

Heat blasted over him from the collapsing roof as the fire rushed outward in a loud whoosh. Sweat beaded across his brow and dripped down his back, causing his shirt to stick to him as he moved. Twisting in his arms, Aria pulled another arrow free of her quiver and fired it at a vampire rushing headlong into the woods. The arrow caught him high in the chest, knocking him to the ground. Daniel drove a stake through the vamp's chest before he could regain his feet.

Aria turned and fired at another vamp as William planted his feet and released a series of arrows. The arrows pelted the small wave of vamps trying to escape around the back of the house. Max, Daniel, and Maeve leapt forward to stake any who

317

had survived William's arrows. To the right of him, Xavier lifted another vampire and drove him onto the jagged, broken branch of a tree.

Bursting free of the woods, Braith surveyed the scene. The guards on top of the wall were firing down on the vamps running through the street. He spotted Gideon, Melinda, and Ashby on top of the wall near the gate, commanding the troops.

To his left, Jack, Timber, and Hannah had also broken free of the woods and were fighting to carve their way through the vampires trying to flee around them. Some of Sabine's followers had shed their brown cloaks in an attempt to blend in, but many were too panicked to have taken them off.

Perhaps some of Sabine's followers would figure out the black streaks on the faces of those attacking them also kept them from blending in, but not many of them would before it was too late. The guards on the palace walls focused on the vampires wearing the brown cloaks, the only ones they knew for certain weren't on their side. No matter that those within the palace knew they had allies on this side of the wall now, the gates wouldn't open before their enemies had been destroyed.

To his right, more vampires were being battled back by the small army blocking their escape at the end of the road. His eyes narrowed when he spotted Sabine walking casually down the street, her hair trailing behind her and her blood-colored cloak bright in the flames spreading through the town.

Her arrogance is her greatest weakness, Aria had said more than a few times and he saw now just how right she was.

At Sabine's side walked the vampire with the shockingly white hair. His uncle, Goran, her possible only other weakness. A dozen or so vampires flanked her sides, looking to keep her protected, but it wouldn't be enough to stop Braith from killing her.

Sabine was outnumbered by those blocking the end of the road, but with her strength she would cut through them with ease. He set Aria on her feet. She pulled two more arrows from her quiver and fired them at the retreating couple. Sabine turned, her eyes flashing red as she snatched both the arrows out of the air and snapped them within her fingers.

"Bitch," Aria murmured as she lowered her bow.

Sabine smiled at her before tossing the arrows away. Then, her gaze slid to Braith and he saw the slightest stiffening of her shoulders and a flicker of unease within her eyes. She hadn't been expecting him, at least not so soon. A smile curved his mouth before he raced down the street toward her.

CHAPTER 37

Aria

Aria fired arrows at the vampires surrounding Sabine and at those trying to escape as she ran behind Braith. She knew he could move much faster without them, but he stayed protectively in front of her. Xavier remained beside her, grabbing anyone she was unable to take out. Behind her, William worked to bring down more vampires with his bow. Daniel, Tempest, Max, and Maeve methodically staked any who survived their arrows.

As a vampire leapt out at Braith, she swung her bow toward him, releasing an arrow that struck him high in the shoulder and flung him back. Daniel pounced on him, driving his stake through his heart before tearing it free. Arrows soared through the air around them, their impacts making a thudding sound when they pierced through bodies or hit the earth.

A whistling sound reached her. She twisted to get out of the way of what she knew was coming from behind, but she wasn't fast enough. The arrow pierced through her right shoulder, knocking her forward and nearly causing her to lose her grip on her bow. Her arm erupted in tingles that made her fingers feel thick. She hadn't made a sound, but Braith must have caught the scent of her blood on the air as he spun toward her, his reddened eyes blazing hotter when they landed on the arrow protruding through her.

"I'm fine!" she shouted to be heard over the growing cacophony of battle filling the town and bouncing off the buildings around them.

He took a step toward her, but she held up a hand to ward him off. They couldn't stop now; they couldn't let Sabine get away, or the fighting and fear would never end. Sabine had to die tonight. Grasping the arrow, Aria bit her lip and braced herself before tearing it from her shoulder. She casually tossed it aside to show him how fine she was.

Blood spilled out of the wound to soak her shirt and skin, but she was able to lift her bow and fire an arrow at the vampire who rose up behind Braith. Though her aim was off, she still struck him. Braith spun as the vamp fell back before his head swiveled toward her once more. His hands fisted and his nostrils flared as he seemed torn between grabbing her and taking from here or continuing after Sabine.

The muscles in his forearms bulged when he finally focused on Sabine once more. Sabine continued down the street with more speed than she'd been exhibiting when she'd first emerged from the house. She was almost to the barricade at the end of the road.

"Braith you have to stop her! No matter what she must be stopped!" Aria shouted to be heard over the noise.

He glanced back at her and she saw the understanding in his eyes. If he went after Sabine, he couldn't stay with her anymore and he had to go. His jaw clenched as he turned away from her.

Aria barely managed to keep her mouth from dropping open when Braith started running again, shoving aside vampires as he moved faster than she'd ever seen him before. Despite the chaos around her, she couldn't help but marvel at the strength emanating from him as he blurred with speed. She rushed forward, trying to keep up with him, but it was impossible for her to do so.

"Go! You're faster than me!" Aria yelled to Xavier as Braith closed in on Sabine, Goran, and the few vampires still trying to protect her. Braith couldn't face them alone, no matter how much stronger he'd become since his death. He was outnumbered and Sabine was extremely powerful too.

It didn't matter if Xavier was faster or not, Sabine and Goran spun to face Braith as he reached them.

***

William

William watched as Braith grabbed hold of Goran and yanked him forward. The red cloak the vampire wore tore in his grasp, but not before Braith wrapped his hands around Goran's arms and pinned them down.

He followed Aria as she cleared a pathway before them with her arrows. Keegan stayed at her heels, lunging at vamps and bringing more than a few of them down with his powerful jaws. Xavier lifted Aria off the ground and held her against his side as a vampire leapt at her.

Thrown off balance, the vamp tumbled onto the ground. Lifting his foot, William drove it into the back of the vampire's skull, caving it in. Daniel bent and drove his stake through the vampire's chest before jerking it free.

"Have to help him!" Aria gasped as she squirmed in Xavier's hold.

William met Xavier's reddened eyes over the top of Aria's head. He knew Xavier was debating keeping her away from the fight unfolding at the end of the road, but Aria wouldn't survive it if Braith died again, and she had every right to fight for both of their lives. William gave a brief bow of his head to Xavier before spinning and firing at two vampires running toward the wood line.

Tempest snatched a staff from a downed vamp and gripped it in her hands as she fell back against William to batter back the vamps around them. He pushed her behind him, swinging out and punching the vampire trying to get at her. His fangs lengthened as he jerked the vamp toward him and drove his hand through the man's chest. Wrapping his hand around the vampire's heart, he tore it free and threw it aside.

Another vampire came at him as they seemed to realize that, if they took him and the others out, they may be able to crush this rebellion. Many of them probably knew what Aria looked like, and they most certainly knew who Braith was. William's gaze shot toward his brother-in-law when Aria released a strangled cry.

Braith and Goran were entangled with each other, tumbling over the ground as they sought to kill one another. Sabine looked on beside them before her head lifted, and she took in the commotion surrounding her. Xavier set Aria down when Sabine launched herself onto Braith's back.

William doubted the woman had ever gotten dirty before, or willingly tangled with anyone, but she had to realize she was losing this battle and the only chance she had left was to take out Braith while he was busy fighting her son. Beneath him, Goran launched a fist straight at Braith's heart when Braith tried to pull Sabine off his back.

Braith lost his grip on Sabine as his hand encircled Goran's wrist to keep it from plunging into his chest. Goran screamed when Braith jerked his hand to the side, snapping the bones in his wrist before throwing a punch over his back. He caught Sabine in the face, knocking her hold on him loose enough that Braith could seize Goran's head.

Sabine shrieked as Braith wrenched it to the side. For the first time, William saw true distress in Sabine's eyes as she tried desperately to free Goran from Braith's deadly hold, but Braith would not be deterred.

When William had first encountered Goran, he'd thought about how much he would enjoy watching Braith tear Goran's cotton ball head from his shoulders, and he did, he really, *really* did enjoy watching it. A smile curved his mouth as Braith tossed the head aside.

Braith sat back, grasping at Sabine over his shoulder when her hand encircled his throat and her blood-red claws pierced his flesh. Blood flowed down his neck and over his shirt.

"No!" Aria screamed and stopped running to release another arrow.

With her wounded shoulder, Aria's aim was off, but Sabine didn't have time to turn and catch this one. She threw herself to the side to avoid the arrow that plunged into the woods beyond her. Braith used the distraction to his advantage and seized Sabine by the hair to fling her away from him. She bounced across the ground before coming to a stop near one of the houses, a hundred feet closer to them. Her eyes were a fiery red, her control finally having unraveled completely as her malicious gaze landed on Aria.

William realized that if Sabine couldn't take Braith down one way, then there was another way she could do it. A way that would make Braith pay even more. Sabine must have realized this too as she launched to her feet and charged at Aria.

***

Daniel

Daniel's hands clenched around his stakes as he planted his feet. Xavier snarled and lunged forward. He jumped in front of Aria when Sabine came at them with the force of a rampaging bull. She lowered her shoulder, crashing into Xavier and flinging him back as if he weighed no more than a child. Xavier's head snapped awkwardly forward as he flew through the air. Landing on the street, he bounced across the ground before coming to a stop against a house where he remained motionless.

"Aria!" Braith bellowed when Aria became exposed to the woman. He leapt to his feet and ran toward them, but with the vampires swirling forward to try to protect Sabine, he'd never reach them in time to stop Sabine from killing Aria.

Aria lifted her bow and fired off a shot, catching Sabine in the shoulder, but it wasn't enough to stop her rush toward them. Daniel would not let everything they'd accomplished over the years be destroyed by this woman, and *no* one was going to hurt his sister.

"No!" Daniel shouted and jumped in front of Aria.

"Daniel, no!" Aria screamed.

She grabbed his shoulder to pull him away at the same time Sabine grasped his other arm and yanked him forward. Something in his shoulder wrenched. It felt as if blood spilled forth, and for a moment, he swore his arm had been torn from his socket. When he looked down, he saw it still hung there, and hung was the right word as it remained limp against his side, dangling at an unnatural angle.

A hand enveloped his throat, lifting him off the ground. Sabine's nails pierced his throat.

William launched forward, slamming into Sabine at the same time Aria threw herself onto the woman, punching and kicking her.

Daniel's feet dangled off the ground as his sibling's weight knocked Sabine back a step. "Aria, run!" Daniel managed to choke out through the crushing grip on his windpipe.

A cruel smile curved Sabine's mouth before she threw him away. Air rushed around him as he soared backward before crashing into a tree. Something cracked in his back, and his skull hit the tree with enough force to rattle his brain. White stars burst before his eyes. His head swayed on his shoulders as he struggled to remain conscious.

Sabine turned to try to grab Aria. His sister threw her head back and then drove it forward. Daniel smiled when blood burst from Sabine's shattered nose before oblivion claimed him.

CHAPTER 38

Aria

"I'll kill you!" Aria screamed as she looked to land any blow she could on the woman with her hands and feet.

The blood had already ceased flowing from Sabine's broken nose. Her eyes were the color of rubies, but Aria barely saw her as the sight of Daniel's limp body soaring through the air replayed in her mind and the scent of his blood hung heavily in the air.

Daniel!

At her side, William released a series of punches that would have shattered the bones of another vamp's face, but Sabine was barely staggered by the blows. Sabine's fingernails tore at Aria, slicing her flesh as she sought to get even with Braith for destroying Goran, but the more Sabine tore at her, the harder Aria and William fought against her.

Aria barely felt the pain or the blood spilling from the gashes in her arms. Tempest dashed to the side and swung her staff out, crashing it against the back of Sabine's knees and knocking her legs out from under her. Max and Maeve leapt forward, beating against the woman who still refused to release her. Keegan circled around them, driving back anyone who dared to get too close.

Sabine briefly loosened her hold on Aria as she swung around, her arm flying out to smack all of those behind her.

William bellowed when Tempest was flung backward, the staff knocked from her hand as she sprawled on the ground. Maeve bounced across the earth and landed near Daniel's body. Like a cat, she bounded back to her feet, but Max remained unmoving in the middle of the road.

More of Sabine's vampires surged forward, looking to protect their leader. Over Sabine's shoulder, Aria spotted Braith battling his way through the dozen or so vampires between them. Blood splattered his face and his clothes were soaked in it. She scented his blood on the air, but most of the blood covering him came from those he ruthlessly carved out of his way.

Sabine's fingers wrapped around her throat, lifting her off the ground. Aria's feet kicked against the woman. She beat at the hand holding her throat and digging into her skin, but it was like pitting a lamb against a lion.

William punched Sabine in the stomach; she never flinched. Lifting her hand, Sabine swung it out to smack it against the back of William's skull. He didn't have a chance to get his hands out to break his fall before he slammed face first into the dirt road.

"I'm going to kill you!" Sabine spat at Aria and drew back her hand in preparation to tear her heart out.

Aria's eyes widened. Her feet kicked against Sabine's stomach and her fingers tore at the iron hold on her throat to no avail. She was going to die and there was nothing she could do to stop it as Sabine's fist shot forward so fast she barely saw it move.

A hard punch crashed into her chest, cracking bone just as another hand shot out and encircled Sabine's wrist before she could tear into Aria's chest. Braith's red eyes loomed over Sabine's shoulder, his massive size dwarfing her slender frame. The power of them both rippled over Aria's skin, causing the hair on her body to stand on end and her mouth to go dry.

There was no denying they were the most powerful creatures on this earth, and they were going to destroy each other.

Pulling his other hand back, Braith drove his fist straight into Sabine's face. As Sabine howled, her grip on Aria's throat constricted and she staggered back a few steps. More blood burst from Sabine's nose and now split lips.

Braith didn't hesitate before unleashing a series of brutal punches on her that pushed her further and further backward. Aria's fingers tore at the hand encircling her throat as Sabine's fingers tore deeper into her flesh to spill more of her blood. Sabine's grip didn't ease as she pulled Aria along with her. Braith jerked the arm he was holding back, snapping bone at the elbow before he grabbed the hand encasing Aria's throat and squeezed the wrist with enough force to shatter it.

Sabine wailed as her grip on Aria finally released and she fell to the road. Aria's hand flew to her brutalized neck as blood continued to spill free. Seizing Sabine by the throat, Braith lifted her up and propelled her off the road and into the woods before smashing her into a tree. The tree shook from the impact but held firm, even as a jagged crack raced up the center of it toward the canopy.

Aria pushed herself back to her feet and took an unsteady step to the side as Braith lowered himself so he was eye level with Sabine. Aria's gaze went to where Daniel remained unmoving against another tree, fifty feet away. Max already knelt at her brother's side with Maeve, while William, Tempest, and Xavier, who had regained consciousness, sought to keep back the remaining vampires. They would all take care of Daniel and get him through this, but first she had to help make sure Sabine was destroyed.

"How?" Braith growled at Sabine when Aria approached them through the woods with Keegan at her heels. "How is it possible we can come back?"

Sabine wiggled in his grasp, her feet kicking against his shins, but with both of her arms useless, she could do little to fend him off. Sabine's eyes narrowed on him. She didn't respond as her gaze flicked between him and Aria.

"Did my father know about this?" Braith demanded.

"No," Sabine finally replied. "I was killed before I could tell him." Sabine's gaze remained on Aria as she stopped behind Braith. "You pollute our blood with this creation," she sneered at him.

Braith pulled Sabine off the tree then slammed her back into it. The crack in it grew, and the tree swayed ominously, but continued to hold. "Do *not* talk about my wife, *your* queen, that way."

Sabine shook her head as if to clear it before she focused on Braith and fairly spit with fury. "Never would such a pollution of our line be *my* queen."

"That's why you're doing this," Aria said, causing Braith to glance back at her. "It's not because Atticus was killed and you sought revenge for your eldest son's death. It's not because you want to rule. It's because you see me as an abomination who will taint your line if we have children."

"You have already tainted it!" Sabine spat. "Just by having *our* blood in your veins you have weakened us. Your children would be abominations of our *pure* blood."

"Do you even care your sons are dead?" Aria inquired, and Sabine turned her nose up.

A sick feeling settled in Aria's stomach as she realized how depraved and indifferent this woman was. She'd lost both of her children, yet all she cared about was the fact she had a turned human on her family tree.

"She's made me strong enough to defeat you," Braith replied, and the look Sabine gave him made it clear she would happily see him dead a thousand times over.

"Our line was created by Lucifer himself and you degrade us with a changed *human*. Let your brother pollute the line with such garbage, but not you."

"So it is the first born of our line only then," Braith said quietly, the muscles in his forearm flexing and bunching as his grip on Sabine's throat tightened. "If I am to die again, would I rise once more?"

The fingers on the wrist Braith had broken flexed before Sabine launched a punch at his face that cracked his cheekbone with an audible thwack. Aria had seen her broken nose heal fast, but she hadn't expected the woman to heal *that* fast.

Braith grabbed Sabine's hand and bashed it into the trunk of the tree. The blood drained from Aria's head, she took a step back when he spun Sabine's hand around and tore it from her wrist.

Sabine screamed, her face turning red as her stumpy wrist flailed against Braith's side and her blood sprayed him.

"I'll tear you apart piece by piece," Braith promised her. "Your next hand will be one finger at a time if you don't tell me what I want to know. I can make your end quick, or it can last years, but you will not walk away from any of it with your head still attached to your body."

A branch breaking behind Aria drew her attention to Jack as he stepped from the shadows of the forest with Hannah at his side. Their clothes were stained and torn; blood and dirt streaked their faces, but they appeared unharmed as they stepped beside her. Hannah visibly paled when she spotted Sabine's missing hand. Jack took hold of Hannah's shoulders and pressed her head against his chest.

Aria's stomach twisted sickeningly when Braith grasped one of Sabine's fingers. Unlike the vampire she'd caught with Xavier and Max, who had been unwilling to speak for hours, words tumbled from Sabine's lips at the possibility of torture. "The only thing that can kill the first born of our line is beheading! Even fire, unless it reduces us completely to ash, is not enough to destroy us."

"What?" Braith demanded and Aria's mouth fell open at the revelation.

"It's a trait that Lucifer gave to the first vampire he created. Each first born of that vampire's line will be able to withstand that which no other vampire can," Sabine said, her eyes darting to Braith's hand when it tightened around her finger. "We will rise as often as it is necessary to do what must be done."

"The phoenix was not a bird," Braith murmured. "But one of our ancestors rising from a fire."

"The legend was changed by an ancestor for our protection," Sabine replied.

"Why do we rise stronger?"

"You have survived death, survived having fallen in your own way. You're closer now to Lucifer than you ever were before."

"Are there any other ancestors of ours out there?" Braith demanded.

Sabine's lips skimmed back to reveal her fangs in a feral grimace. When Braith started bending her finger back, she blurted more words. "Many of our ancestors were beheaded in battle or by their attackers. Some were taken out by their own children after they were killed in order to keep the secret of our line buried, and any others have long since perished. We are the last of the first born children."

With that, Sabine launched forward and sank her fangs into Braith's throat. Braith placed his hand against her forehead as he tried to pry her off of him. The power of his blood caused the bones in Sabine's arm to repair themselves almost immediately as Aria leapt forward to free Braith from the woman's hungry grip. Sabine hadn't been talking because she'd been defeated and concerned about losing her fingers; she'd been biding her time in order to lower their guard.

Aria punched Sabine as hard as she could, but the woman showed no sign she'd felt it as she continued to drain Braith's blood.

"Get off!" Aria shouted. Blood spilled from her battered fists as she continued to beat at Sabine.

Sabine's reddened eyes met hers over his shoulder while his blood spilled from her lips to soak his skin. Aria's heart sank when she realized Sabine truly believed she would kill Braith now, if she was willing to drink his blood. Otherwise, he'd be able to track her anywhere she went.

Jack raced over to them and grasped Sabine's hair. He tried to yank her head back, but she refused to release her hold. Braith drove his hand into Sabine's chest. With a snarl, Sabine switched her tactics and her teeth bit at his neck as if she were chewing on him while his hand continued to work its way through her chest. Keegan growled as he waited for an opportunity to jump into the fight.

Braith yanked back, tearing the heart from Sabine's chest, but she didn't stop biting him. Disbelief swirled through Aria as she gazed at the heart within Braith's hand. The loss of the organ had done nothing to slow Sabine's feeding frenzy. Blood loss may not kill Braith, but if Sabine succeeded in taking him down by weakening him this way, they'd never stop her from doing whatever she sought to do here.

Realizing her attempts at dislodging Sabine from Braith with her hands were futile, Aria pulled an arrow from her quiver. The tip of the arrow was stained red, the scent of Braith's blood drifting from it made her realize this was one of the arrows that had been used to kill her husband.

A cruel smile of satisfaction filled her as she turned the arrow in her hand and swung it forward. She drove it through Sabine's right eye and straight into the tree. The woman howled, and finally released her hold on Braith as she clawed at the arrow pinning her to the tree.

Blood spilled down Braith's neck. His fangs glistened in the fire as he grabbed Sabine's head and wrenched it to the side. A wet cracking sound pierced the air as flesh and bone were severed. Aria stepped away from Sabine's headless body when it slumped to the ground.

Braith's shoulders heaved as he clutched Sabine's hair in his hand. He handed Jack Sabine's head before turning to Aria. His body moved with supple grace as he stalked toward her, lifted her up, and claimed her mouth in a bruising kiss that left Aria momentarily dazed by its intensity.

She sensed his barely controlled restraint behind the kiss and knew he needed her to calm him. Sensed how close he was to coming apart completely and giving himself over to the bloodlust shaking his muscles. Closer than he'd ever been to Lucifer, her husband was stronger, but violence and blood also beckoned him more than it had before.

His fangs scraped against her bottom lip, drawing blood. His hands clutched at her as his hard body enveloped hers. She gave herself over to him, and her own need to feel him against her. His tongue entangled wildly with hers as he licked away the drops of blood his fangs had created. His hand cupped the back of her head before his tongue slipped from her mouth.

An anguished groan escaped him as he lifted his head to look at her. His reddened eyes filled her vision when his forehead rested against hers. Beneath her hands, his body vibrated and beads of her blood glistened on his lips before his tongue slid out to lick them away. The red faded from his eyes and their beautiful gray color slid back into place. In that instant, she knew that no matter how close he'd become to Lucifer, he would never be anything like Atticus or Sabine, because he had her to calm him.

Reluctantly, he lifted his head and set her on her feet once more. "Are you okay?" he demanded as his fingers brushed over the gashes on her neck.

"Fine," she croaked out, her voice hoarser than she'd expected.

A thunderous expression crossed his face before he held his wrist out to her. "Drink," he commanded gruffly. She shook her head no. "You're injured, Aria. Drink."

"So are you," she reasoned.

"I'm nearly healed."

Knowing it was pointless to argue, she took hold of his arm and lifted his wrist to her mouth. She sighed when her fangs pierced his flesh and his blood filled her mouth. He drew her against his chest, cradling her there until she'd taken her fill and released him.

Pressing her head to his chest, he kissed her hair before turning to reclaim Sabine's head from Jack. "Keep the body away from the head. I'm not taking any chances with this bitch until she's nothing but a pile of ashes," Braith commanded.

Jack grabbed Sabine's arm and lifted her to toss her body over his shoulder. Aria glanced behind her, her brow furrowing when she realized the others were nowhere to be seen. If everything had been okay with Daniel, they would be here. She spun and fled through the trees with Keegan on her heels.

"Aria!" Braith shouted behind her, but she didn't look back.

She burst out of the woods and onto the road. She spotted Max and Maeve still kneeling by the tree where Daniel had fallen. Behind them, Xavier, Timber, Tempest, and William continued to battle back the straggling remains of Sabine's troops. Braith crashed out of the woods behind her. He reached for her shoulder, but she was already moving toward Daniel.

She crouched at his side, horror pooling through her when she spotted the blood coating his shirt, the pallor of his skin, and the awkward angle of his arm. His skin had been shredded open around his throat. His head lolled toward her. His glassy blue eyes met hers and he smiled at her.

"You're alive," he whispered.

"Because of you. You're going to be fine," she promised.

"Is she dead?"

"Yes."

His heart gave a lumbering beat in his chest. Aria lifted her wrist and bit into it. "Drink," she commanded when she held it before him.

Despite the growing weakness she sensed spreading through his body, Daniel's voice was strong. "No."

"Daniel, it will help you heal faster!"

"No, it won't," he replied. "It's too late for that, Aria."

"No, it's not," she insisted. "I won't give you enough to change you, only enough to see you through this."

His lips took on a bluish hue that caused her knees to give out on her.

"It's too late, Aria," he said again.

She knew he was right; it would be all or nothing for him now. He'd lost too much blood to reverse this. "You can be one of us," she whispered as she brushed the blond hair from his forehead. "I know you said you didn't want to be, but you could be."

He'd said he didn't want to be a vampire when he'd been healthy and far from death. Now, she could see death creeping through him, steadily taking him over. She opened her mouth to plead with him to change his mind, but the words died on her lips. If he'd changed his mind, he would have said yes to her blood.

Her hand stilled on his forehead as she leaned forward to kiss his cool cheek. There was so much he still had left to do, children to have, laughter to enjoy, plans to design, and life to live. She wasn't ready to let him go, but he'd said he would accept his fate. No matter how badly she wanted to cling to her brother, to plead with him to say yes to trying to change into a vampire, she had to respect his wishes and let him go.

"Daniel…," Max started as realization settled over his features and his lips parted. He closed his mouth against any further protest though.

Aria settled beside her brother and took hold of his limp hand. Tears burned her eyes when she rested her head on his shoulder and her chest squeezed with grief. She refused to shed those tears, not yet. Daniel would go peacefully, knowing they would be okay. There would be plenty of time for tears later.

"The world is a far better place because you were in it," she told him. "We are all better for knowing you, for loving you, and for having you to love and protect us."

Her gaze slid up to her twin as he came toward them. The last of the vampires were falling away before Xavier and Timber. William gazed at her, then her wrist before looking to Daniel again. He opened his mouth, then clamped it shut when he realized arguing would be pointless. William's bow fell to the ground as he walked over to Daniel's other side and knelt beside him to rest his hand on his shoulder.

"William and I never would have lived this long," Aria continued.

Despite the increasing rattle of his breath and the slowing of his heart, Daniel gave a choking laugh. "Tr-true," he stammered as his fingers twitched within her grasp.

"You'll see Mom and Dad again," William said.

"They need one of us there," Daniel murmured and Aria bit back a sob. "Max will lead the humans now."

"I will," Max said and settled his hand on Daniel's leg as tears slid down his cheeks. "Everyone will be safe now."

"Safe, loved," Daniel said and his heart stuttered again.

Aria lifted her head to kiss his cheek. "We all love you so much," she whispered.

"Love you all too," Daniel said, and this time his heart did not beat again.

CHAPTER 39

Braith

Braith kept his arm around Aria's waist as he led her through the bloody streets of the town toward the palace. Smoke wafted around them, and the cries of the dying filled the air before they were able to be put out of their misery. Aria kept her shoulders back and her chin up, but he felt the small tremor in her muscles against his side. Though she tried, she couldn't hide her sorrow from him.

William carried his brother's body in his arms, his expression almost identical to Aria's as they neared the palace gates. The last of Sabine's troops were falling beneath the onslaught of the palace guards and the fighters who had ensnared them within the town.

"Braith! It's *Braith*!" Melinda shouted from the wall when he stopped before the gate and tilted his head back to look up at them. She clapped her hands excitedly and bounced on her toes before spinning away and disappearing from view.

Gideon and Ashby gawked down at them. He lifted Sabine's head into the air to show them she'd been eliminated.

"Open the gates!" he commanded.

Gideon blinked at him before turning away. "Open the gates!" he bellowed, and the cranking of the mechanism within sounded as the battered wooden drawbridge lowered with a groan.

The wood hadn't fully hit the ground before Melinda was running through the gates toward him. She ignored the head in his hands as she threw her arms around his neck. Unwilling to release Aria, or to have Sabine's head touch Melinda, he turned his chin into her shoulder. "It's good to see you too, sister," he told her.

She pulled back from him, her hands staying on his shoulders. "She had your head," she whispered, her lower lip trembling as her gaze ran over him.

"Not mine, but I do have hers."

Melinda grinned at him and slapped him on the shoulders. "Good."

She stepped away from him as Ashby and Gideon emerged from within and strode out to meet them. Behind them, Braith spotted the rest of The Council making their way outside of the palace walls, along with a large grouping of humans and vamps who surveyed the wreckage around them with wide eyes.

"We have to put the fires out, now!" Braith shouted at the milling group.

The command snapped many of them out of their stunned stupor. They ran back inside the walls to gather the hoses and pumps that would funnel water from the nearby lake to the fires.

Melinda's gaze ran over all of them before falling on William's arms. Her hand flew to her mouth and the color drained from her face. "Is that…?"

Her question trailed off as she looked to Aria, who held her gaze, but didn't speak.

"I'm sorry," Melinda whispered to her.

Aria gave a brief bow of her head as Ashby and Gideon arrived.

Gideon's gaze ran over him from head to toe and back again before he grinned at him. "Not your head she had, I'm guessing."

"No," Braith replied. He had to get Aria away from all of this and settle her somewhere safe so she could mourn in peace. Lifting Sabine's head, he smiled grimly at Gideon as he thrust it into his stomach. "Make sure this stays away from her body."

Gideon's lip skimmed back in disgust. His hand threaded through her hair. "With pleasure."

"The fires must be put out, the injured have to be taken care of, and the bodies of the dead collected. All of the bodies of those who followed her are to be burned. There are too many dead to bury them all, and they don't deserve a funeral. Any of her followers who are still alive are to be executed. There will be no leniency and no prisoners. I will help you sort that out shortly, but if you have any questions about who was on Sabine's side and who wasn't, detain them until their loyalty can be determined for certain."

"We will take care of it," Ashby said.

Braith nudged Aria forward, but she planted her feet. "We must stay and see everything through," she said.

"I can take you to our rooms. It will be quiet for you."

"No," she replied. "The largest part of the threat has been eliminated, but we're still needed here. It is the way of *our* world that we can't always do what we wish."

Braith stared at her, torn between carrying her away from here to give her the time he knew she needed right now and doing as she asked of him.

Her head turned toward him; the tears in her eyes didn't fall as she spoke. "These are our followers. They come first, and we will take care of them. It has always been so. It will always be so."

Braith brushed the hair back from her forehead before bending to kiss her. "Sabine was a complete fool. There is no finer queen than you," he whispered against her mouth.

Her hand compressed around his as she stepped back to speak with William. "Place Daniel in the solar where we put father and meet us back here. They will need all of us here to oversee things tonight."

William bowed his head to her and turned away. Tempest stayed close to his side as he walked through the crowd who parted to allow him to pass. Braith would make sure that Daniel's funeral would be the largest they'd ever had once this was all settled; he was the only reason Aria still stood at his side.

"Max will be taking Daniel's spot on The Council. I realize there will have to be a vote to confirm this eventually, but he is in charge right now, and I have no doubt all who vote will choose him when the time comes," Aria said to Ashby, Gideon, and the other Council members who had walked out to join them. "Max has stood by my father's side and then Daniel's throughout. He will help you to calm the humans."

"Come with me," Calista said to Max and jerked her head toward the palace. "It will be best for you to be with the injured and the grieving now."

Max took hold of Maeve's hand before walking beside Calista through the gates. Aria focused on Xavier, her eyebrow raised in question as he stood resolutely by her side. Braith knew there had been something between him and Daniel in the end. He'd smelled them on each other, but he'd never scented Daniel's blood within him or seen Xavier's marks on Daniel. He hadn't gotten the impression of love between them, only a mutual respect and need.

"Xavier—"

"He was a good and loyal man, a dear friend. He will be missed greatly by many, including myself," Xavier interrupted Aria and rested his hand comfortingly on her shoulder. "I cared for him deeply, but I will be okay, Aria."

Aria bowed her head and took a minute to compose herself before squeezing Xavier's hand. Keeping Aria against his side, Braith turned to face the town as water was released onto the flames eating away at the buildings. Keegan brushed against his side, and Braith ran his hand over the wolf's head. Keegan whimpered when he pressed against Aria's legs, sensing her sadness.

"We'll be fine. Go on, return home," she whispered to Keegan as she ran her fingers over his thick fur.

The wolf licked her hand before trotting away between two of the houses not yet on fire. His green eyes flashed in the light of the flames when he looked back at them for a minute. When Keegan turned away and vanished into the woods once more, Braith knew his old friend had said good-bye for the final time.

***

Braith

Throughout the endless night and into the next day, they worked tirelessly to put out the flames, gather the injured, settle those who had been displaced, destroy those who had attacked them, and calm the nerves of the numerous survivors.

The sun had set on the next day when Braith was finally able to lift Aria into his arms and carry her to their rooms. He turned on the water in the large tub before carefully removing her bloody, ruined clothes. The gashes on her arms had healed and the wound in her shoulder was mostly healed, but the skin around it was still red and puckered. She remained unmoving while he worked, her head bowed as tears slid down her cheeks.

She shivered when he bent to kiss her back. He undid her braid, allowing her glossy auburn hair to spill around her shoulders. Carefully, he lifted her into his arms and climbed into the tub with her. He settled into the water, clutching her against his chest when she curled into a ball against him and finally gave herself over to the sobs she'd been holding back.

He didn't try to quiet her, but only held her as she shook against him and her tears wet his chest. He'd give anything to take her sorrow from her, but though there were so many things that could be taken from someone, the worst of them never could be. Grief had to be endured.

CHAPTER 40

Aria

Six months later

William paced anxiously from one side of the room to the other, running his hands through his hair as he muttered to himself. Aria bit on her inner lip to keep from laughing at his nervous movements. "You're going to wear yourself out," she told him.

"What is taking so long?" he demanded.

"You know how women are when it comes to getting ready," Jack replied, and Aria shot him a look.

Jack met her glare with an innocent smile as he adjusted the lapels on his black coat. His hair was brushed back from his face, emphasizing his handsome features. Beside him, Braith wasn't bothering to hide his amusement over her brother's frantic behavior. He grinned as he stood with his arms folded over his chest. Like Jack, his hair had been brushed back from his face to emphasis his gorgeous features. Her heart melted when his eyes met hers and he winked at her.

Stepping away from the wall, Braith strode across the room to her. He drew her into his arms as William started cursing. She melted against his chest, inhaling his crisp, masculine scent. Her fingers dug into his back as she closed her eyes and allowed herself to drift for a minute.

The past six months had been difficult to get through. It had taken them months to sort through the mess Sabine had created, to find any humans and vampires who had survived her imprisonment, and to check on all of the existing border towns. Some of the towns had managed to escape her wrath, others hadn't been so lucky.

They'd discovered the humans Aria had seen with Sabine in the forest had been locked in the basement of one of the homes within the town. They'd been able to get them out before the building had been consumed by the fire. Some of the people had been too far gone to save, but the others had all been set free. The vampires Sabine had imprisoned, starved, and turned into monsters incapable of being saved, had all been hunted and destroyed.

They had increased the amount of the king's guard in every town and recruited more humans and vampires to join the guard. She and Braith were determined to make sure that what had occurred with Sabine would never happen again.

Now they had double the amount of men and women working for the king's guard and received weekly reports from every town. If something were to happen with any town again, they would know as soon as one of their representatives failed to arrive with an update. Before Sabine, they had been confident Braith was the eldest vampire, that there were no more threats out there against them. Despite the fact Sabine had denied any others of their line lived, they would not be caught unawares again if a new threat rose.

Throughout everything that had happened, they had somehow managed to keep Braith's ability to rise from the dead a secret from almost everyone. There was no denying he was more powerful now, everyone could feel it, but most attributed this newfound power to his destruction of Sabine. Though most vampires didn't feed from each other, some believed he'd consumed some of her blood before killing her.

Xavier had told anyone who would listen that Sabine had most likely faked her own death all those years ago, so she could freely roam the earth with no restraints placed on her by vampire society and so she could kill freely. Maybe some doubted this explanation, but no one was willing to question him or Braith about it.

"Perhaps a drink would help," Max suggested to William.

Xavier shook his head when Timber lifted his silver flask into the air. "Here, here!" Timber declared enthusiastically.

"No drink," William muttered.

The Council and humans who resided in and near the palace had unanimously elected Max to fill Daniel's place last month when they'd been able to hold the election. The other human and vampire Council members who had been elected from the border towns over the years had all survived the war and retained their seats on The Council. There were now nearly a hundred members of The Council and the number would continue to grow as the population flourished once more.

When everything was completely settled, Aria had a feeling Max and Maeve's wedding would be the next one they'd all be attending.

Aria released Braith and stepped away from him. As William's best woman, she had to do something to calm her brother; she just didn't know what.

He spun toward her. "Aria, go make sure she hasn't changed her mind," he said.

"She's not going to change her mind," she replied.

"Go, please," he pleaded.

She kept a lid on her impatient reply. It was her role to do these things for him after all, but he had to realize how ridiculous it was to think Tempest would change her mind about marrying him, she was helplessly in love with him.

"I'll go," she assured him.

She kissed Braith's cheek before walking over to take Timber's flask away from him. "Hey!" he protested.

She shoved the flask into William's hand when he paced by her again. "For crying out loud, relax!" she told him, earning her a lethal look before she slipped out the door.

She made her way swiftly down the hallway to the room where Tempest was getting ready. Glancing out the wall of glass on her left, she smiled when she saw the colorful blooms of the peonies, hydrangeas, and roses lining the walkways of the garden and spilling into them.

Within the center of the colorful array of blooming roses stood the fountain she'd come to love dearly. Clear water ran through the fountain to spill into its basin. Red and white rose petals floated in the water and more petals had been scattered over the center walkway to create a rose carpet for Tempest to walk down. Chairs were set out, and all of them were filled with the numerous guests waiting for the ceremony to start.

William had wanted to get married in the woods, but Tempest had fallen in love with the garden the minute she'd seen it. After seeing the fountain, she'd decided they should be married while standing before it, and William had happily agreed.

Sadness slid through Aria as she recalled her own small wedding in the woods and Daniel's loving and wise words as he'd married her and Braith two years ago. At the time, Daniel had been so young. He'd had the whole world at his feet and a lifetime stretched out before him. If only they'd all known how short that lifetime would be, she would have tried to cram in two lifetimes worth of time with him before he'd been killed.

Today, instead of Daniel marrying William and Tempest, William had asked Xavier to perform the ceremony. Glancing back, she realized Xavier hadn't been the one to follow her out of the room, Braith had.

"What are you doing?" she inquired of him.

"Making sure you stay safe," but his eyes were latched hungrily onto the swell of her breasts in her blue gown. She may not be one of the bridesmaids, but the blue of her gown matched their gowns. It also matched the blue cloth square Braith and the other groom's men wore in their coat pockets. Maggie, her friend and lady-in-waiting, had sewn the gown for her.

"I'm perfectly safe within the palace," she retorted.

His mouth curved into a smile as his eyes met hers. "I wouldn't be so sure about that."

She nearly tripped over the hem of her dress and had to resist the impulse to run back and jump him. "I have things I must do," she replied with far more haughtiness than she felt.

"So do I," he replied, and one of his fangs flashed in the sunlight spilling through the windows.

Her teeth sank into her bottom lip as her feet stumbled on the carpet. *Turn away! I'm the worst best woman ever!*

She forced herself to focus ahead of her again, but she heard his stalking steps behind her. She didn't dare look back when she arrived at the solar where Tempest and the other women were. Her hand trembled when she lifted it to knock on the door.

"Who is it?" Hannah called.

"It's Aria," she called back.

"Come in! Come in!"

She dared a glance back at Braith when he leaned against the wall beside her, his thick arms folded over his broad chest as he watched her. "As soon as this is over, you're mine," he vowed.

Aria swallowed and her toes curled in her slippers. "Then I'm going to get their butts in gear," she replied before slipping into the room.

She closed the door behind her and leaned against it until she trusted herself enough to walk away from it. Her eyes widened when she took in the chaos of the room. There were clothes strewn *everywhere*. Hannah hustled from one end of the room to the other with a veil in her hands. Tempest's best friend, Pallas, was fluffing her hair as Melinda pinched Tempest's pale cheeks.

Aria almost groaned aloud when she saw Melinda doing this; she recalled her sister-in-law trying to do the same thing to her. Nora, one of the young orphans from Tempest's town stood in the corner, looking completely overwhelmed by everything. Moira, another woman Tempest had fled Badwin with, was pushing white roses into a thick bouquet while Maeve wrapped a ribbon around the stems.

"We're almost ready!" Melinda declared. Her hand went to her back as she stepped away from Tempest to reveal her rounded belly. She was due to give birth next month, but Aria thought the baby would be coming sooner as it seemed far too big for Melinda's slender frame.

"How is William doing?" Tempest asked anxiously.

"He's nervous," she admitted as her gaze ran over Tempest's exquisite gown. She'd never seen anything like it. The sleeves were off the shoulders and dipped down across her upper arms. The low cut of the bodice revealed the swell of her breasts and the front of it ran down in a deep V that emphasized her slender figure and rounded hips.

Ice blue thread had been stitched throughout the gown to match the color of the bridesmaid dresses. More than the ice blue color gave it a wintry appearance. Icicles had also been intricately interwoven and threaded throughout the lace covering the skirt of the dress and the train spilling across the floor behind her. Tempest came from a town where winter had ruled; she'd loved her mountains and the snow. It was only mid-September, yet she looked like the snow-covered village she'd escaped with William and her friends.

"That dress is beautiful!" she gushed to Tempest.

Because Aria was part of William's wedding party, this was the first time she'd been allowed to see the wedding gown. Melinda had been afraid she'd accidentally reveal something about it to William. Aria didn't like that Melinda believed she couldn't keep a secret from her brother, but she'd been more than happy to avoid all of Melinda's wedding planning. Her interest in dresses was as much as most people's interest in dirt. She'd actually rather deal with dirt.

Tempest gave her a radiant smile as she smoothed her hands down the front of her gown. "Thank you," she said.

"Don't just stand there, help us!" Melinda commanded.

"What should I do?" Aria inquired as she approached, unwilling to get too close to the dress in case she stepped on it or somehow made it dirty.

"Aria's not good around dresses," Melinda said to Tempest, and Aria glared at her. Melinda ignored her as she took the veil from Hannah and settled it onto Tempest's silvery ringlets before flipping the veil back. "She's getting better with them, but let's face it, she belongs with the guys on this one."

Aria rolled her eyes, but she couldn't argue with the truth. She still couldn't walk in high heels and refused to try anymore. However, if it made Braith look at her again like he had in the hallway, she may wear this dress every day.

"Fix the train, Aria," Melinda commanded impatiently.

"If you weren't pregnant, I'd choke you," she muttered as she bent to carefully rearrange all the many layers of lace within the train.

"Yeah, yeah, yeah," Melinda replied with a wave of her hand and stuffed a pin into Tempest's hair.

Melinda placed another pin between her lips as she studied Tempest carefully. Aria smoothed the train out further, careful not to touch it for too long for fear she'd somehow tear the delicate material.

"Was this made by the same tailor who made mine?" she inquired. Her dress had been beautiful, but Tempest's dress was a work of art.

Melinda pulled the pin from her mouth. "No, he retired last year and moved away. A new dressmaker moved into town shortly after he left. She's making quite an impression here."

"Milly is a true talent," Hannah confirmed.

"She really is," Aria couldn't help but agree. Her fingers ran over an intricate design etched into one of the icicles on the train.

"We're ready!" Melinda declared, drawing Aria's attention away from the dress. Aria rose to her feet as Moira handed the bouquet over to Tempest. "Now go do your job, Aria, and get the groom out there."

Melinda placed her hands in her back and propelled her toward the door. Or at least tried to propel her, as Melinda waddled when she walked now. Melinda threw the door open, shoved her out, and slammed it in her face.

"I'm going to kill your sister," Aria grumbled to Braith.

He burst into laughter as he stepped away from the wall and held his arm out to her. "It could be worse. You could be Ashby."

"That poor man," she sympathized while they strolled down the hall together to the room where they'd left William.

***

William

William swore his heart lurched in his chest when Tempest stepped onto the walkway behind her bridesmaids. All the other women vanished from view as his eyes immediately latched onto her. He'd never seen her look more beautiful. She beamed as everyone stood to watch her walk down the aisle; her gaze remained riveted on him as she moved.

At her side walked Abbott, a young, orphan vampire they had rescued from her town when they'd fled it. With no one else to give her away, the young man had stepped forward to offer to do so.

Now, as she walked forward to join him, William realized he'd never been so lucky in his life. Her doe brown eyes shimmered with happiness; her cheeks were prettily tinged with pink as heat crept over her silken skin.

He held his hand out to her, and she took hold of it before they both turned to face Xavier. William would have preferred to have had Daniel standing before him, smiling as he wowed everyone with his eloquent way with words, but he knew that not everything worked out as planned.

Despite the still aching loss of his brother, William was far more blessed in his life than he ever would have dreamed possible just two and a half short years ago. He looked forward to every day he would be fortunate enough to be granted for the rest of his life.

Though his grief for Daniel was still piercing, he hadn't tried to run from it this time, as he had after his father's death. He'd learned there was no running from this, but he had Tempest and all of his other loved ones to help guide him through it now.

Daniel had never run from his responsibilities, had always faced everything head on, and so would he from now on. He would stay and help rebuild this world they'd all fought and lost so much for. Gideon and Ashby had created a place for him on The Council. They both agreed he would be vital in human/vampire relations with his history as a rebel and the fact he was one of the few who had ever survived the change from human into vampire.

There was plenty of room to live within the palace, but it wasn't the place for him. He, Max, Timber, and Jack were currently working on building a home for him and Tempest in the town. Max and Maeve were planning to build a house next to his when they were done. They would visit Chippman and Hannah's family often, but Jack and Hannah would be staying here from now on too. Jack had also earned a seat on The Council and took his role there seriously. For now, Jack and Hannah had decided to remain living in the palace with Jack's siblings.

After his father's death, William never believed he'd settle down anywhere near the palace. Now he knew it was where he belonged, even if he still disliked all the walls. There were plenty of woods to get away to when it became necessary.

William's gaze slid to Tempest, he couldn't help but grin at her when her hand went toward her mouth to bite her nails before she pulled it away. She shot him a sly glance out of the corner of her eye as he tried not to laugh.

His attention was pulled back to Xavier when he asked William to recite his vows, which he did in a loud, clear voice before Xavier turned to Tempest. She proudly repeated what Xavier asked her to say.

"Rings," Xavier instructed.

William turned to Aria. She smiled at him when she handed him the delicate wedding ring with a row of diamonds set into the gold band. Jack and Braith stood behind her, watching him over her shoulder and grinning in that "cat that ate the canary" way they'd both had since the wedding planning started.

William turned back to Tempest as Pallas handed her a band for him. He recited what Xavier told him to say once more and slipped the band onto Tempest's finger. For the ceremony, she'd removed the engagement ring he'd created for her, but she'd proudly worn it every day since he'd first given it to her, and she still refused to let him replace it with something else.

Her hands shook as she slipped his band onto his finger and recited the words Xavier told her to repeat. "I now pronounce you man and wife," Xavier said. "You may kiss the bride."

William didn't have to be told twice. He wrapped his arm around Tempest's waist and pulled her against him. She was laughing when he crushed his mouth to hers. Her laughter faded away as her body melded against his.

"Now it's time to celebrate!" Jack declared, breaking into their kiss as loud applause echoed around the garden.

William turned to face the cheering crowd while Tempest blushed prettily. He led her through the clapping humans and vampires as they threw handfuls of red and white rose petals at them. Within the crowd, he spotted Mary and waved to them as he tried to avoid being covered in the roses. It was a battle he was happy to lose.

CHAPTER 41

Aria

Aria stretched leisurely the next morning and cracked open her eyes to find the thick drapes tugged over the windows, blocking out the sun. She rested her hand on the indent where Braith had slept; it was still warm, but she knew he was gone from their rooms. She climbed out of bed and made her way to the bathroom.

Yesterday had been a day of celebration, the first one in months, but today was back to reality. After she'd showered, dressed, and entered their main sitting room, her gaze fell on her beautiful ice blue gown lying on the sofa where Braith had tossed it. She'd have to see if Maggie could fix the zipper Braith had ruined last night in his eagerness to get it off her.

Lifting her head, her gaze fell on the window seat where she spent many hours with Braith while they read together. Walking over to the window, she peered out the glass and down on the gardens that had already been cleaned up since last night. All of the chairs and rose petals were gone. The dew covering the flowers within the garden glistened in the morning sun.

Her gaze fell to the fountain, the one Atticus had created in memory of Genny. The one where the two lovers would always gaze upon each other, but never touch. The memory of her dream with Braith and the black roses teased at the corners of her mind, but she shoved it aside. She would not think about the unhappiness of that time when they had so much to look forward to.

Turning away from the window, she hurried to the door and slipped out. She walked down the hallway and descended the steps to the main entranceway below. The first time she'd entered the palace, it had all been so overwhelming and foreign to her. She'd been certain she was being led to her death. Now, it was her home.

Her footsteps were silent in the foyer. The call of her blood within Braith let her know he was somewhere in the palace, but she would find him later. He was most likely in a meeting if he'd left while she slept.

A vampire stepped forward to open the front door for her. She bowed her head in thanks to him before stepping outside. She tilted her head back to take in the sun as she savored the noises of the town. Children ran to and fro in the streets, shouting happily to one another. Hammers rang out from the town as more buildings were repaired and new ones were built. Chickens squawked, and the jingle of horse's harnesses and saddles filled the air as their hoof beats sounded on the road.

Descending the stairs, she wasn't surprised when Xavier slipped from the shadows of the stable to fall into step beside her. They didn't speak as they made their way through the town with Aria calling out greetings or halting to speak with those who stopped her. It took far longer than she'd intended to reach the small dress shop at the bottom of the hill situated near the gates.

A sign on the door said the shop was closed, but Aria tried the handle anyway. It remained locked beneath her grasp.

"*You* want a dress?" Xavier asked from behind her.

Aria brushed back her braid and glanced down at her simple brown pants and forest green shirt. "You make me sound as bad as Melinda thinks I am," she muttered.

"You avoid the tailor like cats avoid baths."

She scowled at him as she turned away from the shop, her gaze scanning the crowd. The apartment above the dress shop led her to believe Milly lived above the store. So if she wasn't here, then where else would she be?

Lifting her hand to shield her eyes from the sun, Aria strode back up the hill toward the palace. She didn't go for the main door, but around the side and beneath the trestle to the vast garden beyond. After becoming queen, Aria had knocked out a wall to make it so everyone could enter the garden. Its beauty should be shared with them all.

The garden had been empty when she'd looked out earlier, but it was so large that someone could wander it for hours, enjoying the numerous flowers and trees, before ever making it to the center.

Xavier didn't question her, but she could feel his curiosity mounting as he walked by her side through the rows of privet, fruit trees, roses, lilacs, lilies, and other numerous plants. At the end of the pathway, Aria stopped when she spotted a woman standing before the fountain. The woman had her head tipped back and her hands clasped behind her back as she gazed at the figures in the center.

Aria stood and stared at the woman in the flowing, deep blue gown that hugged her rounded figure and spilled across the earth around her. Her wheat-colored hair had been cut into a bob a couple inches above her shoulders. Aria could see nothing of her features as her back was to them, but if this woman was who Aria believed her to be, then the woman's eyes were blue.

"Stay here," Aria said to Xavier, and he shot her a disgruntled look. "Please."

He glanced at the woman before bowing his head. Aria made her way forward. "Milly?" The woman remained gazing at the fountain, lost in a deep reverie. "Camille?"

The woman stiffened; her clasped hands fell away from her back as she turned. Her mouth parted when she spotted Aria. She dipped into a graceful curtsy that would have had Aria sprawling on her ass, as her feet were twisted awkwardly and she was off balance when she made the move.

"Your Highness," she greeted.

"Please rise," Aria said quietly.

The woman rose before her. Aria's gaze skimmed over her beautiful features before settling on her clear, aqua-colored eyes.

"I didn't mean to intrude. I thought these gardens were open to the public," she said hastily.

"They are," Aria replied as she stopped before her. "You are Camille."

The woman's face became composed, but Aria sensed her distress. "My name is Milly," she replied.

"But you were once called Camille."

Her rosebud lips compressed for a minute before she spoke again. "Many lifetimes ago, yes."

"Your sister was Genny."

Tears filled her eyes before she wiped them away. "How do you know that?"

For a minute, Aria couldn't speak. When her fingers had fallen upon the intricate design in Tempest's gown that had resembled a G, she'd dimly recalled what Atticus had written in his journal. His cousin, Merle, had run into Camille many years ago in a place called Paris. Camille had been designing clothing at the time.

"She seemed happy enough," Merle had told him. "But she told me she misses Genny every day and she actually hides a little G in every piece of clothing she creates."

Aria hadn't dared to hope it could actually be a G she'd discovered instead of some random formation within the lace, but she'd still been drawn to seek out the woman who had created the dress. She had to *know*. This was the one vampire in all the world Atticus had still had some care for throughout his life, the only one he'd sought to protect.

"Atticus kept journals," Aria said to her, and Camille made a choked sound. "He also kept your sister's journals."

"All these years," Camille whispered.

"He loved her very much."

"He did. More than I'd ever believed possible for two people to love each other. Because of what I saw between the two of them, I've waited my whole life for that kind of love and will continue to wait. Atticus was once a very good man."

"I know," Aria said.

"He was once my friend, my brother. What they did to Genny broke him."

"I know," Aria said again and rested her hand on Camille's arm.

The woman looked amazed by the gesture. "Yes, from what I've seen and heard, you would know what it's like to be loved and to love like that."

"Atticus continued to try to look out for you over the years."

"I know. It's why I'm still alive. His men found me in India and brought me to safety before he destroyed much of the world. I stayed in a town a couple hundred miles away while he lived, but decided to move here after he passed. I wanted to see his children. I'd heard they were happy, that they loved deeply and were loved in return. I had to see that at least a piece of him had survived and found the joy Atticus and Genny were denied."

Aria found it difficult to speak around the lump in her throat. "The journals, if you would like them, I think they belong to you." She would remove the information about Melinda's true parentage from them, but Camille deserved to have them.

"I would love them! My sister"—her hand pressed against her chest—"she was my best friend, my protector. We were supposed to always be together. Us against the world. The loss of a sibling..." Her voice trailed off as she gave Aria a sympathetic smile. "But then, you also know what that is like."

A sharp twinge went through Aria's heart at the reminder of the loss of Daniel. At one point, she and her brothers were all going to grow old together, or at least as old as a rebel could. Then, she and William had been changed and faced with the knowledge that Daniel would grow old and die while they remained untouched by the years. They were supposed to have had those years of Daniel's life though, and his children and grandchildren to watch over as they continued his legacy.

And Atticus was supposed to have had Genny, but if they had been granted the life they should have had, I would not have Braith.

She knew life was not always fair and could often be cruel, but there was still much happiness to be found within it.

"I'm sorry for your loss," Camille said to her.

"And I'm sorry for yours."

"How did you know who I was?"

Aria wiped away her tears and smiled at her. "Merle told Atticus you put a little G into everything you create. I spotted a G in Tempest's train yesterday."

Camille laughed. "I'd forgotten I'd told Merle that."

"Would you like to see the journals now?"

"Yes."

"Come with me."

Aria turned to find that Braith, Jack, and Gideon had joined Xavier on the pathway. They were all frowning at her as she made her way to them. Resting her hand on Braith's cheek, she rose on her toes to kiss him.

"You are no longer the oldest vampire, once again," she told him. His brow furrowed as he gazed between her and Camille. He may not be the oldest, again, but he was still clearly the most powerful. Even with her many years, Camille's strength couldn't compare to what Braith radiated. "I'd like for you to meet Camille."

Realization dawned in his striking eyes, and his mouth parted as he gazed at her in wonder. Camille went to curtsy, but he took hold of her arm, stopping her before she could. "No," he said in a hoarse voice. "You do not have to do that, not for me."

Jack's eyes swung between Braith and Camille. Xavier's head tilted in that studious way of his. Aria could almost hear the wheels spinning in his mind. Gideon looked as if he'd been socked in the stomach as he gazed at Camille. Gideon hadn't read the journals, he had no idea who Camille was, but he couldn't tear his gaze away from her.

"Will you tell us about our father?" Jack inquired as he stepped forward.

Shock rippled through Aria as Jack called Atticus his father; most times he referred to him as Atticus, or that man, but it seemed as if most of his anger toward his father had worn away over time.

Camille's smile grew. "I would love to."

EPILOGUE

Aria

Five years later

Aria smiled while she watched the children dashing in and out of the flowers lining the garden walkway. The children's laughter rang loudly through the air as they squealed with delight while trying to catch each other. Melinda and Ashby's daughter, Corrine, ran by with her blonde hair blowing behind her and her green eyes dancing with merriment. Sitting beside Aria, Melinda's hand fell to her rounded belly as her second child grew within her. Ashby smiled at her before resting his hand over hers.

Braith bent to lift Corrine as she ran toward him with her arms extended. He swept her up and out of the way of the pack of boys pursuing her. Corrine turned and stuck her tongue out at her cousins before throwing her arms around Braith and hugging him while the boys all jumped around him.

Braith laughed as he shooed them away, his gray eyes dancing with merriment when Jack and Hannah's three-year-old son, David, stuck his tongue out at Corrine and darted away. Before Jack had named his child after her father, he'd asked William and Aria if they would mind, but neither of them had. Young David's coffee-colored hair was the same hue as his mother's, but his gray eyes were the color of Jack's.

William and Tempest's four-year-old son, James, ran over to them and jumped onto William's lap. His auburn hair shone in the sun spilling over him and his brown eyes danced with mischief. The two of them had been blessed with a son who had William's recklessness and temper, but then Aria's own children had decided to take after her in that way too. Her gaze slid back to Braith as he set Corrine on her feet and opened his arms to embrace their four-year-old twins. Ella slid her arms around his neck. Her black hair fell about her shoulders as her blue eyes danced merrily. In his other arm, Daniel tugged at Braith's shirt before kissing his cheek. Daniel had her dark auburn hair and Braith's gray eyes with the blue band around them.

Her brother had sacrificed himself for her, for everyone, yet his memory would live on forever with their child and the monument Braith erected in his memory a year after his passing. Braith had surprised her and William with the statue of an oak tree with Daniel's face etched into its bark, and the names of all those who had perished in the battle against Sabine beneath it.

Aria knew the monument meant as much to Braith as it did to her. He believed that if Daniel hadn't stepped between her and Sabine, he never would have gotten there in time to stop Sabine from killing her.

The year after Braith had surprised them with the statue for Daniel, he'd had another erected in honor of all of those who had battled against Atticus and lost their lives. This one was a silver horse standing proudly outside the palace walls, and it had the names of all the fallen carved around the base of it. Her father's name was in the center of all the many others; the silver horse of the statue was strikingly similar to the brooch at her neck.

The peace her father and brother fought and died for had held strong for the last five years. There were still some fights, there always would be, but things flowed smoothly between the humans and vampires now. They all worked well together and had found a happy balance between the species. Under her and Braith's rule, and with the guidance of The Council, she knew the peace would continue to thrive for many years to come.

She wished her father and Daniel could have been here to see all that they'd helped to accomplish, but she often felt them looking after her, and occasionally she swore she smelled one or both of them or heard their laughter.

Her son, Daniel, already showed an affinity for drawing. Sometimes, she would find him sitting and staring at things in an assessing way that would make her stop to watch him with her heart in her throat. It might not be true, but she believed a piece of her brother lived on in the nephew he'd never gotten the chance to meet.

Aria's heart swelled with love as she watched Braith with their children. Her hand fell to her belly and the new life growing within. It would only be a couple more months before their family grew even more. Braith caught the gesture and grinned proudly at her as he hoisted the twins higher in his arms.

Her eyes were drawn to Maeve as she adjusted the baby swaddled within her arms. Max leaned over to look down at his son, Dylan. A grin spread across his face when the baby's fingers enclosed around his own.

Braith carried the twins over to her and settled onto the edge of the fountain beside her. Both of the twins leaned over to kiss her cheek before leaping from his arms and taking off after their cousins again.

From around the corner of the pathway, Gideon and Camille strolled into sight. Their hands were clasped together; Camille laughed as Gideon slipped a rose behind her ear. Camille had finally found the love she'd been seeking. Most were amazed it was with Gideon, of all vampires, but he was hugely devoted to her, and they'd been happily married for almost three years now.

"How did your parents keep you two mortals alive?" Braith inquired of her and William when James tackled Daniel, and Ella leapt onto James's back. At three minutes older than her brother, Ella had most likely inherited Braith's ability to not be so easily killed, but it wasn't something Aria ever wanted to find out for certain.

Aria laughed. "Not easily."

"Not at all," William agreed. "I think these little vamps may be tame compared to us."

Aria grinned as she nodded her agreement.

"Impossible," Tempest insisted.

"Not so much," Jack said from where he sat with Hannah on the bench across the way. He had his arms draped around Hannah's waist as she sat on his lap. "I knew those two when they were human teens, and believe me, keeping them alive was a battle."

Aria and William both glowered at him before thrusting their shoulders back. "We didn't need anyone to keep us alive," William declared.

"Agreed," Aria said firmly, and Braith laughed.

Xavier stepped forward and, grabbing Ella by the waist-band of her pants, lifted her easily off of James. She squealed as she kicked and punched at the air. "He jumped my brother!" she shouted.

"That's *your* daughter," Aria and Braith said to each other at the same time and then laughed.

He slid his arm around her waist and pulled her against his side as Xavier handed Ella to Timber before plucking James off of Daniel. Aria closed her eyes, savoring the laughter surrounding her and the warmth of her husband against her.

"I love you," he murmured in her ear.

"I love you too," she replied and lifted her mouth to his. His fingers caressed her cheeks while he took possession of her mouth. A thrill went through her entire body as his tongue brushed over her lips, and she opened her mouth to his invasion.

Peace and love.

It had taken so long to find, but it was here now. She'd never been happier in her life, yet she knew their lives together and with their growing family were only just beginning. There were many more years of peace to come, and she looked forward to loving Braith and being loved by him for every one of them.

THE END

Stay in touch on updates and new releases from the author by joining the mailing list!

Mailing list for Erica Stevens & Brenda K. Davies Updates:

http://visitor.r20.constantcontact.com/d.jsp?llr=unrjpksab&p=oi&m=1119190566324&sit=4ixqcchjb&f=eb6260af-2711-4728-9722-9b3031d00681

WHERE TO FIND THE AUTHOR

Mailing list for Erica Stevens and Brenda K. Davies Updates:
http://visitor.r20.constantcontact.com/d.jsp?llr=unrjpksab&p
=oi&m=1119190566324&sit=4ixqcchjb&f=eb6260af-2711-
4728-9722-9b3031d00681

Facebook page: www.facebook.com/ericastevens679

Facebook friend request:
www.facebook.com/erica.stevens.7543

Book Club: www.facebook.com/groups/545587248917267/

Website: https://ericastevensauthor.com/home.html

Blog: http://ericasteven.blogspot.com/

Twitter: @EricaStevensGCP

ABOUT THE AUTHOR

My name is not really Erica Stevens, it is a pen name that I chose in memory of two amazing friends lost too soon, I do however live in Mass with my wonderful husband and our puppy Loki. I have a large and crazy family that I fit in well with. I am thankful every day for the love and laughter they have brought to my life. I have always loved to write and am an avid reader.

39405089R00209

Made in the USA
San Bernardino, CA
27 September 2016